The Seal's Lair

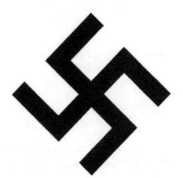

J.A. Gasperetti

authorHOUSE®

AuthorHouse™
1663 Liberty Drive
Bloomington, IN 47403
www.authorhouse.com
Phone: 1 (800) 839-8640

Published by AuthorHouse 03/12/2019

ISBN: 978-1-7283-0322-2 (sc)
ISBN: 978-1-7283-0321-5 (hc)
ISBN: 978-1-7283-0320-8 (e)

Library of Congress Control Number: 2019902687

Print information available on the last page.

DEDICATION

To Anne. She has always been my number one fan.

FOREWORD

This is a work of fiction. However, it has relevance for today's troubled world. To give added emphasis, the physical locations are real, along with some important historical facts of note.

It is a book that wants to alert us to hate, which is portrayed during the story and still plagues us. Caution! The diabolical perpetrators you will encounter are not far-fetched. Their ilk are still in our midst.

Read now about an attempt to stop vile individuals from executing a malevolent action plan. It is good to know that there are still heroic forces at work to prevent terrorists, both foreign and domestic, from accomplishing their deadly deeds. To be sure, it's a fight for all of us to be ever vigilant. For only then will it likely prevent the triumph of evil.

J. A. G.

ACKNOWLEDGMENTS

The author extends his appreciation to the following for the help in preparing this book:

Thomas F. Steinke, Esq. As a long-time resident of San Diego, Tom made sure many of the places mentioned in the book were accurately depicted. Thank you for guiding me through the vibrant venues and avenues my characters traverse.

To my editor, Taney Kurth, my deepest appreciation for your excellent work. This book travels thousands of miles, with many twists and turns, but Taney's expertise kept me on the straight and narrow.

DRAMATIS PERSONAE

MARGARET STARMONT — Manhattan widow and mother of Jordan; her anxiety will be justified

DAMON BROADBENT — Captain, San Diego Police Department; working on the case of his career

DAVID PERCIVAL — A.k.a. Friedrich Vogel; escaped Nazi scientist disguised as an avocado farmer

MARTIN STARMONT — Margaret's deceased husband; father of Jordan and Sela Danby

SELA DANBY — English daughter of Martin Starmont; reluctant friend of Ian Bright in Perth

JORDAN STARMONT — Recruited by the FBI, enlists half-sister, Sela Danby, for a dangerous mission

JOSH HANNIGAN — A.k.a. Rex Murtaugh; American fugitive in Perth, Australia finding intrigue

DAN HERLIHY — San Diego Police subordinate to Broadbent

RICK SANDOVAL — San Diego Police subordinate to Broadbent

IAN BRIGHT — Kooky, gullible English son of Percival; troublesome boyfriend of Sela Danby

THEODORE JOHNSON — Chief of San Francisco FBI office; holds a dark secret

ROSS CARGILL — San Francisco FBI field agent; Johnson subordinate chasing a phantom

YANCEY BIXBY — AWOL Marine; Neo-Nazi henchman of Percival

MONTY CRAWFORD	AWOL Marine; Neo-Nazi henchman of Percival
CASEY DOUGLAS	Navy Seal Ensign; second in command to Percival; provides cover for evil
GRADY DUNHILL	Navy NCO; Neo-Nazi Percival Trooper always ready for action
HOWARD MOORE	San Diego Police Chief; a skilled cop trying to avoid catastrophe
LOIS CARSON	Margaret's housekeeper; has loose lips
JOE PIZZO	San Diego FBI field agent; on a roller coaster ride to nab criminals
CHANNING WILLIAMS	Astute San Diego defense lawyer; plays a pivotal role to avert a calamity
DEIRDRE POWELL	Attractive assistant to Williams; competent at what she does

For even those who receive circumcision do not themselves keep the law, but they desire to have you circumcised that they may glory in your flesh.... For neither circumcision counts for anything, nor uncircumcision, but a new creation

Taken from St. Paul's Letter to the Galatians, Chapter 6.

La Jolla, August, 1969

The dawn's early light began a new day with flat breakers lapping upon the beach of a southern California mecca for surfers. A tranquil Pacific Ocean would be a letdown to the early arriving surfboarders to La Jolla's Windansea Beach. As they alighted from their parked vehicles at the end of Nautilus Street, many of them donned in their wetsuits, they were ready for action. However, their ardor was deflated when they looked out to the shoreline. "Surf's not up," uttered one disappointed youthful surf dog. His buddy observed: "Be no 'Goofy Footing' until we get an on-shore breeze. We got a Santa Ana brewing today?" So, until conditions improved, the two surfers, with bleach blond hair and lithe bodies, decided to take their boards to the four-poled thatched roof open cabana that accented the Windansea landscape. It was a good spot to energize themselves on oranges and bananas while waxing their floating vessels-- sleek polyurethane foam cores wrapped in reinforced fiberglass skins. Waxing would allow the surfer to gain a better grip on the top deck of the board, either for those who use the "Goofy" stance, right foot forward, left in the pivot position, or those who use the regular stance, left foot forward, right in the pivot position. The former stance was coined from a Walt Disney cartoon depicting its Goofy character surfing with his right foot forward on the board.

But as the two approached the cabana something would be more than goofy--and very irregular. The surfers sensed a foul odor and were puzzled why more flies than usual were swirling around their heads as they nimbly walked over the rocky ledge to the beach shelter. Was it an extra accumulation of kelp, large seaweed, driven by the tide across the beach that attracted the winged pests? The answer came quickly, as fast as a wipe out wave engulfs a surfer's oceanic ride. Looking for fun and recreation, the two surfers found the stark reality of death the moment they entered the cabana. A bloated human figure, reeking with the decay of body decomposition, stunned them as they looked down at their feet. Lying face up, the victim had the bulging, stone cold eyes of a grouper. It was a barefoot young man, with stringy black hair, dressed in a red windbreaker, a denim shirt, and blue jeans with holes at the knees. The surfers threw their boards aside, with their heads turned to avoid inhaling the foul odor of the corpse. Swatting away the flies, one of them blurted out:

"What the hell? This dude looks more than wasted. He sure can't board with us."

The second beach boy concurred. "Got that right. Let's not touch him; let's call in the cops."

They decided to get back in their Ford Pinto, parked perpendicular to the beach on Neptune Street, and then drive up the hill to the telephone booth outside Nautilus Drugs on La Jolla Boulevard to call the police. As the two surfers tossed their boards into the bed of the Pinto, they were approached by two athletic looking young men, hatless in casual dress and wearing sunglasses. One of them ambled over to the driver's side. He had chiseled, high cheekbones, in need of a shave, and had a menacing look about him. In a southern drawl, one of them asked the surfer on the driver's side of the Pinto, "This here place Windansea Beach?"

"Yeah, you got the right place. But what makes you guys come this way? Did you bring your boards in search for the perfect wave?"

The inquirer was resolute and purposeful to the question and replied, "We ain't here to splash in the water. But we are looking for someone we're supposed to meet at this spot." Lifting his head, directed at the cabana about fifty feet away, he questioned:

"Is that the only shack on this beach?"

"You got it, but I'd stay away from it now. There's someone lying in there in pretty bad shape."

"What makes you so sure?"

"The body has a foul odor. That's never good."

Frowning with disappointment, the stranger said to his buddy, "Let's see if these guys have a nose for dead meat." Then in a demanding tone, he admonished the surfers by adding, "Stick around! Don't go anywhere until we check this stiff out."

Flanking the body and kneeling, the strangers were business-like in handling the remains. Gently, one of them checked the victim's jacket pockets by inverting their contents. Nothing found. Then they rolled the body over and found a set of car keys and the attached Hertz rental car agreement on the rocky floor beneath the body. One of the searchers read aloud the paperwork to the other. "This is our man. Says here on the paperwork that car is leased to a Jordan Starmont."

His more assertive buddy concurred:

"Got to be only one like him. How much cash is he carrying? Check the body for any money."

They discovered a wallet in the back pocket with some greenbacks. One of them began counting them: "One, two, three, four.... Holy shit, man. Just a wad of singles—not the amount we were looking for."

"Quiet! Keep your voice down. Those surfer shags don't need to know our business. That's not enough cash. We were told he was supposed to have much more than that. This poor bastard is driving a Ford--if this car tag is right. Let's see if it's parked around here and if he has more dough in it."

They made one final search of the deceased. Finding nothing besides a wrinkled red and black pattern bandana, they scooped up the car keys and wallet, making a hasty exit from the cabana. The one who initially spoke to the surfers stopped several paces away from the driver's side, pulled out a pistol, and gave a warning in a hushed but audible voice as he pointed the barrel at the only witnesses on the beach who saw what just transpired:

"You boys best know that this here firearm will do bodily harm to you if you move one inch from this spot until we are out of sight. Do you read me?"

Both surfers responded by giving frightened nods that they understood.

As the strangers skirted past the front of the Pinto, the surfers locked their eyes on them through the open driver side passenger window of the vehicle. Tensely glued to their car seats, they could see the pair frantically searching through the now filled parking area. Using the information on the Hertz tag, they scanned the beachside parking spaces for a Ford with California tag number CGY 129. It didn't take long to find the vehicle in question. Like a vulture descending on a carcass, the threatening one pounced upon a white four-door Ford Fairlane. He unlocked it and directed his pal to help him search through the car. They combed the interior, looked under the seats, and surveyed the glove box. Finding nothing, they went to the trunk. Upon opening it, one of the thugs looked away when a miasmic smell fumed out. Holding his nose, he peered in and found it empty. Slamming the trunk in anger, he signaled his cohort to get to the curb of the parking lot. Once there one of them raised his arm in a forwarding motion. Suddenly an approaching vehicle stopped and picked up the disappointed evil pair. The car sped up Nautilus and headed east up the rise to the heart of La Jolla. Just as mysteriously, seconds later two other cars, with wheels squealing, came out of nowhere in pursuit of the first car in the same direction.

Reacting to what just transpired, the surfers shrugged their shoulders in unison. The one spoke with bewilderment to the other:

"What in the hell is going on here? This is the ultimate in weirdness."

2
CHAPTER

New York, September, 1969

"Is this the residence of Margaret Starmont?"

A distinguished looking forty-five-year-old woman, with svelte lines, high cheek bones, and sleek black hair, who heard those words at her New York City Park Avenue residence sensed there was bad news emanating from the voice on the other end of the telephone line. Because the caller had the sound of authority, she presciently answered:

"This is she. Is there something wrong?"

"This is Captain Damon Broadbent of the San Diego Police Department. It's taken us awhile to finally locate your family, Mrs. Starmont. We need your help to confirm some important identification information here in San Diego."

"Confirm? What needs clarification?"

"Do you know or are you related to a Jordan Starmont?"

In a foreboding tone, the woman replied:

"Please, please. Do not tell me you have bad news for me. Jordan Starmont is my son."

"Ma'am, we are not sure if it is bad news for you, so I do not want to be premature."

A frightened mother asked:

"Premature about what?"

"We need you or some other family member to come to San Diego to identify a dead body."

Hearing this, Starmont was shaking. She stumbled to find a chair next to the telephone and replied in a quivering voice:

"What gives you any idea the body you have could be Jordan?"

"I apologize for being so presumptious, Mrs. Starmont, but our investigation has led to your home."

"What investigation?"

There was a pause as some shuffling was heard on the telephone line. Broadbent then said:

"I'm referring to our initial investigation. We traced a Hertz rental car back to your son. This car was found abandoned. The investigating officers discovered the Hertz rental agreement near the body, which revealed a Jordan Starmont rented a Ford Fairlane at the San Francisco International Airport. We confirmed he gave a New York driver's license to Hertz to rent the car. We traced the home address from the license back to your residence."

With hope in her voice, Starmont said:

"So, you have a car, not my son?"

"Ma'am, the potentially bad news is that we found a dried pool of blood in the car's trunk. We found the car when our officers were called to a city beach, in La Jolla, where some surfers discovered a dead body. We found no I.D. on the body, but our crime lab took a blood sample"

Starmont interrupted:

"Why would my son have a reason to drive to San Diego? He did call me recently and said he found a way of life he loved in Haight-Ashbury in San Francisco."

"I don't know his motivation to drive to our city, but let me continue. We presumed the car was stolen and driven to where we found it. The lab matched the blood samples from the victim and what we found in the car. Still, we need a positive I.D. to confirm if it is, unfortunately, your son."

Starting to sob, Starmont sensed the connections Broadbent made about her son:

"Okay, okay. What do I do next?"

"How soon can a family member fly out here to San Diego? Have you visited our fair city before?"

"Yes, La Jolla is familiar to me. My husband and I vacationed there several times in the past. I can arrange to fly immediately...."

She stopped and wept for a few seconds and continued:

"...to see if you have my son."

"Ma'am I hope we are wrong, but we appreciate you assisting us with our investigation. Please do call me direct when you arrive, 555.425.1000, Captain Damon Broadbent, Detective Bureau, San Diego Police Department. Can we help you with a place to stay when you come to town?"

Trying to compose herself, Starmont scribbled Broadbent's number on a pad on the telephone stand. She replied:

"No, thank you, that won't be necessary. I'm familiar with the La Valencia Hotel in La Jolla. I'll stay there."

After Broadbent brought the conversation to a sympathetic close, Starmont put down the telephone and tried to get an emotional hold on herself. The instant shock to the system made her tremble and feel empty. Things were compounding. First, the sudden death last spring of her husband, Martin, ten years her senior, from a coronary. Secondly, now this awful news--the apparent loss of her only child. After emitting a mournful wail, she headed for the bathroom. There she found the comfort of another dose of Librium to compose her nerves. Placing a tablet in a shaky palm, she cried out:

"Lois, Lois. I need you."

Lois Carson, Starmont's housemaid, came rushing to the bathroom. Carson saw a disheveled woman, with teary eyes, drooping hair over her brow, and a dangling beige scarf that had fallen off her shoulders.

"Mrs. Starmont, why are you crying? What's wrong?"

"It's Jordan; I'm afraid it is something terrible."

The maid was stunned:

"Oh, no. This can't be. What happened?"

Clutching a handful of Kleenexes to dry her eyes, Starmont tearfully replied:

"I just received a call from the San Diego Police Department that they have a dead body out there they need me to identify."

"Is it Jordan?"

"Based on what they told me I fear it could be Jordan."

Clutching Carson's sympathetic hand, the distraught mother was a bit more stable:

"Please pack a bag and call the airlines. Book a flight from LaGuardia to San Diego as soon as possible. Also, call the La Valencia Hotel in La Jolla for an extended stay. The number is in the directory."

"Do you want me to call Dr. Ramsey to help settle you down?"

Gaining a badly needed injection of inner strength, the crestfallen woman thanked the maid for her help and concern. She walked to her decorative bedroom, with large windows that looked out to the East River, trying to compose herself by combing her black hair back into a tighter beehive look. Mournfully, she gazed at the photograph on the nightstand of her late husband, Martin, a successful Wall Street broker. The two had met shortly after World War II, 1946, in Greenwich Village. Margaret was finishing her liberal arts degree at NYU; Martin was starting a career with Smith Barney. She came from money, her father was an executive for General Electric in Groton, Connecticut; Martin was trying to make some, after serving as an intelligence officer in Europe with the U.S. Navy during the war. They had a big wedding back at the bride's home and found a modest apartment on the lower east side of New York City.

Margaret was very fertile; Jordan was born ten months after they wed. The couple tried to expand their family but two miscarriages ended that plan. Martin concentrated on building his career at Smith Barney; Margaret played the dutiful wife with an eye for upscale furnishings, a rich Fifth Avenue wardrobe for the three of them, and hosting gourmet dinners. With the cold reality that her son might be dead, Margaret began the self-flagellation of where she went wrong as a mother. She stripped off her prim and proper formal wear for something more casual: slacks, a long sleeved blouse, a camel hair blazer, and some Italian leather flats.

While preparing for her anxious journey, Margaret waxed philosophical. Was it a crazy world that claimed her son? Life was good for the Starmonts until the turbulent 1960's arrived, when America looked into the mirror and did not like what it saw. The last five years had been rife with profound changes that racked the nation's psyche. Jordan was affected by all of it. He often had deep discussions about society's ills with his mother. More with her than his father, who wasn't around much, preoccupied by his career. The national landscape was under duress. Was it the expansive and endless Vietnam War, with its truculent anti-war demonstrations on many college campuses? Was it the rise of the drug culture, with its pernicious appetite for marijuana, heroin, and LSD? Was it the onset of the civil rights movement, with its convulsive demonstrations in the segregated south and riots in the country's urban centers? Was it the beginnings of the sexual revolution, calling for a new definition of femininity and the urge to "find someone to love"? Was it the new defiance of authority, which admonished not to "trust anyone over thirty?" Could it even be the great appeal of popular music, with its new themes of protest, alternative life styles and drug-induced highs?

Many young people during the 60's could not control events; events controlled them. Jordan was particularly affected by the shockwaves that hit the nation in 1968, viz., the assassinations of the Rev. Martin Luther King, Jr. and Senator Robert Kennedy, civil unrest in a number of major cities, and the vehement opposition to the Vietnam War, climaxed by the violence at the Democratic National Convention in Chicago. Jordan became disillusioned and confused. He inexplicably left Princeton at the end of his junior year. He began a profligate existence living off the generosity of his parents, both voicing their displeasure with his misguided life. Shortly thereafter, hearing the hedonistic call from the "Flower Children," who would rather make love than war, he was drawn from the comforts of his Manhattan home for to the psychedelic kingdom of Haight-Ashbury in San Francisco. For the young Starmont, it would be the journey of his young life.

3
CHAPTER

Perth, August, 1969

Josh Hannigan was on the run, wanted for a criminal escapade that occurred in San Francisco's Haight-Ashbury district in December 1968. To avoid arrest, he had to leave town in haste. He luckily found an employer that did not ask for references—a Panamanian freight line that put him to work on the *S.S. Marquez*. The ship made stops at Manila, Djakarta, Surabaja, and then slipped south for Australia. When the Marquez stopped in Fremantle, near Perth, Hannigan jumped ship with a new identity. This came about by stealing the wallet and passport while aboard ship from a fellow American exile from San Diego, Rex Murtaugh, the day before they dropped anchor. Hannigan had a wild dream of coming to Australia because he was a tennis player in high school and followed the exploits of many of the Aussie court greats: Roy Emerson, Lew Hoad, Rod Laver, John Newcombe, Tony Roche, Ken Rosewall, and Fred Stolle. Well, he realized his dream, all right, but he wasn't sure if it might become a nightmare.

Australia is described by many outsiders as the "The Land Down Under." The term refers to the fact that the Australian continent, unlike Africa and South America, lies completely below the equator in the southern hemisphere. And with Antarctica to its south, positioned at the bottom of the world, most global maps depict the Australian landmass looking up, or under, most of the world's continents. So, too, Hannigan was down and under with the reality that his life was without a compass and needed to regain a safe course. For now, Australia was his escape, away from the evil of a heroin drug deal gone wrong back in the States.

As an undocumented alien, how long could he realistically finesse his stay here under a stolen name? Would the local authorities discover he was wanted by the law back in America? Could he eke-out a livelihood, with a dwindling amount of cash he brought with him? Sure. Why not? It was in his bones to defy the odds and start a new life in a land of second chances. For after all, the British settlement of Australia was highlighted by the exporting of its undesirable prisoners to penal colonies, especially to New South Wales on the eastern side of the country. Many of them eventually gained their freedom and started a lawful existence as new pioneers in a hardscrabble environment. Hannigan hoped that he could also find renewal as an undesirable in a land of redemption.

Using the stolen identification of Rex Murtaugh as cover, Hannigan was compelled to lead a clandestine, laid back, and anonymous life. His first order of business was to find a cheap, convenient, and low-profile place to stay. He thought of a youth hostel, where strangers were not viewed suspiciously. Recommendations from the locals led him to the Marbury House on Goderich Street in East Perth. This haven for tourists on the cheap was conveniently located near numerous cafes and central to public transportation. It also was close to Perth's city center along the peaceful banks of the Swan River estuary, which empties to the southwest into the sea at Fremantle. The hostel's amenities were austere. Hannigan's room had a tiny kitchen, with a kettle on a small stove, but no plates. He had to share a bath down a narrow dark hall with a pervasive smell of cigarette smoke. However, at ten Australian dollars per night it was a bargain because his American greenbacks had a favorable currency exchange advantage.

Hannigan needed work sooner rather than later because what cash he had in his pocket would not last long. It wasn't hard for Hannigan to find a job as a bartender at a Perth watering hole because the owner didn't require references and did not ask many questions. It helped that the Cricket Club was only a few blocks from the Marbury House on Hay Street and was aptly named because it was directly across from the WACA (Western Australian Cricket Association) Oval, the historic playing field in the city used for cricket, rugby, soccer, and Australian rules football. The club drew a hard drinking clientele, many of them WACA spectators. They drank before and after matches, and even during if things on the playing field were disappointing or dull. The spirited patrons took to this "Yank", who had an Anglo first-name--Rex. He poured generous drinks at bargain prices, often serving free "shouts" (a round of drinks). This often filled the tip mug next to the ale handles on a heavy mahogany bar. So far, he was liked, making some money, and, most importantly, undetected.

After a month or so it was apparent that Hannigan couldn't stay at the hostel much longer because of their limited stay policies. He fortunately saved his generous tips, over $200 (Australian) and found a better one bedroom flat on Riverside Drive, which had short-term and month-to-month leases. As time passed, the Rex Murtaugh alias was working because of his hermit existence outside of work. At the club, more than a few Sheilas thought him a cute catch, with his athletic six-foot build, shaggy brown hair, and ingratiating demeanor, he parried off the more ardent tries by the opposite sex to get to better know him. He'd get teased but was good at denying them entry into his world. Hannigan liked women; he just didn't want to get attached especially now when he might slip and reveal his true identity.

Most days were sunny and dry in a part of the world that cried out for rainfall. It allowed Hannigan to stay lean and mean in his free time by either taking walks along the Swan River esplanade or a long jog down to Fremantle via Canning Highway. At times he ended a run at the historic Round House Gaol, a twelve-sided limestone edifice that once housed the insane and prisoners and was the oldest standing building in Western Australia. At this site, one day near sunset, Hannigan sat on the steps above the tunnel of the Round House to take an inventory of his sanity. He was trying to stay self-assured and confident. Life was better now, being removed and far from the turmoil in a past life. No more drug dealers, no more counter culture crusades, no more anti-war protests to break America apart at the seams. Yes, Hannigan felt a cold sense of relief in a newly found warm and stable environment astride the Indian Ocean. He felt fortunate to make the right moves with a calculating mind and an uncanny ability to save his hide from imprisonment and even a close encounter with death. Such was the life of a survivalist, now living on the western edge of the world's most remote continent. But his cocoon of apparent safe anonymity was about to be penetrated.

Months had passed. It was now August. On his way to work on a late Friday afternoon, Hannigan stepped into his apartment's hall and locked his door. Preparing to walk to the stairwell, a young woman was also exiting her room and locking her door, directly across from his. The two were virtually butt-to-butt and they turned inward to become eye-to-eye. Despite the dim light, Hannigan saw beauty a foot away. A lass with sandy brown hair, radiant blue eyes, stunning cheek bones, and sensual lips froze him in place. The visual connection between the two elapsed in a flash; the impact it made would last much longer.

Hannigan reacted first:

"Excuse me. I didn't mean…."

Before he could finish his line, the beauty interjected with a voice more like an Englishwoman than a Sheila:

"I'm glad we finally have met. I've noticed you since I got here ten days ago and I've wanted to meet you."

Hannigan was pleasantly surprised that he had a secret admirer and stayed speechless, lowering his head in modesty and letting her continue.

"So let me formally introduce myself. I'm Sela Danby."

"Well, hi."

Hannigan caught himself by keeping up his masquerade and continued:

"I'm Rex Murtaugh. You visiting Perth just like me?"

"Yes, for now I am a visitor; however, my stay could be longer."

Hannigan sensed some conflict with Sela's last line:

"Oh, what might prompt that?"

"Let's just say I am waiting for the right person to direct my future."

Hannigan pointed to the stairwell and the two continued their departure from the building. Sela shared more of her background as they continued the conversation. She was originally from England and was on an extended holiday that had taken her from London to Western Australia. As they got outside into the warmth of the afternoon sun, Hannigan stopped and said:

"Sela, this is all very interesting. Can we continue this conversation later? I'm off to my bartending stint at the Cricket Club. You know where it is?"

"Sure do. I've mingled with the mates and that's where I first saw you."

Hannigan was becoming more intrigued by this alluring woman, who had a veil of intrigue about her. As they were off to different directions, Hannigan offered:

"When can we continue the conversation? How about my day off? Can we make it dinner tomorrow evening?"

With an air of angst in her voice, Sela beckoned:

"No, this can't wait. Can we talk after you take leave from work this evening?"

Hannigan knew he had to be suspicious of strangers wanting to know him better. But this lovely and seemingly forlorn creature melted his defenses:

"I'm done at ten or so, depending if I get the hard core drinkers out of the club. How about the K on Hay Café? It's not far from the Cricket Club."

"I've seen it on a stroll. I will meet you there."

She tenderly took his hand, said good-bye, and was on her way up Goderich Street. Hannigan moved on about twenty yards up the walk but was compelled to turn and look again at the feminine splendor, dressed in a light blue cotton dress that clung to her shapely narrow hips, retreating from view. Hannigan got a grip on his libido and returned to his cautious side. Who is this girl and why is she so trusting and friendly in a far away place? But whatever Sela Danby may or may not be he had to know her better.

4
CHAPTER

San Diego, September, 1969

The beauty of the morning belied the gloomy purpose of Margaret Starmont's flight as her plane landed at San Diego's Lindbergh Field. Despite the inner turmoil she felt from her son's apparent death, there was a bit of solace to return to a region she had enjoyed in times past. By her calculation this was her sixth time back, being a favorite vacation spot when her husband was alive. Martin Starmont became familiar with the San Diego area while a U. S. Navy intelligence officer during WW II. He made more than a few trips on business the last ten years of his life, and some of them included taking Margaret with him. This was Martin's dream place to retire. With San Diego's benign Mediterranean climate, where ice and snow were aberrations and extremes in hot and cold temperatures the exception rather than the rule, many thought it an Eden. He once observed that if the French and English explorers and settlers had come to this California landfall first, then would they have even bothered to go east into the North American hinterland? Nevertheless, all Margaret knew was that she had to go from east to west to maybe reclaim her son's body in a place of bittersweet dreams and memories.

Starmont had a skycap find her luggage at the terminal carousel and then went to a payphone to call Damon Broadbent. After she described to him what she was wearing, black slacks and a camel haired blazer, Broadbent instructed her to wait at the curb of the TWA terminal for an unmarked white police car to pick her up. It wasn't long before two plainclothes detectives spotted the distinguished looking woman, who looked like a mature movie star with lithe body lines, long dark hair tied at the back by a black silk scarf, and looking at the late morning sun through Gucci sunglasses. The officers pulled up to the curb in a semi-official looking four-door Oldsmobile 88, with front-door mounted floodlights, and a wrapped wire antenna over the car roof and tied at the rear bumper. They approached Starmont politely, identified themselves, and helped to seat her in the back seat. Located close to the airport, it was a short drive to arrive at San Diego Police headquarters, located on Market Street just off Pacific Coast Highway. The Spanish bell tower accented the station, which was built on a historic site, eerily called Dead Man's Point, a name it got because it was a burial place for sailors and marines during the charting and surveying of San Diego Bay. Broadbent knew they were arriving via car radio and was at the entrance and came out to greet Starmont. He was wearing a dark brown business suit, a white shirt, and a beige tie. As he approached her, Margaret was initially struck by Broadbent's handsome features. She surmised he might be about her age-- mid-forties. With a stout build and a curl to his jet black hair, he reminded her of Victor Mature, who was now past his filmmaking prime but was one of Margaret's favorite actors. He offered his hand to her:

"I'm sorry we had to bring you here, but welcome, Mrs. Starmont. I trust you had a good flight?"

"Thank you, Captain Broadbent. The flight was uneventful. It was nice of you to pick me up."

"Our motto for the department is to 'To Protect and Serve'. We certainly want to do that for you while you are with us. Please follow me to my office."

Along with the two staff detectives, Rick Sandoval and Dan Herlihy, who met Margaret at the airport, the four of them wended their way down a sunlit hall on a tiled floor that created an echo to their footsteps. Broadbent must have had some clout in the department, for he had a corner window that looked across the Pacific Coast Highway and the adjacent picturesque San Diego Bay, with moored sailboats in the foreground and Navy ships ported at Coronado in the background. When they sat down, he offered Margaret coffee, which she declined. Her stereotype of a police environment, the first she has ever encountered, was out of focus. Maybe it was the perception of too many movies and television shows that conveyed police stations as crowded, noisy, and redolent with cigarette smoke. But this one seemed civil, almost neat. Broadbent's office had no cluttered bulletin boards, was devoid of cigarette smoke, ashtrays, and even had an upscale touch with attractive ferns flanking his window. In an initial state of dissonance, she tried to listen attentively to Broadbent's report after he made some perfunctory remarks about his department, a homicide unit, why he is handling the case, and what they uncovered so far. He was blunt but tactful when he told her:

"We believe the person, who might be your son, may have been murdered. Suicide can't be ruled out because he had severe trauma to his neck, which was broken and the cause of his death. With constrictive bruises around the neck, it looks like he was possibly garroted, perhaps murdered. Am I being too indelicate here?"

Starmont appreciated Broadbent's paternal demeanor:

"No. I understand this is important to your investigation."

"Okay. Before you view the body, let me say, his face will appear bloated and somewhat distorted. I hope this will not offend you."

Starmont rolled her eyes in anguish:

"Detective, can we please make the confirmation now, while I still have a handle on my feelings?"

"Yes, by all means. I am sorry. I didn't mean to sensationalize things."

Seeing that she was ill at ease, Broadbent immediately directed Herlihy to ready his car to transport the group the San Diego County Medical Examiner's Office, which was located in the Kearney Mesa part of town. The unmarked white Oldsmobile made its way through downtown San Diego and entered the freeway, just to the south of San Diego's beautiful Balboa Park, and headed north. Broadbent, seated next to Starmont in the back seat of the police car, made small talk about the attractions in the Park, to include its famous zoo. He talked about how the city was changing and growing from a sleepy Navy town into a major west coast metropolis.

She appealed to Broadbent for a moment of silence to collect her thoughts, ones that were not so pleasant. Not only was Starmont reeling from the dreadful fate that may have befallen her son, she was trying to come to terms with a letter Martin wrote to their son. Jordan gave it to her before he left home to go west. She thought a moment about delaying the re-opening of the letter until after she viewed Jordan's body. But she could not abstain from revisiting its mournful contents. Her husband's recognizable handwriting was on the front of a wrinkled number 10 white envelope:

Open in the Event of My Death.

Starmont was stunned by the fact that her husband, whom she trusted, might be keeping some family secrets from her. Why did he not tell her there was some vital information that their son, not her, should be the first to know? She nestled in the corner of the car to keep Broadbent's eyes off the letter. With renewed anguish she read:

February 1, 1969

Dear son:

I trust you honored my memory by reading this after I have left this life. My doctor told me I had an inoperable tumor near my heart that could cause sudden death. I kept my condition from both you and your mother because I found no value to increase the anxiety in a world with too much of it. Rather, I thought it best to hide my illness to keep things stable.

Unfortunately, life does not completely conform to our wishes. Jordan, we have high hopes for you. There must be a reason you seemingly want to reject all the comforts your mother and I provided. With all the country is going through, where almost everything is questioned, we live in a troubled age. I sensed college reinforced this by changing you and your values. Perhaps that explains your desire for a new perspective on the world by leaving Princeton and going to San Francisco. Your return will be welcomed in a flash by your mother. She loves you more than you know. Don't be ashamed to be a prodigal son!

Now, for the real purpose of this letter. You should know that I was always true and faithful to your mother. I truly loved her and avoided temptation with the many attractive women I encountered socially and in business. If you ever marry, you will find virtue by being friendly but not too close with the opposite sex. That's the danger we men carry with us--the loaded pistol between our legs that reacts and does not think. I had to keep a dark secret to avoid losing your mother's trust. It is this, Jordan: you are not my only child. You have a sister, or more accurately, a half-sister.

While I was a Navy officer stationed in England preparing for the D-Day invasion of France, I met a woman who was a British Navy communications aide. We got involved and it led to unintended consequences. She wanted to return with me after the war, but I could not commit to that. I guess I wanted to leave the world of war by detaching myself from everything, and, yes, everybody associated with it. In early 1946 the woman contacted me by mail through the Naval Reserve. She claimed she gave birth to a child, naming me as the father. Subsequent letters, with baby snapshots, painted a bleak economic picture and she demanded child support. You see what happens when you react and you don't think! I really could not confirm or deny that I was the father. I was in a fix and unable to send her financial help. I had just started at Smith Barney and was barely eking out an existence.

She continued to write, even after I married your mother. Finally, in time, I managed to save $10,000. Unknown to your mother, I sent it to the two of them in England, where they lived southeast of London in Tunbridge Wells. The money apparently stopped the contacts and ended "the affair."

But this story continues. From out of the stormy past, I took a call at work from a young lady calling from England. Because I never left Smith Barney, I was easy to reach. She informed me that her mother died several years ago from a rare form of cancer and she had to stop her college studies. But before her mother died, the young lady was finally told about her unseen father. She said enough to convince me that I was her father. There was no demand for more money but the girl insisted she wanted to finally meet me--her father. Even though her intent was honorable, I said that would not work. Rather, as awkward as it appears, I thought a better way to know her family was to meet you--the connecting bloodline you both have. So, forgive me if this is too sudden and creates problems for you, but I think you young people would rather bond with each other instead of the older generation. For after all, don't we represent what you are rejecting?

The young lady, a few years older than you, has your contact information in San Francisco. I suspect she'll be contacting you soon. Maybe she has already done so. I leave it to you when and if you want to share this story with your mother. I hope she understands why I kept it from her. So, please keep me in your memory and, more importantly, accept this blessed surprise in your life: your sister--Sela Danby.

With my love, I beg your heartfelt understanding.

Dad

With tears in her eyes, Margaret reached for a handkerchief in her purse. Broadbent noticed her discomfort:

"Mrs, Starmont, are you upset? I apologize if this has all been so abrupt...."

Before Broadbent could say more, she put her left hand tenderly on his right arm and softly said:

"If you found Jordan, you have to be a better detective by finding someone else who may know something about his death."

"And who might that be?"

"Sela Danby."

Perth, August, 1969

When Josh Hannigan (Rex Murtaugh) came into Sela Danby's life, she was unaware of his personal baggage. He was a fugitive from America, using an alias, trying to avoid the law. But she had her own issues. By trying to find her past, seeking to find a father she never met, Sela had an anxious future. Her family search was more dangerous than she imagined. What she needed, thousands of miles from her English home, was some direction and, yes, based on what she has encountered these last few months, some protection. She was vulnerable and afraid that she was on the brink of committing a crime. That's what happens when you are involved with a shady skinhead, Ian Bright, and his gang culture. The specter of Bright, whom she met at a Carnaby Street pub in London earlier this year, made her cringe. Sela has been paranoid since she came to Perth with him nearly two weeks ago. He was away from her for now, taking a flight the day before to Melbourne to meet some Sharpies, Australia's version of skinhead youth gangs. Sela wanted out from Bright's dark approach to life. Would Murtaugh be her savior and show her the light? Rays of hope in the present is what was needed because of a gloomy past.

⊷ ◈ ⊶

Sela Danby was a social outsider growing up in Tunbridge Wells, located thirty miles south of London in the glorious Kent countryside. She was working class, the daughter of a house servant. There was a certain smugness here because in 1909 the town's name was changed by royal decree to Royal Tunbridge Wells. Her hometown was founded in the 17th century as a spa around Chalybeate Spring, intended to cure a number of human maladies. It was often referred to in English literature and had one of its great writers, William Makepeace Thackeray, take up residence there. Its recent claim to fame occurred in David Lean's epic 1962 film, *Lawrence of Arabia,* which closes with a comment to capture the community's good feel from actor Claude Rains, playing Mr. Dryden, who answers a question posed by Saudi Arabia's King Feisal, played by Alec Guinness, where he would rather be than the Middle East:

"Me, your highness? On the whole, I wished I'd stayed in Tunbridge Wells."

It was a settlement primarily composed of the prim and proper middle and upper classes. Despite the place's fame and comforts, it did not make for a good fit for Sela, especially since recent developments beckoned her to leave it.

Sela was the daughter of Sarah Danby, an unmarried woman who became pregnant during her service with the British Royal Navy during WWII. Fortunately, this occurred at the time the war ended, enabling her to hide her pregnancy just before she gained an honorable discharge. The two lived with Sarah's parents, but it was a bleak existence during the austere economic times in post-war Britain. Sarah came into some money, sent by a source she would not reveal, to improve their lot. With good jobs scarce, two years later she went to work as a servant, maintaining the home of Trevor and Darcy Sutherland. Mr. Sutherland was the managing principal of the largest bank in Royal Tunbridge Wells and owned a spacious two-story brick home on Ramslye Road, to the west of the town center. Sarah has been a loyal employee to the Sutherland's, who paid her well, to include year-end gifts of extra cash. At Christmas, Sarah and her daughter were part of their annual "Twelve Days of Christmas" gala, even though the Danby's were out of their league with the other elites invited to the fete. Sarah's employers were flexible and understanding, allowing her to work those hours when Sela was in school. Eventually, the two moved out of Sarah's parents home, finding a modest two bedroom flat in the southern, older part of town. With stable employment and a new found independence, things improved for Sarah and her daughter.

When Sela reached puberty, her mother sat her down for the most meaningful conversation in the young girl's life. Sela was precocious and wise beyond her years, a good time her mother thought to tell her how babies were made and finally answer a daughter's questions about her father. Had the conversation been recorded, it would have sounded like this:

"Sela, your father lives and works in America, in New York City. I worked with him when I served in the Royal Navy during the war. He was a dashing, kind man, an officer in the United States Navy, who I met on leave outside the Plymouth Naval Base. We fell in love--I thought. The war was ending. I wanted to be his wife, but he returned to America without me. I did not reveal to him when he departed that I was pregnant--carrying you. So, you are a wonderful mix of America and England. I think it best at this time not to reveal his name or how you can reach him. He wants it that way and has taken steps to provide for us. For that we should both be grateful. Someday I'll tell you more, when the time comes."

As the young girl grew older, she would press her mother for her father's identity and presumed whereabouts in America. But her mother sidestepped the inquiries. Then, a moment of truth arose. Sarah was diagnosed with pancreatic cancer in late 1967. The treatments were painful and her demise went fast. In a fatal state, six months later, Sarah had another profound conversation with her daughter. On her deathbed, the gaunt woman, still young at forty-three years old, rallied her strength to leave her daughter with the truth:

"Sela, dearest, my time is short. Do not think me cruel for keeping what you need to know about your father for so long."

Sela was trying to hold back her tears:

"Mom, the last thing you might be is cruel. Through the years I've come to terms with your silence about him."

"That's a comfort for me to know. Please take my hand, dear one. Hold it tight."

Sela offered her right hand, while swabbing away tears with a hankie with her left. She firmly grasped her mother's deathly white hand, mustering her courage for what she was about to hear:

"Sela, your father is the only man I ever loved. My wish is that you will meet someone you can cherish--but to have and to hold for a lifetime.

When it comes to your father, you will find him in New York City. His name is Martin Starmont."

Before her mother's weak utterances could go on, Sela injected:

"Starmont. That is an English sounding name."

"That may be, but don't forget your American side."

Propped-up in her bed, the failing woman pointed to the dresser in her bedroom:

"In the top drawer of the bureau is a large envelope with the name 'Martin' on it. You'll have the letters we exchanged and his contact information. But, dear one, be delicate and do not upset his personal life."

The daughter found it hard to restrain her sorrow and embraced her frail mother and tearfully said:

"Oh, mum, my sweet mum. Thank the Lord you guided me through life this long. I will honor your wishes."

Sela continued to hold her mother for a few precious moments longer. But she heard no further words or felt any movement. At around 8:30 A.M., Sunday, June 16, her mother died in her arms. It was Father's Day.

⊱ ◉ ⊰

It took Sela over a year to have the courage to initially telephone her father. That's when he told her about Jordan, her half-brother. Martin, while not mentioning that he knew he was dying, told Sela that the timing was not good for them to finally meet. He begged her to not contact his wife. Rather, he encouraged her to make connection with her brother, Jordan, now living in San Francisco in the Haight-Ashbury district among the "Flower Children." Martin stressed that the best route to begin some family bonding was to cultivate a relationship with Jordan because they were of the same generation. The emotion filled call ended with long distance tears and sobs.

After the maudlin conversation with her father, Sela was reluctant to seek out Jordan. It all seemed too awkward. Finally, in the spring, she wrote several letters, to include a photograph of her, to the New York address Martin gave to her. There were no replies until two months ago, when Jordan finally wrote her. The letter was typed no less, so this appeared to be a message with a purpose. She read pensively:

August 20, 1969

Dear Sela:

I hope you received this in a timely fashion. It took a bit for the mail to be forwarded to me. I now live in San Francisco. You indicated in one of your letters that you might be traveling to Australia. It's too bad we have not met, but I think that eventful day is coming. However, since things are changing fast for me, I cannot predict where or when they will normalize. So, please try to call me as soon as you can—it's important. Call me at 555.747.2815. Although far apart, our lives are bound together by a person of common interest you told me about—Ian Bright. There is reason to believe he is about to be complicit with a rash act of some kind. Sorry to alarm you. At this time I really can't tell you why I know this. Eventually you'll learn more.

Like you, Ian has never met his father. He is the illegitimate son of Dora Bright. Ian's father, who now lives in California, recently tracked down Ian's mother in England. She gave him Ian's contact information. Now engaged in a long distance relationship, father and son are likely up to no good. Ah, my dear sister, if you will allow me to call you "sister", here's where you come in. Earlier this summer, Ian's father called him to say "something big" is going to happen, and he needs his help. Ian is doing that right now in Australia. The conversation had few other specifics but it looks like the two will finally meet—here in America in San Diego, California.

Wow! Isn't this something: two children, you and Bright, who have never met their fathers! And this ironic set of events links you together. Don't know what Bright looks like but the picture you sent in one of your letters identifies who you are. You need to stay with him, somehow, if and when he comes to San Diego. We hope that the two of you together will lead us to Bright's father. When you arrive, you will be under major surveillance and protection by American authorities. I'm sorry if this sounds very dangerous and too hard to believe, but your help is needed. I guess you can become a female James Bond. Some joke, huh?

Please call me as soon as possible. Can I contact you at Western Union to keep this under wraps? I know this is bizarre and precarious, but you can be playing a vital security role for both of our countries. Therefore, we can't allow Bright to know what's happening. So, whatever you decide to do, help us or say no, please destroy this letter. And, either way, you are at the top of my list to finally set my eyes on you and hug you. You are a dear through all of this.

My love,

Jordan

P.S. Thanks again for the picture. You are lovely!

Sela could not believe what she just read. Indeed, what Jordan wrote about could have been found in one of Ian Fleming's James Bond tales. Only this was different—it was fact and not fiction. All of this seemed too confusing. Jordan's letter exacerbated the presumed danger she was living under by staying associated with Ian Bright. Seeking a half-brother she has never met has all of a sudden put her in the middle of a manhunt. How could this be? Her mother told her to be careful of the men she would meet, especially if they seemed too different from Sela's prim and proper approach to life.

The unheeded advice made Sela's current predicament dire. Despite the fact she felt troubled being Bright's girlfriend, she reluctantly agreed to go to Australia with him. He was a little older than her, and that gave her comfort. But she was essentially held captive, since Bright carried most of their money and the plane tickets back to London. Was it a reach to believe Rex Murtaugh would help her find a way out, or at least give her some protection? Indeed, not a good bet to rely on a total stranger and an unknown quantity as a defender. Choosing between Bright and Murtaugh was a Hobson's choice. It was obvious to Sela that her life was in the balance. She had to make the right selection--now.

6
CHAPTER

San Diego, September, 1969

Still in disbelief and shaken by the hidden past her dead husband had kept from her, Margaret Starmont almost called off the ride to the San Diego County Medical Examiner's Office to view her son's corpse. Martin's letter was a stunner. The last few days have become one shock wave after another. But she gathered inner strength and decided not to postpone the identification of Jordan's body. She was trying to cope, as difficult as it was in a police car that included three City of San Diego detectives, essentially three strange men who had control with a sad grip on her life. Seated next to Margaret, Captain Damon Broadbent could sense the woman's angst after she put the letter down on her lap. Staying quiet, Broadbent detected the fragrance of Margaret's exquisite perfume, far from the stale stuff many women wore. Her clothes were upscale, the coif of her hair was chic, and her nails were beautifully polished and manicured. He'd only known her for almost an hour, yet he surmised this was a woman of distinction—maybe with money. Oh, yes, he thought, she was different, unlike any woman he had encountered. If he wasn't careful, he could lose his professional objectivity. But Broadbent was an ethical, very thorough cop. He wasn't given to dalliances on the job. Nevertheless, Margaret's attraction compelled him to satisfy his basic instinct, to confirm her marital status, when he broke the silence:

"These things are never easy. We discovered in the phone directory that the home address your son had on his driver's license was only listed in your name. Will your husband, or any other family member be joining you to lend you some support?"

Margaret wasn't prepared for the detective's question. To this point it was not asked and she did not volunteer any information about the rest of her family. However, she was candid with her answer:

"No, my husband is deceased. If Jordan is gone, it's only me."

Broadbent sensed the woman's vulnerability but he did not dwell on it. He reached into his jacket and found his package of Kool's and said:

"Do you mind if I smoke? I'm trying to kick the habit. I don't dare smoke at the office. But I sneak a cigarette in at times to break the tension."

Margaret, who last smoked a cigarette when she was in college, needed something to get the edge off as well:

"Go ahead, Captain. But only if you offer me one, too."

To satisfy his nicotine habit, Broadbent conveniently had his car come with a rear ashtray and a companion cigarette lighter. He offered Margaret a cigarette, waiting for the lighter to recoil from its housing when it became aglow. Looking into Broadbent's eyes, Margaret clumsily withdrew the long-stemmed Kool. She tenderly held his hand as he lit it for her. As Broadbent pressed the power window buttons to crack the rear windows to allow the smoke to vent, she gazed out her window, taking a slow drag on the cigarette. At first the smoke taxed her lungs, but she did not cough when she asked:

"How much longer to the coroner's office?"

"The next ramp is Claremont Mesa. We'll be there shortly. Are you okay?"

"As good as I'm going to be—until I see the body."

"We'll take it slow once inside. I must say you appear to be a strong person, given all the personal loss in your life. But don't hesitate to tell us to back off if you feel we are too pushy."

Margaret liked Broadbent's composed manner, which made him appear more like a clergyman than a detective:

"Thank you, Captain, for all your concerns. I'm bracing myself as best as I can."

But Broadbent came back to business:

"I'll leave it to you when you want to tell us more about the person you just mentioned. With your flight alone, I think you've had a tiring day. Was it a Sela Danby?"

"Yes, that's the name. Maybe tomorrow I'll tell you why she's important. After I see Jordan, could you kindly take me to the LaValencia?"

"By all means, Mrs. Starmont. I'll have a car bring your bag from my office to the hotel"

With their cigarettes nearly consumed, the two smokers extinguished their butts in the ashtray as the squad entered the County Medical Examiner parking lot.

Once inside, Broadbent gave Margaret an orientation to what she was about to witness, emphasizing again the disfigurement and some discoloration to the body. He advised her to look for those distinguishing characteristics that would be vital to confirm the identity of the person she was about to view. He also added:

"We haven't performed an autopsy. You have a legal right to prevent it."

The sound of the word "autopsy" made Margaret feel a little faint as they approached the entrance to the morgue room. She grabbed Broadbent's arm and said:

"Captain, can I rest a moment? Things are moving around."

"Sure, sure. Herlihy, get some water for Mrs. Starmont."

Broadbent sat next to Margaret on a padded bench in the corridor. Herlihy brought a large plastic cup of water in less than a minute. Margaret took a deep breath, sipped the water, and closed her eyes for a moment to regain her equilibrium. After a minute, Broadbent commented:

"You appear better. Do you want to proceed with the identification?"

The grieving mother gave a reluctant nod of consent. Inside the room, which appeared cooler to Margaret than it really was, things were stark and unadorned, with white walls, stainless steel examining tables and the vault, which looked like oversized filing cabinets holding the dead in its wall. The diener (morgue attendant) slowly pulled back the sliding cabinet that held the body. Broadbent clung to Margaret's arm as they approached the corpse, shrouded in what appeared to be a rubber blanket. The diener calmly withdrew the covering, exposing the milk white body from head to foot. Margaret gave it an initial glance, then suddenly looked away. When her eyes returned to the body, she looked for the identifying characteristics she was advised to confirm: color/type of hair and eyes, any scars or moles, body type, or any other unique body characteristic. It has been almost a year since she last saw her son. Her initial scan of the body began with the head, seeing some likeness to Jordan's high cheekbones and the straight texture of the black hair. She glossed over the discolored and bulging neck, and moved down the torso. Then, with a burst of curiosity, stopped at the pubic region. Her mouth opened, taken by surprise Something was not right. She needed clarification.

"Can I get a better look at the genitals?"

Broadbent instructed the attending pathologist in the room to elevate the limp penis. With a bit of consternation, she asked:

"Is this person circumcised?"

Uplifting the genitals with a small towel and rubber gloves, the pathologist examined the foreskin on the flaccid organ. He responded:

"Based on what I see at this first observation, the individual was never circumcised."

The answer gave Margaret a ray of unanticipated hope and joy. She broke out with an air of certainty:

"This is not Jordan."

It was as if only Margaret stood erect, with Broadbent, the pathologist, the diener, and detectives Herlihy and Sandoval drooping their shoulders in disbelief. Broadbent demanded:

"Mrs. Starmont, what makes you so sure?"

With a maternal assurance, Margaret gave her reply:

"Detective, mothers know their sons. We had Jordan circumcised, it's the religious custom in our family. You've got the wrong person!"

Perth, August, 1969

It was dark in Sela Danby's apartment. The lack of light symbolized her current state. Drowsy after awakening from a two-hour nap, she became startled when she didn't know what time it was. There was fear that she would miss her date with Rex Murtaugh. She pulled the metal chain of her lamp on the nightstand and nervously turned her wristwatch to the dial. Whew! It's only 9:10—enough time to freshen up and make her date at the K on Hay Café. Reinforcing the need to be free from so much, she napped in the nude. Unclothed, it expedited her jarring, cold shower. Given the pile of clothes both she and Ian Bright had in the room, finding suitable apparel was a challenge. She toweled briskly and found a pink top with spaghetti straps and a pair of white chinos, which clung to her lean, sensual torso. Her hair cooperated as she brushed it into a flip hairdo. Her bangs accented her forehead. She looked like Marlo Thomas, only she had sandy brown hair. A spray of Givenchy Cologne gave her the scent of a woman—needed to excite a man.

Ready to go out the door after twenty minutes of preparation, she was startled by the phone ringing. She thought about not answering it, but she did not want to arouse his suspicions if Ian Bright was calling. In an agreeable voice, she picked up the receiver:

"Hello, is this Ian?"

Bright had lusty intentions:

"Sela, dearie. I trust you've been missin' me caressin' your sweet loins. You best be ready for me when I come back to Perth."

Trying to humor him, she stayed amiable:

"When might that be? My date book is always clear for you."

"Ooh! Just my bad luck. Need to stay here two maybe three days more. These sharpie mates I'm meetin' with here in Melbourne want to know more about my business. I trust you've best behavin'."

Sela needed to placate him:

"You know we are tight. What are you about with your business?"

"Only can say it is crunch time—need a way to get to San Diego. That's in America if you don't know, dearie."

Sela was mystified:

"San Diego? Why there? Aren't we going back to London in a week?"

"Can't say much more, dearie. It's a change of plan. I'll tell you more when I come back to Perth."

"Okay. I understand."

"Don't fret, dearie. Got to run off to a meetin'. I'll call you tomorrow 'bout the same time to let you when I'm comin' back to give you a squeeze. Sweet dreams, now, even without my warm body next to yours."

Sela was cheered by the fact she had some time to think things through. She didn't want to hasten Ian's return:

"I understand. Take your time. Miss you, love."

Sela was renewed with hope after the call. It gave her a bounce to her step as she left the apartment. The warm, comforting breeze in the night air was refreshing when she hit the sidewalk. Even though the benign Perth climate was growing on her, she knew she had to leave it. Bright has given her the opening; Murtaugh has to see her through it.

The K on Hay Café was doing a brisk evening business. Located in the Comfort Hotel Perth City, the restaurant's nightlife was alive most of the time. There was always a steady flow of tourists and it had an attraction for athletic types, especially the cricketers and soccer players who performed at the WACA athletic grounds. The eatery was modern, airy, and bright. She was struck by the wall behind the bar, studded with stone pebbles. No sooner did she approach the bar, the host approached her:

"Forgive me, but are you a Miss Sela Danby?"

She was surprised:

"Why, yes. How did you know?"

The host played his assigned role and did not answer the question:

"Right this way, ma'am."

She followed him to an alfresco area, an excellent choice on a balmy evening. There, she saw the smiling face of Rex Murtaugh, dressed as if he should have been at the Royal Perth Yacht Club. He was wearing a navy blue and white ringed short-sleeved mariner's shirt and solid navy bandana tied around his neck. He looked handsome in the subdued outdoor light that gave him a sexy, bronze look.

Sela was concerned:

"Rex, here I thought I was late."

Murtaugh stood up with a beaming smile, seated Sela at a cozy, candle-lit rattan table for two, and put on the charm:

"No, no. You look lovely, Sela. It's good to see you again."

Sela wasn't sure if she should she begin on a serious note or start the evening with small talk. She settled for a little of both:

"Thank you. I'm so delighted you agreed to meet with me tonight. I need this more than you know."

"Okay. Sounds important. How has life been treating you?"

No need wasting time. Murtaugh's response gave her the segue she needed to get to the point:

"Frankly, not the best. I have a serious matter to contend with."

Murtaugh winced when he heard she was troubled. He was hoping for a leisure evening, not a profound one. To relax things, he poured each of them a glass of a popular Australian wine, a Yellow Glen Bella Chardonnay, he had chilling in an ice bucket. While pouring, he was comforting and interested:

"I hope we can have a good time this evening, but I sensed earlier in the hall you had some important business to discuss. Tell me about this 'sign' you are looking for."

"Oh, Rex, I don't mean to be impolite. I apologize for coming on so strong. I must say I'm a little tense just now."

Murtaugh reached for her hand and looked into her eyes and tried to reassure her:

"You know, I have a confession to make. I've been in this country for almost nine months. I couldn't think of a better choice than you for my first date. So, I'm here to listen if that makes you happy."

Murtaugh shunned the waiter who offered them menus and told him to hold off. Sela gained composure knowing she had a sympathetic ear:

"I won't mince words: I think I am in danger. I'm traveling with a man, Ian Bright, who I believe has evil intentions. Fortunately, he's in Melbourne—out of my life for a bit, thank goodness."

Murtaugh immediately grew suspicious:

"That doesn't sound good; he wouldn't approve of us meeting tonight. I take it you are total strangers in Perth and no one knows about our meeting?"

"Ian scares me because he's mingling with this 'sharpie' crowd. But I don't think he's got one of them watching me in his absence."

Murtaugh raised the caution flag:

"They're also known as 'sharps' here in Perth. I've seen a few at the club and their dress, high steel-toe boots, levis, and vulgar slogans they write on their personally designed cardigan sweaters and crest-knit black shirts, give them away. A fellow employee told me they have a taste for violence and are part of the seamy side of recent newcomers to Perth that work at the BP refinery."

"So, they are out and about—right here?"

"Well, don't worry. I doubt you'd find these undesirables in this place—too upscale and no reggae or Jamaican ska music in the room. They literally march to a different beat."

"Yes, I know. Ian thinks the Beatles music I adore is not cool and does not like the way I dress. Thinks I need a new look--clothes, hair--you name it."

"Sela, from what I have seen, don't change anything. I like you just the way you are. But--do tell me how you and Bright got together."

Sela rambled a little. She said she met Bright through an offbeat girlfriend earlier this year, who had a boyfriend in a skinhead band in London--the East End Boys. Sela went to one of their gigs in Soho and was introduced to Bright. She'd been dating him on a regular basis since. He said the band was going international, with some bookings in Australia. Bright offered her to go with him. Not mentioning the information about

Bright Sela received from her half-brother, Jordan Starmont, she told Murtaugh about her other misgivings. Once they arrived in Australia, there were no band members to be found. She stressed it was her good fortune that Bright had to suddenly run off to Melbourne for an apparent meeting with some Sharpies.

Murtaugh wasn't sure where to go next with the conversation. Rather, he steered the talk to the niceties of Perth, i.e., the great weather, fine restaurants, a casual environment, and a fun place to be. He then paged the waiter and ordered for the two of them--a shrimp special. But midway through the entrée, Sela had to get back to her major task at hand:

"Rex, this may sound crazy, we really don't know one another. But I need a way out of this place. Can you help me?"

Murtaugh sensed the young woman was in distress by the tears in her eyes. But he had to keep his guard up, even though her cute English accent, the smell of her perfume, the outline of her breasts protruding through her tight top, and the glow of her lovely face excited him:

"Sela, this all seems too fast a pace for the two of us. Besides, you really don't know much about me."

"When you are in the dire straits I am, you need to gamble. You look trustworthy."

Murtaugh laughed inwardly. If she really knew about his diabolical past, Bright would seem like a choirboy in comparison. However, he let her plead her case after he ordered a second bottle of wine.

"One of the reasons you appealed to me is that you look and act smart I saw that the first time I saw you work behind the bar at your club. Women look for intelligence, you know."

Murtaugh gained a perspective he never knew before. Maybe that was his problem--he tried to assess himself through the impressions men held for him, rather than women, for most of his young life. He was amused:

"Ah, yes, that's just another reason your sex lives longer than men--you look before you jump. Let me offer an alternative to you, to confirm my intelligence quotient."

Murtaugh sensed Sela was dangling on a string, the effects of the wine notwithstanding. She leaned a little closer to him and said:

"Rex, I am all ears."

"You need a sanctuary to allow us to build an escape plan for you."

"And where would that be?"

"Across the hall from where you are staying--in my room."

San Diego, September, 1969

Damon Broadbent's livid state raised his body temperature above the early afternoon heat. Steaming behind his desk back at his San Diego Police Department office, he questioned his expertise as a detective. He had just returned from viewing a corpse, whose identity was now more unverifiable than ever. Never in his ten years as a detective has he mistakenly called on the wrong next of kin to identify a homicide victim. Requesting Margaret Starmont, who believed she was to see her dead son at the County Coroner's office, to come over 3,000 miles on a wild goose chase was the ultimate ineptitude for a cop. He has an impeccable record, who has solved most of the cases that he's been assigned. With no positive identification, he had little to go on to pursue the perpetrator of this heinous crime. He was surly as he shouted through his open door:

"Herlihy, Sandoval, get in here please!"

Detectives Dan Herlihy and Rick Sandoval were discussing the case over coffee at the latter's desk when they heard the order. Fearing the worst based on Broadbent's sour tone, they dutifully came into his office and glumly took a chair. Broadbent cut to the chase:

"Once it leaks out at what happened this morning at the coroner's it will give the papers a field day. The chief is really interested in this one because it's in the news and is high profile. Right now, he's not happy with my report. Let's call it our version of L.A.P.D.'s Black Dahlia case, only it's a dead man on our watch."

Sandoval's curiosity was aroused:

"Black Dahlia? Tell me more."

"Sorry, Rick, we're both off task. Let's table that one for now. Our job is the big problem on our plate. This town is still small enough to have the locals nitpick us to death. You both know there is a large law and order crowd that lives here, especially the military firebrands. We've got to get a handle on this one--fast!"

Herlihy tried to be positive:

"Captain, from a procedure standpoint we did nothing wrong. We all know this case borders on the bizarre."

"Dan, I appreciate you trying to be objective on this one, but we need an action plan pronto to get the egg off our faces that is sure to come our way. I want you to get on a PSA flight up to San Francisco this evening for some TDY. I'll call Blake Sheridan in the San Francisco PD homicide division to tell him you're coming; give him the facts of what we know."

"Sure thing, Captain, so my objective is to track down this Starmont guy?"

Broadbent paused a bit before he answered the question. He wanted the focus on the son, not the mother:

"Yeah, we presume he might still be there. Mrs. Starmont did confide that her last contact with Jordan was when he supposedly was still in hippyville --the Haight-Ashbury district. That's a place you'll have to scour to find him."

Herlihy had a sense of humor:

"Do I pack my beads and my Grateful Dead tie-dye shirts?"

Broadbent smiled but thought there was substance to Herlihy's question:

"Hmm? Dan, that's more than funny. You may have to go undercover. Hey, with your youthful looks you might just fit in with the flower children up there. We'll cover your expenses if you have to purchase psychedelic duds."

Herlihy reinforced the counter culture lingo:

"Right on, brother!"

Broadbent reinforced the good vibrations and gave the peace sign. Then he directed another order for Herlihy:

"Find out from the SFO Hertz location what they might recall about the person who rented their car. Work backward from there. I think that might bring you into LSD country in what they call 'The Haight.'"

Sandoval was amused and ready to get into the hunt:

"So, where do you want me to sniff around?"

Thus far, Broadbent was pleased his associates did not bring up Margaret Starmont. Broadbent wanted her to be his--all his. He also gave Sandoval a big assignment to keep it that way:

"Rick, there is plenty of action for you, too. Start with the Marines, especially up at Pendleton. The surfer witnesses at Windansea think the two seedy characters inquiring about the corpse in the cabana might be military types because of their short hair and southern drawls. Anyone AWOL or on a 'bad boy' list? Then we need to identify who the hell is in the Coroner's cooler. That's missing persons territory for you to explore--on a national level. So, that means the FBI. I think you know a little bit about Al Taggart's FBI shop here in town?"

Sandoval dutifully responded:

"That will work. I try to get together with the Bureau's Joe Pizzo once a month for happy hour at the 'old boys club'--Lubach's. Gets the edge off."

Good, Broadbent thought. He was free and clear to pursue Margaret. Wanting to keep it that way, he suddenly ended the session:

"Great, guys. Dan, call with daily reports from San Francisco. Tell your girlfriend you may be out for awhile. Rick, we'll be close enough to debrief daily. Good hunting, men!"

The three rose from their chairs almost in unison. Broadbent began paternally ushering his subordinates out. Putting one arm on Herlihy's shoulder and the other gently pressing Sandoval's lower back, he was extolling their abilities. As soon as Broadbent got them outside his office, he closed the door and returned to his desk to ponder his next moves. He began thinking about Margaret and how he was going to approach her, now that he bumbled his way into her life. He called the La Valencia to check in on her. He was heartened to hear her soft, tender voice after he was connected to her room:

"Hello."

"Mrs. Starmont, this is Captain Broadbent again. I trust the La Valencia is up to its usual high standards and comforts?"

"Many things change, captain. Fortunately, this grand place always remains at its elegant best. It sparkles this time of year."

"Yes, as you might know summer really begins in August and September out here. Not as much fog and overcast in La Jolla to boot. I'm sorry we gave you a scare and inconvenienced you."

Margaret was not too upset about Broadbent's miscalculation. In fact, the woman was gleeful, now that she knew the body she inspected was not Jordan's cold remains. Besides, coming back for another stay at the lovely La Valencia Hotel atop La Jolla Cove overlooking the Pacific had its amenities. What a one-eighty for Margaret. The ride to the coroner's office was dreadful; the scenic ride to the hotel over the ridge of Mt. Soledad, descending to La Jolla by the Sea, was like a journey in Cinderella's carriage. Never before in her lifetime has she gone from agony to ecstasy in so few heartbeats. What Broadbent did not know was that she appreciated his display of vulnerability, even though he was in a macho profession. Feeling better about herself, she started to assuage him:

"Don't be so hard on yourself, captain. Based on the circumstances, you thought you had good reason to bring me out here. Now that I'm back in this jewel of a place, I might extend my stay. That's what La Jolla means—'the jewel'?"

That was music to Broadbent's ears:

"Yes, if you use the Spanish derivation from their word for jewel: 'la joya'. There is some thought it also comes from an Indian word. No matter its source, it's beautiful anyway you spell it, or cast its meaning."

"That's almost literary. You take a lot of pride in this place."

Broadbent could feel her appreciating his charms:

"Sure do. That's why I do police work. To me, criminal acts mar the reputation of the place. I try to do my best to lessen their negative impact."

Margaret continued to stroke him:

"It's good to know that you really believe in your 'to protect and serve' motto. I appreciate how you have been mindful of my feelings throughout this experience."

Broadbent had professional and personal motives in mind when he asked:

"Good. Good. As I mentioned when I dropped you off at the hotel, we need to follow-up on some things, especially what you know about this Sela Danby. Do you have any plans later this afternoon?"

"No, but I do need some rest. The anxiety of the last few days and the early flight out here have drained me. I can see you – say, seven? Would that meet your schedule?"

Broadbent jumped at the opening:

"Great. That will work. I'll meet you in the lobby at that time, Mrs. Starmont."

Perhaps it was the peace of mind knowing her son still walked this earth somewhere. Or maybe it was the delight of returning to La Jolla. But Margaret put a different spin on their relationship:

"Tell me something, Captain. What about Mrs. Broadbent? Does she condone your irregular hours?"

"There was a Mrs. Broadbent, but we divorced five years ago. She couldn't handle me not being around much. My kind of work has its personal hazards."

Something was in the air with these two when she said:

"I'm glad you have the time to see me then. My friends call me Maggie."

Broadbent seized the moment:

"My friends call me Damon."

9
CHAPTER

San Francisco, September, 1969

When Detective Dan Herlihy's Pacific Southwest Airlines (PSA) flight landed at dusk at San Francisco International Airport (SFO), he was dressed for his assignment: denim pants, a leather vest, a paisley shirt, and an unruffled look to his brown, curly hair. The air was noticeably cooler than San Diego's warmer temperature, but he found it refreshing after he claimed his bag and waited at the terminal for his lift--a San Francisco Police Department squad car. His boss, Captain Damon Broadbent, had alerted the S.F.P.D. that he was coming--with an incognito look. It wasn't long that one of their cruisers with two uniformed officers spotted him and pulled to the curb. Herlihy hopped in and requested that they first stop at the SFO Hertz office. But the officers said that was "not necessary." Instead, they headed north into the city. Herlihy sensed there was something out of the ordinary. But, he stayed cordial and chatted about what was preoccupying their time. With no lulls, the S.F.P.D. had had plenty of action, primarily controlling the marches for social justice, sporadic race riots, college student anti-Vietnam War demonstrations, especially at San Francisco State University, and the hippie movement based in Haight-Ashbury. By comparison, Herlihy felt lucky to be based in staid San Diego. But he had an itch for something more exciting, the reason he got into police work. He wasn't going to be bored with this assignment.

Once they arrived at the S.F.P.D. Hall of Justice, it had a familiar look. It was the film site of the current and very popular *Perry Mason* television series and in a few more years would gain future acclaim for the locale of the *Dirty Harry* films. Herlihy wasn't a television or movie star, but he was going to have an important spotlight cast upon his assignment. Blake Sheridan, a chief homicide inspector, was waiting for him in his office. Sheridan looked atypical because he was in his dress uniform, having come from a funeral earlier in the afternoon for an officer killed in the line of duty. A stern looking man with salt and pepper black hair, he got to the point:

"Detective Herlihy, I am glad you arrived. Based on what Captain Broadbent told me about your problem in San Diego, maybe the pieces start coming together up here. You'll work through us as long as you are in our city. No solo work. Is that clear?"

"Yes, sir, I gather that is one of the reasons your people told me I could not go to the Hertz shop at SFO to start my investigation?"

Sheridan deflected the question, having his own agenda to stay in charge:

"How long have you been a cop, Herlihy?"

Herlihy was puzzled by the query but answered forthrightly:

"This November it will be nine years, four as a homicide detective working with Captain Broadbent."

"Okay, from what I have researched on your boss, you sure are lucky to be working for Broadbent--he's one of the best."

"Yes, I'm learning so much from the Captain. He's thorough and fair."

"When I spoke to him about your purpose for coming up here this afternoon, he was frustrated and embarrassed on what happened at the San Diego coroner's office. It's too bad your department is a step behind the science that is now becoming an excellent investigative tool."

"Oh, what's that?"

"They, and I should say we because we have a new department for it, call it forensic science. It's designed to recover and corroborate evidence. That includes bodies found in a La Jolla cabana. Much of it has to do with trace evidence. Stuff beyond fingerprints, to include hair, fibers, bloodstain patterns, and glass and soil residues. It's all becoming more scientific, my friend. Had you used these new tools you would not have been so red-faced at your coroner's office."

"Yeah, I've heard about some of the new stuff, but they'll still need wise old owls like us to make the connections and come to the bottom of things and make good collars."

Sheridan nodded. Then he reached into the middle drawer of his large wooden desk and retrieved a manila envelope. He pulled out a document from it and said:

"Here, this might make some sense as to why what you have in San Diego does not appear what it was presumed to be. Let me read:

> *From: Theodore Johnson, Chief Investigator, Federal Bureau of Investigation, San Francisco Division*
>
> *To: San Francisco Police Department*
>
> *Re: Undercover Surveillance in Your Jurisdiction*
>
> *With the increased use and distribution of illegal drugs in your city, the Department has increased its activities to interdict the flow of these substances, many of which have come from sources outside your state, and some from foreign dealers. Much of the illegal activity has been occurring in the Haight-Ashbury district. To assist this effort, the Department is using undercover agents, many of them first-time apprentices under the tutelage and guidance of our staff. They are college age individuals, who would strategically fit in with the counter culture youth who are the primary users and dealers of illegal drugs, viz., hallucinogenic LSD and heroin. These undercover agents are working hand in glove with our people and have been highly effective.*
>
> *As you know, the Department is also very vigilant with its national security responsibilities. Because of their misgivings about the country's involvement in the Vietnam War, we are also monitoring subversive anti-war activists with a penchant for violent and destructive behavior. In fact,*

we are diligently pursuing a potential terrorist plot from an old adversary: the Nazis! We have good reason to believe a neo-Nazi group is in its early stages to perpetrate a violent act somewhere in California. At this time, the primary target may be in San Diego, likely at one of the many military facilities in that region.

In that regard, please call our agent in charge, Ross Cargill, who is spearheading our surveillance operation. He can be reached at our usual contact telephone number. Agent Cargill can bring you up to speed as to where we are with our activities. As usual, the Department appreciates your continued cooperation and assistance with this endeavor.

"So, it's funny. The FBI has scooped us again, Detective Herlihy. They have agents closer to the ages of the hippies and recluses roaming 'The Haight'. Are you sure you are not too old to be working undercover for the San Diego PD on our hippie turf?"

Herlihy laughed:

"That might be, but I do know there are a number of counter culture types roaming your streets who are my age and older. I think I'd fit in."

Sheridan smiled:

"I think you are right. Our department has undercover types, both male and female, your age doing a good job keeping the lid on. But, I'm sure you want to know what this all means to you folks to help your investigation down in San Diego."

"That's why they sent me up here."

"If you prod Cargill hard enough, he'll open up. He gave us a roster of their apprentices working with the Department just in case we stumbled into them to avoid embarrassment for all concerned. It's a well-kept secret that the public is being protected from the crazies more than they know—and that's a good thing to keep them ignorant to make our work pay dividends. At any rate, one of the names on that list makes your assignment worthwhile. And, as you will find out when you make your first move, which is to contact Cargill immediately, you will discover the sub rosa that is clouding your investigation."

Herlihy became impatient:

"C'mon. Let's get to the point."

"The point is, Detective Herlihy, I just learned yesterday that the FBI apprentice at the heart and soul of the quirky happenings that just occurred on one of your beaches is none other than Jordan Starmount."

10
CHAPTER

Perth, August, 1969

The morning after Sela Danby's date with Rex Murtaugh she hoped for a new beginning in her troubled life. Given the assurance that he would help her extricate herself from the clutches of Ian Bright, it would also be the onset of a different direction her life would take—one that still had peril along the way. Sela knew she had no choice and accepted Murtaugh's assistance to stay with him until she had the resources to go back to England. He allayed her fears that despite the fact she was moving just across the hall, within Bright's sense of sight, sound, and smell upon his return, this gambit would work. Murtaugh was convincing when he last saw her:

"Bright has never seen me and does not know who I am. I'll be your lookout if you need to leave the building. When he finds you gone, the last place in Perth he will look for you is right under his nose. Guys like him lose their objectivity and go ballistic when something they think they own is missing."

Sela spent the night in her current apartment alone after Murtaugh politely brought her home from dinner and only gave her a peck on the cheek when he said, "Good night". In the early morning, she scurried to get dressed after awaking from a short, fitful sleep. But before she packed her belongings to transport them to Murtaugh's room, she felt compelled to telephone her half-brother, Jordan Starmount, to give him an answer if she would agree to help him keep track of Bright. Rather than call from her room, where a call could be traced, she decided to go to the Western Union office to use their telephone and to see if there were other messages or letters from Jordan. Dressed in a casual sweater and denims as she locked her door on the way out, she thought of knocking at Murtaugh's adjacent apartment to tell him her whereabouts. However, she thought differently, believing he might convince her to stay low and off the streets. Besides, she still was not ready to reveal who Jordan was and what he knew about Bright's dangerous intentions. It was not quite 7:00 A.M.; she only hoped the Western Union office would be open at this early hour.

Once outside, another sunny day brightened a morning to dissipate some of Sela's dark outlook. She was a bit paranoid, wearing sunglasses and a scarf covering her head, still worried that someone was watching her or that, heaven forbid, Ian would suddenly return from Melbourne unannounced. Walking at a fast pace, in minutes she got to the Western Union office. But her fears were realized when she saw no lights on when she came to the glass doors. The posted hours stated they did not open until 10:00 A.M. But, luck was with her. There was enough light from the sun's rays to reveal a man was stirring behind the counter--a Western Union agent. She knocked on the glass door to get the agent's attention. He came to the door and with a raised voice said:

"Sorry, ma'am. We do not open for another several hours."

Sela got inventive:

"Sir, this is an emergency. Big strife as you people down here would say. My brother in the United States is not well and I have to see if he's contacted me. I need to use your telephone to contact him."

The agent hesitated, grimaced, and then relented by reaching for his keys to unlock the glass doors. When he had it slightly opened, he ordered:

"All right. But please follow me to the office in back. Can't have other mates see me giving you any preferences."

She entered the office, dutifully followed him to a small office behind the counter, and thanked him for this exception:

"Sir, I really appreciated this. My name is Sela Danby. Do I have any messages from my brother—Jordan Starmont?"

"Let me check. We did get a wire before we closed last night from San Francisco. Please wait here; I'll see if it's for you, Ms. Danby."

Hearing where it came from, Sela just knew it was a message from Jordan. The agent came back with the message in his hand:

"Yes, here it is. Our log shows it came for you at 9:21 P.M., Western Australia Time, from a Jordan Starmont."

Sela couldn't wait to break the envelope's seal. She read with an excited heartbeat:

Sela:

Urgent! If you are ready to help, we need your assistance. Please call me at 01. 555.747.2815. Call collect! I'll be standing by for the next 24 hours. If we don't make connection, call a higher authority at 01.555.272.4000. Again, this is for "your eyes only." You are needed. Thank you.

Jordan

Sela put the wire down and reflected. Wow! What timing! We are on the same telephone wavelength. Yes, Jordan is right. This is a little like a James Bond escapade. *For Your Eyes Only* was an Ian Fleming book she heard about and a directive for top secret documents. Without further hesitation she requested:

"Sir, I need to make a collect call in private."

"Here's what we do. Give me your number. I dial it. You look like an honest sheila, but if I get your call through there are no worries. Sound fair?"

Sela heartily agreed. When the agent told her it was a sixteen hour difference between Perth and San Francisco, making it around 3:00 P.M. the previous day, she thought the call might be taken by someone. The agent dialed the number, connected to the operator, and told her he had a "collect call for Jordan Starmont from a Sela Danby." The agent brought Sela to the telephone after he heard Jordan's phone ring and then left the room to give her privacy. After several rings, Sela heard Jordan and the operator interact. He joyfully approved taking the call and said:

"Sela! I'm so glad you got my message. Are you safe with Bright?"

"I think so. Ian is still in Melbourne, but he'll be back perhaps tomorrow."

"Fine. But we have little time. It's time I level with you. I'm working for the Federal Bureau of Investigation, our FBI as we call it. That's why I have inside information about what Bright is all about."

Sela found a hidden reserve of humor to help her cope:

"And here I thought you had some ESP ability. I'm impressed. How'd you get such an important position?"

"Can't reveal that. But, to the point, we know Bright has been instructed by his father to come to San Diego soon. I can now tell you that Ian's father is a David Percival. They speak in code. We know Percival told Ian 'to bring the ignitor to deliver the blow'. Not really sure what that means, but they are getting ready to strike--somewhere in San Diego."

Sela was having misgivings:

"So, does Ian have to bring me along? I want to get away from this bloody fool."

Jordan had to be persuasive:

"Sela, the guy has a 'thing' for you. He convinced Percival that you have to be with him—just in case he can't go back to England from America after they complete their mission."

"If he loves me so much, why did he run off to Melbourne?"

"That's where the 'ignitor' might be. He can get it from a no questions asked provider in Melbourne that has the key piece to pull off their dangerous stunt."

"I'm confused. Again, why do you need me to come to San Diego? Can't they just go out and arrest Percival without me? Then they could stop whatever damage you think he will cause?"

"Good suggestion but there are two reasons why the authorities do not want to simply nab him now. First, the evidence we have against him is primarily circumstantial; won't hold up in court. Second, we believe Percival is part of a larger terrorist ring. If we take him into custody too soon, his unseen and unknown accomplices will be free to cause additional harm."

"Oh, Jordan. This sounds really dangerous. I don't know. I must tell you I think I have a way out of this drivel without Bright at my side."

"What do you mean?"

"I met a man, an American, who is my protector. He lives in the same building I'm in. I trust him to relieve my burden."

"Sela, I understand why you are looking for a way out. But let me assure you that we will be at your elbow the moment you land in San Diego. Once we see you land with Bright, the two of you will lead us to Percival. The hope is that Percival brings us to whomever else is part of this plot. Bright told Percival he needs to safely 'stash' you away before he makes contact with his father."

"So, I will be out of harm's way?"

"Trust me. I work with very professional, competent people. Once you are no longer needed we will have you well protected. I think Bright will try to put you off to the side probably as soon as you arrive. Then you are ours; then we'll have Bright alone in our sights."

"That's reassuring, but this other option is appealing--and I won't have to risk my neck."

"I presume this must be a real impressive guy. What's his name?"

"Rex Murtaugh, a strong, resilient type."

"Just to be sure. We'll run an ID check on Murtaugh. You just never know about total strangers, no matter how appealing they seem. But, can you help us? It will be a noble act."

Sela had a moment of truth to make. Murtaugh seemed to be legitimate, but he was no guarantee to assure her deliverance. Bright was now a bona fide bad guy, but Jordan was persuasive to keep her unscathed. She hemmed and hawed with Jordan for a few more minutes, discussing the pluses and minuses of her next move. Finally, she relented:

"Jordan, I'll do it. Not because I'll be some brave heroine but because I finally will get a chance to meet you--my brother."

Jordan was ecstatic and ended the call by giving Sela the telephone number for the US Consulate in Perth and instructed her to reference "Operation Odessa". Wrapping up their conversation, he advised to call the Consulate once her flight to San Diego was booked:

"They'll know what to do. Sela, you are a brave soul. Our father was an intelligence officer. It's funny, now we are following in his footsteps. He'd be so proud of us. Stay cautious and God bless you."

Sela put the receiver down, feeling confident that she could help do something constructive in her young life. Maybe it was the spiritual connection she felt to her parents, or the persuasive arguments Jordan made, or maybe it was the rush of adventure she finally appreciated. But she had to awkwardly reverse herself. Yes, Rex Murtaugh tugged at her heart. It would not be easy rejecting a newly acquired guardian angel for a return to the dark side in her life without him.

La Jolla, September, 1969

Captain Damon Broadbent had two immediate goals. First, to solve the murder on one of his city's scenic beaches; second, to get to know an attractive widow, Margaret Starmont, better. In his mind, both were related to the other. When it came to the gaffe about the misidentified murder victim, he had little to go on. When it came to Mrs. Starmont, well, let's just say he was attracted to the woman. He had to be sure to temper his ardor for her, else it would complicate his investigation as to who was murdered, why it happened, and who did it. It was nearly 7:00 P.M. when Broadbent found a parking space on Prospect Street, one of America's more elegant thoroughfares, accented by world-class museums, upscale shopping, gourmet restaurants, and the street address to the posh La Valencia Hotel. He was about to keep his date with Margaret, who would be awaiting him there. As he approached the hotel entrance, his professional ego was bruised. Police work was a demanding profession. This was a challenging case, but Broadbent knew what he had to do. Only this time he had a pleasant bonus--the comfort of Margaret's company.

Broadbent appreciated the La Valencia's trappings, an inspirational edifice of old-world Mediterranean elegance. It's soothing pink exterior stucco walls, accented by a domed tower, outdoor patios, flanked by palm trees and graced with fresh flowers in cobalt blue vases on tables with white umbrellas, and an opulent lobby, with Persian rugs and baroque furniture, would place it perfectly along the Amalfi Coast in Italy or on a Greek island in the Aegean Sea. Broadbent looked first for Margaret in the corner bar off the lobby. The usual clientele he interacted with might be found there. Of course, he knew Margaret, who oozed with social class, wouldn't be in the bar with a drink in hand. It was his basic instinct that drew him to this spot. But Broadbent resisted the urge for a shot of alcohol. He did not want the look of a vice squad officer. So, he waited at the end of the hotel's foyer to appreciate the magnificent vista through a large picture window. The view was stunning. With a background of the sinking sun's rays glistening on the blue Pacific and a foreground of a descending hillside of palm trees that surrounded the beautiful La Jolla Cove up to the water's edge, Broadbent looked upon the beauty beneath him.

He turned from nature's beauty and found a chair next to a narrow table with an ashtray. A bit edgy, it was the right spot to reach for a Kool. With eyes glued to a gold lighter poised to light his cigarette, he discerned Margaret, comely in gray slacks and a cream-colored gypsy blouse made of pure silk. Margaret's svelte, sleek lines gave her an athletic look. The blouse's billowy long sleeves further helped defy her chronological age. Her make-up accentuated her features. It didn't have to be; she was attractive enough. What Broadbent did not know was that she appreciated his softer side, even though he was in a macho profession. She was apologetic as she approached Broadbent:

"Good evening, Captain. I am sorry if I kept you waiting."

Trying to stay all business, Broadbent arose out of chair and looked at his watch and said:

"Yes, good evening Mrs. Starmont. I try to be early for my appointments. No, you are very punctual--it's first seven o'clock now."

"I appreciate you giving me some time to catch my breath after what happened earlier today at the coroner's office."

"Again, the whole department is not happy we put you through a false alarm. I assure you, this is not the norm with our force. We are bound and determined to get to the bottom of what really happened not far from here down at Windansea."

"Oh, please, you did what you thought was right. Let's not dwell on what went wrong."

Broadbent wanted to stay in control:

"Where do you prefer we discuss this further, especially how your son is a still a very major part of our investigation?"

"It's a warm, lovely evening. The patio looks inviting."

The two strolled to the adjacent patio, and were lucky to be seated on a busy evening. Broadbent was glad the large gathering created a general hubbub to keep their conversation muffled for adjacent patrons. When the waiter came to their table, Margaret was ready to unwind:

"I need something relaxing. Please bring me a glass of Claret. One of the Bordeaux's I know you serve here."

Broadbent was impressed with the lady's knowledge of fine wines. He followed his on-duty protocol with a tame order:

"Tonic with a lime, please."

The waiter left and Margaret wanted to extend the joy of freedom from anxiety she was experiencing:

"Can I trouble you for another cigarette? I guess I have to control an old habit, but the smell of tobacco has that old allure for me right now."

Broadbent dutifully reached for another Kool, offered it to Margaret, and was titillated by the touch of her hand holding his when he re-ignited his lighter for her. He let her draw a puff and asked a probing question whose answer might keep her close to the San Diego scene:

"Well, you should know our department is devoting much of its energy to properly identify the corpse of the young man you viewed, and with that solve his murder. In that regard, I have sent detective Herlihy, whom you have met, up to San Francisco—in search of your son. It would aid us if you were close at hand. Any idea how long you will be with us in San Diego?"

"That is real good to know, Captain. I have an open return to New York. If it will help you solve the murder and to confirm where Jordan is, I'll stay here as long as I have to."

"That would be helpful. It has been over a year since you saw him--correct?"

"A long, troubling year. I have the fervent hope to see him again. I just know he is somewhere in San Francisco, likely still living in Haight-Ashbury It would make me so very, very happy to know that he is safe."

Broadbent appreciated the outpouring of a mother's love. But it also satisfied a selfish desire that she wasn't leaving town soon. Now he focused on Sela Danby:

"Rest assured I will inform you of what Detective Herlihy discovers up there. Now, you mentioned a Sela Danby in the car. Can you tell me more?"

Margaret took a deep drag from her cigarette and gazed at the sky to collect her thoughts:

"Captain, I think I can trust you? Right?"

Broadbent saw his chance to get closer to the woman:

"I hope so. I like to be all business. But, as I surmised this afternoon on the telephone, you offered to be on a first-name basis. When that occurs, it implies a friendship. Right now, I don't know where this might go with our relationship, but I can't get to the bottom of things if you hold back key information--which, I assure you, is confidential."

"Okay. That colors things differently. Sela Danby is Jordan's half-sister. I was stunned to confirm this in a letter written by my late husband, addressed to my son, not me. I found that unusual and a little hurtful. I am glad Jordan gave me it to set the record straight. Things are tangled together with Jordan and a half-sister he has never seen."

"Can I call you Maggie, as you confided earlier, or is it Mrs. Starmont between us now?"

"Make it Maggie--but only when it's you and me alone."

Hearing the sultry sound of Maggie, Broadbent thought he was making progress with the alluring woman in his company. But to win her confidence he had to stay all business:

"Maggie it is. Yes, letters can have unintended consequences, especially if they have more questions than answers. Honestly, this is a case where things are not as they appear to be."

"Where are you going with this, Damon, or is it Captain Broadbent?"

"As you say. It's the two of us--alone. Damon will do. I can't put my finger on this yet, but there are external pieces, as disjointed as they are, that have a bearing on this case. This Sela Danby might have a role to play with everything that's swirling around our fine city."

Margaret's curiosity was at a high pitch:

"Meaning what, Damon?"

"On a hunch, I think she's been in contact with Jordan, and it has likely been recent. Maybe Herlihy can confirm that if he finds Jordan in San Francisco."

"So, that means it's a waiting game for your detective's findings?"

"Yes, but we are moving rapidly, to include working locally. The other detective you met, Rick Sandoval, is working with the local San Diego FBI. I'll have him expand his investigation to see what we can pick up on Jordan's sister--this Sela Danby?"

"That sounds good. Do you want to see the letter? I had no idea Martin had fathered a daughter."

"Maggie, I think that is too invasive for me to request at a point when you have been on such an emotional roller coaster. Oh, no, for now keep it in your possession. However, we might want to dust if for fingerprints, which means we'll have to get your prints to see if there are others we can compare them to."

When hearing this, it reinforced Margaret's high opinion of Broadbent--the guy had a soft side to the hard profession he plied his trade:

"Damon, you really do care about how I feel about things. A woman needs that tenderness, especially when she is vulnerable."

"Maggie, I want you to know the truth as we uncover it. They'll be no secrets we will keep from you. Once we locate Jordan, and find out more about Sela, you'll be the first to know."

The conversation then shifted to less profound topics. Margaret learned that Broadbent had been too busy to have involvement with someone special. She reflected on the times she and Martin would vacation in San Diego, often staying at the La Valencia. Broadbent got the impression that her extended stay would not be painful--La Jolla was like a home away from home. After refills on their drinks, Broadbent offered to foot the bill. Margaret would have nothing of it, insisting with a light touch:

"You gave me free cab fare when I arrived. Let me get this."

Broadbent thanked her and thought it best to end this business and pleasure session:

"Thanks, Maggie. The City of San Diego appreciates it, too. Although I have a budgeted account for such interviews."

He then paused and looked directly into her lovely eyes, still shimmering in the fading dusk:

"Maggie I must confess. I find you an attractive woman. For that reason, I think it best we keep our visits to a minimum until we learn something substantive about Jordan and Ms. Danby."

Maybe it was the emptiness Margaret was feeling. Or perhaps the time had come for a widow to begin a relationship with another man. That Broadbent was at the forefront of solving some personal mysteries for her might complicate things.

Broadbent was attracted to her scent:

"That is an attractive fragrance you are wearing."

"It's my favorite, Chanel."

There was a sexual tension she could not resist:

"Until we meet again, I can preoccupy myself with some good books I can find not far from the hotel. Damon, I find you appealing as well. You can call upon me anytime--I'm not going anywhere."

12
CHAPTER

Perth, August, 1969

When Sela Danby ventured into the world on her own after her mother's death, she did not intend to be a risk taker. She did not think living on the edge was an existence her mother would have approved. But playing it safe went out the window the day she contacted her father in America earlier this year. Not knowing if Martin Starmont would have believed she was his unseen daughter in England had its own set of perils. However, risks bring unseen rewards. The fortunate by-product of contacting Martin was the joy of knowing she had a half-brother, Jordan, who seemed so rock solid at such a young age. He could be the familial, masculine protector she never had in her life while growing up. Given the uncertain situation Jordan was in, linking Ian Bright to neo-Nazi's, she owed her brother support and trust. Rex Murtaugh, a great prospect to replace Bright and his evil machinations, could be her way out of a difficult situation. But she decided to move on without the former—an action she might deeply regret. Sela just hoped that, in Murtaugh's eyes, she could maintain some credibility by reverting back to the nemesis she wanted to shake.

It has been several days since Bright left for Melbourne to acquire an instrument of destruction: "an ignitor." Jordan did not tell her what it was meant to ignite, but Sela surmised it had to detonate something very explosive and destructive. All of a sudden it hit her: she was on the cusp of something spectacular, as dangerous as it might be. But that only compounded her decision to forsake Murtaugh for Bright. Sela was not sure she could be persuasive once inside Murtaugh's room without her belongings he expected her to bring to his quarters:

"Rex, it's like things have swirled too fast for me. I hope you feel I'm not mad, but I think it best that I stay with Ian--at least for a little while longer."

Murtaugh was astounded by Sela's change of heart:

"Whoa! I was afraid sleeping separately wasn't going to work. Did Ian Bright's ghost spook you last night?"

To save face, and any hope of seeing Murtaugh again, Sela had to reveal the truth about who she was and what she needed to do:

"Let's sit down--together. There is more to me than meets the eye."

Murtaugh chuckled inside when he heard this. If only she knew who he really was. The two looked romantic enough, sitting side-by-side on a love seat in the early morning sunlight peeking through a window with a half-raised shade. They were poised for carnal contact, but a mating game was not in the offing when Sela held his hand and said:

"For the first time in my life I really feel moved by a man. You affect me with sincerity, and strength. I've had all I can do to restrain myself from having you make love to me."

Murtaugh tried to be cute to lessen the seriousness of the moment:

"Hey, don't you like my after-shave? Or is my place too messy? Maybe I need a woman like you to reform my ways?"

Smiling, yet trying to stop a tear, she responded:

"You are a kick--and that's what I am doing to myself now by staying with Bright. Rex, I hope you can keep this in all confidence…."

Sela hesitated and took a gulp. Murtaugh ran his hand tenderly across her brow and he exhorted her to bring it out:

"My past is now my immediate future. Earlier this year, for the first time, I made contact with my father--a successful American businessman: Martin Starmont. He met my mother during the last great war, before the invasion of France. He returned to the United States when the war ended, without my mother. I came along as the result of their ill-fated union."

Sela began to sob. Murtaugh knew she was hurting:

"Go on. This is nothing shameful."

She drew a hankie out of her slacks, dried her eyes, and continued:

"Oh, thank you for tolerating me in this state. Well, this story goes on. For the last few months, I have been in touch with the half-brother my father said I had when I had a telephone chat with him. His name is Jordan--Jordan Starmont. He's living in Haight-Ashbury in San Francisco. Does this all sound zany to you?"

Zany, Murtaugh thought? Hearing the words San Francisco again had more of an impact, hitting him like a sledgehammer. It recalled his reviled past, back in the nightmare days of "The Haight", a sense of déjà vu that troubled him. He had to verify if this was real:

"Are you sure he's in San Francisco?"

"He's there--the location of the telephone calls he's made and letter he's sent confirm that. However, I am not sure why he left his home in New York City and why he's involved in what I think is some hush, hush spy business. He said it's vital I stay with Ian if and when he leaves Perth. Jordan thinks he's bound next for San Diego--in California."

Murtaugh made a flippant response:

"So, you are leaving me to stay with Bright for some kind of James Bond caper?"

"No, no, although we have joked about being part of an Ian Fleming story. But, Rex, I'm convinced it is serious business. I think I have a duty, to a brother, to help him. He needs me."

"I'm confused. Why does this Jordan know so much about Bright? Who does he work for?"

"Can't tell you that just now."

"From the sound of this, you are on a bigger roller coaster than I thought. You ready for this ride with Bright, your brother, and whatever landmines may await you?"

"Rex, I guess I surprised myself by tagging along with Ian to come to Australia; going to the United States just adds to the adventure. I do want to meet my half-brother badly."

Murtaugh sat back in the love seat, reflected a moment, then slowly moved his head to about six inches from Sela's lips:

"You've done something wonderful for me in the very short time I've known you. I'm so excited now that it is hard for me to resist you. I have to do this…."

He pulled her close to him, gave her a deep kiss, and moved his hands to squeeze her shapely buttocks. Sela did not resist him. But in the heat of a moment that might lead to a conjugal encounter, Murtaugh broke off the passion. Instead, he drew back and said softly:

"I've got a proposition for you. I'll let you go back to Bright so you can do what you have to do. But, Sela, I'm not letting you go so easy. I'm ready to return to America on the same plane you take to get there. Bright doesn't know me; he shouldn't be suspicious if you don't call attention to me. Look at it that if I'm on board, you have a guardian angel to watch over you."

Sela was still excited, at a point of allowing Murtaugh to penetrate her, when the romantic clinch broke off. She was flushed and bent over a little. With a diminished libido, she looked back directly up to Murtaugh:

"Rex, you have some kind of power over me. It's the reason I was drawn to you. Yes, it would make what peril I might face better to survive if you were near."

"That's funny. Are you afraid I might really be a demon in disguise?"

"Life is one big chance. I like it with you, even if it is against all odds."

"Sela, that's good to know. Let's coordinate your movements out of Perth. You can always slip your itinerary under my door as soon as you know it. Let's make it that you contact me, either with secret notes or a telephone call out of Bright's earshot. Assume I'm always right behind you."

That gave Sela more reassurance that what she was doing for her brother, escorting Bright to San Diego, and what she was doing for herself, not losing Murtaugh, gave her the best of both worlds—as dangerous and risky as they both might be. The two then agreed that notes under Murtaugh's door would be the best way to stay close. Sela assumed Murtaugh bought into the change of plan. She then got up and was ready to return to her room and said:

"Rex, thank you for understanding what I must do. Knowing that you will be close at hand makes me feel better about what I must do."

Murtaugh gave her another kiss and checked the hall before he let her leave his room. If Sela only knew how experienced he was at operating under clandestine conditions. When she scooted across the hall unseen, safely back in her room, he had to get a grip on what he just did. Murtaugh took an internal inventory of his situation. This was so unlike him to let a woman run his life, especially as a fugitive. Could his Rex Murtaugh alias get him a plane ticket back to the USA? Would Murtaugh's passport get him through American customs? And just how good a shadow would he be over Sela once she arrived in San Diego? More importantly, was this an ill-advised return to California, taking a chance of being arrested and jail-time, rather than staying under cover thousands of miles away? In the end, his hot emotions were overruling his cool logic. The exotic appeal of an English lovely had lowered his defenses and opened the door for foolhardy actions. He was fooling around all right--and he was falling in love.

Portsmouth, May 14, 1945;
Fallbrook, Summer 1969

Lurking, twenty-four years after the demise of the Nazi menace, were the residual survivors of Adolph Hitler's Third Reich, many of them with new identities to disguise their sordid past. This hunted quarry had slipped through a wide net cast by the victorious allies and more vociferously by Jewish Holocaust agents led by Simon Wiesenthal. Fugitive Nazis were still at large in other parts of Europe, South America, and the United States, blending into the unsuspecting general population. One of these post-war renegades was Friedrich Vogel, camouflaged under his alias: David Percival. He used his pre-war background, educated in English schools, including a chemistry degree from Oxford, as a protective shield. His English accent, natural and uncontrived, was a perfect disguise. Percival sounded just as British as the famous Shakespearean actor Laurence Olivier.

Ever since Percival miraculously avoided incarceration that momentous day in Portsmouth, New Hampshire, May 14, 1945, he led a charmed yet paranoid life. Germany had quit the war and ordered its at-large U-boat submarine fleet to surrender at the nearest Allied base. When the *U-234* ventured into North American waters along the Atlantic coast, Percival was one of its high-profile passengers, which included a German general and his staff, four German naval officers, civilian engineers and scientists (experts in rocket power and nuclear technologies), and two Japanese naval officers. The mission of the *U-234* was to transport a nuclear cargo, 560 kilograms of uranium oxide-Uranium 235, to Japan--enough to produce two atomic bombs. If successful, it would create a huge danger to the war effort still raging in the Pacific against Japanese forces. The uranium was stored in eighty gold-lined cylinders. The gold had highly protective radioactive shielding properties, as effective as lead. It was an excellent choice when storing or shipping enriched uranium. At the time it was Vogel's assignment to shepherd the cylinders to their ultimate destination and use.

For those on the *U-234* it was their good fortune that the ship did not surrender to Canadian or British forces at Halifax, Nova Scotia. The ship's captain felt it likely the Americans, unlike the Canadians and British, would not imprison them and simply send them back to Germany. However, the two Japanese naval officers could not stand the ignominy of surrender and committed suicide before the submarine docked in Portsmouth. It remained for those who survived to be sorted out for processing and a determination what to do with them. This gave Vogel his chance, given his glib, believable British accent. If questioned by the Navy, he could claim he was unable to return to England when war broke out and was forcibly detained to help the Nazi war effort, using his scientific background, to build super weapons. He could further plead that he was on his way to build atom bombs, under duress, for Japan from the uranium the *U-234* transported.

Prior to the ship's surrender, Vogel packed a uranium cylinder and some American dollars into a satchel. If Naval interrogators uncovered the uranium, he felt he could use it as a bargaining chip to gain his freedom. There was confusion with the questioning of the submarine's passengers and crew. Vogel eventually debarked the boat in custody. But in one reckless moment, the US Navy Shore Patrol (SP) officer accompanying Vogel, was called upon to assist other SP's to restrain a nearby German submariner, who refused to be shackled and controlled. Seeing an opening, Vogel slipped away undetected at a brisk pace on foot. Coming to the main gate, he got off the base by convincing a naïve SP that he was a British Broadcasting Corporation (BBC) reporter covering the *U-234* surrender. Toting a bag weighing thirty pounds, most of it coming from the heavy uranium load, he quickly scurried away from the base into obscurity. It is another separate tale in itself to describe how this fugitive avoided capture and transformed himself into an accepted avocado farmer near Fallbrook, California under the alias of David Percival. But he was one of more than a few others in hiding who had the clever intelligence to remain outside the grasp of the vengeful Nazi hunters.

Carrying his deadly contraband since 1945, Percival knew he had a potential weapon of mass destruction. He had the nuclear ammunition; what he lacked was the triggering mechanism to ignite a catastrophic explosion. Deep in his soul, Percival carried a deep seeded anti-Semitic animosity. His parents often conveyed in their family discussions their envy of the intellectual prowess, good business sense, and general superb abilities to live by their wits, at the luxury of avoiding manual labor, of many of their fellow Jewish neighbors. The pre-war Jews living in Germany enjoyed a life of comfort, a position they earned through hard work and perseverance in the face of discrimination. They thrived as best they could as professionals, bankers, academicians, and successful business entrepreneurs, much to the dismay of their gentile counterparts. But when Hitler came to power in 1933 as German Chancellor, the polluted environment of revilement and hatred was ratcheted up with anti-Semitic laws. It prompted many to look the other way when eventually many of their Jewish neighbors were whisked away for deportation or concentration camp confinement for the Nazi's "final solution" to dispose of them.

But Percival and his parents would be sympathetic spectators to the anti-Semitic cauldron that would boil in Hitler's Germany during the 1930's. His father, Heinrich Vogel, was appointed as a staff member to the German ambassador in London, England in 1925. Vogel's only child, Friedrich, was eight years-old at the time but was speaking fluent English. The elder Vogel had an English grandmother, one of the main reasons he was given his assignment to England, and was an Anglophile. He mandated his only child, Friedrich, to learn English at an early age in Germany. When immersed among English school children, the younger Vogel soon mimicked the accents of his peers. A bright student with a penchant for mathematics and science, Friedrich made it through English prep school and an eventual degree in chemistry from Oxford in 1938.

He had a sexual liaison with a local woman, Dora Bright, and gave birth to an illegitimate son, Ian, whom Friedrich never saw.

Heinrich Vogel was no longer a part of the German delegation since 1932, but he liked England and found a position with an export business that needed his international skills. The Vogel family managed to stay afloat in England amid growing German-English tensions. Despite their life in pre-war England, all the Vogels never lost their fondness for things German, to include the Hitler regime.

Then, in September 1939, England and Germany went to war. The Vogels were forced to leave and return to their home in Mannheim, Germany. Mannheim was a major industrial town. Friedrich stayed out of the military by utilizing his scientific expertise to head a defense plant there. To increase his status, Friedrich gained general membership into the Nazi party, known as the *Parteimitglieder*. The Third Reich was committed to building super weapons, to include nuclear devices.

In 1942, Friedrich was selected to join other German scientists to work on an accelerated secret project to develop fissionable material for atomic bombs at the Kaiser Wilhelm Institute in Berlin under the general leadership of Nobel Prize recipient Werner Heisenberg. Fortunately, for the free world, Hitler's attempt to develop an atomic bomb failed. With Nazi defeat imminent in April 1945, Friedrich Vogel was assigned to a special operation to help an Axis ally, Japan, build a bomb in World War II's last desperate hours. It got him a ride on the *U-234* and a chance for revenge to finally inflict damage on one of Nazi Germany's major adversaries--the United States of America.

Living with impunity as a successful avocado grower among the rolling hills of Fallbrook in northwest San Diego County, Percival was now ready to strike--but he needed willing lackeys, his own subservient little army of hate mongers. Percival's farm was a short distance from Camp Pendleton, the sprawling 125,000 acre United States Marine Corps installation 38 miles north of downtown San Diego. It was an ideal location to find recruits with a military background who could naively fall under his evil spell. One day, while parked outside Camp Pendleton's east gate, Percival spotted two Marines, Monty Crawford and Yancey Bixby, who exited the base. They were likely on a weekend pass, dressed in civilian clothes and were looking to find a ride with the next Marine out with a car. Percival drove up with his bright red Pontiac GTO, which was an attractive muscle car for the day's younger generation, and stopped beside the two and called out through his rolled down front passenger window:

"You guys want to impress the ladies in Oceanside, or any other place your heart desires?"

The two Marines had puzzled looks on their faces when they heard the offer. Bixby mumbled something to Crawford and ambled up to the open window:

"This here looks like a fine coaster wagon. Be nice to ride in, but our NCO's have warned us to stay clear of strangers offering us rides, given war time and all."

Percival knew he had a sales job to do:

"I understand your caution. But I'm local, live nearby in Fallbrook, and I just want to help you brave Marines for keeping us safe from those commie bastards over in Nam. It's my way of thanking you, compared to those anti-war nuts who have no idea what it takes to put one's life on the line to keep the country free."

"Much obliged for your kind words, but we are sure we can get a ride with a fellow Leatherneck."

Percival had to be more persuasive. He reached into his pocket and pulled out a roll of dollar bills. Holding the wad up, he stated:

"This will pay for anything you want to eat, drink, or even find a place where you can get laid. If there is anything left after we have a good time, it's yours. Call it a reward for putting your life on the line for the country, one does not appreciate its fighting men."

"Naw, we ain't out looking for a handout. We're Marines. We are expected to fight for our country first. The money ain't why we stay in the Corps."

"That might be, but I think I'm your best bet for some well-deserved liberty. Your buddy can sit in back to be sure I don't do anything you don't like. You can even search my car if you think I've got a weapon. You can even drive the car if you think this is too good to be true. That puts you in control as to where you want to go"

A chance to drive a flashy car hit Bixby's hot button. He put his head just above the open car window and ordered:

"Sorry for this, but we ain't nobody's fool. Please get out of the car so we can search both you and it. Besides, you talk funny--like you are English or something"

Percival knew he struck home and immediately exited the car without protest and a smile. Bixby hopped in the Pontiac and searched under the seats and the glove box. Still suspicious but with a plan in mind, he called Crawford over:

"Monty, pat him down. If he's clean, tell him to hop in back. He sits in the right rear back seat; you sit right next to him to make sure he makes no sudden moves. I'll drive."

Percival discovered that Crawford, with piercing blue eyes imbedded in a bronzed, gaunt face, accented by high cheek bones, had the grip of a heavy duty vise when he shook his hand. His search of his person was firm and professional. These guys were trained to frisk enemy combatants. Crawford knew what to do. The keys were still in the ignition. As instructed above, the three men took their positions in the GTO. Bixby, all aglow behind the wheel, was gleeful to impress any car or pedestrian outside the gate that he had some horsepower under his command. He revved the engine and sped off down the road for some fun in the California sun, compliments of an apparent friendly stranger. Then Percival laid his propaganda on the two warriors as Bixby pushed the speed limit when he got to Highway 76, on the way to Interstate 5 and unlimited destination options:

"Let he explain my funny speech? You see I'm originally from England, but now call Fallbrook my home. You know, it's too bad you brave warriors are getting no support for your defending our country's honor in Vietnam. There's a reason for that."

Bixby nodded his head in agreement and stated:

"Yes, sir, Monty and me fought our butts off in I Corps over in Nam. We both survived the 'Meat Grinder' against the NVA at Con Thien near the DMZ. If I had the power I'd wipe North Vietnam off the face of the earth, the wretched bastards. One night they threw 1200 artillery and mortar rounds at us."

Percival had a sympathetic ear and a malevolent motive:

"I really feel for you guys. And to think all this anti-war shit you are dealing with now that you are back. Did you guys ever think about pay-back for the abuse you have to endure?"

Crawford became interested:

"Sir, what's the reason for these protests? Don't they know we are protecting their asses?"

"Son, let's dig down and see where all this misguided anti-war bullshit is coming from. Many of them are Jews, guys like Abbie Hoffman and Jerry Rubin, who have stoked up the hatred for America's fighting forces. Most of them are gutless. Military service is not high on their list. Got any Jews in the Corps?"

Bixby volunteered:

"None in my company--I think. We pretty much know who's on board. Guys get the raspberry based on their background."

"See what I mean? Jews have traveled to different countries throughout their history, with no loyalty and looking for a better deal. If not, they move on. In this country, too many Jew boys in Hollywood and other media. We get pictures of what they want us to see, not the whole truthful story. They slant things to their political liking, which right now is not pro-America in Vietnam."

Bixby wasn't initially buying Percival's anti-Semitism. He turned to his fellow Louisiana buddy:

"Man, can't say any Jew I've met, which I don't think I came across many in my home in St. Tamany Parish, Louisiana, has done much wrong to me. Monty, what's your take on Jews living among your kin in Slidell?"

"Can't say I ever met any."

Percival's hate wasn't taking. He tried a different approach:

"Guess I'll have to tell you more why we can't trust these devious pricks. You guys looking for some extra pocket money? Not sure the Corps pays you that well for sticking your necks out."

Bixby was interested:

"What you got in mind?"

"When you get to I-5, let's stop at the Denny's on Harbor Drive in Oceanside and have some lunch--on me. Is that a plan?"

"You hungry, Monty? Sounds good to me."

The three men bantered informally about a lunch break and agreed to eat at the suggested spot. The Marines were initially interested in the food, rather than conversation, when they got to Denny's. After demolishing double-hamburgers, fries, and large strawberry shakes, they sat back in their booth and listened to Percival's pitch:

"Can I call you Yancey and Monty?"

The two Marines nodded in agreement. Percival continued:

"The time is right for Americans who care for their country to take a stand against those you wish us ill. I'll offer you two $500 apiece every time you help me out. I need you to make contact with someone who wants to help us strike a blow against the anti-war mob. You'll be my runners, if you will."

Bixby needed more clarification:

"Come on. We are in the Marines; don't have much free time. Money looks nice, though."

"I realize your commitments to the Corps. But now is your chance to kick these protestors in the ass. You simply can work for me when you get weekend passes, or if you get some leave time. For example, I need you guys to help me enlist a guy who wants to join our crusade against the anti-war crowd. Might commit some money to our cause."

Bixby inquired:

"Is he in the area? Where's he from?"

"He flew into San Francisco from New York, but he wants to relocate down here in San Diego. We've arranged for a meeting location when he drives down here from San Francisco."

"When and where does that happen?"

"Soon. Likely some rendezvous spot in La Jolla."

"What's his name?"

Percival paused a little, not knowing if he had commitment from these two wary warriors. But he didn't think the name really meant anything to them at this point:

"The guy in question is Jordan Starmont."

14
CHAPTER

San Diego, September, 1969

Damon Broadbent got to his office early in the morning. He couldn't get Margaret Starmont out of his mind after their meeting last night at the La Valencia in La Jolla. For Broadbent, it was an enchanted evening. Just thinking of her stimulated him sexually. His interest in her was more than to solve a murder on a beach. But his sexual ardor cooled when the telephone rang around 8:30:

"Captain Broadbent, this is Herlihy up in 'la-la land'. Man, they sure are weird in Haight-Ashbury."

Damon Broadbent was not surprised by his subordinate's impressions of the Hippie kingdom in San Francisco on his end of the telephone line:

"Dan, you still under-cover, looking like one of the 'flower children' I told you to fall in love with?"

"Have no fear, sir. They even have many gray-haired freaks in their numbers that look older than me. No one has questioned if I'm a cop. In fact, they are friendly and are only locked into the present. They are not concerned about your past and, with their mellow approach to life, not worried about the future."

"Good. Glad you are fitting in. Now, what's the status on Jordan Starmont?"

"Well, I made connection yesterday with the FBI, this agent Ross Cargill. Yeah, he acknowledges they are in touch with the Starmont boy, but he's hands off."

"What do you mean? He's not carrying any infectious disease, is he?"

"I wish it was that simple. This case might be bigger than a simple murder on Windansea Beach."

Broadbent was getting animated and raised his voice an octave:

"What can make Starmont off limits? He's nothing special as part of this lost younger generation--defying authority and looking for a handout and some free love. Is he?"

"Again, Captain, not that easy to explain. You see Starmont is involved with the FBI in a matter of what Cargill called 'national security'."

"National security? C'mon, Dan! This can't be real?"

"More than real, Captain. It's got teeth in it. Cargill advised our department to temporarily suspend our investigation of properly identifying the corpse found in La Jolla and to not try to make any contact with Starmont."

When Broadbent heard the restrictive directive, Maggie Starmont came into focus again. He thought he could make strides with her, professionally and personally, if he could deliver her son to her. With Maggie in mind, he pressed Herlihy:

"Did you explain to Cargill what happened--how we made an understandable misidentification of Margaret Starmont's son? That it is our obligation to get to the bottom of who the corpse is and how we can give her solace by finding her son? Did you tell him we've got egg on our faces and we need to wipe it off--before the public gets wind of this and blows us all away?"

"Sir, I gave him all the details of what we've done with our investigation, to include how we gave Starmont's mother a false ID on her son's death and scared the hell out of her. Not sure if they want us in the picture."

"What are you saying, Herlihy?"

"Ah, I just get the sense it is FBI arrogance--thinking they are above and beyond local police forces—you know they are the 'el supremo' of law enforcement."

Broadbent was in no mood for compromises:

"We've got a job to do. But tell me, how do we save our reputations now that we can't try to repair them?"

"Cargill would not tell me too many details, but here is what he wants us to know for now. Captain, this is all hush, hush stuff. Make a note of this:

One. There is a neo-Nazi movement alive and well in the San Diego area.

Two. They have a hot lead on a suspected Nazi scientist living in our area, who they believe is planning 'something big'. No details on what that means.

Three. The Starmont boy is a vital cog to the FBI investigation. Seems he knows a girl who may lead them to the Nazi in question.

Four. Jordan is off limits until the FBI tells us we can talk to him.

Five. The FBI really doesn't need us now. They'll give us marching orders direct when they do."

Herlihy paused for a moment while leafing through his notes, then continued:

"That's all I can really tell you. What's my next directive up here?"

Broadbent found it hard to digest what he just heard. Nazis on the rise again in a very conservative, pro-America town like San Diego? But, he thought it was perfect cover for a war criminal to hide--right under the noses of his fiercest adversaries. He had a few strategic questions to ask, both related to the investigation and his desire to get closer to Maggie Starmont:

"So, we are to help their investigation when they need us down here but not pursue Starmont up there?"

"That's the order, sir."

"Stay where you are for now until I direct your next move. Pester Cargill for more information. Tell him the misidentifying a dead person is causing realistic emotional problems with Jordan's mother. Did Cargill instruct us to stay away from Margaret Starmont?"

"No. No mention of her. Might be fair game."

"All right. Now, tell me, who's the girl that might help us solve this intriguing mess we find ourselves?"

"Would not divulge the name. Only that she is presently in Perth, Australia."

Perth, August, 1969

Sela Danby was trying to steel herself for what was to be the most dangerous journey of her young, complicated life. After telling Rex Murtaugh she could not leave Ian Bright, her actions, words, and steps had to be carefully calculated. That was apparent when Bright came back from his brief journey to Melbourne, where he became more candid why he went there.

When he returned last night back to the flat they were renting on a temporary basis, he had a serious mien. They were seated on the bed when Bright revealed:

"Well, love, I guess I owe you some answers. Took you half way 'round the world and didn't give you the whole story. Now it's time to ramp up the craziness. You know why we came here?"

Oh, oh. If this was about his next steps in San Diego, she had to be guarded as to what she knew:

"Ian, pray tell why? So far, it's been fun 'down under'".

"You mean you haven't wondered why the East End blokes in the band haven't appeared for any gigs yet on this journey?"

"Well, they seemed to have been distant; thought they might show yet."

Bright gave a half-hearted smile of surprise:

"No, love, they ain't showing. You see, my Sharpie pals are more important. I thought they were based in this borough--Perth. No, they were in Melbourne and that's why I left you, dearie. The 'Sharps' are the reason we came here—to get what we need to go somewhere else where we can really make a big bang."

"Big bang? How do you mean?"

"Sela, what I tell you now is to be kept close to your tights—it's a life and death secret between us two. Am I clear, love?"

Sela wasn't surprised to hear this dire ultimatum—she saw it coming. But she reinforced her surprise by sitting closer to Bright on the bed and took his hand to show her earnestness:

"Ian, I wouldn't have come here with you if I did not think what you do is important. Trust me, we have a bond. I vow not to break it, love."

Bright believed Sela's contrived candor and loyalty:

"Okay. That's good to know. We have to get to San Diego as soon as possible. You see my father needs me there. It's important, and I've told him about you. He's anxious to see you, too. You see, I've never seen my father before. We came in contact about a year ago by mail. It's a long tale, but he met my mom before the war, left her to do his own thing, and then I was the bun that popped out of the oven for my 'ole mom' to raise on her own."

Sela could not believe the irony. They both were products of unseen fathers. She was beginning to wonder what was real or fantasy. She prodded Bright with concern:

"Go on. This is tender."

"Besides a chance to meet for the first time, he needs me to bring a special package. It's something important for his work on his farm north of San Diego in a place called Fallbrook. Grows avocados out there. What I am bringing is a special detonator for explosives so he can clear more land for his trees."

So far, this sounded somewhat practical, but Sela knew this was the veil of deception Ian was placing over his real objective. Staying innocent and curious she offered support:

"Fallbrook, hey. Sounds like it belongs in England. Yes, you have to see your father, more than anything. It's a bonus that you are bringing him something vital for his farm. I want to meet him and see what I might do to assist his work."

When he heard that, he drew Sela near to his excited body. Without another word, he put his hand under the back of her blouse and unhooked her bra. He fondled her breasts and sensed her nipples growing erect. After he slid her top over her head, he stretched himself over the top of her compliant body. Slipping his slacks off, Bright's manliness was firm and ready for carnal penetration. Sela could feel his organ on her warm pubic zone. She had to keep the charade going by complying with his desires. In one passionate tug she slipped off her jeans and panties. She was now bare and flushed. Bright entered her without difficulty; she was moist from the passion. But her libido was aroused as well as her suspicions. While feeling his forceful thrusts, she wandered in space. Too bad this is not Rex inside of me--what she really wanted. After the climax of two disjointed souls, Bright resumed the pillow talk:

"I had to do that, dearie, to know you are still with me. Now I know that you are. We can do big things together if you keep our life under wraps. We got a seal of love on that?"

"Sure, love. When do we leave Perth for what you... no... what we need to do?"

"Likely in a week or so. Have to call my dad in an hour to get particulars. It's funny. We are in bed in the evening time, ready for slumber. Where he's at he's just waking up."

"Yes, we are ahead of most of the world as it turns."

"I know he has to tell me more about his chap who is to fetch us at the airport when we arrive in America."

Sela knew who it might be but she needed confirmation to keep her clever disguise:

"Oh, is he British or American?"

"My dad didn't say much about him. Only that we might hit it off. Said he's a young lad—close to our age".

Sela posed a question to get more definition on Bright's father:

"I can't wait to meet the elder Mr. Bright—your daddy."

"No, love, Bright is my mother's name; my father is a David Percival."

16
CHAPTER

Coronado, Summer, 1969

David Percival was now meeting regularly with two young US Marine warriors, Yancey Bixby and Monty Crawford, primarily after their duty hours on weekdays and on weekends when they got their usual passes from their Camp Pendleton assignment. Percival was confident they were under his spell, giving them both $50 apiece each time they met to buy their devotion. They were to be the first of others Percival wanted to recruit to build a neo-Nazi para-military force in the United States. He generally would buy them dinner at a restaurant, imbuing them with his anti-Semitic hate and why America was on the wrong path. Percival called the Vietnam War a "stalemate" because the Jews ran the national media and gave the enemy hope by portraying American military forces in Southeast Asia as "child killers" and "perpetrators of genocide." According to Percival's twisted sense of things, the Jews were also at the forefront of the anti-war operatives demonstrating on college campuses and protesting in the streets. Both Bixby and Crawford had sympathetic ears to the odious message Percival was spewing, especially since they had several buddies killed near the North Vietnamese border not so long ago. It only made them more committed to Percival's cause.

One Saturday evening, Percival decided to bring the Marines into his web of intrigue at his Fallbrook home, where he would finally give them their first marching orders to execute his belligerent plan. Percival's estate was on sixty acres of rolling hills, accented by avocado groves he harvested to give him a comfortable existence. The house was a 4,000 square foot white stucco ranch, with five bedrooms, four baths, a large kitchen, a dining room with a table that sat twelve people, a great room with a rounded stone trimmed fireplace, all comfortably placed on cool tile floors to dissipate the summer heat. In back, was a casita, for guest quarters, and a detached four car garage.

To impress his youthful guests when they drove up to the property, Percival displayed the contents in his garage first. In addition to the Pontiac GTO muscle car they were riding in, he opened the doors to a sporty forest green MG convertible, a black Lincoln Continental, and a blue Ford pick-up truck. Each automobile impressed the Marines, since Percival's "motor pool" had a varied sex appeal, depending what function you wanted the respective vehicle to perform. Bixby was taken in by the horsepower on display:

"Yes, sir. The sports car will really impress the ladies. That Lincoln is a nice ride for a larger group to be comfortable. The truck is down home 'country' for the rough and tumble for any job to do."

Percival reinforced the young man's appetite with his lures on wheels:

"Yeah, you and Monty can take any one of them at your convenience. I'll even have one of my workers deliver it to you at the east gate of Pendleton."

Bixby and Crawford were almost salivating as they took turns getting behind the wheel of their new found toys. But Percival had more serious matters to discuss. After the Marines got over the fascination with the autos, Percival took them to the great room inside his house. He had his maid, Consuela, bring them some beer and nachos. Sitting on deep leather furniture, Percival induced the Marines's relaxation by making sure they downed at least three Dos Equis. He could see they were starry eyed but alert enough to consume his pointed message:

"Fellows, you'll be my guests here tonight. Tomorrow, we go for a ride where the Navy lives and breathes in this place—Coronado. Yes, I know you Leathernecks aren't particularly fond of the swabbies, but they hold ground where we need to make a big splash."

Bixby, now dealing on a first-name basis with Percival, laughed at the mixed metaphor:

"Yeah, David, the Navy can't splash on dry land."

Crawford joined in the merriment as the two chuckled over their beers. Percival wanted to stay on task:

"You guys need to go back to your barracks tomorrow to fetch your dress blues. I need you to look prim and proper to gain entry into our command post, if you will."

Bixby was puzzled:

"Why do we need to dress so formal, David?"

"You'll see. Best be getting some winks for our big day tomorrow."

Percival got them high but not drunk so they would be usable the next day. The young men went sheepishly to bed, spending the night in the casita. When Bixby and Crawford arose, they were sober and pliant for their assignment. Percival, cleared at the gate as a temporary guest, drove his "recruits" to their barracks on Camp Pendleton so they could exchange their civilian clothes for their dress blue Marine uniforms. Percival fully expected them to look impressive and sharp, as if they were ready for a military parade. He wasn't disappointed. Clean shaven, with well-chiseled faces, Bixby and Crawford projected a regimented elegance. Their white dress hats had the sparkling gold cluster of the Marine trademark: the eagle, globe, and anchor, the oldest military insignia in continuous use. The black dress coats were accented by brass buttons, red piping, and a white belt with a gold buckle. Each man's rank, Lance Corporal, was on their sleeves, designated by red stripes with crossed rifles. The service ribbons and weaponry medals bedazzled each man's chest. The scarlet "blood stripes", signifying all comrades lost in battle, ran down the sides of their blue trousers. The black dress shoes were spit polished to reflect the rays of the morning sun, completing an impressive look. The Marines looked like persuasive recruiting models, but Percival had no intentions of keeping them loyal to their country. He was about to have them renounce their Marine Corps motto of *Semper Fidelis* (Always Faithful) and their service to their country.

The site for the betrayal was about a forty-five minute drive to the major US Navy installation on the Coronado Peninsula. Bixby was at the wheel of the Lincoln Continental as it crossed the newly opened Coronado Bay Bridge, resting on thirty distinctive blue box-girder towers, rising two-hundred feet at its acme over the water below. The span replaced the ferry between the City of San Diego and Coronado. Once off the bridge,

Percival instructed Bixby to drive south down Orange Avenue until they stopped at the gate of another prominent military installation with its own unique history.

In June 1943, the Navy Department approved the creation of the Naval Amphibious Base (NAB) located in the San Diego area. About 1,000 acres in size, most of NAB was a man-made development of land-fill dredged from the bottom of adjacent San Diego Bay. It was situated south of the much larger Naval Air Station North Island (NAS). The NAS was located on the broad terminus of the Coronado peninsula, connected to the mainland to the southeast by a narrow arm called the Silver Strand, which divided San Diego Bay on one side and the Pacific Ocean on the other. The NAB was at the northern end of the Silver Strand and had the luxury for surfside and bayside landings.

The City of Coronado was sandwiched between the NAS and the NAB and offered an attractive, upscale community, populated by active and retired Navy personnel and well-to-do civilians. Coronado had an amiable relationship with the large Navy presence in a region where its major installations and contingents were facts of life. The city's landmark was the Hotel del Coronado, an elegant example of Victorian design that opened in 1888. The hotel was the playground for many Hollywood stars and a prominent location for the hit film *Some Like It Hot,* released in 1959 with an all-star cast that included Tony Curtis, Jack Lemmon, and Marilyn Monroe. But there was also something else that would create heat on this beautiful piece of geography, and its purpose was not to entertain.

There was an embarrassing oversight upon the completion of Complex 320-325, located on the grounds of the NAB. Flanked by roads with names of naval operations in the Pacific during World War II, Bouganville Road on the north, Tulagi Road to the south, Eniwetok Road to the east, and ROI (ROI Namur atoll) Road to the west, the shape of a series of three-story barracks represented a dreaded symbol that came from the other major military theater during that great conflict--Nazi Germany. It seems, unknown to the Navy architectural planners, a series of "L" shaped buildings, repeated three times and set at 90-degree angles to one another, created the symbol of Adolph Hitler's Third Reich. When viewed from the air, an unintended consequence of its design, Complex 320-325 took the form of a clearly outlined swastika--the insidious Nazi identifier the free world fought valiantly to extirpate in World War II.

Ironically, a Marine was the duty officer at the NAB main gate when the Lincoln Continental came to a stop. He peered into the luxurious car at the driver's opened window and queried:

"Good morning. What's your business here today, Marines?"

Bixby gave his prepared lines that Percival preached to him on the drive down to the NAB:

"Yes, sir. We are here to see an officer on base to arrange the transport of the body of one of your Seal's who was killed in action over in Vietnam."

"Sorry to hear about that. Who's the officer I can page and who is the civilian next to you?"

"The officer is Ensign Casey Douglas; the man next to me is the father of the deceased. Ensign Douglas is awaiting us at his on base quarters."

The guard was sympathetic to the ruse and was impressed with the specificity of who to call and where to find him. He went to his kiosk, to the directory, dialed his telephone, and responded to the person on the other end of the line:

"Sir, we have two Marines and the father of a deceased Navy Seal here at the gate."

The guard nodded his head several times from his conversation, not knowing that Casey Douglas was a Percival plant inside the bowels of a strategic military complex. He returned to the car and had the trained decorum to console the survivors of the all too frequently lost Naval and Marine personnel in Vietnam lately:

"My sympathy for your loss, Mr. Percival. You are free to pass. Have a good day."

Bixby drove onto the NAB without hesitation, following Percival's directions on how to get to Douglas's location, on an upper floor of the bachelor's officer quarters on Tulagi Road. Crawford, seated in back, was all eyes and made an observation:

"This place has the look of something special. Almost mysterious-like, made for action for the guys based here. What's it called besides Navy Amphibious Base, David?"

"The Seal's Lair."

17
CHAPTER

San Diego, September, 1969

It was early afternoon and Captain Damon Broadbent had a hangdog attitude. Earlier in the day his report from his subordinate Dan Herlihy, on special assignment in San Francisco, was not what he wanted to hear. Herlihy's investigation on the whereabouts of Jordan Starmont was stonewalled by the FBI until further notice. That didn't sit well with Broadbent, not so much that it hindered his investigation to properly identify a dead body on a La Jolla beach, but that he would not score any points with a woman who preoccupied his thoughts—Maggie Starmont. Having gotten bad news from Herlihy, he requested his other detective working the case, Rick Sandoval, to stop by his office.

Sandoval was a bright, handsome detective with a keen mind and a quick wit. When he strode into Broadbent's office, he knew his boss was surly because of the frown on his face that was ready to break out into a scowl. Sandoval tried some humor to break the ice as he took a chair:

"You know what the last guy I pinched said when I told him 'Anything you say will be held against you'".

Broadbent gave a smirk as Sandoval delivered the punch line:

"The guy said: 'How about Raquel Welch's tits'"?

Broadbent cracked back:

"C'mon, Rick. You got nothing better than to run down our profession? Our asses are in a sling here!"

"Sorry, sir, but I thought I'd start out light, especially after I just talked to Herlihy on the state police band. I know we are facing an investigative stonewall."

"You got anything for us to hang our hat on?"

"Maybe. I had lunch today with the Bureau's Joe Pizzo at Lubach's. He told me there's something brewing in town that has the potential to make a national, maybe an international headline, if they can make the collar on their prime suspect."

"Oh, what did he volunteer? Herlihy told me the San Francisco FBI is smelling the same rat--a neo-Nazi in our backyard. You got a name?"

"Pizzo was guarded, as you might suspect. It took all I could do to eke out from him that they are focusing on a shadowy avocado grower up in Fallbrook. He did say we should coordinate daily with his office."

"Hmm. There are legs to this story. That's the same thing their San Francisco office wants us to do. They want us to stay away from the boy but possibly help the Bureau in our bailiwick. What can you tell me about the Nazi in north county?"

"Little. I think they will spoon feed us tidbits on a need to know basis."

But Broadbent had to comply with Maggie Starmont's desire for information about a mysterious girl and asked:

"Did Pizzo mention anything about a Sela Danby?"

Sandoval scratched his wavy black hair with a puzzled look:

"Who's this now? Madame X?"

"Maybe not as sinister as that. I've got a hunch she's the linchpin to getting at the bottom of this. Herlihy was told by the Bureau that some unnamed girl is in contact with Jordan. See if you can loosen Pizzo's lips about her."

"Sure thing. And you should know the FBI has nothing on missing persons in our area that would go back to the unidentified corpse. I'm awaiting a call from the Camp Pendleton Public Information Officer on AWOL Leathernecks."

"Good, Rick. Ride herd on all this. Did you check with the crime lab for any prints found in the car with the body? Did the pathologist get any identifiable leads on the corpse in their possession?"

"Yeah, the scene inside is a mess--given it was a rental car. More smudges than distinct prints a lab tech can get a handle on. But they think there are some fresh prints of interest on the outside of the trunk. The human remains are still a mystery."

"Well, stay on it. The FBI wants us to leave that corpse on ice and stay away from it. But watch your steps here. We need to ID that body ASAP. Good hunting."

As Sandoval was leaving the office he turned and inquired at the door:

"Where you bound today? Can't see you riding this desk when you are sitting on a hot seat."

Leaning back against his chair, Broadbent had Maggie on his secret itinerary. He played his cards close to the vest:

"Got that right. I'll be ambling about. Keep tuned to the radio. You'll know where to find me."

Broadbent then got up and ushered his skilled aide out of his office extolling his virtues. He then closed his office door and returned to his desk trying to catch up on some department reports. After twenty minutes he violated an office rule and lit a Kool. The cigarette smoke wafted out his open window as he telephoned the La Valencia for Maggie's room.

His heart raced a bit when he heard her voice on the phone:

"Damon, good to hear you again. Any news on Jordan?"

With that response, Broadbent knew he was still no higher than second on Maggie's man chart. He had to better position himself for her consideration:

"Well, I've got good news for you. Can I stop by and discuss it--it's somewhat involved to describe on the phone?"

"Yes, yes. By all means, Damon. I need something positive."

Now Broadbent was getting places with Maggie. The 'Damon' tag was sticking with her. He reciprocated the first-name attachment that seems to be growing:

"Maggie, I can get to the hotel in an hour."

Maggie was a worried mother for her son, but she was also a lonely, attractive widow who suddenly felt uplifted in the care of a handsome man. She felt it time to play the latter role rather than the formal and reveal a little more of her sensual side to him:

"Good. Meet me at the pool, Damon, say about three?"

"That will work. See you shortly."

Broadbent put the telephone down on the receiver and started to get erect just thinking about Maggie looking more revealing to him. Still, he was a professional and composed himself quickly as he informed the sergeant on duty of his afternoon schedule. He checked with the department scanner to be sure nothing related to his case had been sent to him. In fifteen minutes he was at the wheel of his unmarked Olds Cutlass and headed up I-5 to La Jolla. The radio band was open and he picked-up when Rick Sandoval was paging him:

"Captain Broadbent? I've got something you should know. Where's your location? Over."

Broadbent misrepresented his true destination:

"Rick, I'm in the car on the way to the Windansea to investigate the crime scene. Over."

"Can that wait? Over."

Broadbent wanted no diversions from Maggie now:

"What's so important that it can't wait? Over."

"Once I left you I got a call back from the Camp Pendleton Public Information Officer. He has an updated list of AWOL Marines. There are two names on it that they especially need us to coordinate with their activities if we can get up there this afternoon. Over."

Broadbent was subconsciously off task by not connecting Marines and the importance to the investigation. Maggie was probably clouding his decision making:

"This better be good, Rick. Over."

"Sir, just a reminder of the importance of this lead. I think we've got something to chase now. Over."

Broadbent knew the error of his ways:

"Sorry, Rick. Guess I'm not myself today. The Chief sent me a pointed memo as a reminder to get at the bottom of the Windansea case. He's been evasive with the press. So who do you have of interest for us?"

"Yancey Bixby and Monty Crawford."

Perth, August, 1969

After a long night of tending bar at the Cricket Club, accented by a rowdy gathering celebrating the victory across the street at WACA by Australia's national rugby team, the Kangaroos, winning a pre-World Cup match over the visiting New Zealand team, the All Blacks, Rex Murtaugh was still spent as the morning light awakened him in his bed. Given the mayhem that hit the Cricket Club, several disputes erupted among drunken blokes that required him to play referee until calmer heads prevailed, he rubbed his aching shoulder and the bruise on his cheek bone—souvenirs from the previous night's disagreements. But, battle scars and all, the revelers were in a giving mood. Hannigan picked up nearly $250 in tips last night, his best reward yet for keeping the pints filled at this raucous Perth watering hole.

The Cricket Club was giving him sustenance, but he wondered if he has been there too long. Nothing has changed his status with the law since he came to Perth last winter. He was still a fugitive and not home free by any means. Would trusting his luck with his stolen identity as Rex Murtaugh give him a permanent reprieve from possible incarceration? If and when he arrived at US Customs, he had Murtaugh's driver's license, which at this time did not require an imbedded photograph on the document. But the Murtaugh passport did, a troubling fuzzy likeness to Josh Hannigan. If a sharp investigator queried Hannigan about Murtaugh's home background in San Diego, he would be on tenuous ground, since he'd never been there. To add to his anxiety, just two weeks ago his heart skipped a beat when a known Perth undercover police officer had a long conversation with the club's owner when Hannigan was tending bar. The fact the two looked at him several times while talking out of earshot increased his anxiety. He still wasn't sure if he was under suspicion for whatever they were discussing. Time to leave Perth and find a different place to hide?

The answer to that question wasn't easy. Despite the fact the authorities might be zeroing in on him, where else could he go without a misstep? Western Australia was as good a place as any to stay anonymous in the English-speaking world. The Aussies hold the view that their country is unique, differentiated by its geographical location, climate, topography, and unusual flora and fauna, because "God created Australia last"--away from it all. It still would be a good bet to stay undetected in this remote, distant location from America.

However, any notion to move on was more complicated by a woman, which made for a potential emotional trap. Sela Danby had a romantic hold on Murtaugh. His involvement with her would severely limit his options of where he could or wanted to go. Sela's appeal was hard to resist. She was beautiful, intelligent, intriguing, and adventurous, all qualities Murtaugh had succumbed to in the little time he has known her. In many respects she was just like him—a risk taker. He thought it wise to cling to a mate with the same outlook on life, as precarious as it has been for the two of them. If Sela was headed out of Australia for San Diego, he had to be with her. She was too dear to him to lose at a time when there really was nothing else for him to gain.

When Murtaugh arose from his bed with Sela on his mind, it was if she was thinking of him as well. He saw an envelope awaiting him that was slipped under the door. He went to it immediately, tore it open, and read Sela's note about another round of secret meetings they'd had the last few days:

Rex:

Time is short. Ian has returned and there is mischief on his mind. He's also not in a good mood and he takes it out on me. We are planning to go to America—soon. I have to see you this morning. I hope you are home to make this happen. I'll be sitting close to my door for the next hour or so. Pretend you are walking past my door and give a loud cough. I'll know it's you. I'll make an excuse to leave Ian for a bit. Leave your door unlocked and I'll slip right in. It's fun being a sneak. Oh, the wonder to see you again!

Sela

Murtaugh got a rush reading Sela's message. He liked her sense of enjoying the dangerous thrill of it all. Their deceptive game of meeting in Murtaugh's room in the morning has been working. It didn't take long for him to slip on some Bermuda shorts and a souvenir rugby jersey he was given last night by the manager of the Australian national rugby team. It was dark green with a gold collar, with a kangeroo nestled on two gold chevrons on the front. The shirt was part of the gratuity he earned by pouring generous pints for the victorious Kangeroo Gladiators. Knowing he would be conspicuous and did not want to be confused as a national hero by someone who might see him in the hall, he cracked the door open to see if the coast was clear. With no one in view, he made little noise with his bare feet as he walked about ten feet past Sela's opposite door. He turned to reverse his course, stopped at her door, gave a loud cough, and slipped behind his open door. Sela, dressed in red tank top and white shorts, carrying a small purse, entered his room in minutes.

Even without make-up she was sensual to Murtaugh. When he quietly closed the door to conceal their tryst, the preliminaries were over for the two of them. The urge for an intimate embrace was in control. Sela was more aroused then he was when she greeted him with a hug and a deep kiss:

"I can't stay long. Make love to me now in a way I'll remember."

Murtaugh needed no further instructions. He gently grabbed her hips and placed her on a waist high foot wide trim shelf that marked the top of a wainscot wall in his cramped living room. He took off her top, dropped his shorts, and kissed her erect nipples. She slid off her panty-less shorts and invited him in. They met each other with vigorous thrusts, keeping the sighs down to a minimum to stay concealed. It didn't take long for the two of them to climax, almost simultaneously to finally unleash a paroxysm of pleasure.

In a soft voice, Murtaugh said:

"I hope you don't forget what I'll always remember at a time like this."

"Rex, that was memorable. How can I forget?"

After kissing and caressing one another, they gathered themselves for a hurried strategy session. Sela went into the bathroom to dress and to straighten out a slightly disheveled look; Murtaugh went into the galley kitchen and started to brew coffee. But Sela was all business when she returned to him and instructed:

"That coffee may be for you only. Can't stay much longer. I told Ian I had to get some feminine product at the chemist shop. I think he bought the story, but no time to dawdle. He's been in a snit."

Hannigan knew he had to get off the physical and focus on the cerebral with Sela:

"What's got Bright pissed?"

"Been uppity because he's not really sure of himself?"

"How do you mean? Something he can't handle?"

"Well, he wants to help his father but he's starting to realize if he does that he might be part of a catastrophic outcome that he might regret--with me a part of it."

"Hmm. Now I know why you want to shake this guy. Together we can still do that, you know. You sure you want to hang on to the consequences and dangers Bright can create for you? Is it time for another option?"

"You mean the two of us blowing away from Perth? Where do we go?"

"Well, for starters, how about back to 'merry old England'? Once we get there, we'll decide where we can fit in there or move on to another country."

"No, I have to see this through with Ian. A few days ago you said you would shadow my trip, possibly on the same airplane flight, to act as my guardian angel, if you will. Still up to doing this?"

Murtaugh knew a return back to his country was dangerous for him. But it was a chance he would take to not break contact with Sela. He encouraged her desire to aid and abet Bright:

"Okay. Times a wasting. You win. Yes, I'll be there for you. This last week brought a special excitement and meaning to my life. It's you, Sela, that has uplifted my world."

Sela knew the boy was hooked:

"Rex, I feel the same way. Here's what I know about our travel plans. Ian said we must fly to San Diego shortly--in three or four days. Not sure when. Later today he makes flight arrangements for us. Once I have them I'll slip the details under your door. Again, I dearly hope you will be along for the ride."

Against his cautious nature, Murtaugh could not back away now. He made a reply to cut the tension a little:

"Sure thing. Getting too many battle scars working at the Cricket Club anyway. Besides, my mother does not know where I've been the last nine months or so. Have to check in with mom, you know."

"Good, darling. I do not use that word lightly. We just have to hope whatever bloody mess awaits us in San Diego does not hinder our future. I must go. Ian is a clock watcher. Said I'd be back in a flash."

"Before you do, you mentioned Jordan, your brother, or half-brother, is somehow involved with Bright. I take it when you arrive in San Diego you'll be greeted by Jordan?"

"No. Probably won't see Jordan immediately. Ian has a very important person to see first. He'll be at the airport to meet us."

"What's his name and why is he important?"

"What little I know about him does not sound good."

"Okay. Does Jordan know who'll be meeting you? Again, what's his name."

"It's Ian's father, who now lives in the San Diego area. I believe his father is part of some dangerous plan that involves Ian."

"So, can I surmise that perhaps Jordan has alerted you to this—the reason why you and Ian have to be inseparable?"

"Yes, you might say that is true."

"Hmm, Jordan must work for somebody in the know back in California. Whom does he work for?"

Then Sela gave an answer that injected instant fear into Murtaugh's body, and the reason why he was on the run:

"He works for a special government investigative group or something"

Murtaugh now knew things could be dicey on an eventual American homecoming. This investigative group could only be The Federal Bureau of Investigation.

19
CHAPTER

The Seal's Lair, Summer, 1969

The national security of the United States was in jeopardy because a saboteur was in its midst. Ever since he miraculously eluded the United States Navy in May 1945, Friedrich Vogel, a Nazi Germany fugitive, had been on the loose. For lo these twenty-four years, he had escaped capture by making his alias, David Percival, work to conceal his true identity. But there would be no rest for the wicked. Percival was well aware that Nazi hunters were in a frenzied search, especially for individuals who committed crimes against humanity. Percival was fortunate that he was not in the company of Holocaust perpetrators. His biggest sin was being an undocumented Nazi still, at-large and unaccounted for, and kept him off the most wanted list that included such genocide villains like Adolph Eichmann, the "architect of the Holocaust", who was captured by Jewish Nazi hunters and was executed in 1962. Nevertheless, it was incumbent on Percival to vigilantly work quietly but purposefully while appearing above suspicion.

Living by his wits, he cajoled a naïve banker to lend him enough money to buy a failing avocado farm in Fallbrook, an agricultural region north of San Diego. His masquerade as a likable gentleman farmer with the charming English veneer gave him cover in an off the mainline Southern California community like Fallbrook. The farm was not far from the major U.S. Marine installation at Camp Pendleton. What a great place for Percival to lie in waiting before he could commit a dastardly deed.

Would Nazi hunters really look seriously at a place so close to American military might? It also played into Percival's hands to recruit his own neo-Nazi army in a convenient location filled with trained killers. He found a committed band of brothers to strike. It took him over twenty years to finally approach sufficient financial resources to be positioned to commit a terrorist act. And the blow, if struck, had to be a cataclysm, one with mass destruction and numerous deaths. The weapon in his possession would provide the results he desired—a nuclear cylinder capable of unleashing devastating results.

Percival was on a vengeful twofold mission: to inflict damage on America, one of the major Allied powers that helped vanquish and destroy his beloved Germany, and to remind those Jews who escaped to America that they were not safe, wherever their diaspora has taken them. Despite his simmering anti-Semitism, it did not play well with some of the converts he needed to execute his plan. Rather, Marines like Yancey Bixby and Monty Crawford fell under Percival's beguiling spell more for their dislike of the way the war was unsuccessfully being conducted in Vietnam, killing and maiming their buddies, and the attraction of easy, good money now coming their way. Percival's antipathy for Jews never resonated with them because they had little or no contact with them in their backwater Louisiana hometowns and in the Marine Corps. The slick, fast cars and a good time during their off-duty hours were the ultimate persuaders that brought them closer to Percival. Until today, Bixby and Crawford did not know that their ties to Percival would involve nefarious deeds against the country they swore to defend.

With access granted to enter the Naval Amphibious Base (NAB) on the Coronado peninsula, Crawford, Bixby, and Percival pulled up in their Lincoln Continental outside of the bachelor officer quarters of Ensign Casey Douglas on Tulagi Road. They parked the car on the south side of Complex 320-325 in a lot adjacent to San Diego Bay, an unlikely den of iniquity. Douglas's location was on the top floor of the three-story barracks. He resided at an ominous address: 88 Tulagi Road. The number was benign enough, but the sordid significance was for the first letter in "Heil" and "Hitler", with "H" the eighth letter in the alphabet. The Navy did not pick up on that, nor the unintended swastika shape of the building. The place was a repository of repugnant Nazi stench, which became more apparent when the two Marines and Percival climbed the flight of stairs and approached Douglas's door. They could hear muffled sounds of people cheering, with a strident call from a frenzied audience: Sieg *Heil! Sieg Heil!*, the Third Reich's paean to Adolph Hitler.

The cries ended when Percival knocked on the door. Sounds of footsteps could be heard inside the apartment. There was a pause. The man who opened the door was the one who ended the cheers for Hitler when he turned off a tape recorder. Bixby and Crawford were stunned when they saw Douglas dressed in a military uniform, but it wasn't one they recognized. Douglas was donned in a black long-sleeved shirt, an arm band, with its red field, white circle, and black swastika in the middle, a black pistol strap over the right shoulder that connected diagonally across the chest to a black belt with a holstered German Luger. His pants were also black and bloused at the top of black, smooth, and non-laced Nazi jackboots. It was as if he was ready for one of Hitler's Berlin rallies--in the United States of America! Douglas, with closely cropped brown hair, bright blue eyes, and a round face accented by a ruddy complexion, opened his arms to the three arrivals and said with a subdued voice:

"Fellow believers of our departed, but not gone *Fuhrer,* please enter."

The men came into Douglas's quarters, which had two large posters of Adolph Hitler on the living room walls. As soon as the door was closed, Douglas took center stage:

"To my Marine friends, do not be alarmed. You are now in the right military force, not the one controlled by communists, Jews, and leftists who are leading our country to defeat in Vietnam."

He extended his hand to Bixby and Crawford and shook theirs with a firm, forceful grip. He then acknowledged Percival:

"*Reichmarschall,* all is ready for our meeting."

Douglas then faced toward the bedroom that adjoined his living area and called out:

"Storm Troopers of the new *Reich,* please join us."

On cue, out stepped four more men, identically dressed like Douglas. It was apparent to the Marines, their faces agog and their mouths opened, that they were in the presence of a cadre of neo-Nazis. Douglas instructed them to form a tight parade line as he joined them on their right. They then all gave the classical Nazi salute to Percival with the uplifted right arm:

"Heil Hitler!"

Percival stepped forward and acknowledged them with the same salute and salutation. Then he turned to the Marines:

"From this day forward, you are part of a new movement, one designed to cleanse America from the influence of appeasers dominating the news and college campuses, racially inferior people, namely black men and Jews, and tyrants in government undermining a failed war in Asia to aid and abet their communist cronies, which will only kill more of your fellow Marines."

To Bixby and Crawford, that was quite a mouthful. Percival's true identity and motivation were now unmistakable. He wanted a changing of the guard in the country, back to the hateful ways of fascism. Percival then stepped forward and directed his words to Douglas and the four new arrivals in the room:

"My Aryan brothers, meet two more loyal combatants to our cause: Lance Corporals Yancey Bixby and Monty Crawford."

Percival then introduced the Marines to their new comrades, who respectively came forward to shake hands as they were introduced:

"First, we have our host, Casey Douglas, originally from Stone Mountain, Georgia, but grew up here in San Diego. Then we have Grady Dunhill, from Raleigh, North Carolina. Next is Mack Smith from San Marcos, Texas. This handsome lad, as all these fine men are, is Bobby Montag from Gadsen, Alabama. And, finally, and certainly not the least of all of us, is Curtis Wyatt, from Tupelo, Mississippi."

After some friendly bantering, it was discovered that three of the men, Douglas, Dunhill, and Smith, were all in the U.S. Navy. Douglas was an officer and was residing at the NAB as a Navy Seal; Dunhill and Smith were enlisted men assigned to the USS *Ticonderoga,* a carrier that was out at sea. They missed the ship's last six month Pacific cruise because they were assigned to training at a special radio/communications school offered at the nearby North Island Naval Base. Montag and Wyatt were fellow Marines, who returned from Vietnam six months ago. Given this was the first time they'd met Percival's para-military force, Bixby and Crawford didn't know he had a secret cadre of believers.

When Douglas broke out some beer, and laid out an array of cheeses, cold cuts, vegetable munchies, potato chips, pretzels, and popcorn, Dunhill brought out his camera and took several shots of the men fraternizing. That's when Bixby became suspicious. He got Percival's attention and took his arm and steered him to the bedroom as the men ate and drank in jocularity:

"David, what's going on here? I ain't no expert when it comes to military law, but aren't these guys insubordinate? I mean German military outfits and praising Hitler and all?"

"Yancey, there's no turning back for you and Monty now."

Bixby was animated and starting to boil:

"What do you mean? I had no idea doing these odd jobs for you would lead to possibly betraying my country. My kin back in Louisiana would not like this."

Percival had an answer:

"Son, you and Monty are in too deep from this point forward. If your friends and relatives knew what is happening to this country, they would be right here with us. Shortly, when you both will vow to spread the principles of fascism, you will be part of a special force that will cleanse this country of those who wish it evil. You should feel proud to be at the vanguard for a new way for America to rid itself of its internal enemies."

"Come on, David. What's to stop us from leaving this place and report what we saw to the base commander back at Pendleton?"

"We won't be here if you do. We will move somewhere else. I've got the financial resources to make it happen. You leave us now and we send those pictures to the appropriate Marine Corps officials. With proof you attended a meeting of this kind you will face a court martial for sedition and treason, something that could get you life or worse."

"So, it's play ball for the two of us or suffer the consequences?"

"Come on, Yancey, I want you to feel good about this—not suspicious. This is a way out for you and Monty from a losing war effort. I have in mind a special assignment for you two. And the money's good-- $3,000 for the two of you to split!"

Bixby could not resist the almost hypnotic hold Percival had on him as he spun his words. He was pliant again when he said:

"Okay. That will make it better, but I think from this point forward we need cover because we will be through with the Corps."

"Good. I'm glad you realized that. My home will be your new home and base of operations. The Corps won't find you if you obey my directives, and stay, as you Marines say, 'Hunkered down'."

Bixby inquired:

"So, what's our new assignment?"

"Can't tell you now. Let's rejoin the group so we can relay an important task at hand."

Returning to the full group, Percival told them to give him his full attention. He reeled off what he termed "the noble causes of the fascist agenda" to include the quest for racial purity by negating and possibly eliminating Communists, Jews, Slavs, gypsies, blacks, homosexuals, and the mentally and physically disabled.

"Men, starting tonight, Operation Sea Lion begins. The name harkens back to the *Fuehrer*'s military plan in 1940 to invade Great Britain across the English Channel. That did not happen, but we are renewing the fight here in America. We have one advantage the German Army did not have: we are already behind enemy lines and in the midst of their major naval forces at this location--what we will call the *Seal's Lair*. And what an appropriate place for us to strike. I'm not sure the Navy knows that when they built the structure we are in they subconsciously dedicated it to our cause. As viewed from the air, the roof outline is in the shape of our symbol of trust and faith--the *swastika!*"

The men stirred a bit when they heard this. Douglas echoed what they heard:

"Fellow Storm Troopers, our plan is to extricate ourselves from defeatists, Communists, Jews, and radical mongrels that corrupt American life and society. In so doing, we will establish a true Aryan nation, one free from the vermin that affect and pollute pure Caucasian life. Let's vow to secrecy and unquestioned loyalty by paying homage to our new *Fuhrer--David Percival!*"

That was Percival's cue to get specific. He stepped forward to clench Douglas's right arm at the elbow and gave him a hug. Composed, resolute, and erect. Percival paused for a moment before addressing the group:

"I know some of you feel betrayed by the feeble effort the United States is making to win the Vietnam War. You've been used and abused risking your lives. That's why you are here. However, your opportunity to redeem your worth is at hand. I will now tell you that I have the power to bring this country to its knees. Shortly, we will make an ultimatum to the United States government to give us sanctuary and give us a homeland within America to attract others we choose to live with in our carefully select world. From there we will expose the undue influence of the enemies of America-- Communists, Jews, left-wing liberal academicians and ideologues, shiftless blacks, and anti-establishment hippies and malcontents. The truth will shock this country to revolution, which will prompt a majority of white American citizens to re-frame and re-cast the Constitution."

That got applause and a whoop from those assembled. Percival railed on a little more on the righteousness of their cause and good reasons why they had to prevail and make a foothold for fascism in America. He then took a penknife out from his pocket and made a small slit that drew blood on his right thumb. As a gesture of solidarity he invoked this decree:

"Now let us show our unity to our fascist purpose. I will pass the knife along to each of you, so you can make a cut to call forth your blood to mingle with us all. Let us each press our thumbs together to make a blood brother bond, from this time forward, to keep our identity secret and to vow to give our sacred honor to defend each other to the death, if need be!"

The men co-mingled and pressed their bloody thumbs as a sign of their fealty to one another. After Percival exhorted them to pipe down a little, he reminded them that they could be exposed and snuffed out on a major United States military base, he again drew Bixby off to a vacant corner of the apartment. With his arm firmly clasping Bixby's shoulder, Percival commanded:

"After we leave the base, we'll stop by Pendleton. You and Crawford take all your personal possessions, a set of khaki's and your cunt caps, all civilian clothes, and any weapon you can get a hold of. A pistol would be fine. You and Monty will get your assignment, one I know you both can perform and will be rewarded with the $3,000 I said you two can divide."

Bixby's reply showed he was instantly indoctrinated when he curiously asked:

"*Reichmarschal,* we are yours to command. Can you tell me anything now?"

"I will simply state you will meet an important ally soon. I'll give you his name and what he brings to us at my house."

"Where will we meet him?"

"Some place that is light, breezy, and laid back--a spot like Windansea Beach in La Jolla."

20
CHAPTER

La Jolla, September, 1969

Captain Damon Broadbent's unmarked Oldsmobile police cruiser was headed north up I-5 after he left his downtown San Diego office. It was a drive Broadbent had made many times, but this one was far from routine. Making this trip special was the thought of meeting Maggie Starmont again at her La Valencia Hotel in La Jolla. Yes, for Broadbent, it was part of his ongoing investigation to solve a murder, but it also excited his sexual juices. When it came to Maggie, he was torn between business and pleasure.

With this emotional tug-of-war on his mind, Broadbent shifted to the professional side of his internal struggle. He got back on his radio and contacted his competent associate, Rick Sandoval, who had found a hot lead:

"Rick, come in and let's talk about your Marine contact up at Pendleton. Over."

There was brief static on the line. Sandoval then made connection:

"Captain, good to hear from you again. I'm driving to Pendleton as we speak—going to see their Public Information Officer, a Captain Julian Desmond. Over."

"Yeah, you told me he had several jarheads of interest up there. Was it a Bixby and a Crawford? Over."

"That's right. Any chance you can zoom up here in the next hour or so? Over."

Broadbent had other priorities, so he falsified his location:

"Yeah, I think so. Right now I'm going to Windansea to try to find more witnesses who might know something about the corpse in the cabana. Things still too delicate and hot on this case. We need something to hang our hats on—like suspects. Stay put up at Pendleton Public Information Office until I get there. I'll radio you when in route, over."

"Copy that. Over and Out."

After exiting I-5, Broadbent's car was at the summit descending Ardath Road, which gave him a spectacular view of the blue Pacific. La Jolla's verdant foreground of palm trees accented the base of the road. Broadbent now enjoyed this route so much he was driving in a rapture to get to his destination. Once he hit the light at Torrey Pines Boulevard, he instinctively turned left. Then a short jog up the hill and a right turn unto Prospect Avenue. In a flash he was at the front door of the quaint and lovely La Valencia. At the hotel, with the luxury of police license plates, he avoided the congested parking and used a sidewalk stall reserved for temporary loading. To Broadbent, parking where one pleased was one of the few perquisites that came with the job. More importantly, it got him faster to meeting Maggie after he acquired directions to the pool from the hotel bellman.

The hotel pool deck had a scenic view of the ocean at the back of the building. When Broadbent left the interior shade of the La Valencia hallways, he was bathed in spectacular sunshine. On this warm summer day, the pool was crowded, with a small combo playing *I Only Have Eyes For You* near the adjacent bar on the left. How appropriate the song was. As if guided by a laser beam, Broadbent's tunnel vision drew him to Maggie, sitting on a lounge at the far end of the pool in front of a plexiglass wind screen that framed the Pacific in the distance.

Broadbent's dark brown suit made him stand out among the more scantily clad hotel guests cavorting in the pool area. Maggie, clad with a white terrycloth top over a one-piece black swimsuit, saw Broadbent the moment he entered the pool area. She gave a friendly wave, which gave a lilt to Broadbent's step as he walked along the pool's edge to Maggie's relaxed perch. Pulling up a patio chair, he drew it near to her. He was stimulated when he furtively saw her shapely legs, inviting hips, and the cleavage of her breasts:

"It's good to see you again, Maggie. I'm glad you have a chance to relax after all we've put you through."

"Yes, I must admit I've gotten a better grip on my emotions now that I believe Jordan is out there alive--somewhere. Do you have any updates about his location?"

Broadbent knew he had to give an answer that gave a mother hope but he had to be wise and not give too much information:

"Detective Herlihy has discovered that Jordan is, in fact, living in San Francisco. But, for now, he's off limits for us to contact him."

Maggie removed her sunglasses to better reveal a look of disbelief:

"Damon, I don't understand? We can't have the police locate a missing person, my lost son, because he's 'off limits'! Do they think my boy is a leper?"

"I can't tell you specifics, which I'm sure will not comfort you, but let's give this some time to sort itself out."

"Okay, can I at least call Jordan--to hear his voice and give me the assurance that he is safe?"

"That's not an unreasonable request. But I need to clear this with higher authorities."

This evoked a sardonic laugh from Maggie:

"Higher authorities? My, my, Jordan has become a celebrity of sorts. This sounds serious—right?"

Broadbent knew he couldn't say much, so he deflected Maggie's inquiring mind by injecting a red herring:

"Of course. It's all that. But I can tell you that Jordan could lead us to Sela Danby, this girl you wanted us to get a handle on."

Hearing Sela's name diminished some of Maggie's negativity:

"Oh, what can you tell me about her?"

"Just that she could be in touch with your son. My department has no means to get a beat on her at this time without knowing her whereabouts."

"You said you would keep no secrets from me. What's changed here?"

"There are no secrets, Maggie. I hope you appreciate that my hands are tied. Believe me, I really don't know much more than what I have already told you."

Maggie was clinging to the belief that the detective at her side was truthful—but she wasn't sure. She had to test his sexual desires to determine his veracity:

"Damon, you are an appealing individual. You are thoughtful, responsive, and a very handsome man. I do want to know you better, but I am a woman looking for a lost son. That's at the top of my list. Right now, what's more important to you: bringing Jordan back to me by solving this murder or just enjoying the pleasure of my company?"

Broadbent was taken aback by the profound nature of Maggie's question. The woman had a keen mind in addition to her attractive physique. He paused to ponder an answer that would dictate the future direction of his relationship with Maggie. To give him more time to reflect on his critical response, he reached into his suit pocket, drew out a Kool, lit it, and then took a slow drag while looking into Maggie's pensive eyes:

"I have to solve this crime, because I am convinced that, if I do, Jordan will come back to you to make you happy. And, to be sure, the driving force behind my investigation is your happiness."

Good. Maggie felt she had the man right where she wanted him. She knew Broadbent found her alluring, but she believed his priorities were straight when it came to her son:

"Damon, you are good man, who also happens to be a perceptive detective. Keep me posted on what you find next--and if I can possibly call Jordan."

"That goes without saying. I trust you still won't roam far from La Jolla until we crack this case? It could take a long time, you know."

"I'll be here, even if I have to buy a house in La Jolla and take up permanent residence."

Broadbent was pleased to know Maggie was in this for the long run. He put his cigarette down, got up from his seat and reached for Maggie's hand, holding it tenderly with both of his:

"I'm so glad we have this understanding. Trust is a wonderful thing when you believe in it. Now I have to get up to Camp Pendleton to qualify a lead on the murder—the corpse you saw."

"I understand. Tell me, what might you find there?"

Broadbent got up and was ready to depart. He was a bit disappointed because this latest visit with Maggie was more routine detective work.

What he wanted to do was to hold her and dance to the music of the poolside combo, which was now playing *The Very Thought of you*. The song captured the reality of the moment, because he felt Maggie thought of him more as a cop, rather than a romantic opportunity. So, he answered the question directly to keep the woman's confidence and trusting that she would not divulge specifics to another:

"Have to determine if two Marines are linked to the Windansea corpse."

Margaret's mood was now testy:

"This whole situation seems so odd to me. My son's identity is mistaken; he's taken for dead but isn't. Right now, some girl, this Sela Danby, might know more about Jordan than we do. We think we found him but we can't really see him. And now the Marine Corps has an interest in him? What prompts the military to get involved with this?"

As Broadbent began to walk away, against his detective nature he gave Margaret some specificity, hoping it would placate her and give reasons for the two to stay close.

"That's why my next stop at Camp Pendleton is to make any possible connection between the Marines and Jordan. But this whole case is bigger than we know because it involves an old adversary not yet defeated that still threatens this country."

"Pray tell. Who can that be?"

"Nazis."

21
CHAPTER

Perth, September 1969

Sela Danby slipped a note under Rex Murtaugh's apartment door around midnight, while he was still tending bar at the Cricket Club. Several hours later, a fatigued Murtaugh stumbled to his dingy residence after another long night of satisfying the unquenchable thirst of Australian mates. He was pleasantly surprised to see Sela's message at his feet when he unlocked and opened his door. It gave him an instant jolt of energy. Behind his closed door he then tore the envelope open to read Sela's latest news. A piece of yellow ribbon accompanied what he read:

Rex:

No time to waste now. Ian has plane tickets in hand to fly to San Diego, via Los Angeles. As we agreed, you will try to be on this flight. You have to be my guardian angel, you know! Here's our itinerary:
  Friday, September 13:
  Leave Perth for Sydney on Qantas Airlines, flight 235 at 7:00 A.M.;
  Arrive Sydney at 12 noon;
  Transfer to Qantas flight 150 to Los Angeles;
  Arrive Los Angeles the same day at 8:00 P.M.;
  Transfer to PSA flight 2777 at 9:45 P.M.;

> *Arrive San Diego at 11:00 P.M.*
>
> *Things are moving too fast and Ian has a tight grip on me. Not sure I can see you until we get on the plane. Again, you must make the flight!*
>
> *To confirm you read this and will be making the trip to San Diego, please tie this piece of ribbon on your doorknob. That way I'll know you'll be there for me.*
>
> *Miss you and need you.*
>
> *Sela*

Murtaugh knew he now faced a critical moment. He had to dig deep through his conflicted psyche if he cared for this girl enough to risk his neck by going back to the United States. Throughout his young life, Murtaugh had been a risk taker. He was active with a radical anti-establishment group, the SDS (Students for a Democratic Society), during his college days at the University of Wisconsin. After college, he got involved with heroin drug smugglers, thinking the junk they sold would weaken the American power structure, which was one of the SDS's goals. The drugs led him to San Francisco and the hippie kingdom of Haight Ashbury, where things went terribly wrong. His thoughts wandered back to why he was a fugitive from the law:

In his college days at the University of Wisconsin in Madison, which was at the forefront of strident college student protest across the country against the Vietnam War, Josh Hannigan was an ardent member of the Students for a Democratic Society's, a New Left movement dedicated to a major overhaul of American social, economic, and political life. When the War escalated in Vietnam, the SDS focused its energy to denounce America's involvement. Hannigan made friends and foes during his student days as an SDS protester. His political arch-enemy at Wisconsin was Gil Landon. Landon loved another UW student, Becky Morris, who Hannigan tried to recruit into the SDS. Morris rejected Hannigan for Landon.

After leaving Wisconsin, Hannigan would pay for his sins by making a deal with the devil. It became apparent that his radical views to transform the government and end the war were not creating the desired effect by taking to the streets in protest. The ruling establishment held the upper hand by quelling whatever convulsive protest groups like the SDS could throw at them on college campuses, political conventions, and troop embarkation points. Rejected for the military draft and working in Chicago, he was approached by Corsican drug dealers (known as the CABAL), who convinced him that there was a better, more effective way to subvert those in control—pollute them with heroin.

Things went bad when his scheme, using a US Army accomplice, Johnnie Krupke, to acquire heroin in Thailand with the $50,000 in cash the Corsicans gave to Hannigan. Hannigan mailed the money via special delivery letter to Vietnam-based Krupke, who was to acquire the drugs on an R and R (rest and recuperation) trip to Bangkok. By accident, that sinister piece of mail fell into the hands of his old college nemesis, Gil Landon. Without the letter, Krupke couldn't go to Thailand to make the buy. The CABAL wanted their money back; Hannigan did not know where it was.

Hannigan was frantically trying to find the Krupke letter. He enlisted the help of the Krupke's: Johnnie (now back from Vietnam) and his hitman brother, Stan. Johnnie told Hannigan that he and Landon were in the same outfit in Vietnam. That prompted Hannigan to call Landon's home. His mother answered and told him her son was out delivering six unopened letters addressed to his Vietnam buddies he mysteriously had in his possession, one of which belonged to Johnnie. Hannigan surmised Landon had the letter with the Corsican drug money. With Landon on the road, he was unknowingly being hunted by Hannigan and the Krupke brothers.

Hannigan led a charmed life in his search for Landon. Through another Wisconsin classmate, he became aware that Landon's lost love, Becky Morris, was living with the "flower children" in the Haight-Ashbury district of San Francisco. She would be the lure to bring Landon west with the Krupke contraband cash. Johnnie made contact with Landon and told him to bring his letter to San Francisco. If the letter was unopened, a stipulation made to keep the money secret inside, Krupke would lead him to Becky. While driving through Texas, Landon sensed a trap and enlisted the aid of one of the letter recipients: Charlie Toogood. Toogood knew Landon would be outnumbered, by Hannigan and the Krupke's so he rounded up three other letter recipients, C. J. Wellington (Washington, D.C.), Sal Baccione (Philadelphia, PA), and Wendell Rucker (Horse Cave, KY) to form an ad hoc Vietnam veteran cadre to protect Landon and rescue Becky, who had now been kidnapped by Hannigan and the Krupke's. Landon now had an able strike force to assist him, one Hannigan was unaware of.

With Hannigan awaiting Landon to come for Becky, things became dangerously murky for him on a foggy night in late November 1968 at a rendezvous point with the Corsican heroin dealers on Treasure Island in San Francisco Bay. It was there that his big problems with the law compounded. Hannigan didn't have the money or the heroin the Corsicans demanded. In a showdown, he exchanged gunfire with them and fled the scene in his car. The dealers gave chase but lost control of their car, careening into San Francisco Bay and drowning the occupants after hitting another vehicle head-on in a fiery crash. Two Corsicans and an innocent man and woman in the other car were killed. If uncovered, this fatal result made it likely that Hannigan has a second-degree murder charge on his head.

In the end, Landon and a fellow band of Vietnam veteran brothers, Toogood, Baccione, Wellington, and Rucker, cleverly turned the tables and get the drop on Hannigan and the Krupke brothers. Before Landon left with Becky in tow, Toogood and company tied up Hannigan and the Krupke's, bound back-to-back, in a compromising position. Struggling on the floor in early December 1968 in a tawdry Haight-Ashbury apartment, Hannigan was regretting about how he got into a conspiracy to bring high grade heroin to the United States. This plotting troika failed in their attempt to lure a returning Vietnam veteran, Gil Landon, into a trap. At least Hannigan avoided the deadly consequences with the CABAL.

The police got wind (through an anonymous tip from Landon) where Hannigan and his bound-up accomplices could be found. Hannigan miraculously freed himself from the attached Krupke's, who eventually also freed themselves before the police arrived, potentially facing charges of kidnapping, drug dealing and extortion. Slipping through the law's net, Hannigan was fortunate to find a tramp steamer to vacate America for the Far East. Because he was involved with foreign drug smugglers, there was a distinct possibility that both the FBI and the local police wanted him. Although Hannigan had been on the lam for nearly a year, the stark reality was that it might be way too soon to return to America. His trail was cooler, but he had to assume it was not forgotten.

⊰══◉══⊱

Hannigan was now back in the present. After taking off his work clothes, redolent with the smell of the alcohol spills he absorbed at work, he collapsed into his unmade bed. He thought about the potential dangers that lay ahead--for both Sela and him. No matter, not knowing why, he was beyond the point of no return and had to go forward. Having made his decision, he got out of bed and returned to the yellow ribbon he left on the kitchen table with Sela's note. He complied with her wish and carefully opened his door half-way, not wanting to be seen at this crucial moment. The hall was dark and unpopulated at this late hour. After he tied the ribbon around the knob, he quietly closed the door. He returned to bed, took a deep breath, and fell asleep.

When the sun beamed through his windows, it awoke Hannigan with a start. There was no time to dawdle. He dressed in a rush, donning sunglasses, chinos, a hooded sweatshirt, and a navy blue knit cap. Hannigan had the look of tough guy who didn't want to be bothered as he hit the sidewalk for the Qantas ticket office located on Wellington Street across from the square with the same name.

The Qantas office was modest. It had several simple chrome framed chairs in the narrow waiting area in front of the counter. A large world map accented the wall behind the counter, showing the international Qantas air routes, which took its passengers to every continent on earth. Standing at the counter, Hannigan's eye was drawn to the uninterrupted red colored route line that connected Sydney with Los Angeles. As he readied to hit the desk bell to page an agent at the unattended counter, he had his speech rehearsed to avoid answering any embarrassing questions, especially any specifics on his background.

But just before his hand drew down to ring the bell, Hannigan's epiphany began. His eye was drawn to the miniature Australian flag that was mounted on a tiny staff on a small marble base next to the bell. The dark blue field was accented by a Union Jack in the upper left corner and a cluster of stars that compose the Southern Cross constellation distributed across the rest of the banner. This heavenly grouping was clearly visible throughout the year in Australia's southern hemisphere sky. To this country's aboriginal peoples, the juxtaposition of stars looked not like a cross but a giant footprint of a wedge tailed eagle called Waluwaru. The two pointers represent a spear that is used to hunt the eagle; the dark patch between the two brightest stars of the Cross represent its nest.

Hannigan saw himself as the hunted eagle, but this time he could only be saved through atonement. From out of nowhere he suddenly recalled a religious memory from a life that had not sought God's guidance. He remembered a priest in his boyhood days in a Jesuit high school counsel:

"The sages tell us to repent exactly one day before we die. But, you may ask, how do you know the day before you die? Exactly!"

Hannigan's life was full of peril. Any day might be his last as a free man. So, while he had the opportunity, it was time to make things right. The return to America would be a trip of redemption by helping someone in need, regardless of the consequences that would befall him. His new good intentions were rewarded by getting a break. A prim and proper Australian Sheila came from the back room to the counter at the sound of the bell. She had a Qantas uniform on: a light gray shirt, a matching vest, and a long sleeved white blouse. Hannigan surmised that a young woman could be better manipulated, something he had been doing for much of his young life. It made for a no questions asked purchase of his plane tickets—in the name of Rex Murtaugh

With tickets in hand, Hannigan still knew he had a major problem. He wasn't sure he could finesse the veracity of Murtaugh's passport to custom officials, especially in the United States. They had the same hair color, but Murtaugh's facial features differed, for he had a wider face, compared to Hannigan's lean, high cheek bones visage. Customs could question the likeness on the passport photo. Time to go muddle his visage by growing a beard and mustache. He hoped the ambiguity would work.

22
CHAPTER

San Francisco, August, 1969

Jordan Starmont was wise beyond his years. For sure, he was bookish, but the many man-to-man talks he'd had with his late father about the realities of life were interred in his bones. A Dean's List scholar at Princeton, he found academia stimulating but not exciting. He decided to leave college at the end of his junior year. His new destiny was prompted by the beck and call he heard from the west. It beckoned for a new life with the "flower children" in a kingdom found in the Haight-Asbury district of San Francisco. Unlike many of the youthful emigres who came there, Jordan had amassed sufficient financial resources from his parents to meet his day-to-day existence. Most struggled through an austere existence--if they even cared about their humble state. The alternative lifestyle environment had a distinctive appearance (bell-bottomed pants, brightly colored shirts and blouses, and long-haired men and women), a predilection for drug use (to include LSD consumption), and a wallowing in psychedelic music (laden with drug induced euphoria). All this new behavior exhibited by prodigal sons and daughters provided the impetus to reject the standards and values of their parents.

Jordan chummed around with a new generation of carefree friends and found a flat on Baker Street in the Haight. It was a center for merriment. Life was to be celebrated by consuming both the spirit and the flesh of the moment. Leisure and self-indulgence were to be optimized. At a quasi-bacchanalian party, he came close to swallowing "acid" (LSD) but rejected it because he saw the bad, sometimes fatal, effects it had on some of its users. But that did not prevent him from losing his virginity rather quickly with a free-love maiden who found him attractive. It all seemed too beautiful and other worldly to believe.

Then, after only a few months, it hit him: was this apparent Shangri-La sustainable without consequences? What he was about to embark upon would require all the maturity, intelligence, and even some bravery he could muster. An epiphany came one afternoon while sitting forlorn and pensive at the Blue Unicorn restaurant. A fellow counterculture lad came up to his table. He was atypical because he seemed to be at least five years older than most of the general population in The Haight, but, with a droopy mustache, he was wearing the uniform of many of the avant-garde in the area: a suede vest, a parson's shirt, and denim pants. With a voice of non-threatening authority, he stated:

"Mind if I join you? You look a bit puzzled?"

Jordan introspective mood made him open for a dialog.

"Sure, man. Right now I've got time on my hands."

The stranger took a seat and got to the point:

"Are you Jordan Starmont?"

Jordan was taken aback with this pointed intro:

"How'd you know my name? We meet at some bash in the Haight?"

"No, but we have been trying to find you ever since you got to San Francisco."

"Who is we?"

"Before I go further, let me allay any anxiety you might have about me and where this conversation will be going. I mean no harm and need you to listen to a proposition."

Now Jordan was really circumspect:

"Are you a narc? I know they have been floating around the neighborhood to stop the drug consumption. I'm not a rat."

The stranger bent back in his chair in a relaxed fashion to avoid a confrontational look:

"If you are Jordan Starmont, then I can tell you your father's name was Martin. So, again, are you Jordan Starmont?"

Jordan gave himself away when he heard this penetrating revelation:

"How did you know my father's name? Why are you talking to me?"

"Okay. I'll come clean. My name is Ross Cargill. I work undercover for the Federal Bureau of Investigation. No worries. You are not in any trouble or a target for arrest. Can we talk business, Jordan?"

Jordan gulped and his pulse raced a bit when he heard this. Trying to be composed, his voice had a quiver to it:

"Did my mother send you to look for me? I did call her and told her where I was living, unlike most of the people out here."

"Jordan, this is not about your mother. It's about your father, a patriot who served his country well. You see, when your dad came home from England after World War II he continued to do Naval intelligence here at home before he went to work for Smith Barney. Did you know this?"

"All I know is that my father was an officer in the Navy and worked for Smith Barney. He never got into specifics about what he did in uniform or civilian life."

"Well, that is why your father was so useful and competent--he could keep a secret about his military assignment. Jordan, like your father, do you want to do something in full confidence for your country? I emphasize in full confidence. If yes, then we can proceed. That's the proposition."

Jordan had to make a quick decision of extreme importance. He was savvy enough to ask:

"What if I say no."

"Again, no worries. I'm out of your life and you are free to pursue your own. But I think you feel, deep down, that this unconstructive existence you find yourself is not really meeting your expectations. Right?"

Cargill's question captured Jordan's present dissonant outlook. He needed clarification:

"What makes you so sure? You really know me well enough to say these things?"

"All I know is that in dealing with more than a few of your friends in the Haight that they have misgivings about the life they are leading. The smart ones come to realize a decadent present leads to a bleak future. I put you in the extra smart group with your Princeton background."

"Hmm. You FBI guys can get real personal. What else do you know about me besides where I went to college?"

Cargill knew he had to disarm Jordan with some humor:

"Don't worry, Jordan, we don't follow you into the bathroom, although we might know what you eat that gives you a bowel movement."

Chuckling, Cargill continued trying to appeal to Jordan's parental pride:

"Yeah, sure. We are getting off task. Do you want to follow your father's example and help your country?"

Jordan injected with flippancy and earnestness:

"All right, you put me on the payroll, my funds are shrinking. I consider myself high priced help. Right? My father once told me that really important things in life come rarely and at times you don't expect them. I'll play ball. But how in the hell did you find me?"

Cargill was reassuring and jocular:

"First, the Bureau has an intern program that will compensate you. Come to our field office with me now. My car is outside. We can then tell you what your father uncovered and put some meat on what we propose for you to do. Second. Find you? You were easy to locate—you were not on our 'Most Wanted List'."

The two shook hands in agreement and stepped briskly outside the Unicorn for a ride in Cargill's unmarked blue Ford sedan. Cargill engaged in less serious badinage with Jordan on the short jaunt to the FBI location on Golden Gate Avenue. When they arrived, Jordan expected a high security environment, complete with guards and steel gates. Rather, it was an open setting with serious minded clerks typing in a large office bay surrounded by offices with doors with dark wood on the bottom and opaque glass on the top. Cargill whisked Jordan to the office of Theodore Johnson. It read in big black letters on the glass: Chief Investigator. Jordan felt this had to be big.

One of the clerks paged Johnson that he had visitors. When his office opened, Johnson was there to greet Jordan and Cargill with a smile and requested they take a seat. Seated behind a large desk, cluttered with files and legal pads, Johnson paged the receptionist on his intercom to not be interrupted. Dressed in a blue business suit, white shirt, and red tie, he had an avuncular face befitting a man in his 50's. This first impression relaxed Jordan a bit as Johnson started to discuss why he was sought by the Bureau:

"Can I call you Jordan?"

"No problem."

"Good, Jordan, we want you know that my office is so happy you agreed to help us. I apologize for keeping you in the dark as to why we need you, but we had to be sure you wanted to assist the Bureau. However, from this point on, I want you to completely understand that your participation in our operation is of dire importance for national security. You will be provided a different residence in the city to allow our agents to have immediate access to you and to tap into every telephone call you make with a phone we will provide for you. Am I clear here?"

Jordan was now very concerned:

"So I'll be followed and restricted in my movements as well?"

Johnson wanted to be a bit unrelenting:

"We will not confine you, but you must call us first where you are going, why you need to step out, and who you might be meeting. We'll either allow or deny your request. You'll likely be followed."

"This almost sounds like a witness protection program?"

"Jordan, you are perceptive. Same modus operandi. Again, by agreeing to meet with us today you are now part of a top-secret activity which has potentially grave consequences for the country."

Jordan was now anxious to know specifics:

"Right now it's all so vague. What is so urgent about what your office is engaged in?"

"Sorry for rambling, Jordan, but by beating around the bush I noticed that you were intently interested in what I had to say. You exhibited nonverbal signs of composure and concentration, all valuable assets to have when under duress. I think you got that from your father, who I worked with in 1945."

Jordan, quickly retorted:

"Agent Cargill told me he worked with you guys for a bit. Is he the center of all this?"

"A big part but not all of it. Jordan, here's the situation:"

Johnson then went to a credenza and brought out a file. He opened it and showed a photo of his father, Martin, in a Navy uniform, sporting a handsome smile. Johnson then relayed the background of Friedrich Vogel and how he slipped through the hands of the US Navy when his submarine surrendered at Portsmouth, New Hampshire in May, 1945. Martin Starmont was back in America at about this time and was assigned, along with both military and FBI operatives, to find Vogel's whereabouts. Vogel's trail was cold, but they had a loose description from the surrendering U-Boat captain to assist the chase. Martin was quick to the scene a day later when the Navy discovered one of the nuclear cylinders was missing from the sub's manifest. He followed a tip that a Portsmouth cab driver gave a ride to a man fitting Vogel's description to the nearby railroad station in Dover. Martin queried the station master and boarding conductors of the Boston and Main (B & M) line that serviced Dover. They said a man that matched Vogel's description bought, in cash, a B & M ticket to Boston, which connected to a New York Central (NYC) train headed for New York's Grand Central Station. The fare included a ride on the NYC's westbound Twentieth Century Limited to Chicago. From there the suspect would board the Union Pacific's Super Chief, bound for Los Angeles.

At this point in the narration Jordan interrupted Johnson.

"Hmm, how did this Nazi scientist have American dollars to pay for the train rides?"

Johnson clarified:

"We assume that Vogel's family amassed American dollars while living in England in case their travels would take them there. As I understand it, Nazi banks could exchange gold for American greenbacks from Swiss banks during World War II. It's not surprising that he carried our currency."

Johnson asked if there were more questions. Hearing none he continued.

"Martin, attempting to interdict Vogel, took a short-cut via a military flight from Portsmouth to Meigs Field in Chicago. From there he went to the LaSalle Street Station, the terminus of the Twentieth Century Limited. Martin tried to get a glimpse of the arriving NYC passengers from New York. No luck in sighting Vogel. The chase continued. On a hunch, Martin had the credentials to board the westbound Super Chief. Carefully patrolling the aisles of the train in route to Los Angeles, no one close to Vogel's appearance seemed to be on board. But there was a glimmer of hope when the train reached the Los Angeles Union Station. Still on board the Super Chief, Martin looked through a window and saw a man carrying a trench coat on one arm toting a satchel with the other on the platform. Martin scrambled through debarking passengers backed up at the exit doors of the train, trying to intercept Vogel. He frantically searched the platform and then inside the station until he eventually went outside into the bright California sunshine. Poof! Vogel was gone."

Jordan queried Johnson at this point:

"Were you a part of trying to find Vogel with my father?"

"Yes, at that time I was a young agent based in LA. I met your father that day and he debriefed me about his futile search. We stayed in touch for a while, then he left the military for civilian life."

"You got my curiosity up. Any luck finding Vogel?"

Johnson returned to the saga:

He explained after many years of fruitless investigation, the Bureau finally got wind of Vogel, now living in Fallbrook, California, in northern San Diego County, as a mundane avocado grower. He invented an alias, David Percival. The break came when we received an anonymous tip. Our source relayed that there was an unnamed person who was enticing types to join his covert organization. When pushed to identify the perpetrator, the contact only said the individual spoke with an English accent and farmed avocados in Fallbrook. We hustled down there and combed the area, questioning residents about a person who might fit this description. That's when we discovered Percival, disguised as an ordinary avocado grower. Rather than alert him that we were on to him, we wiretapped his telephone.

Jordan again interjected:

"Why did you not arrest him?"

"Insufficient evidence for a warrant. Too early in the process. We wanted to cast a wider net to round up any and all accomplices. Also, Friedrich Vogel is not accused of any wartime atrocities, which would make him a white-hot criminal for immediate arrest."

Johnson went on:

From the wiretaps we discovered that Percival has a son, Ian Bright. Ironically, he's never really met him, for he was a lovechild with a British woman. Percival has stayed in touch with the mother, she not knowing that Percival is a Nazi fugitive. Percival has talked to Ian more than a few times lately at his London home. He instructed his son to purchase a detonating device in Australia that he found in an explosives engineering textbook. Percival indicated he would pay for Ian's trip and the device by wiring the money. In the USA, these devices have restrictions on them and require a background check on the purchaser. That's not the case in in Australia, with its wide open and sparsely populated terrain. Percival told Bright to make an excuse why he had to suddenly go to Australia. But Bright told Percival he wanted to go with an important other person.

Jordan was really curious:

"Who was that?"

The answer Johnson gave blew Jordan's mind:

"A Sela Danby."

Jordan explained with surprise:

"That's my sister, who I have been trying to reach since my father explained in a letter how she is related to me."

"We know that and that's why it was vital to find you and where you come into this whole intriguing web. You see, your father also sent a copy of the letter he wrote to you, the one that said: 'Open in the Event of My Death', to the Bureau to keep on file in case any legal/financial repercussions would affect his estate. We opened it when he passed away this year and kept its contents confidential. You read it, right Jordan?"

"Of course I did"

"Did you share its contents with anyone else?"

"My mother, Margaret Starmont."

Johnson had a devious smile when he said:

"Good, now it's a good bet your mother won't be a problem in this investigation because she knows where you are, here in the Haight, but she might be more curious to find your sister when she knows you are safe."

Johnson then leaned forward at his desk and his eyes narrowed ready to execute his authority:

"Jordan, Agent Cargill, here is the battle plan. We are going to create some subterfuge to draw Percival and hopefully some of his cohorts out into the open to build our case against them."

Cargill was inquisitive:

"What's the bait we use here?"

With a wry smile, Johnson said:

"Jordan Starmont."

Fallbrook, August 1969

David Percival paced the floor of his north San Diego County home in pensive thought. Escaping the net of allied forces after World War II, it had taken almost twenty-five years for this Nazi with bad intentions to strike a blow. But was this the right time? With an apparent clever camouflage as a modest avocado grower, he had successfully avoided detection. Could he afford to lose his cover, given all the physical amenities he had accumulated since he arrived in southern California? He mentally harkened back to where he came from.

A man of wits and daring, when he left a surrendering German U-Boat in Portsmouth, New Hampshire in May of 1945, he fled by train across the United States to Los Angeles, paying the fares in cash. This was possible because Percival exchanged his Reichsmarks for $20,000 American dollars. There was a supply of US dollars in the German Reichsbank because it exchanged gold for foreign currencies with Swiss banks in order to purchase vital materials like tungsten and oil from neutral countries. He patted himself on the back for stashing away the money while still living in Nazi Germany, just in case he had to make a run from a dying Third Reich regime. The English accent also did not hurt him, for he sounded at the time like an ally, not a German enemy.

Once a free man on American soil, he eked out a clandestine existence by working at odd jobs where employers would not ask too many questions about his background. He knew Nazi hunters were looking for his ilk around the world. Gradually, avoiding any close personal relationships, although he did have some sexual pleasures with poorly educated, naïve American women. In general, the smarter the person he met, male or female, he avoided for fear they would get too inquisitive about his background.

Not losing his hatred for Jews, it rankled Percival extremely to see how well they were existing, especially in southern California. More than a few were leading luxuriant lives in the entertainment industry in Hollywood. It rankled Percival that Jews thrived in America. In addition, a racist to the core, the prevalence of people of color, especially blacks, mingling with whites openly stunned him. This vitriol for humankind did not abate and was reinforced by his shadowy association with the American Nazi Party, founded in 1959 by George Lincoln Rockwell. Ironically, Rockwell, like Martin Starmont, was a former US Navy officer, serving in the Atlantic and Pacific theaters in WWII and in Korea. Percival read the ANP literature and went to one of Rockwell's speeches at UCLA in May, 1967, staying on the fringe of the audience. Rockwell's primary party hierarchy were ex-US military individuals, a thought that Percival later would seize upon.

After amassing enough cash, Percival saw an advertisement in the *Los Angeles Times* for a sixty acre avocado farm, with a large house and outbuildings in Fallbrook, a quiet community about thirty miles north of downtown San Diego. This was perfect to give him a base of operations in near privacy. The harvests were always bountiful and profitable, enabling Pericval to build some wealth. Maybe he did not realize it, but he was living the American dream, a man who came with modest resources and was now something.

So, on this hot summer afternoon, Percival stopped pacing the floor and took a chair. He became less engaged in the past and thought about a destructive future, one that could be accented with destructive consequences of the uranium canister he had buried in a secret cache in his house. That's when his telephone rang:

Never answering a telephone call by name, Percival answered:

"Hello. Sunrise Ranch"

An unfamiliar voice was on the other end:

"Yes, hello. Is this David Percival?"

Always the very cautious type, he responded:

"Who might this be? What is the purpose of your call?"

"Okay. If you are or are not Mr. Percival, does the name George Lincoln Rockwell mean anything to you, or perhaps to Mr. Percival?"

Percival knew the answer but asked the question:

"Whom might that be?"

"He was the founder of the American Nazi Party, the ANP. Tragically, he was shot and killed two years ago by an expelled member from his group. Believe it was a George something or other."

Becoming more trusting:

"His name was Patler, George Patler."

"Yes, that's him. You sound like you know something about the ANP movement. I am very sympathetic to their cause."

Still probing, Percival demanded:

"How did you get this telephone number?"

"I have friends in the telecommunications industry. I found Mr. Percival's unlisted number. But tell me, does the name Matthias Koehl mean anything to you? He said Mr. Percival is on their mailing list for ANP literature, particularly the *Storm Trooper Magazine*."

"You know Koehl?"

"Oh, yes. Koehl succeeded Rockwell as ANP commander. I recently gave a check for $15,000 in person to him when we met in his Arlington, Virginia office. He was very grateful for the contribution. Now he wants me to branch out and support other ANP followers by donating more money."

After hearing this, Percival surmised that the caller knew too much about the ANP and how he was connected to it. What really lowered his suspicions was the financial contribution. With a growing corps of followers, whom he paid, he could use a new cash source.

"I hope you appreciate that the ANP is carefully monitored by the government as a subversive group. We live in a world where we have to be careful with whom we associate."

"I fully understand. Do you think Mr. Percival would be open to a financial gift to start a Storm Trooper group in your area?"

"Tell me more about yourself. Where are you from and where are you now?"

"I'm originally from New York, but I just flew into San Francisco to meet an old friend. Another reason for the call, is that I want to relocate to San Diego. Nice place to retire and escape the cold and snow in the winter. Besides, too many Jews in New York. I've kept them out of my business, for fear they would be too bossy and siphon away my profits."

Percival was now locked in when he heard the enmity:

"Back to the contribution. What range are you prepared to give?"

"Like I said, I own a company. I'm ready to sell with a buyer in tow. Money is not a problem. Let's start with $10,000, with more to follow if you get an ANP chapter going."

Percival was won over:

"Okay, enough of the games. Money talks. You are talking to David Percival."

"Great. I am glad you were cautious. This will make for a secure partnership with a man who can be trusted."

"It's funny. We've been in a serious conversation and I never did get your name."

"You see it works both ways. As you say, it is vital to be careful with the company you keep. My name is Jordan Starmont."

Still a bit leery of the caller, Percival queried:

"Mr. Starmont, can I call you back tomorrow about this same time to arrange for a meeting in San Diego soon. What's a number I can reach you at?"

"It's a deal to meet. However, I am calling from a pay phone because I am traveling. Hard to reach me, so let me call you again, Mr. Percival."

Percival conceded somewhat reluctantly:

"Okay. But this is strictly between you and me."

Starmont wanted a quick, reassuring close:

"You have my strict confidence about our relationship. Talk to you tomorrow. Long live the ANP!"

As the call ended, Percival was both apprehensive and satisfied. Apprehensive that he gave a stranger confirmation about who he was and his political sympathies. Satisfied that he had potentially a new influx of money to expand his local converts. He had a somewhat fitful sleep that night, recalling that the caller did not ask about his English accent. Strangers almost always brought that up. Well, maybe it was nothing.

Back to business. He had a laidback rendezvous site with Starmont that should not attract too much attention with the people who populated it: Windansea Beach in La Jolla, a spot he had frequented several times to just relax and get some sun.

Starmont called back at the appointed time that day. The two men agreed to meet at Windansea Beach in seven days just after sunrise. Not much stirring at that time to attract attention. Percival convinced Starmont to bring $10,000 in cash to verify his intentions to support his Nazi recruitment. Starmont said the seven days would give him sufficient time to have the cash and to drive south to La Jolla. Again, doubt entered Percival's mind when he ended the call. He needed a contingency plan. Hmm. This Starmont offer was too good to be true. To be sure he would not be captured by the authorities, he was thinking of abandoning his Fallbrook location for a more secure location. But where? Could the Seal's Lair be his safe house?

+▸━ ◉ ━◂+

Percival's suspicions about discovery were prescient. Because when the telephone clicked during the Starmont call yesterday, two would-be captors were at the other end of the line. One of them, FBI agent Ross Cargill, beamed with pleasurable disbelief and lauded what he heard:

"Wow, Commissioner Johnson, the way you wooed Percival you missed your calling—you should have been an actor."

24
CHAPTER

Camp Pendleton, September, 1969

Approaching 3:00 P.M., Damon Broadbent left Maggie Starmont at the La Valencia Hotel in La Jolla with business and pleasure on his mind. Work came first. Acting upon the work of detective Rick Sandoval, who was investigating possible AWOL Marines at Camp Pendleton, he headed out of La Jolla for I-5. This scenic thoroughfare would take him to the huge Marine installation that straddled the Pacific Ocean about thirty-three miles north. The weather had a soothing effect on him. It was a classic Santa Ana day, typified by clear blue skies, variable on shore winds, 90 degree temperatures, and low humidity. Such benign conditions belied the grisly occupation Broadbent was in. When he hit I-5, he radioed Sandoval:

"Broadbent here. What is your location, over?"

Sandoval picked up on his radio:

"Captain, as you ordered I am sitting in my car outside the office of Pendleton's Public Information Officer, a Captain Julian Desmond. Over".

"Rick, good man. Stay there. I'm on I-5 now. How do I find you? Over."

"Take the first Pendleton exit to the main gate. Have the MP direct you to Vandegrift Boulevard. Follow the signs to the Public Information Office. Park in the space for 'Official Vehicles'. Don't think the Marines would give a cop a parking ticket. Over."

"Funny man, Sandoval. See you in about 40. Over and out."

Mentally putting the police work aside, Broadbent had time to ponder the pleasurable--Maggie Starmont. She had a sophisticated allure to her, unlike any woman he had known. However, with the latest information about Jordan, she was acting more like a mother rather than a woman who might take a fancy to him. Given the botch up in the morgue, the secret to her heart was to deliver her son back to her. Broadbent knew he owed her the decency to make amends. If only they could identify the body on the beach. Who was he? Why was Jordan's name on a rental car agreement? How are Jordan and the corpse linked together? Most importantly, who was responsible for orchestrating such a confusing scenario?

These were baffling questions. He hoped for some positives as he spotted Sandoval's police cruiser outside the Camp Pendleton Public Information Office. The two detectives wasted little time leaving their cars and heading inside. Sandoval went right to a uniformed receptionist to have her page Captain Desmond. The detectives waited on a wooden loveseat. Sandoval's debriefing to Broadbent contained no new information: just two AWOL Marines, who may or may not be relevant to the case. Broadbent hoped he could get something of substance when Desmond came out to engage in the introduction process and escort them into his office.

Desmond, a handsome, chiseled man with glistening double bars designating his rank on the erect shoulders of his olive green jacket, was a commanding presence. He was made more impressive by battle ribbons on his chest. Sitting in front of a map of Vietnam, he visually sized the two San Diego police officers up for a moment to get their attention before he spoke:

"Gentlemen, what's all the fuss about some errant Marines? I did tell Detective Sandoval that we have two members of our organization, E-4, Lance Corporal Yancey Bixby and E-4 Lance Corporal Monty Crawford, absent without leave. That's somewhat unusual because most of our force is deployed in the country behind my back."

Broadbent was hoping to ingratiate himself with Desmond:

"Captain, this country owes the Corps much. By chance have you been over to Nam?"

"Just got back three months ago. Survived Con Thien near the DMZ in I Corps. Lucky, I guess. Came back without a scratch but a lot of near misses. Lost too many loyal Marines. Either of you got anyone over there?"

Sandoval volunteered:

"Yeah, I have my youngest brother in the Army with the 4th Infantry Division near Pleiku, a real hot spot near the Ho Chi Minh Trail."

Desmond concurred:

"Yeah, it's hot, as every nook and cranny of that forsaken place is. But let's talk about domestic warfare. Why are Marines linked to a body on a La Jolla beach?"

Broadbent explained:

"The surfer witnesses have a good feel for who visits their surfing domain. They've bumped into Marines before who have brought their boards asking for current and optimal wave tips. Such newcomers generally have skin tight hair, in contrast to the shaggy manes their known buddies sport. Many also have southern accents. Two of those types were seen frisking the corpse."

After hearing this, Desmond was puzzled:

"So you two are operating on a hunch?"

Broadbent countered:

"In police work, hunches many times make good leads. How long have Bixby and Crawford been AWOL?"

"Captain, the exact date of absence is privy only to the Marine Corps. Let's just say it's been more than a day or two."

Broadbent was hopeful he was on to something:

"Hmm, that fits in within the timeframe of the discovery of the body. Did they leave behind any personal items or clothing in their barracks?"

"They emptied their closets, both Marine Corps issue and civilian clothes. But Bixby did not empty the contents of his desk."

"What did you find of note?"

"Simply skin magazines, assorted junk, a letter from back home in Louisiana, and a scratch pad."

"I see. Is it possible either or both Marines would have access to a pistol?'

"Simply prohibited to have a weapon of any kind in the barracks."

"Back to the letter. Can we see it?"

Desmond was adamant:

"Strictly no can do because it is a personal item belonging to a member of the Corps."

"Okay. Can you briefly describe its contents?"

"As I recall, it basically was a plain vanilla letter from Bixby's mother and her usual concerns about a son just back from Vietnam and the fear he would have to go there again."

Broadbent drilled down:

"Any unusual person or things mentioned in the letter?"

"Let me think. Yes. Bixby's mother did have a concern about an older gentleman her boy recently met, who had an English accent and farmed avocados,"

"Did he have a name?"

"None mentioned. She just mentioned to be careful with non-Marines off base, something we stress during these war-time days to all our Marines."

Broadbent was pressing for more specifics:

"How about photos of Bixby and Crawford? It would help us immeasurably."

Desmond looked at the ceiling in pensive thought before he answered:

"That could be a tough proposition, considering the Corps is in a major armed conflict. We don't like putting a public face on any of our warriors for fear that the anti-war crowd would target them. But I'll see what I can do."

Then Sandoval injected with a brain storm:

"Captain Desmond, do you have this scratch pad in your possession? If so, can I see it."

Desmond opened his desk drawer and handed it to Sandoval:

"Hmm, nothing written on it--see for yourself."

Sandoval immediately pulled out a pencil from his coat pocket and began to apply a light film of lead across the entire top sheet of blank paper. An image of writing that was previously impressed above the empty paper was emerging from the lead imagery. While making this application, both Desmond and Broadbent looked at Sandoval's activity with silent amusement. Then Sandoval blurted with accomplishment:

"Eureka, Captains Broadbent and Desmond! It says: 'Directions to Windansea- Take La Jolla Boulevard to Nautilus'."

Broadbent exclaimed in delight:

"A man with an English accent, avocados, and Windansea. Now we are getting somewhere!"

Perth, August, 1969

Sela Danby was cringing inside her apartment, awaiting the return of Ian Bright from his trip to Melbourne. Bright called her two days ago and explained he was heading back to Perth the day after tomorrow, with his "important purchase" in hand. Sela wanted safe passage for her travel plans to San Diego, which could only be done with Rex Murtaugh, close-by on the airplane along for the ride. According to plan, she continued to contact Murtaugh via written messages under his door. This last one had some urgency to it:

> *Rex:*
>
> *Ian called. Sounds anxious to go to the USA. Got your tickets for the flights I gave you? We've got to talk. Getting cold feet to go on this trip with Ian. Tie a ribbon or string on your doorknob to let me know when you are around. I'll knock when that happens.*
>
> *Need you now more than ever.*
>
> *Sela*

Murtaugh now came to the realization that his last days in Perth were upon him. His exit strategy included telling his boss at the Cricket Club that he needed about ten days off. It was a fair request because for months Murtaugh was putting in regular six-day work weeks, sometimes seven when there were lengthy tournaments at the WACA. Working eight to ten hour shifts, the continuous toil was starting to wear on Hannigan. His boss understood his request for leave but wanted him back. The "Yank" was popular and well-liked by the Club patrons. In ninety minutes he would be off to his flat on Riverside Drive. When it was time to shed his bartender apron at quitting time, an empty feeling was in the pit of his stomach upon leaving the club. The past was a land of merriment; the future was a world of risk. It hit Murtuagh with a thud: he was saying good-bye to a protective safe haven from the law.

In a dour mood, when Murtaugh opened the door to his flat, he found a pleasant surprise --Sela's note. Any reminder of Sela made his heart race. Tired but with a sudden rush of energy, he collapsed into the one soft chair he had in his residence. Reading with intensity, Sela's message was disconcerting. The girl may not go to San Diego now? This flew-in the face of him quitting his job and preparing to risk his neck by going home. After serving a plethora of malt beverages at the Cricket Club, he needed a quaff to settle himself down. He got up and went to the refrigerator and found a Foster's beer, taking a heavy swig. Pondering for only a minute. Knowing that Ian Bright would not be present, he subverted the way he was communicating with Sela with ribbons, strings, and written messages. So he left his place and stepped out to knock on Sela's door across the hall to create an immediate dialog. He hoped she would be there.

Fate was kind, as Sela said in timid voice from behind her closed door: "Yes, who's there?"

"Sela, Rex. Please let me in."

Obeying the request, Sela was dressed in a filmy, baby blue nightgown. Her alluring body radiated through it. Without saying a word, Murtaugh closed the door behind him and immediately embraced Sela with a romantic embrace, kissing her deeply and running his hand across her back down to her shapely buttocks. Murtaugh felt the warmth of a woman who was under his skin and could not be resisted. In this height of passion, he restrained himself from going further. Breaking away from her, Murtaugh took her hand and bade her to sit together on the sofa.

Looking into her eyes, Murtaugh tried to be tender:

"Sela, your note is troubling. What's wrong?"

"Rex, we are becoming close. This has happened so fast, but my spinning world needs assurances that I will not be harmed."

"By Bright? Someone or something else?"

"Both. Ian is a shaky, volatile person. That's one trepidation. Believe me, I want to shake myself free from him. But now it's a bigger concern, from my brother."

"Jordan Starmont?"

"Love, recall I said he was involved with a special investigative group interested in Ian and his father. Well, I got updated information when I called Jordan this morning."

Sela hesitated. Hannigan wanted her to continue:

"And?"

"Rex, you have to keep your lips sealed for what I am about to tell you. Can you keep a secret?"

Hannigan was measured when he said:

"Sela, keep a secret. With all the candid revelations I've picked up at the Cricket Club, the bar patrons have been confiding in me since I landed in Perth. It's in my nature to be a confidante."

"Don't let me down, Rex. Jordan is working with the American Federal Bureau of Investigation to intercept Ian when he meets his father--David Percival I told you about."

"This is not surprising to me Sela. I sensed they would be in the picture when you talked about the urgency surrounding this whole episode. With the FBI nearby, and remember I'll be at hand, too. I have my plane tickets. What do they want you to do when you arrive?"

"Bring Jordan to the baggage claim area of the San Diego airport. Like Judas, give him a kiss there to confirm his identity and stay with him until someone of interest meets us. Then I run."

"Let me guess who the third party is--Ian's father, this David Percival?"

"Rex, you are so wise and perceptive. All Jordan would tell me is that Ian's father is a fugitive that is most wanted by the FBI."

"Sela, we have become intertwined with intrigue and secrets. Trust me, what is said here stays here."

"Rex, that is reassuring to me. But I am curious. What will our future be like in America together?"

Murtaugh revealed the ironies of ironies:

"When we get to the states we need a new identity to shake off this messy present--we'll start by changing our names."

26
CHAPTER

Fallbrook, August 1969

David Percival sensed that the walls might be collapsing on him. Since May of 1945, this wanted Nazi scientist had carefully avoided detection. The day after he arranged to meet Jordan Starmont at Windansea Beach in La Jolla he now felt he made a serious mistake. He believed at the time that Starmont was credible. But why was he coaxed into it? Was it greed, i.e., the money Starmont offered to give him? Was it vanity that a stranger from nowhere sought him out to support his malevolent creed? Or maybe he just felt impervious to arrest. Whatever he said or agreed to is now mistrusted and required immediate action to counteract any possible chance of apprehension by the authorities.

Time to take action. It was early evening on a warm summer night. Percival disguised his casual attire of sandals, chinos, and a tee-shirt with a baseball cap and sun glasses. He was bound for town to find a pay phone to make a call. But he had to rein in Yancey Bixby and Monty Crawford. The two AWOL Marines left the casita to live full-time in Percival's spacious home. Scurrying from his bedroom, Percival went downstairs to the game room, where the two Marines were playing pool. Bixby just broke a rack of balls when Percival came in with a purpose:

"Guys, listen up. First off, as I instructed to keep your location secret, you two have never made any telephone calls or left the house without me since you have been here? Right?"

Crawford meekly replied:

"Yes, *Reichmarschal.* Being AWOL and such Yancey and I have been real low profile."

"Good. To make sure that continues, go around the house and yank all the telephone cords from the outlets. I'll take care of the phone in the garage. You talk to no one until I come back. Understood?"

This time Bixby answered sternly:

"Loud and clear, *Reichmarschal.*"

Percival was annoyed and snapped:

"From this point forward drop the title. No longer use the name *Reichmarschal.* Just call me David. Got it!"

Both of them nodded meekly.

"I'll be back shortly. Start rounding up all your stuff. Understand?"

Used to taking orders, one reason Percival liked recruiting military types, the Marines dutifully went to their rooms and started packing their possessions in their duffle bags and other luggage they brought with them from their Camp Pendleton barracks. Percival immediately went to the wall phone in the garage, yanking the line from the outlet. In a cupboard in the garage Percival found some self-defense. He unlocked a metallic box of a reminder of the Third Reich military: a holstered 9mm short-nosed German Luger, a weapon he purchased at a gun show ten years ago with no questions asked. He slipped the weapon under his pants at the waist and covered its protrusion with his shirt. As animated as he is now, any hostile encounters would draw gunfire from him.

Climbing into his Ford pick-up, the automatic garage door went up instantly. With a revved engine, he bolted from the garage and sped along the long avocado tree lined drive of his property until he came to De Luz Road. It was a winding drive that brought him to the community of Fallbrook, a small town of just under 7,000 people in ten minutes. He pulled into the parking lot of the Bank of America on Main Street because there was an adjacent telephone booth. With the sun starting to set it was not in clear view for passers-by. Percival brought a wad of coins with him to keep him viable in conversation. Dialing the operator, he wanted to make a long-distance call to Coronado. With the number in hand, he placed his call to a key individual's quarters on the US Navy Amphibious Base. The answer came after two rings:

"Hello, Douglas here."

"Casey, David Percival."

"Good evening, *Reichsmarschal*. Good to hear from you again."

"Casey I appreciate the formality, but trouble is brewing for our organization I'm afraid. From now don't use the *Reichsmarschal* salutation again. Instruct Dunhill, Smith, Montag, and Wyatt to also refrain from using it. Am I clear here?"

Quick on the take, Douglas complied:

"Very, David."

"Important. As we agreed, you have never attempted to call my home? It was always me calling you. Is that procedure correct?"

"Yes, that is right. In fact, you never told me where you lived exactly in San Diego County."

"That's not important now."

"So, what is alarming you? As far as I know, the Navy knows nothing about our organization and the few meetings we have held in my quarters."

"That is reassuring to know. Casey, I have a strong feeling that some law enforcement agency and/or the Navy will likely attempt to close down our operation, possibly with arrests."

Douglas wanted to be reassuring:

"I have no reason to believe that anyone on the base knows who we are. Got any sources here?"

"I can't tell you much, but I believe my telephone has been tapped by law enforcement. They are trying to lure me into a trap."

"How long have they been eavesdropping? What do they know about us?"

"Hard to say, maybe just a few months, but one day is too long and too implicating."

"Hmm. Trap, hey. How can we help?'

Percival was recharged when he heard that he had trusted support:

"Casey, I knew I could count on you, as second in command of our Troopers. Let me run this by you. Is it possible to drive three of my vehicles onto the base and have them parked there without being towed or confiscated?"

"As I recall, you told me you own a large sedan, an MG, a truck, and a GTO. The last two would not raise eyebrows; no Seal drives a luxury sedan or an MG--those are red flags."

"Okay. How's about I drive the truck and GTO to your base in the next day or two? Can you obtain parking base decals to make them look official? I'll call you when ready."

"I think I can work that out. I know the master-at-arms who commands the SPs at the gate who regulates the parking area. However, here's a better plan. Allow me and another trooper to drive your vehicles through the gate and onto the premises. Fewer questions asked if an active duty person is at the wheel."

"Great idea. Now, another request for the survival of all of us. You have enough room for me, Bixby, and Crawford to live in your quarters?"

It was not so simple for Douglas to comply:

"David, that might be a bit tougher. Can't predict when we could receive a surprise inspection. If discovered, you three would immediately look out of place and be sent to the brig. And that would be my ass as well. Why are you looking for shelter?"

"My home is no longer safe. This would not be a long-term proposition--maybe a week or two. Is that a better possibility for you?"

"Yeah, that might work. We just got inspected last week. Next one not due for another thirty days, but let me check on that."

"Can we take our chances and have us show up in the next two to three days? We'll let you know when we are coming so we can meet you off base to have you and one of the troopers get our cars parked near your quarters."

"Sounds like a plan. Presume you'll call me before this happens?"

"For sure. In preparation for our arrival, one more favor. See if you can steal three sets of license plates so we can replace them on my vehicles. Can do?"

"Not a hard task. Plenty of vehicles in the Coronado hotel parking lots we can heist the plates late at night. From the looks of it, are you planning to make a big move soon?"

"Very perceptive, David. Don't get too comfortable yourself. Be ready to vacate as well."

The two conspirators wrapped things up by emphasizing their zeal for the Nazi cause. Douglas reaffirmed he would have the four other troopers apprised of their new duties to accommodate Percival's move to the base.

With new found hope Percival could pull off a quick relocation, he left the booth to gas up his truck and go to the local Safeway store to buy a plethora of food, especially meat, fruit, and vegetables. Back at the ranch he found the two Marines both asleep, each one on a loveseat in the game room, with the television blaring. The screen was showing the movie *The Night of the Generals,* about the hunt for a Nazi general twenty years after he committed a murder during World War II. Percival was not gentle. He kicked the couch of both Marines:

"Not good, troopers. Sleeping on the job. Get anything done while I was gone?"

A groggy Crawford responded:

"Sorry, sir. I think we are in good shape. Been living out of our bags since we came her a few days ago. Only have to wash a few things and we'll be raring to go."

"All right. Now come upstairs and help me get my things together."

Percival selected the clothes he thought were essential from his large walk-in closet and from two chests of drawers. This included his black shirt, pistol belt, black riding pants, and brightly shined jackboots, the diabolical uniform of Nazi perfidy. But the nonpareil to this evil costume was the swastika armband he had buried in a drawer. When he pulled it out and let it hang from his fingers, the Marines were mesmerized by it.

Percival almost revered it:

"Troopers, this symbolizes our reason for being. For you fellows, it will be payback for several of your buddies you lost in Vietnam."

Both Marines agreed with the chance to avenge the death of buddies in the bloody I Corps theater of operations in Vietnam.

Crawford asked:

"Where are we going to relocate?"

Percival looked at the two of them and said with a serious intonation:

"The Seal's Lair."

27
CHAPTER

San Francisco, August 1969

Jordan Starmont was trying to adjust to being a secret agent for the government. Compelled to live undercover, the FBI ordered him to vacate the Haight-Ashbury district for an assigned more mundane residence on Columbus Avenue. Living on the third floor of a traditional walkup building, he was across the street from Washington Square and had an unobstructed view of a famous San Francisco landmark: Coit Tower. Starmont saw symbolism being so close to the Tower, an art deco structure paid for by Lillie Hitchcock Coit, a wealthy socialite who loved to chase fires in the early days of the city's history. As he was close to a memorial honoring firefighters, Starmont recognized the irony that he too was being asked to help extinguish a fire--an ideological one raging in his country.

Using the name of Jordan Starmont, FBI Chief Ted Johnson was sure he duped David Percival on the telephone that he was a domestic Nazi sympathizer, luring him for a potential meeting in La Jolla—with cash in hand. However, the real Jordan Starmont was confused and a bit upset that his name was at the head of the spear. Johnson felt the surname was as good as any. But the real motivation to use the name was to confirm the young man's allegiance to the FBI.

Johnson used some emotion to mollify Jordan's concerns. Revisiting what Jordan's father did back in 1945 to apprehend Percival, Johnson appealed to continuing the proud legacy his father established to bring wrongdoers to justice. Thus, the operation would have the Starmont name on it, another means to cement Jordan's energy and commitment to assisting the FBI.

It was around 8 A.M. on a foggy morning when Starmont heard a knock at the door. Aroused from sleep by the sound, the banging continued as he struggled to get to the door. Speaking in code, Starmont said:

"Who goes there?"

"Agent Cargill. Open up."

Starmont was unprepared:

"Could you wait a bit until I get my pants and a shirt on?"

"Okay. Don't delay. Remember, I also have a key to this place if you take too long."

Starmont didn't particularly like the FBI's control over him in a secret location. Dressed in a pair of hole-riddled jeans and a paisley shirt, the uniform of those who populated the Haight, he drew back the bolt and let Cargill in. The FBI agent had a new appearance: now clean shaven in a business suit, a solid red tie, and a black fedora, a radical change from the "flower children" raiment he wore undercover. He was blunt:

"You ready to leave this place? Things are moving quickly. We just got the flight schedule for Sela Danby and Ian Bright from the U.S. Consulate in Perth."

Starmont was happy to hear this:

"Good. Good. I told Sela to work with the Consulate. I think she is cooperating."

"I'll get to the flight business in a moment. But to be sure we have another opportunity to nab Percival, we are setting a trap for him before Sela and Bright even arrive."

"Tell me more. Am I involved?"

"Not in person, but your identity is."

Starmont was really confused:

"My identity?"

"Yes, Commissioner Johnson made a telephone call to David Percival, convincing him that he was a Nazi sympathizer. The plan is to meet at a La Jolla popular surfing location. The person Percival is to meet is none other than you, 'Jordan Starmont'."

"Hmm. Now I see why my name is front and center here—it's part of the commitment thing Commissioner Johnson talked about."

"You are a perceptive young man, Jordan. But your physical presence will eventually be required in the San Diego area"

"I am so happy to hear that my body, and not a ghost, will finally be useful."

"Lighten up, Jordan. You are more vital than you know. You told us that you received a photo of Sela Danby. Correct? Can we see it?"

"Sorry, agent Cargill. No way. You are getting too personal here. You can insist on my cooperation, but not the body and soul of my family. It's my trump card in this whole operation. You have this wrong—you need me more than you ever know."

"Now I know why you went to Princeton--you are nobody's fool. We suspected you might not agree to our request. If we don't nab Percival at the coastal location your attendance will be required at another important San Diego location."

"This better be good, agent Cargill"

"It's better than good--it's vital. We need you to identify Sela Danby when she gets off the plane at Lindbergh Field. The assumption that Bright will be next to her."

"You guys are really blind in this whole caper."

"More than blind—we have no idea what Ian Bright and David Percival look like."

28
CHAPTER

Perth, September 1969

For Sela Danby her dangerous journey to the United States with Ian Bright was yet to begin. After being assuaged by Rex Murtaugh that she would be out of harm's way when she landed in San Diego, she committed to him to take the trip. To confirm her intentions, she had to inform Jordan Starmont that she would be alongside Bright at journey's end. That required a visit to the U.S. Consulate in Perth, to reveal her flight information, as Starmont instructed. Fearing Bright would be returning from Melbourne at any unannounced time, she left her flat and walked swiftly, almost a jog, to the Consulate on Adelaide Street, about a six-block distance. Her heart was racing as she avoided pedestrians and crossed several busy streets when the "walk sign" told her not to. The Consulate was close to St. Mary's Cathedral. Almost to the front door of the Consulate, she heard the Cathedral bells toll out the hour: 10:00 A.M. The holy sounds encouraged her. Perhaps there was a guiding light looking down upon her.

Once inside, she was greeted by a youthful young man, about her age, in the small reception area. Behind him on the wall was a list of duties the Consulate complies with. She was drawn to the one that said: *The Consulate makes efforts to prevent and counter threats to civilian security, such as violent extremism, mass atrocities, and weak governance of law.* Based on Starmont's importance for her to assist him, she wasn't sure which one of those bad things Bright may be up to, but it had to be one of them.

She timidly stated:

"I am here to see someone who is familiar with Operation Odessa. It's important."

The young man was taken aback, as if Odessa was some secret he was not aware of.

"I'm not sure what you mean, but please stay here and I'll find an individual to assist you."

He quickly got up and knocked on several office doors in a frenzied way. It took him four tries for success. That occurred when she saw him talking in an inaudible voice through an open door for about five minutes. When he walked back to his desk, he was followed by a gentleman with a serious mien, dressed in a stiff white shirt and a red tie. He greeted her:

"My name is Richard Donovan, chief consul for the United States in the Perth office. Would you kindly follow me back to my office?"

He seemed a bit edgy once he got her to his station; but sat her down and asked her if she wanted a beverage. Sela said a cup of tea would be fine, which Donovan requested over his intercom for her. On either side of his large cluttered desk was an American flag inserted into a floor stand holder in one corner; an Australian flag in the other. Directly behind him were two large photographs: Richard M. Nixon, President of the United States and William P. Rogers, Secretary of State, whose auspices the Consulate was under. Donovan briefly described what the Consulate does in Perth and then made a bold assumption:

"I presume you are Sela Danby. I hope no one else in Perth knows about Operation Odessa."

Sela had to be resolute to be believable:

"You would be correct, sir."

At that point, a young woman brought in cups of tea for both of them. Sela stirred hers with a spoon, quivering a bit while holding the supporting plate. She worried she might be detained and not be around when Bright returned. She needed to speed things up:

"I am on a tight schedule. I was told you would be interested in my flight plans to your country."

She opened her elongated purse and gave a folded sheet of paper to Donovan, who was speechless while reading it with a look of delight:

"This is what we have been waiting for Ms. Danby. I can't tell you how much we appreciate your cooperation in this matter. I presume no one other than Ian Bright knows about your travel plans?"

Sela responded instantly to give her responses a continuing air of truth:

"Again, that is absolutely correct, sir. However, let me ask you a question before I leave: Do you know Jordan Starmont?"

Donovan sat back in his chair, made a sigh, took a sip of tea, and then said:

"All I can tell you is that, yes, my office is aware of Starmont, but I can't elaborate much further. I will say, though, I want to reassure you that to compensate for your help that the full measure of protection will be provided to you once you arrive in California by the American Government."

These were words Sela wanted to hear. She finished half of her tea while discussing her willingness to assist a convincing and insistent Jordan Starmont. When she arose from her chair, she offered her hand in farewell to Donavan, and saw herself out his office and the Consulate. Whew, she felt as she started to walk briskly and more buoyantly on the usual sunny streets of Perth back to her flat. Upon arrival, she wrote a quick note to Rex Murtaugh and slipped it under his door. She wrote that she was beyond the point of no return--off to San Diego, emphasizing the main reason for her decision was that he would be her guardian angel on the airplane. For her, it was an act of love to be close to the man she hardly knew but deeply trusted.

Sela was emotionally spent after completing an obligation filled with consequences—good and bad. She slumped into a soft chair and dozed off, only to be awakened shortly when she heard the key in the door and an animated Ian Bright walking through it carrying a medium-sized cardboard box, but no other luggage. He was tempestuous as he walked rapidly past Sela without acknowledging her and plunged into the bedroom. She could hear him rummaging through the dresser and the closet, as well as opening the drawers of a small desk. He then came out and said brusquely:

"How much of value do you have here in the flat? Can you do without for our trip?"

Trying to disarm him:

"How do you mean, love?"

"I spoke with my father and he wants us to travel light to America—just minimal clothing and personal items in a carry-on bag. I just found out neither of us has anything in the bedroom we can't replace, which my daddy said he would pay for."

"I think I can make do. Your father is a generous man."

"I take it you will have minimal luggage for your things?"

"We have a few days before we leave--that's doable."

"Very well, then. You booked the tickets for us without any problems?"

"Yes, it's a long flight with several connections: one in Sydney, a long venture to Los Angeles, and a short flight to San Diego. But it all starts and ends on the same day as it turns out. It's funny how the great distance has the sun constantly at our back."

Then he hit her between the eyes:

"You been true while I've been gone? No dallying with these aggressive Aussie blokes. I got an eyeful in Melbourne. They find it hard to keep their hands off Sheilas, especially if they are alone and vulnerable."

Sela was struck by Ian's suspicion. She had to come up with some convincing show of affection. Playing the forlorn lover, she immediately went up to Bright and put her arms around him:

"Ian, let's have a shag and then see if I have lost my fire for you."

Sela had to resort to Ian's active libido. He acquiesced and brought her to bed, almost tearing off her clothes. In an attempt to reduce his suspicious ardor, Sela's sexual thrusts were more pulsating than his. Her pleasure was faked; Bright's was quick and satisfying at orgasm. When their passion abated, Bright became reflective and apologetic:

"Sorry for the suspicion, love. Been under some pressure to comply with my father's wishes. He's a demanding man. Here's the deal. As I said, we travel light, but I was told that we do not sit together on the flight to San Diego."

"Why the distance between us? Doesn't make sense to separate us."

"My father prefers that I get a seat up front in first class, and you sit at the rear. He wants to meet me first to be sure I have the item he requested."

"Is this the detonator?"

"You'd be right. I just want to get this over with and then go back to England and play gigs with my band. That's all."

"That's enough, love. I understand."

The two appeared to be amicable and started to cull out what clothing they would take with them on the flight. Just one more important thing for Sela to do--keep Rex in the loop.

It was mid-afternoon and Bright was in a deep sleep. Sela was now becoming risk averse. She slipped out the door and glided to Murtaugh's and gave it a rap, hoping he would be there. Luck was with her, when a surprised Murtaugh opened his door. Sela didn't dally:

"Rex, let me in, not much time."

He complied, closed the door, and held her hand:

"Where are we in the scheme of things?"

"Ian seems very weird about the trip. Wants us not to sit next to one another; get off the plane separately. It's like he fears being seen together makes him stand out."

"You know that is well and good. The further you stay away from him upon arrival the better. That will allow us to make a run for it."

Hannigan sensed there could be trouble at journey's end. He needed a solution:

"You think that will work?"

"It has to. Bright's father is a thug and I think he knows whatever his son is carrying cannot be discovered. He's extra cautious to get the delivery from him—not you."

"This will be a slippery one to pull off. I have to go back to my place before Bright awakes."

As she reached the door, he gave her a quick kiss on the cheek and said:

"I have my tickets and look forward to our new life together."

"Yes, I want a new start too. Rex, I hope the stars will be aligned for us. We arrive in San Diego on Friday the 13th."

29
CHAPTER

Fallbrook and Coronado, August 1969

David Percival agreed to have Jordan Starmont meet him on a late August morning at a well-known La Jolla surfing locale. However, sensing a ruse, Percival would have surrogates to represent him: Yancey Bixby and Monty Crawford. Percival previously called Bixby's barracks and told him to write down the directions to the rendezvous site. Windansea Beach in La Jolla. He instructed him to memorize it and discard what was written. Several days later, with the two Marines now AWOL and living in his home, Percival outlined the battle plan for the seaside meeting:

"Troopers, we move three of my vehicles, fully loaded with our stuff out of here tomorrow morning. Monty, you drive the GTO, Yancey you drive the truck, and I will drive the Lincoln Continental. I have arranged for troopers Casey Douglas, Grady Dunhill, and Bobby Montag to meet us at the Hotel del Coronado guest parking lot. Then they will drive you and your vehicles onto the amphibious base and unload them at Trooper Douglas's quarters--the Seal's Lair."

Crawford was curious:

"So, you are not going to the Lair right away?"

"That's right. Trooper Douglas will drive me to the La Valencia Hotel in La Jolla tomorrow. We'll both stay overnight there. The morning after that he'll play a big role at the wheel since he knows the beach area rather well."

Bixby had questions:

"So, who gets us to the beach and what are we looking for?"

"Trooper Dunhill will take you there in the GTO and drop you off at the Windansea Beach parking lot. You've got the directions, right?"

Bixby confirmed:

"Take La Jolla Boulevard and turn onto Nautlilus."

"Good, you'll be going north, so turn left down the hill when you get to Nautilus. Trooper Montag will follow you in the truck but will stay parked at the top of the hill. If someone follows us after we pick you up from the beach he'll block the roadway. Now, the big prize: Jordan Starmont."

Crawford queried:

"Where do we find him on the beach? What does he look like? You think this guy could be hard to handle?"

"All great questions, Crawford. Remember, the Marines trained you to be on guard at all times in a strange environment. He's an older guy, likely my age, and is supposed to be alone. Look for him near the cabana--an open sided, thatched hut. Let's assume he might be armed because he's carrying money, which we will get to."

Percival then brought the Marines into a sealed room at the back of the house. He unlocked the door and turned on the light switch. The eyes of Bixby and Crawford bulged at the glistening gun metal in the room, which was a mini-arsenal. Mounted on the wall were:

- Eight pistols: two .45's, two 9mm Glocks, two APX Berettas, and two single action, long barreled Colt revolvers, the gun that won the west. All had accompanying holsters.
- Four Remington 740 semiautomatic rifles
- Two M-14 automatic rifles, with scopes
- Four M-16 fully automatic rifles
- A recoilless bazooka (rocket launcher)

Directly beneath the mounted weapons were ammunition cases for the arms displayed, to include two dozen rockets for the recoilless weapon.

"Troopers, here is some firepower we might need."

Bixby was a bit dumbfounded:

"How'd you get such good armament? The Corps arms us with some good shooting hardware, but I am impressed with the firepower. That recoilless is a gem."

"Yancey, you'd be amazed what you can buy in this country from catalogs or gun shows.

I assume you know how to handle these pistols?"

They both nodded.

"Yancey, here's the .45 caliber for you. Monty, this 9mm Glock will be your protection. Fire if only you think you will be fired upon. We don't want to make a scene. To me, the power of suggestion will work here if you just display your weapon. You'll make your point."

Bixby was happy with the weapon he was to use:

"Yes, David, the .45 caliber is a keeper. It's a large round that will lift a man off his feet at close range when it hits him in the chest."

"The pistols are precaution. Things could get dicey because, as I said, money is involved."

Percival then told the Marines that Starmont contacted him to make a $10,000 donation to his Nazi movement. He was to have cash on hand, wrapped in currency strips.

He cautioned:

"If he forks over the cash, tell him that I will contact him with next steps; if not, get your asses out of there right away. Trooper Douglas and I will be close by and pick you both up at your signal. Any questions?"

Having none, Percival told them to complete their packing to include the weapons and ammunition. Then to get some sleep. The house was quiet and dark around midnight. That's when Percival slithered quietly to the kitchen. Once there, he drew back a throw rug, which concealed a trap door. With a flashlight, gloves, and a claw hammer, he opened the door, descended the steps, and stepped into an old wine cellar. Percival had retrofitted it with a four foot by four foot steel safe, with a combination dial and a large spoked wheel opening device. He looked up the steps and listened quietly to be sure no one was near. Then he dialed the combination:

4-20-89—Adolf Hitler's birthday of April 20, 1889. Turning the wheel to open the door, he once again saw the contraband he smuggled off a German U-Boat over twenty-four years ago. Stored in a wooden crate, he used the claw hammer to lift off the slats, where the deadly uranium cylinder was packed in saw dust. Also in the safe was a Swiss dosimeter, used to detect any ambient dose equivalent of gamma rays or other harmful radiation emissions. Scanning the cylinder, shining brightly once more with its gold protective casing, no elevated levels of radiation were present. And, as if he was back in time to celebrate his triumph of escaping to his safe haven in Fallbrook, he reached for the satchel stored in the safe to again re-pack the cylinder, weighing about twenty-five pounds. This time this diabolical package would have catastrophic consequences if unleashed onto the general population.

One more stored item in the safe of value. A jumbo cash box, with a combination lock, was opened using the same combination for the safe. When Percival lifted the lid, approximately $100,000, in $20 bill denominations wrapped in strips, was stashed away. This was the savings from numerous bountiful avocado harvests, but was dwindling with payments to Ian Bright's trip to Australia and recruiting his new storm trooper cohort. It was another reason he needed Starmont's financial contribution.

He went back up the steps with the satchel and the cash box, covered his tracks, and then took both into the garage, loading them into the trunk of the Lincoln sedan. However, Percival had one more dastardly deed to accomplish before he would depart the Sunshine Ranch. As a scientist, he had enough knowledge to make an explosive device, with a timer, to unleash fury. He took it out of a locked cabinet, again opened with the same combination for the other locks, and placed it between two 50-gallon gasoline drums, used to fuel his farm vehicles. To destroy as much as he could about his physical presence at his home, it would detonate several days before Ian Bright came to San Diego. Percival wanted a dramatic diversion prior to Bright's arrival, hoping the blast would create a blaze that would not only destroy the house but spread to the surrounding tinderbox vegetation of grass, scrubs, and trees. All of this as a dire warning to investigative authorities that they were dealing with a wily adversary. As a final testament to his living among serene hillsides of avocado wonder,

Percival would bolt the doors and windows and leave a cryptic note for Consuela, his valued housemaid for nearly twenty years, taped to the front entrance of the house with an envelope with $500 in it:

Consuela:

Sorry this came on so suddenly. I have to take leave of Sunrise Ranch for an undetermined period of time, which I can't tell you why now. There is also a note and a bit of money for the field hands, Diego and Pedro, attached to the main door of the large shed. The hope is we will be together again.

Buena suerte!

David

Locked and loaded for trouble, the following morning Percival and the Marines drove their three-car caravan from Fallbrook to Coronado, about a sixty-mile drive. As they reached downtown San Diego, they came to the Route 75 ramp, leading to the newly opened Coronado Bay Bridge, a curving span of steel and concrete over 11,000 feet long, mounted on 21 piers, and with a high point of 200 feet above the water to allow US Navy vessels to sail unobstructed from south San Diego Bay around the tip of Coronado to the open Pacific.

After paying the bridge toll, it was a short drive to the historic Hotel del Coronado, built in 1889 in the late Victorian, Queen Anne style, with a custom wood exterior, painted in white, a red shingled roof, several large cupolas, and a distinctive pointed tower above its famed dining room. Percival picked this meeting place because it also came of age the same year as Hitler. Like the rooftop swastika shape of the Seal's Lair, the man had a fetish for symbolism.

Back in the rear of a quiet, empty part of the parking lot, troopers Douglas, Dunhill, and Montag had walked from their base quarters to await Percival and the Marines. When they arrived, Percival gathered them together in a close huddle and gave final instructions in a subdued but commanding voice for the Starmont rendezvous:

"Troopers good to have you assembled again. Glad you have a mini-pass to be away from your duties. Trooper Douglas, I take it you have three new sets of plates for our vehicles?"

"Sure do. Tried a better approach--took them off cars in a San Ysidro auto disposal yard. They may no longer even be registered. And, yes, I have the powerful Navy Seal field glasses you requested."

"Great work. Transfer the plates just before we depart, shielding what you are doing.

Trooper Dunhill and Montag, you will each be provided with a Beretta pistol—just in case. Trooper Crawford will show you how to make it armed and dangerous. Then assist troopers Bixby and Crawford to offload the contents from the truck to trooper Douglas's quarters, what we call the Seal's Lair. Be mindful there is other armament besides personal possessions. Be cautious to avoid detection and unload after midnight."

Percival's last instructions reviewed how Crawford and Bixby would be transported to La Jolla, trooper Montag's role to obstruct traffic, and where Percival and Douglas would be positioned. As if giving a final pep talk salvo, Percival exhorted:

"To success in two days at Windansea Beach!"

30
CHAPTER

San Francisco and Windansea, August/September 1969

Jordan Starmont was beginning to question if he was just a pawn in some FBI web of intrigue and deceit. Sure, he was committed to interdict a catastrophic plan by a fugitive Nazi scientist, something his late father almost accomplished in 1945. But it might not have the desired effect if things went wrong--his good name could be associated with former, much maligned international criminals. The saving grace of all of this, he thought, was that, by chance, he would finally meet his half-sister--Sela Danby.

With Sela on his mind, Jordan decided to check in with the Western Union office. To keep things secure, it was the preferred way to communicate prior to Sela's arrival to the United States in September. Since the office was across the city peninsula on Golden Gate Avenue, Starmont called FBI agent Ross Cargill for a lift:

"Ross, I need a ride to the Western Union office on Irving Street."

"What's up? You need to touch base with Sela Danby?"

"Come on, Ross! What other women of note do you think I have a relationship with? The FBI has confined me like a monk to a Dark Ages abbey. I am curious? You getting any during this hush-hush gig for God and country?"

Cargill was not amused:

"Okay. Cut the sassy shit. I'll be there in ten minutes in the usual drab gray Chevy we drive with tender love and care."

Then Starmont got a grip on his irreverence for the FBI and its associates:

"Cargill, you are a good sport. Sorry for the bull. You've really been a valued person—almost like an older brother--to get me through this."

"Jordan, this undercover work is never easy because we don't know what you will find or if it will solve anything. Stay loose. Meet you outside your building in ten.! 0-4."

To both Jordan and the FBI, making sure Sela Danby came to San Diego with Ian Bright was the lynchpin to hold the elements together to capture David Percival and his fellow Nazi thugs. And, of course, Starmont had personal reasons--to finally meet his half-sister. It would be like ending a family saga, one his father wanted him to complete.

It was a sunny morning, but there was a chill in the late summer air when he stepped outside without a jacket. The external conditions reminded him of the famous Mark Twain remark he came upon in an American Literature class at Princeton:

The coldest winter I ever spent was a summer in San Francisco.

No matter, he reduced the discomfort by staying out of the chilly breeze in his doorway. It didn't take long for Cargill to show up. He climbed in the car and they headed west to the Western Union office. They traveled two blocks when the car radio blurted out. It was FBI Chief Investigator Theodore Johnson:

"Agent Cargill, what is your situation? Over."

"Morning, Chief. On my way with Jordan Starmont to Western Union so he can make contact with Sela Danby again. Need to confirm her end of the deal. Over."

"That's all well and good. But we need to make a change to how we will lure David Percival out into the open at the La Jolla beach. Over."

"Major or minor change? Over."

"Let's just say it's a bit involved. Ironically, it's based on an old deception by British Intelligence in World War I, called Operation Mincemeat, that helped fool the Nazis. Unfortunately, we are still trying to fool them--in our country! You'll know more when you bring Jordan to the office after he cables the Danby girl. Jordan, you there? Over."

Jordan grabbed the radio microphone:

"I'm here. Chief Johnson, you amaze me with your creativity. Over."

"Son, I'm no genius. The secret to my success is having average citizens like you help us with our work. There are never enough agents to cover the criminal waterfront. Again, my thanks for your perseverance throughout this operation. See you both shortly. Over and out"

Cargill then briefly told Jordan about the scheme, to include a money transfer, to drive a rental car from San Francisco International Airport to a beach in San Diego to lure Percival out into the open. If not in hiding and on the run, his chances for a mistake increase. The gambit was only days away. This caught Jordan by surprise:

"So using my identity I'll to be there on the beach, but it really isn't me?"

Cargill went into the strategic explanation. First, he cautioned about entrapment:

"We cannot misrepresent ourselves first by trying to induce a crime. That's false pretense. Rather, Percival has to confirm he is talking to the person he was planning to meet with a wrongful motive--Jordan Starmont. He might want some confirmation of the person's identity. When he gets it, then he, David Percival, asks for the cash he's expecting that I told you about. It's not handed to him first. If that occurs, it won't stand up in court as criminal intent to do bodily harm with the money."

"In other words, you can't give this guy a defense or legal out?"

"Exactly, my perceptive fellow. Besides, we think this David Percival is really the fugitive scientist Frederick Vogel, but we don't have the proof until we find the nuclear device. It's not a crime to be a professed Nazi in this country--there are more than a few of them running free spreading their hate."

Jordan reconciled in his mind using his good name to snare a fugitive:

"I guess that makes me feel better about why I might be central to all this."

Cargill told Jordan he would wait at the curb when they arrived at the Western Union Office. Getting out the car, Jordan's head was spinning a tad from the twist and turns the law made him comply with. Why can't this all be so simple? No matter, in the office he composed himself and sent his wire to Sela:

September 1, 1969

Sela:

I hope this message finds you well and prepared to make your journey to America. Can't wait. I can't emphasize enough that you will be in safe hands when you arrive. Are you still close to this Rex Murtaugh guy? So far the authorities have no criminal record on him. Is he still coming with you? Please advise your next steps as soon as possible.

Best,

Jordan

After finishing this task, Jordan took a deep breath and sat down for a moment. He pondered: this all wouldn't have happened had he not left Princeton. But, rather than dwell on the negative, he reconciled internally that he was living through a dramatic moment few people ever experience. Dissipating the self-pity, he got back up to return to Cargill's vehicle. It took another ten minutes to get to Chief Johnson's office, who put some meat on the bones of the plan:

Johnson started out explicating the deception the British used in Operation Mincemeat, designed as a ploy to place false papers on a dead body in a strategic place an adversary will find it. It was successful in the Allied invasion of Sicily. By placing false information on a corpse, it was possible to deceive one's foe to make critical mistakes. He brought this ruse into the present, but he sounded mournful:

"We've got a body, a drifter who was just found hanging in his seedy apartment, identity unknown. We find these types all the time, and all too often now, Jordan my boy, from where you were: Haight-Ashbury."

"Yeah, chief, I saw my share of both happy and depressed folks in the Haight."

"We will indicate to the rental car agency at San Francisco Airport that you, Jordan Starmont, a resident from New York, will be leasing the vehicle. That's consistent with what we told Percival to be aware of. No worries, Jordan, agent Cargill will be assuming your identity when he picks up the automobile--it's all been worked out with the car people."

Johnson then instructed Cargill to drop by the morgue to have the corpse loaded into the trunk.

Cargill interrupted:

"What do I do with the stiff when I get there? How is it to be disposed of properly?"

"There's a cabana on the beach I told you about. Lay it out there before sunrise, you'll get help from agent Joe Pizzo's people."

"Hmm. Does this bring the San Diego Police into play?"

Johnson was adamant:

"That's precisely part of the plan. The dead body is a diversion for them as well. They will investigate and likely bring the body to their coroner's location. We don't want them muddling into our investigation--this is national in scope, not local. By the time they are aware of what's going on we should have Percival in hand."

Johnson concluded by instructing Cargill to drive south to La Jolla to get there before the appointed time for the beach meeting. He also stressed that this tactic would be the first attempt to catch Percival. If this failed, the back-up plan was to intercept him and Ian Bright when Sela Danby arrived with him next month at the airport, reiterating that was where Jordan would be needed. Johnson rationalized that you always need "more than one way to skin a cat", in this case a fugitive. He lamented previous failures to capture wrongdoers on the first attempt and to charge them properly. Percival's guilt would be enhanced if they found the missing uranium cylinder, which made him revert back to his true most wanted identity: Friedrich Vogel. When Cargill got to San Diego, he was to contact Pizzo's San Diego office to finalize how they would be positioned to make the collar. The fateful journey to Windansea Beach was on.

David Percival chose a luxury La Jolla hotel, the La Valencia, knowing this might be the last place of comfort he may have for some time. Always the inquisitive kind, he wasn't sure where Jordan Starmont might be staying before their meeting. The guy had money and the La Valencia was within his price range. Upon checking in, he gave a pseudonym, Wilfred Tanner, and he asked the receptionist coyly:

"I'm supposed to have dinner with a Jordan Starmont here at the hotel. Has he arrived yet?"

The receptionist searched through his records and indicated no one by that name had a reservation. But Percival wanted to confirm a hunch if Starmont has been to San Diego before, sniffing around for him. To Percival, an alarm went off because it was the first time an outsider identified him as a Nazi sympathizer. Things were dangerously bizarre, he thought, with the Starmont connection.

"Hmm? No Starmont on the property now. I'm curious. Has he ever been here before?"

The receptionist then became guarded:

"We really can't give these details to the public without authorization."

Percival didn't hesitate to induce more cooperation by giving the receptionist two $20 bills:

"Could you go back six months to a year to see if he's been here?"

"Please wait a moment? I have to go to our office to research that."

"I'm not going anywhere. I'm staying here tonight. I'll wait in the lobby."

Casey Douglas was nearby with their bags. He told him to have the bellman take them to their room. In about ten minutes, the receptionist returned with a slip of paper in hand:

"Mr Tanner, we have no record of a Jordan Starmont as a guest recently, but in early December of 1968 we had a Martin Starmont and his wife, Margaret, as guests for a week."

"Good. Any address for them?"

"Yes, a Fifth Avenue location in New York City."

Secure in knowing something was not adding up, Percival ended his inquest and went up to his room with Douglas. After he closed the door, he gave a warning:

"Trooper Douglas, tomorrow seems like a set-up. It seems the Starmonts have been poking around to reel me in. Keep your pistol locked and loaded when we hit the beach,

something I know you Navy Seals always have at the ready."

Douglas nodded in agreement before they headed down to dinner. If Percival only knew a Starmont would again frequent the La Valencia. This time it would not be for pleasure, but, in an indirect way, to make things very difficult for him.

⊹⊶◎⊷⊹

Before the dawn of the following morning, FBI agents Cargill and Pizzo offloaded the corpse from Cargill's rented Ford sedan and placed it in the cabana of Windansea Beach, certain that no one saw their movements. They placed the car keys and the rental agreement under the dead man's body. It was a grisly act in a beautiful environment of luxurious homes, many with huge glass windows, designed to visually appreciate the adjacent beauty of the blue Pacific lapping on white sandy beaches. The agents needed a good vantage point of the beach and a convenient way to get to Neptune Street. Cargill, with another agent, parked his car just slightly up the hill on Bonair Avenue; Pizzo, also with another colleague, backed his onto a driveway of a beach property facing Windansea. They both were in a good position to observe anyone approaching the beach in general and the cabana in particular. The agents were armed with Smith and Wesson service revolvers, as well as a 12-gauge Remington shotgun in each car's back seat, fully loaded if needed.

As sunlight began to fill the seascape, the agents scanned the area through their front windshields with binoculars for human activity. Several surfers came to the beach, oblivious of an impending showdown. Trouble was ready to rear its head. After being dropped off by Grady Dunhill, Yancey Bixby and Monty Crawford began their two-block descent down Nautilus Street to the beach. Bixby wanted to touch base with Crawford:

"Monty, got a round in the chamber of that Glock--just in case? As I told you, something does not seem right. I hope it's only one of him and two of us."

"Yancey, I agree. I am wondering if Percival bought into something too good to be true."

"We'll find out."

They reached Neptune Street, astride the beach with parked cars. Coming to a stop, they looked half a block north up the street and saw Percival and Douglas parked in the Lincoln Continental. There was no traffic on the street. Things looked innocent and clear. They gave a wave to Percival and Douglas and proceeded to the beach, encountering two surfers.

Agent Pizzo instructed that the car windows be rolled up to ensure secure communication between cars on their radios. When Bixby and Crawford came into view, Pizzo radioed Cargill in a low voice:

"Ross, two dudes coming on scene. See them? Over."

"Yeah, Joe. Let's keep an eye on them. I know the surfers found the body and went back to their Pinto. I'm sure they are dazed and confused. Over."

"Ross, you seeing anybody middle-aged that might look like Percival? Over."

"I guess a man that old doesn't surf. No one in sight like that. Over."

"You'd be surprised, Ross, of some of the idiots trying to recover their youth out here with surfboards, if only to get a better look at the dollies. Over."

Cargill was hoping to see a more realistic suspect to reach the cabana. But he wasn't ready to jump to conclusions:

"Joe, stay in place. Let's see what these two guys do before we erupt with authority. Remember, we need Percival to show up, the grand prize in this hunt. Over and out."

Bixby and Crawford left the body in the cabana and went to a car in the lot, an unusual but suspicious move. Cargill zeroed in on them with the binoculars that aroused his curiosity:

"Joe, these two are getting hot. After they left the body, they went to the leased car, and I think are rummaging around. Are these guys what you call beach poachers? They have a lean and nasty look. Stay at the ready. Over and out."

But the evil that men do was also overseen from the front seat of Percival's sedan. While peering through his high-powered Navy Seal field glasses, he nudged Douglas:

"Casey, my suspicions are coming true. Bixby and Crawford haven't met this Starmont character. If they did, it looked like he was asleep or passed out on the cabana floor. They have a look of disbelief. Now they are in a car, searching feverishly. Start the engine and come about that so we can make a quick exit up Nautilus."

The timing was apt. Douglas was in position on Neptune for a getaway move. He drew out his German Luger and put a round in the chamber, just in case the Marines needed cover. Bixby signaled to pick them up. Douglas backed the car to the curb so he could drive up Nautilus Street. Then Bixby and Crawford jumped up in the back seat. That caught the eye of very interested spectators:

"Joe, Joe. I smell a rat. The two suspects are signaling someone. Could they be Percival hooligans? Over."

"Ross, they went into that black sedan that's in a hurry. Not good. Let's go get them!"

The FBI vehicles both squealed out from their positions in pursuit. In two blocks they got to Nautilus and made a hard right. As they turned all they could see at the top of the hill, La Jolla Boulevard, was a large white Ford pick-up truck at an angle blocking across the entrance to the intersection. They came to a frustrating halt. Cargill jumped out of his car and went to the driver of the truck in a rage:

"What the hell are you doing here? Move this rig now!"

The driver, Percival ally Bobby Montag, was well schooled for the response:

"Sorry sir. I think I have a dead battery and this was the only spot I could pull over."

"Did you see a black sedan come up this way?"

"It was some big car. The son of a bitch almost sideswiped me when I came to a stop."

"Which way did he go? Get this thing started and move out!"

"Hey, man. This is all a blur. Guess he could have gone one of three directions."

Montag knew how to make an engine sound that it was ready to turn over and start--but then would cut the gas to prevent ignition. Montag shrugged his shoulders in not giving the desired effect, much to the ire of Cargill, slapping his hand against the cab of the truck.

Obvious that he was thwarted, Cargill went to Pizzo's driver side window:

"We are in a fix, Joe. Whoever they were are long gone."

Pizzo wanted to offer relief:

"Should we radio San Diego Police for an A.P.B. on the car? Sorry. I didn't pick-up the plate I.D."

"No, damn it, no. Chief Johnson does not want them involved for now. Would only complicate things and scare the community with what we may be up against. Let's find another way out of here and go downtown to your office."

In disgust, Cargill returned to the car's steering wheel and conveyed to his partner:

"The old Chief was wise to have a backup plan to catch these creeps. We'll get them--when they arrive at the airport."

Meanwhile, an animated Yancey Bixby felt anguished in the back seat:

"David, I don't know what happened—but it seemed so fuckin'strange. A dead bastard, with car papers that said he was this Starmont guy, but no big-time money."

Crawford chipped in with his analysis:

"Can't really confirm who that stinking body was. He seemed too young for the guy you said we had to meet. Who knows? Could be he had some heavy-duty cash and was robbed and wiped out for good measure."

From his front passenger side, with a devilish smile on his face, Percival felt vindicated:

"Guys, I really felt this would happen—lulled into a trap to lure us out into the open. I'm just glad trooper Montag knows how to do a roadblock. At least you guys kept your cool and didn't use your weapon after you showed it to that surfer bum. There's no one following is there, Casey?"

"Naw. Have to watch for cops, so I'm regulating my speed. They probably thought we turned onto La Jolla Boulevard, but this shortcut taking Soledad Mountain Road will get us back to the Interstate much faster and out of sight."

Percival wanted them on alert:

"Troopers, from now on assume the law is looking for us. Stay quiet and out of sight when we get to the base. It's good we have the Seal's Lair--a perfect place to be hidden from civilian cops who shouldn't suspect we are on a military base."

As the sedan was approaching the Coronado Bridge, it was apparent they were undetected. Once on Navy property, Percival previewed what was next:

"The master plan will be the big show. It will fulfill our goals to threaten a government that coddles our enemies--foreign and here in America. We will have at our disposal a monster weapon to get everyone's attention."

Douglas inquired:

"What could that be?"

Percival replied in a sinister tone:

"Something that will strike fear in the hearts of everyone if they only knew."

31
CHAPTER

San Diego, September 1969

Back in his downtown San Diego office, Damon Broadbent was trying to piece together the three clues he discovered after his trip to Camp Pendleton. There was a strong possibility that Yancey Bixby was present at Windansea Beach the day the dead body was discovered in the cabana. He had directions to get there. But how to connect him, and possibly fellow Marine Monty Crawford, to a man with an English accent, who possibly lives in Fallbrook? With detective Rick Sandoval seated in his office, Broadbent, puffing pensively on a Kool cigarette, reviewed these leads out loud:

"English accent, directions, Fallbrook. Rick, what's the key here: finding the Marines or some guy with an English accent up in North County?"

"Both, captain. I think they are linked. My hunch is the accent guy is the one who gave the Marine the directions to Windansea. Finding either one will lead us to the other."

"Makes sense and is very plausible. Now, for the Fallbrook part. It's unincorporated up there so you need to visit the County Sheriff and quiz them about any guy in the area who might be an Englishman. Drill down on this hard and find out what you can."

"Will do. I can get up there early this afternoon."

As Sandoval was leaving the office, Broadbent arose and stated:

"Rick, you are a smart cop. As simple a task as a lead pencil imaging a piece of paper, it was brilliant. You may have my seat someday."

Sandoval shrugged and replied:

"Captain, thanks for the kind words, but I'm in no hurry to drive the busy train you manage for this city. I'm just glad that as a kid I liked playing with tracing paper. Now it came in handy in the adult world of violent crime."

After Sandoval left, he needed to check in with his undercover detective, Dan Herlihy, up in San Francisco. It was still early in the business day that he might catch him by telephone. That happened after the third ring when Herlihy answered by singing:

"It's a beautiful morning I think I'll go outside for a while."

Broadbent was caught off guard:

"What the hell, Dan. Stop singing lyrics from the Rascals. Can't you be normal when the phone rings."

"Sorry, captain, but if you want to fit in as a hippie you have to be off beat, even with something as simple as answering the phone. That Rascals musical lyric greeting fits right in with the culture."

"Okay, glad you seem to be mainstream up there. Now, just some police talk. Any more details on the Starmont boy? His mom is pressing me hard."

"Hmm, Damon. She's a nice-looking woman. That can't be that bad if she is that close to you."

Broadbent had to take pause when he heard that. Did he give clues that he was enamored with Maggie Starmont?

"Dan, let's cut the fun and games. We have to appreciate a mother's concern for her son. What do you have?"

"Sorry, just wanted to lighten things up a bit with all the duress you must be getting. However, not much more than last time. FBI wants control over their efforts to ferret out some Nazis operating under our noses in San Diego. But, the last time I spoke with the FBI's Ross Cargill he was a little more informative."

Broadbent was in need of more:

"And, and...?"

"It seems Jordan Starmont will be coming to San Diego sooner rather than later to help their operation. No specifics on where or when—all tight lipped about it. If it will help, tell the mom it's something the kid wants to do. Damon, above all—the kid is safe and protected."

"Did Cargill give a timeline on this? It appears something significant is about to happen soon back here again, and to me it's all related to that stiff found in the cabana on the beach. Did Cargill put any substance who the corpse was?"

"Captain, the guy is measured and said it's a local law enforcement issue—we have to solve it."

Broadbent was piecing together a ploy by the FBI:

"Dan, I've got a hunch this whole thing is a red herring to keep us chasing ghosts rather than uncovering a more serious crime that may or might have been committed."

"If that is true, then the action is in San Diego, not up here in flower land in San Francisco. You still need me to stay here?"

"For now, yes. Check back with the San Francisco Police Department. Find out how close they are to the local FBI. Again, emphasize the mess they have made with the Jordan Starmont misidentification. Do they know the identity of the corpse at Windansea?"

"Will comply, Captain. You got anything with meat on it?"

Broadbent then showed his cards:

"I think so. We are trying to patch together two AWOL Marines, who we think were at the cabana, and some unknown Englishman who lives in Fallbrook. To put pressure on the FBI, tell Cargill we are pushing hard to solve this puzzle. Maybe they will relent and clue us in to what really is going on."

When Broadbent ended the call, he was a little angry. Why couldn't law enforcement agencies cooperate? What's pride got to do with it? Not willing to keep Maggie Starmont waiting for information about her son, he called her and indicated he was on his way to the La Valencia with an update on Jordan.

Broadbent parked in his usual convenient space, reserved for hotel loading, to hasten his meeting with Maggie. The front desk paged her; she indicated she would meet Broadbent at the outdoor patio restaurant. The eatery had a large white canopy over it, with an unobstructed view to the pool area below and the blue Pacific beyond. Broadbent told the waiter he needed a table for two in a quiet corner, among other talkative guests enjoying their breakfasts. Good, he thought. They would be consumed with themselves, not Maggie and him. Directed to his table, she arrived shortly, dressed in a white coordinated outfit; silky long-sleeved blouse and a knee length pleated skirt. With her hair pulled back and tied by a white scarf, she had the glamour look of a woman of distinction.

Standing as she approached the table, Broadbent greeted her with a broad smile as he seated her:

"I am so glad we can meet again. Can I still address you as Maggie?"

She was coy with a smiling reaction:

"Only if I can still call you Damon?"

"Sure. I am happy we are on a first-named basis. With what you have to deal with, it assures an honest and open relationship"

The waiter then interjected and asked them what he could bring them. Coffee for two would be fine. They got to business when Maggie inquired:

"So, as you said there is an update on Jordan?"

"My detective in San Francisco reports that he is safe and wants to assist the FBI in its inquiry about possible Nazi activity here in San Diego."

"I did not know Jordan had this in him. He was so anti-establishment when he left for Haight-Ashbury."

"Apparently he had a change of heart. To me, it's a patriotic act. I guess your late husband would be proud."

This struck a chord for her:

"Yes, Martin would approve of such gallant behavior. Still, I am concerned for his safety."

"I have to reassure you that the FBI will keep him well-protected. I believe they are using him to provide information services, not apprehend criminals--that's their job."

The coffee came. Broadbent ever so briefly talked about how they were diligently trying to identify the mistaken corpse in an effort to clear the association of Jordan's identity. There was no mention of AWOL Marines and an Englishman in Fallbrook. Broadbent saved the best for last to mollify Maggie's anxiety:

"You have talked about going up to San Francisco to seek out Jordan. That's understandable. But it looks like that will be unnecessary. Better yet, rather than you go there, he will come here."

She was ecstatic:

"When, Damon, when?"

"Maggie, hold on. We must be patient. Something is up that will bring him to San Diego sooner than later. I have no specific timeframe as of yet. I'm working on it."

This was music to her ears. She drew near to him and looked around to see if anyone was noticing their tête-à-tête. In the clear, she took his hand and gave him a kiss on the cheek:

"Damon, I can't tell you how much I appreciate the work by you and your department. I wonder what is in store for all of us."

His admiration for her entered into the picture:

"Happy outcomes for you and Jordan. Who knows? Maybe big things for you and me."

32
CHAPTER

Perth, September 1969

A testy Ian Bright had been hen-pecking Sela ever since he returned from Melbourne. It seemed she could do nothing right for him, i.e., preparing meals, packing the right clothes and personal items for their impending trip, and questioning her daily activities. Perhaps, this control freak mentality came from qualms about his mission to purchase and deliver a clandestine device for his father for unknown purposes. Thinking back on what he bought gave him some angst. He recalled the curiosity of the explosives merchant at a Melbourne blasting equipment and supply emporium:

"Young man, this is a very unusual request you have of our limited available inventory for a device with explosive bridge wires and a power source. It creates an implosion on a very volatile energy core, pressuring it enough to reach supercritical density and set off a chain reaction. Are you aware of this?"

Bright looked mystified. The merchant continued:

"This device is not unlike, as I understand it, the one that detonated one of the atom bombs over Japan."

Bright wasn't prepared for a scientific inquiry, which would confirm his ignorance. Rather, as his father instructed, avoid confusing questions and just hand over his letter of explanation.

To Whom It May Concern:

I am an avocado farmer in southern California (USA) in need of an exploding bridgewire detonator (EBW). This will be utilized to clear new ground to expand the acreage for tree plantings on my property. It seems the terrain needed to be cleared and modified for cultivation is resting upon a very large rocky formation. This will require a non-traditional explosive with sufficient energy to break up and disperse the rubble of this impediment.

You should know the central energy core for the explosion will be a high-grade, very dense TNT metallic cylinder. Based on advice from detonation experts in my area, it will require an EBW detonator to produce the desired effect.

I am not in a position at this time to travel to your location, but my son, Ian Bright, has agreed to make the transaction for the EBW product. Based on your catalog, the price for this item is $1,000 (Australian dollars). I made arrangements with a Melbourne bank to provide a cashier's check in that amount, payable to your firm. My son will give it to you to complete this transaction. I hope this will be sufficient to cover the transaction.

In conclusion, I trust you will pack the device in a plain cardboard carton, sufficient for transport via air. Thank you for your assistance and understanding.

David Percival

San Diego County, California (USA)

The merchant read the letter and placed it on the counter. He confirmed why Bright was there:

"Yes, now I understand, Mr. Bright. I take it you have the payment in your possession?"

Bright took the check from a small carrying case and dutifully handed it over. He had questions:

"How much will this weigh? Can I transfer it around without difficulty as an airline passenger? As you can understand, I need to keep it close at hand to deliver directly to my father."

"Yes, it is wise to keep within your grip such an expensive, unusual item for safety's sake. For your convenience, we'll package this for you in a box with built in, durable cardboard handles. The EBW product has really been miniaturized to make it less bulky and more lightweight. You'll be carrying roughly 8.5 kilos, just under 19 pounds. You look like a sturdy lad, and you should have no problems toting it to and from airports."

Bright wanted this transaction to end as soon as possible. It was foreign to him and he wanted to spend a little time with a Melbourne band he made contact with during this trip, which was composed of Australian Sharpies, taking that name because they wanted to look and dress "sharp." Bright liked their style in clothes, as he came dressed for the part to mingle with them in Melbourne, a Sharpie enclave. He casually strutted around in a Sharpie wardrobe of Levi's, jumpers, and T-shirts, individually designed by group members to outdo themselves with best patterns, color, and detail. Attending bands at town halls and urban discos, Sharpies were associated with violence, given to regular brawls. Fortunately for Bright, there were some tense moments at a Melbourne night spot, but he avoided any altercation with the local police. You always had to be ready for conflict in the Sharpie sub-culture, especially when it crossed the turf of a rival gang.

Bright was enjoying himself on his brief hiatus from Sela. He even thought of sending for her so they could immerse themselves in the youthful frivolity for a few days. But he knew he had to go back to Perth and then move on to the United States with the package his father clearly wanted--the EBW device. To sweeten the pot for Bright's cooperation, he threw in an extra $1000 for his personal use. Not too bad for a young English bloke of modest means and a cavalier approach to life.

Bright's return to Perth accelerated the onset for the day of reckoning for two conflicted souls about to embark on an uncertain journey. One of them was Sela Danby. Like a chronic itch that could not be relieved, she still had not completely dissipated her misgivings for her participation in a plot to implicate her rogue companion, Bright, with aiding and abetting a potential domestic terrorist--his father, David Percival. However, the latest communique by wire from her never-seen and convincing half-brother, Jordan Starmont, to travel to the United States and help bring a fugitive to justice armed her resolve to take the plunge. That and her unbelievable reliance on a total stranger, Rex Murtaugh, the other conflicted person in this unlikely triad. He was her fallback position for support. In the end, it was a strength of character for a young lass that was developed by a hard-working single mother in Tunbridge Wells, England, who imbued her with the value to be devoted to some great expectation—as implausible as it might be. With that notion at the forefront of her mind, it stimulated her to give a response to Jordan's latest message. She wasn't going to let him down. It was now or never to rid Bright from her life.

She responded with this latest Western Union wire to Jordan:

> *September 7, 1969*
>
> *Thank you for thinking of me. Yes, for the last time, I am committed to helping you and will travel to San Diego. No changes in the travel plans I sent to you. Yes, Rex Murtaugh will be on my flight. Glad you checked his background. This will likely be the last message I will send to you. Look for me when I arrive and safely reach out to me so I can be rid of Ian Bright. I hope to point him out to you to end this whole sorry affair.*
>
> *Fondly,*
>
> *Sela*

The other conflicted soul in this exceptional twist of fate was Rex Murtaugh, pondering when his true self, Josh Hannigan, once again might be viable. It had been nearly a year since his flight from justice brought him to Perth. As an unknown outlaw, Hannigan was at the point of settling into the mainstream local population. He wasn't sure his best course for personal improvement would be tending bar at the Crickett Club, but, with the influential contacts he made by satisfying the alcoholic desires of influential Perth dignitaries and businessmen, it was a realistic launching pad for a more productive career. The second-guessing was constant, and he questioned why he did not move on to bigger and better things.

All that changed when he was suddenly smitten by the lovely charms and physical allure of Sela Danby. The man was moonstruck by her and she penetrated his inner being. He knew what was upon him was different: she was a continuous image before him. He thought of her when he ate, she was the last thought before he fell asleep, and the first lovely image to awake him in the morning. Hannigan, with all the imbedded nastiness to do untoward things in his checkered past, was now a more mellow personality. With that in view, he, too, was committed to take a fateful ride to America. For Sela, it would be a new experience; for Hannigan, it would be coming to terms with old headaches. But, ah, together he thought they could be a new personality that would find a way to say farewell to their troubled present predicaments.

To allay Sela's anxieties and to establish some survival objectives, he had to contact her one more time before their imminent flight to the western hemisphere. He tied a string on his entry doorknob to his flat to alert her that they needed to communicate. He would not vacate his flat until he heard her knock. Awaiting this moment was a tormenting test of patience. Hours passed without a sound, prompting Hannigan to pace and fret. Much to his dismay and dislike, he reverted to bad habits. The first came when he found a gift from a Crickett Club admirer, a carton of Chesterfield cigarettes, buried in a kitchen drawer. It didn't take him long to break the carton, find a package, break the seal, and slip out a king-sized filtered nicotine creation. Taking a nervous puff, he found his revisited vice bitter to the taste but somewhat soothing to his nerves. But he still needed another elixir. Alcohol had been removed from his life, but its tempting reminder was provided by another Crickett Club fan who gave him a quart of Jack Daniels Tennessee Whiskey as a tip one raucous night after a big rugby victory. The bottle still had an unbroken seal and was under his kitchen sink. He quickly found a glass for its bronze colored contents. Trying to lead a clean life, with a cigarette in one hand and an ice filled drink in the other, he thought his friends, at times, provided some bad substances in his life. It was heaven sent that it only took fifteen minutes after his return to tobacco and booze to hear Sela knocking at his door.

Hannigan sprung to the door, not caring who was on the other side. The sight of Sela gave him instant relief:

"You are so dear to me."

He took her hand, closed and locked the door, and gave her a sensuous kiss. She broke the passionate clinch, clutched Murtaugh's hands, and looked into his glowing eyes:

"Rex, you are so close to my heart, too."

Gazing at him she said:

"You smell of smoke and of drink."

Murtaugh had to justify the foul aroma:

"Yes, I needed a smoke and a drink to calm me a little. You know the stakes are high for us both."

Sela concurred:

"There's been a time or two when I needed a jolt myself."

Murtaugh had to get the conversation on point:

"What's Bright up to?"

"I got away when he left to bid farewell to some Sharpie pals at a pub near the Swan River Esplanade. I can't stay long."

"Sela, this won't take long, as much as I find it harder to let you go. Please sit down so we can go over what we know and what we are both getting into."

"Fine. I guess we need to pin things down for my swirling head."

"Okay. Let's give this some stability to rehash where we are and what's next as we prepare to step onto American soil. First, you have a half-brother, a Jordan Starmont, whom you've never met who is assisting the FBI to bring Bright's father, a David Percival, to justice."

"That's correct."

"Second, it appears Bright purchased a dangerous device in Melbourne for his father, something with potentially profound consequences."

Sela was in a cooperative mood with some important detail:

"Let me clarify: it's an ignitor. Jordan said it is 'to deliver a blow'."

"This sounds like a sophisticated apparatus to me that might be a part of exploding a large weapon. Any details you have on this?"

"Nothing more specific. But it all seems very horrifying to me."

"Dear, I understand. We can't let this happen. I am glad you have been cooperative to Jordan and the FBI. Let's go on. Third, Bright has been acting very peculiar. Not wanting you to sit next to him on the plane is very odd. But, that's an opportunity for increased safety for you. When you get to the airport, be sure you designate a seat at the rear of the plane from Los Angeles to San Diego. I'll get one nearby to stay within your sight."

"Yes, that is important. The farther from Ian the better."

"Four, and this is very critical. To me, Bright's old man, Percival, is a crafty animal. He knows he could be set-up to be nabbed when Bright arrives in San Diego. But, the unknown is that no one, probably not even the FBI, knows what Percival and Bright look like."

"That's a vital fact. You are so smart, Rex."

Murtaugh paused for a bit to reflect before continuing:

"However, I have to assume that Jordan knows what you look like. Is that correct?"

"You are correct. I sent him a photo in one of my letters to him."

"Voila, Sela. You are the tie that binds in this whole scenario. The FBI wants you to be next to Bright and stay with him until he meets his father, Percival. I suspect they want Jordan to point you out to help the FBI. This is crazy. Do you even know what Jordan looks like?"

"Why, no. He never sent a picture."

"Again, you can't go to Percival direct since you never met him. Only Bright can lead the FBI to him, but the FBI won't know who Bright is without you next to him. And, yeah, has Bright ever met his father? Does he know who he's looking for?"

"Ian did say he'll know him by the package he's carrying."

"I see. That's the detonator."

"Must be. I saw a good-sized box that Ian brought back from Melbourne. He was evasive about it."

Murtaugh surmised with an air of self-righteousness:

"This whole rendezvous is chock-full of things that could go wrong."

"That might be, but Jordan assured me that I would be protected when I land."

"I don't want you to be alarmed, but that is easier said than done. Once we enter the terminal that's when we both make a dash for it. I'll be with you at that point and we'll let the chips fall where they may."

"But won't this upset Jordan and the FBI if they can't catch Percival? I do want to meet my half-brother."

"Sela, I do understand your emotional bond here. But your safety is paramount to me. Trust me, I've been in tight spots before. I think Jordan has painted a too simplistic picture for a happy outcome for you. There'll be time and a place for a pleasant meeting for you two once we are safely away from the clutches of Bright and his diabolical father."

Sela had a look of disappointment and gave a sigh:

"Rex, I feel you are right. I've never accepted this whole idea that things would be peachy keen for me. Love, I trust you and have confidence in you. You are the one I need to stay close to for the foreseeable future."

That gave Murtaugh the assurance that he had a handle on the situation and had Sela committed to him. They briefly discussed that they would be visually mindful of each other on each leg of their long flight. It would become a rousing journey of thousands of miles--one with a final destination that was taking them into uncharted territory. Upon leaving, Sela gave Murtaugh a warm embrace and deep kiss. He went to the door and spied down an empty hall, giving an all clear sign for Sela to cross the hall and return to her flat.

With Sela gone and silence his only companion, Hannigan still had vital points to ponder. To give him a chance to pass through American customs with Rex Murtaugh's stolen passport, he clouded his appearance with uncut hair and an unshaven face. Fortunately, the Murtaugh passport photo had the visage of a man with no facial hair and short hair. It helped that both Murtaugh and Hannigan had brown hair and brown eyes. But clearing the entrance hurdle back into the States was minor compared to what would be next. To be sure, he knew he was operating in a crisis mode. But a crisis is both a danger and an opportunity. A wanted man had to atone for his sins. Always the perpetual schemer, Hannigan mentally searched for a way to receive a reprieve from the law by making a grand splash. What if when he came to San Diego the person to lead the FBI to Percival would not be Sela, but the notorious one and only Josh Hannigan?

33
CHAPTER

San Diego, September 1969

Waiting for Damon Broadbent like a lurking barracuda was San Diego Police Department Chief Harold Moore. Broadbent was bracing for a meeting that would have specific questions, but he knew it might fall short with his vague answers. Moore always requested early morning meetings to allow the most from the remains of the day to solve the problems he posed to his law enforcers. Taking the short walk down the tiled hall from his post to Moore's office, Broadbent gave a wave and a nod to the staff officer, Johnnie Tobin, who was Moore's gatekeeper. Tobin laid it on the line:

"Good morning, Captain Broadbent. The old man is waiting for you and he's in a bad way."

Broadbent wasn't surprised:

"Tobin, that's nothing new."

"Yes it is. The chief never complains about the coffee I prepare for him. He came out twice this morning to have me remake a pot to his liking."

"What's the matter? Doesn't he know that the world is an imperfect place? That's why we are all employed--to correct its shortcomings. I have no fear of your cooking. Pour me a cup"

Tobin went to a nearby credenza filled with a coffeemaker, rows of Styrofoam coffee cups, and supplies of artificial sweeteners and creamers in plastic bowls. He poured a cup and gave it to Broadbent by offering his perspective:

"Captain, you know it never ceases to amaze me the simplistic philosophy you have for the world we live in. How do you cope so well with this danger business we call police work?"

To get the edge off the things, Broadbent pitched a curveball:

"You know I am curious why you have a lock on the credenza. Is that where you store your coffee?"

"Hey, there's a reason for that. I don't want my drinkers to see my coffee source—they may not like the brand. And, if they see the same can all the time, they may think it is dated."

Broadbent gave a response that encapsulated the enigma of the unidentified corpse on the beach:

"Apparently that did not work today. Looks can be deceiving. Tobin, maybe you can fool Mother Nature, but you can't stop Father Time. Anything sitting for too long loses its zesty taste, regardless how new or mysterious it may seem."

"You are Mr. philosopher."

"Tobin, have no fear, your coffee passes my taste test. But, to answer your question, I guess I try to solve crimes with a simple approach: get to the bottom of things by acting on the information you have, not what you really want but may never obtain."

The officer smiled and then got on Chief Moore's squawk box:

"Chief, Captain Broadbent is here."

Moore was at the ready:

"Good. Send him in. Officer Tobin, I'll presume this time that your coffee meets your usual standards if he has a cup in hand. Have the captain come right in."

Tobin nodded towards Moore's door. Broadbent took the cue and entered Moore's space and was wide-eyed. The chief was in a dress uniform, not his usual blue suit, white shirt, and any assortment of matching ties for the day. Sitting erect in his chair, Moore was clad in a dark blue serge jacket, accented by department insignias on his lapels. Above his breast pocket was his black plated and white lettered nametag. His white shirt was so stiff it looked like it was treated with extra starch. The chief had the bloated look of a heavyweight boxer who took too many blows to the face. A veteran of D-Day with the 4th Infantry Division during World War II, he came west after the war to San Diego, the hometown of an Army nurse he met after suffering shrapnel wounds near the Ardennes Forest during the Battle of the Bulge. They married the same year, 1946, Moore joined the ranks of the San Diego Police Department.

A recipient of several citations and awards, to include the Medal of Valor he earned after saving the life of a fellow officer during a bank robbery, the chief was a no-nonsense guy who demanded respect and gave the utmost support to his officers in the field. Broadbent was one of his favorites because of his unblemished record and the quality of his work in solving some tough cases. But the latest crime at Windansea Beach had him perplexed and upset that the investigation was stuck in neutral. He had justification for his sour mood:

"I've got some time before I am off for an awards ceremony for two fellow officers. Damon, what's it been, at least a week since that nameless body was brought to our morgue?"

"I wish it weren't so, but I've been on this during all my waking hours."

"I know that to be true, since it seems you've been leaving your office after I do--at dusk. But, as I have harped on it, the mayor knows what happened and has tried his best to keep the story out of the papers. It's too bad a few snooty, elite types in La Jolla got wind of what happened and feel violated by this. As a minimum, they want this investigation concluded with the peace of mind that this was an exception to the norm for beach safety."

"That's not an unreasonable expectation, since that part of the city is tranquil and basically a crime-free area."

"So, let's start with what I know. Got the coroner's report on the corpse. The cause of death was twofold: hanging and if that wouldn't have done him in he had enough heroin in his veins to kill three people. The body was too decomposed to extract a sufficient smear for fingerprints. I guess if the guy was in the service, committed a crime, or applied for a high-level government position, then prints could give us a name to go with the flesh and blood."

"That's too bad, but what may be helpful is to know where he came from? The assumption is the San Francisco area because of the car rental connection. Any help from Blake Sheridan and San Francisco homicide? Detective Herlihy seems to think investigative progress is slow because of FBI roadblocks."

"One of the biggest regrets I have had on the force is the lack of cooperation between law enforcement agencies—may they be on the local or national level. However, this Nazi stuff gives them justification for taking the lead on this whole case because the home-grown ones cross state lines regularly. Damon, fries my ass that I had to fight those dogs in Europe and now we have to crush them on our turf."

"It's unfortunate that Nazism has been so deep rooted. That's why hateful minds are still drawn to it."

Then Moore was looking for a cause and effect relationship:

"Is it your feeling, though, that the body has a relationship to the Nazi who wants to do something big?"

"Not only that but the two AWOL Marines in my reports are under the spell of an avocado grower up in Fallbrook. They were there at the cabana when the body was present, I am sure of it."

"Yeah, that directions stuff on how to get to Windansea detective Sandoval uncovered accounts for that. I know the FBI wants to collar this guy. But I want his ass just as bad. Can we assume this nameless grower is the one who wants to strike the big blow?"

"Things point in that direction. I have to believe his telephone was bugged by the FBI. That's why they have some specifics. If we could only find out more detail from the FBI findings it would aid our investigation."

Moore then reflected by looking up at the ceiling for a moment. Perhaps he caught a creative moment by doing so:

"Do you think the mother of the FBI apprentice, Jordan Starmont, could give us some of those specifics."

"Chief, I've done all that I can to placate her concerns for her boy after we misidentified him. If she had her way, she would already be in the Bay area. She is being stonewalled by the FBI from doing so."

Moore then came forward leaning over his desk, looking Broadbent sternly in the eye, and asked a profound question:

"Damon, instead of having Mohammed go to the mountain, how about the Mountain coming to Mohammed?"

"You saying if Jordan can't come to us, let's have his mother go to him? Yes, I see. She can shake out unknown facts that he won't give to us because of FBI interference. A mother's pleas for help would be hard to reject."

"Precisely. FBI or no FBI they can't stop a mother from seeing her son. And furthermore, I want a good integrator and a capable sleuth to go with her."

Broadbent hoped it would be him, but he wasn't sure:

"Who?"

"I'm looking at him."

The Seal's Lair, September 1969

Fresh off avoiding capture at Windansea Beach, David Percival caught his breath after he safely passed through the security gate of the Navy Amphibious Base (NAB). Casey Douglas was at the wheel of the getaway Lincoln Continental when he parked the vehicle outside his quarters on Tulagi Road. In the back seat Yancey Bixby and Monty Crawford shared idle chatter amongst themselves, happy they also got away without consequences. Percival lauded Douglas's driving abilities:

"Casey, how long have you been stationed here in the San Diego area? With the driving twists and turns you took, you appear to be a native."

"David, as a matter of fact I am. I'm an old beach child, growing up in Pacific Beach. I am familiar with all the beach communities along the coast, from Oceanside to Coronado and the South Bay."

The four of them got out of the car and walked up to Douglas's quarters. Once inside, Percival could see that Douglas was expecting company:

"Casey, I presume the sleeping bags on the living room floor are for Bixby and Crawford."

"Got that right. Have to keep the rank and file at their proper station. You've slept in worse, right Marines?"

Crawford answered for the two of them:

"This is heaven compared to what we lived and slept in Nam."

Percival was curious:

"So, where you got me laying my soft head."

"You have my bedroom--you are in charge here."

Percival was gracious but not accepting:

"No, Casey, this is your residence. I can sleep on the couch."

"David, no, no. That's where I will put my head down."

Percival wanted to get back to business:

"You are very accommodating. Thank you."

Douglas then went to his refrigerator to offer a stiff beverage he thought his comrades could use:

"You guys up for a brew? I know it's not even noon yet, but this might calm you down."

Bixby declined the beer but wanted water, Percival asked for a cup of coffee, and Crawford made the same request. With drinks in hand, Douglas was ready to return to the car to off load. He had an inquiry about something unusual in the trunk:

"David, besides our bags we took to the hotel, do you want that satchel?"

Percival was quick and adamant:

"Under no uncertain terms does anyone touch that item. Casey, give me the car keys after you bring up the bags. I'll explain what needs to be divulged when troopers Dunhill, Smith, Montag, and Wyatt get here this evening."

"Sure thing. Better yet, if you don't need your other bag, why don't I wait until it gets dark to get mine. Still too much base activity; don't want to arouse suspicion."

Percival concurred:

"Good move. That's when we can also get the stuff that we packed in the truck that Montag is driving. I hope he was able to rid himself of the law when he blocked traffic. You think Dunhill is returning to the base and not speeding around town in the GTO?"

Douglas sounded assuring:

"Montag was to call me if he had a problem. I told Dunhill to return here. He's quartered on the *Ticonderoga*. Just like Smith. I assume they are both there. Right now, no news is good news."

"Where's Wyatt?" Percival asked:

"Unlike Montag, he can't get away from the Marine Corps Recruit Depot until duty hours end today. He'll be here tonight."

Percival then gave the group a dose of reality:

"Gentlemen, for Monty, Yancey, and me this is home. Given the circumstances, this is as good as place as any to stay removed from any contact with the law. And in your situation, Troopers Bixby and Crawford, away from the Marine MP's. Besides, only the military has jurisdiction on base. Right, Casey?"

"Correct. In my eight years in the Navy I have never seen a case where a civilian cop arrested a sailor or a Marine, let alone seen them snooping around on military property."

Douglas was on extended leave for ten days, so he had no military duties to attend to. This allowed him to move about with no obligations to the Navy and to stock his refrigerator with plenty of food, to include meat, fish, chicken, fruit, assorted vegetables, and plenty of beer and pop. Percival wanted to know the cost of these items and gave Douglas $90 in cash: $80 for the actual cost and $10 for what Percival called "wear and tear" money. Percival was always generous and rewarded exemplary efforts. Douglas's quarters weren't a mess hall, but it would feed the troopers well for the at least the next week.

After rehashing what transpired, the assembled renegades from the law then tried to get some rest after an early start to a frenetic day. Percival had some time to think about his son, Ian Bright, and his imminent trip to San Diego, carrying the item that was essential to his plan with earth shaking consequences. Needing to give Bright some last instructions, he decided to telephone him in Perth. Douglas assured him that his line was not bugged because he had a security clearance. Being sixteen hours behind Perth, this was a good time to call. It was approaching 1:00 PM in San Diego and it was close to 5:00 AM in Perth, the next day. Percival guessed Bright should be able to take the call, even though he would not be pleased to be roused from bed. It took eight rings, but a bleary voice answered:

"If this is a wrong number, bloke, there will be hell to pay!"

"Ian, this is your father, David. Sorry to awake you so early, but with the time difference I thought my chances of reaching you were good at this early hour. Judging by your surly disposition, I succeeded."

"Yeah, my head is foggy. Sorry for the grumpiness but I am really knackered."

"Knackered, hey. Been a while since I've heard that term for tiredness. Well, I'll cut to the chase so you can go back to bed. To review, you are all set to arrive in San Diego on Friday, September 13 via PSA Airlines at 11:00 P.M. And, most importantly, you made the purchase we talked about in Melbourne."

"No changes to the flight plan; I have the package in hand. As instructed, it is in a plain cardboard box with handles, which allows me to carry it at all times."

Percival was pleased:

"Nice work, Ian. Although we have never met, that will identify you when you arrive and have us finally meet. I owe you so much, son, for not only this business favor but for not being a more responsible father."

"I understand. But, I have been thinking about this. Have I been taking a risk by bringing the detonator to the States?"

"How do you mean, Ian?"

"Well, this lovely I've been involved with has questioned why the secrecy and the unusual seating on the plane?"

"Is this the Danby girl you spoke of?"

"It's her. I told her not to worry. Things will be cool after we all get together in California."

Percival had to drill down on this issue:

"Good, good. That's right. As I said in my letter to the supplier, the detonator is to remove stubborn obstacles on my ranch. If she questions you further on this, tell her simply that it is for clearing some ground. By the way, what does Sela Danby look like?"

"You've heard of the Herman's Hermits song, *Mrs. Brown You Have a Lovely Daughter*."

"Can't say I have. Who do we look for so we can pick her up as well?"

"Let me sing you the descriptive lyrics from the song to help single her out:

Walkin' about
Even in a crowd, well
You'll pick her out
Makes a bloke feel so proud

Really, look for a beauty with sandy brown hair and high cheek bones--very English, I'd say."

"I'd say as well and why, as the song reveals, 'makes a bloke so proud'. You've got a good voice. Perhaps you have a future in music."

"Yes, and coming to California maybe I can find some contacts to book our band some day. You know any?"

"Well, sort of, but we'll discuss at the appropriate time. But, back to your arrival, I will have two men, about your age, who work for me pick you up. I think you young people will hit it off."

Bright was realistically inquisitive:

"What do they look like? Where should I go to meet them at the airport?"

"They will pick you out by dint of you carrying the carton. One will call himself Yancey; the other will say he is Monty. In the interim call this number to reach me: 555.589.1900. If I don't answer, leave a message with anyone who does."

"So, you are not at the old number? And, by the way, it's also good to know your people have English first names."

Percival responded with deception:

"That's correct. My home is being remodeled and I am staying at one of my trusted workers place. It seems the people I hire and trust do have names that remind us of our English roots."

As the call went on, Percival confirmed that Sela was important to Ian. They rounded out the conversation with the mutual anticipation they had to finally meet. Putting down the telephone, Percival surmised that Sela could be a complicating impediment for their introductory meeting. He wasn't sure what to do with her. Nevertheless, he was heartened to know the detonator would finally be in his possession.

It was nearly 7:00 P.M. when Percival had all of his assembled troops together in Douglas's living room, for only the second time. Smith and Wyatt were updated as to what happened at the beach earlier in the day. With everyone up to speed, Percival gave more specifics as to what was next:

"My troopers, it is good we are all gathered together. I am confident that we can be a small but effective strike force. If it comes down to using firepower, when you off load the pickup truck you will see we have sufficient arms and weapons. Troopers Wyatt and Smith will be given the colt .45 revolvers. The heavier weaponry, the rifles and recoilless cannon, will be assigned later. Now, for the bigger picture. I have in my possession a weapon of mass destruction which we can use to intimidate the ruling class of this country, both civilian and military. If need be, it will be a bargaining chip to meet our demands. On Friday, September 13, my son from England, Ian Bright, will arrive at the airport with a device that will trigger the volatile explosive I have in the trunk of the Lincoln, which is off limits to all of you."

At that point, the men squirmed a little, which prompted Douglas to ask:

"What specifically is the explosive?"

"Minimally, all I can say it has the capability to destroy the whole Coronado Naval Base, as well as much of adjacent downtown San Diego. But we lose our capability if we do not have the detonating device Ian is to bring to us. Therefore, because of their fine work at Windansea Beach, I am again assigning Troopers Bixby, Crawford, and Douglas to meet my son. It is vital that we meet him and safely escort him and the detonator to the Seal's Lair. I will await your arrival here. Now, Troopers, here's the rub. After what happened this morning, I fear the authorities are aware of who I am and will try to destroy our movement. They are cagey and are full of trickery. So we should know that we are to be extra cautious by keeping our sacred secret oath to keep our activities only known to us. One thing more. You also noticed that I am not calling attention to ourselves with Nazi symbols, uniforms, names and expressions. We have to stay low key for now. Am I clear here?"

The men all nodded in agreement.

"I will give specific instructions on Ian's arrival at Lindbergh Field and how to spot him as September 13 approaches. But, we also have to be mindful of a person who stood us up today and may also be at the airport when Ian arrives."

Douglas knew who that could only be:

"You mean this phantom, Jordan Starmont?"

"Exactly, I don't know what he looks like really, but I think he and maybe others will try to intercept Ian and the package he carries. My sense tells me he might be a younger person, one interested in Ian and a female companion who is coming with him. A girl named Sela Danby."

Douglas offered his caution:

"This could be trouble, David. How do we handle her?"

"I don't know yet. For sure they are realistic threats. That's why, if need be, they both need to be eliminated."

35
CHAPTER

San Diego and San Francisco, September 1969

"Maggie? Damon. I have good news".

Margaret Starmont had a sudden rush at the other end of the telephone line:

"Is it about Jordan?"

"Yes, and it has come about with the blessing of the San Diego Police Department to have you see him in San Francisco."

"What prompted the change of heart? I thought the FBI was a roadblock for a meeting?"

"Well, legally, because your son has not committed a crime, as a parent, you have every right to see him, regardless of the cloistering they have done to him."

"This is great. I can make reservations to fly you there. Do we know where Jordan is living?"

Broadbent had to temper a mother's elation:

"Maggie, it's all arranged, courtesy of our department. We fly via PSA to San Francisco the day after tomorrow. Because of our coordination with the San Francisco bureau of the FBI, it will occur at their location."

Margaret felt a setback:

"Oh, you mean I may not have unconditional visitation rights?"

"That's one way to put it. But, given the circumstance of Jordan's involvement in a critical investigation, he has to stay tethered to the FBI. To be sure, they will allow us to speak with him at a different location, say a restaurant or hotel, to relate in confidence."

Hanging on every word, Margaret was curious:

"Damon, who is 'us'?"

"It's you and me."

"I like that combination."

Broadbent was tingling inside when he heard that answer. He then went on to give the particulars on the flight, to include picking Margaret up and where they will stay in San Francisco for two nights--the Days Inn near Columbus Avenue. As an attempt to impress Maggie, Broadbent tried for the upscale Mark Hopkins, but Chief Harold Moore could not justify the expense. At the end of the call, Broadbent achieved two objectives. The first was all business: the broadening the Windansea investigation. But the second was personal: an affair of the heart to be in close proximity with Margaret again.

Broadbent's next telephone call was to alert his temporary duty assistant, Dan Herlihy, up in San Francisco, of his impending arrival. Herlihy was spinning his wheels trying to get anywhere, with the FBI as an impediment and the San Francisco Police Department of no help. He was glad to see his boss come to town to get things moving in the right direction. Besides, he liked his current location. Wearing the costume of "flower child" made him feel ten years younger.

After checking with Herlihy, Broadbent received a call twenty minutes later from his other subordinate working on the case, Rick Sandoval. Broadbent was hoping for more good news:

"Sandoval, go ahead—make my day!"

"Damon, that line is so good they should put it in a movie."

"Who knows, maybe this whole escapade we are on will be a movie. So, what do you have?"

"Captain, another captain of the Marine Corps, Julian Desmond, has relented and just gave me the photos of Bixby and Crawford, the AWOL Marines. They both have a lean and hungry look, and one of them comes close to matching the description the surfers gave us at Windansea"

"That's a good break. Bring the photos in so we can disseminate to the entire force and put them on an APB alert."

"Through Directory Assistance in Louisiana I found out that Yancey Bixby's father, Earl, is a deputy with the St. Tammany Parish in the area. When I told him who I was, he was very cooperative with a fellow law enforcement officer."

Broadbent thought: finally, a law enforcement agency that will help his investigative cause:

"Hmm. This is good stuff. Go on."

"It seems there has been little or no communication with their son for several weeks. His wife has written several other letters to him, with no response. He doesn't even call any more. His father does not like the fact that his son is associating with an individual who does not have Yancey's best interest at heart."

"Can we give a name to this Svengali?"

"I pressed for it, but their son never said more than what we know: he's an avocado farmer and has an English accent. By the way, I had to explain why I was calling and did mention his son is AWOL from the Marines and may be involved in some illegal activity."

"I am sure that did not please him."

"For sure. The guy is a World War II veteran and indicated the extreme loyalty his family has for America, although he is not very happy with the lack of support the country has for our efforts to succeed in Vietnam."

"That's understandable. Where did you leave it with him?"

"As a law enforcement official, he even volunteered his services to help us. I cooled him down and said we would keep him and his whole family in the loop."

"That's the right move. Continue to sniff around Fallbrook and see where this avocado farmer may be living."

"Will do."

⊷◉⊶

Meanwhile, the mood was testy in the office of FBI Chief Investigator Theodore Johnson. He was notified by San Francisco Police Homicide Inspector Blake Sheridan that he would have company tomorrow: San Diego Homicide Captain Damon Broadbent and a person he was hoping to keep at arm's length to not complicate his intricate plan to collar David Percival--Margaret Starmont. Johnson tried to prevent any possible meeting between mother and son to no avail. It would only make matters too emotional, with a loss of investigative objectivity. Nevertheless, he did have a leash on Jordan, as tenuous as it was around his neck. He called both him and agent Ross Cargill to his office to keep his game plan in place.

"Agent Cargill, Jordan Starmont, it seems there is a change of plans. In fact, tomorrow. Things need to be clarified. Jordan, I imagine you have been in touch with your mother since you have been a part of our team."

"No, that's not true. She knows I am in Haight-Ashbury living in a world of my choice."

"All right, I'm glad we have that straight, Jordan. But she knows more than you think about your whereabouts and activities. She was called to San Diego by their homicide bureau to help identify the body we put on Windansea Beach."

Jordan made a disgusting laugh:

"First you identify me as leasing a car I have never driven. Second you give a dead body my name. Of course she was notified--to possibly identify the stiff you put there? This is so incredibly bizarre. I never thought I would be a part of a murder investigation with homicide detectives."

Johnson wasn't amused and stuck to his eccentric scheme:

"On the contrary, it's what we wanted--to keep the local police out of our hair and to have them chase down possible perpetrators of a killing on one of their pristine beaches. More importantly, to not get wind of the real target in this case--David Percival. My guess is that she probably didn't identify you stretched out in a coroner's cooler."

"Man, I sure hope so. You guys are going to have to do something good for a woman with noble intentions and an unquestioned code of ethics. My mom didn't deserve to have additional grief, given the recent death of my father."

"Jordan, I concur with everything you said, but let's give you a pleasant surprise to lessen your anger toward the department. You'll meet her tomorrow at 9:00 A.M. in my office. I must level with you, we did not want to have this reunion until we nabbed Percival. But, legally, we can't prevent it."

A sarcastic Jordan responded:

"Gee, thanks Chief Johnson for the favor. But, oh, yes, given what has happened, I can't wait to see her. At least I'll know the love and attention will be genuine."

"Jordan, I appreciate your misgivings, but there is a problem here. Your mother will be accompanied by a San Diego Homicide Detective, a Damon Broadbent, who as I was apprised, is a slick inquisitor. Let's go over, given the agreement you bought into for secrecy in this operation, and what I command you not to reveal."

"That does not surprise me. I know this is a lockstep operation. I'll be careful what I tell him. You know why?"

"Jordan, I admire your patriotism and your courage. What is your motivation?"

"I am in too deep now. I can't upset the plan, because, deep down, I feel my father wants to grab David Percival more than I do."

The Seal's Lair, September 1969

Casey Douglas came into his quarters in an animated state with a slip of paper in his hand:

"David, as you know, I have a security clearance and have access to both base and civilian communications that affect security and safety. While on duty today, here's what I picked up on the teletype:"

He handed over to an aroused Percival, who read feverishly:

TO: All San Diego Police Units

From: Chief Harold Moore

Re: All Points Bulletin (APB)

Be on the lookout for two AWOL Marines, Lance Corporals Yancey Bixby and Monty Crawford. Both left their duty posts last month from Camp Pendleton and are presumed to still be at large within the San Diego city and/or county limits. They were both last seen at Windansea Beach in La Jolla and are possibly connected to a violent crime there. Witnesses say one of them brandished a pistol; therefore, consider them armed and dangerous. Physical characteristics: they have military style short haircuts, are about six feet tall, have athletic builds, and perhaps approach 180 to 185 pounds.

*They both are originally from Louisiana, so they speak with
a southern accent. For more information, contact Captain
Damon Broadbent, Homicide Department.*

Percival read the directive with a sense of dismay and realism. The
escape from Windansea did not go unnoticed, given that Trooper Bobby
Montag encountered the law with his effective roadblock. However,
Percival was puzzled: who gave chase--the FBI or the local police? No
matter, his paramilitary force had been partially identified and now was
under surveillance. That was the setback, for he wanted as much anonymity
as possible. He confided in Douglas:

"Casey, I rely on your maturity, good judgement and the fact you
are the senior member of our group. As I mentioned to everyone, you are
second in command, so I value your appraisal of our situation. Given this
police bulletin, what red flags must we be mindful of?"

"First, this is no surprise. We fought the law and this time we won—by
getting away. Second, Bixby and Crawford must be confined to quarters.
Now they have more than the Marines looking for them, although I doubt
the Navy SPs will make their AWOL status a big deal on this base."

"Why is that?"

"It's the old bad blood rivalry of Marines not mixing with the Navy.
I can't recall any time either branch helped the other with disciplinary
problems. They've been like gasoline and matches forever. Still, it's not
wise to risk exposure for Bixby and Crawford at this location."

Percival nodded:

"What else you got?"

"Third, your three vehicles do not leave the parking area until we make
any significant moves. Remember, all three were at Windansea, and we
can't be sure if they were ID'd. It means nothing if they got license plate
numbers because it will lead them to literally a dead end in a junkyard
of cars. Still, they saw the make and colors. If we need anything or have
to leave the Lair, we can use my Camaro. Montag and Dunhill also have
wheels."

"Yeah, Casey, that's good. For now, I'm not going anywhere either.
Anything else?"

"David, while we have this private moment, can we stop playing word games with the explosion power of what you have in your trunk? Frankly, some of the guys are a bit edgy about it."

Percival leaned back in his chair and paused before answering:

"Casey, haven't I given enough clues as to what the explosive consists of? If I literally tell our force it may spook some of them out and render our mission impossible. Again, use your imagination but don't discuss it with the fellows."

Always the dutiful subordinate, Douglas acquiesced:

"I can see your point. I'll keep it under the lid and squelch any discussion about it."

"I appreciate that. Now let's check our loyalty pulse on every man in our command. From your level, are they all committed, who has voiced some discomfort, and who, my worst nightmare, may play turncoat and report our activities?"

Douglas then gave an assessment of every man in their cohort. He rated Grady Dunhill and Bobby Montag reliable and trusted under fire, especially with their cool, exemplary performances at Windansea. Mack Smith and Curtis Wyatt, the youngest of the group, were attracted to Nazism more as a defiance of authority and the allure and excitement of it all. Monty Crawford seemed steady and sure of himself in his own skin. However, when it came to Yancey Bixby, Douglas was leery:

"Yancey came up to me last night after we ate and was worried that he is risking everything by being a part of our unit. He mentioned the loaded word--treason."

Percival had to respond immediately:

"If you can get him aside, tell him the treason has been committed by those who have subverted America's values and decries its military: the Hollywood and media Jews, the anarchists in the streets subverting the American presence in Vietnam, communists spewing their class warfare and socialist views, and general apologists who accuse the white race as the root of America's problems."

"I agree with that and it's why I espouse your cause. But he's young and has only been touched by the impact of a no-win situation in Vietnam. I guess we have to convince him, and all of us, that we are true Americans, by opposing the persons in influential places from bringing it down."

Percival was pleased to hear this:

"Casey, I could not better state it myself. To get their minds off the philosophy of our cause, let's give them a battle plan. This includes having all Troopers familiarize themselves with the rifles and pistols in our arsenal. I want every man to be capable of firing any of these weapons. Would Montag be a good candidate to be assigned the recoilless?"

"His MOS in the Marines is small arms, to include this type of weapon. He'd welcome that."

'Then here is the big objective they should be prepared to accomplish. Once we have the detonator in our hands, we leave as a unit to take up our battle stations, where we make our demands and force the country to listen to us."

"I was wondering what our next big move is after we get the detonator."

"Dunhill and Smith are assigned to the carrier *Ticonderoga,* but they missed sea duty because they went to special school for communications. Dunhill told me it is due in to port at North Island the middle of this month. The day it arrives, amidst all the fanfare of dependents, we take over a strategic location, which gives us an unrestricted view of the beach area astride the Pacific and within sight of the whole naval base."

"I like the timing and puts a spotlight away from the Lair on NAB. But will we have problems getting in position?"

"No, my friend. It's a place a short jaunt from the Lair. We should have no difficulty contending with pleasure seekers to take over a pool house. The Hotel del Coronado welcomes guests."

37
CHAPTER

San Francisco, September 1969

On the directive from San Diego Police Chief Howard Moore, Damon Broadbent was to accompany Margaret Starmont to San Francisco to visit with her son—Jordan. The local investigation was not going as planned, with skimpy leads and information. Moore pressed both the San Francisco Police and the area FBI office to accommodate the meeting between mother and son. The hope is that Jordan will reveal significant information that would cast a better light on the Windansea episode. To be sure, Broadbent relished the thought of being close to Maggie again to accomplish a twofold objective: solving a crime and perhaps enhancing his personal attraction to her.

The morning of the flight to San Francisco, Broadbent had a uniformed police officer drive a cruiser to where Maggie was still residing at the La Valencia Hotel in La Jolla. When he left the squad car to page her in the hotel lobby, Broadbent had to temper his excitement to see her again. He had the look of an executive, dressed in a blue suit, red tie, white shirt, and a black fedora. But, first and foremost, he was still a cop. Carrying his holstered .38 caliber revolver, he made sure there was no inordinate bulge at his waist by keeping his suitcoat unbuttoned. Maggie had never seen him armed, and given her tense state, now was not a good time to increase her anxiety.

In minutes Maggie reached the lobby. Filled with anticipation, she was ready to go an hour ago. As fate had it, she too was dressed in blue--a fashionable two-piece business suit, with a multi-colored print scarf accenting her neck. She was the type of woman who looked good wearing anything. Broadbent saw the glint in her eye. He wasn't sure if it was more the desire to finally see her son, or to see him again. He could only hope it was the latter as he greeted her and took her small suitcase from her hand:

"Good morning. It's a day we both have been waiting for."

"Oh, Damon, I must say I'm excited to see Jordan again. It's been unnerving coming back to San Diego, especially since there was a chance he would not be alive. I owe you much for making this happen."

Broadbent proffered his arm for her to take:

"Maggie, I am glad you were confident our department would finally get you and son together. We had to do this, given the unjustified fright you had at the morgue"

"That was the past. Now I look forward for an eventful future with Jordan close at hand again."

Hearing this, Broadbent knew he was making progress with Maggie by mollifying her fears. This helped to endear him closer to her heart. Broadbent escorted her to the vehicle, put her suitcase in the trunk, and seated her in the rear seat. Sitting beside her, he previewed the trip as they drove to San Diego's Lindbergh Field for the PSA flight to San Francisco. Maggie was taken by surprise when Broadbent said several things. First, once at the terminal, she would act like she was traveling alone, doing her own check-in. Broadbent would delay and go to the ticket counter five minutes later for his flight confirmation. Second, once on board, they would take separate seats, several rows apart, a fact Broadbent did not readily appreciate. These were all restrictive movements ordered by Chief Moore, who did not want to give the appearance the two were comingling. He wanted this to be all business, knowing that a handsome man and an attractive woman makes for unforeseen consequences. Lastly, they would address one another formally to reinforce the decorum when they were with others.

However, what Broadbent did not tell Maggie was not revealed during their short flight to the San Francisco International Airport. He met her at baggage claim and quickly whisked her out the door, seeking a police cruiser that strategically was not far away. He raised his hand to be picked-up. When the car came to them, detective Dan Herlihy jumped out from the front passenger side and greeted them with a warm grin:

"Captain, Mrs. Starmont. Did you have a good flight? Hop in the back seat. Allow me to take your bag, ma'am."

Once seated, it occurred to Maggie the number of suitcases, or the lack of one, gave her pause:

"Captain, did you not take any luggage?"

"No, as you can see I just have a small personals case. I won't be staying long. Besides, you see these nice flower child clothes Herlihy has on? If need be, I can always borrow some from him. Right, Dan?"

Herlihy, dressed in a parsons shirt, leather vest, and denims, played off the humor:

"Yes, Captain, these clothes feel so comfortable. Hey, maybe it will be our new plainclothes uniform when we get back to San Diego?"

With some levity in the air, Broadbent had to give Maggie a dose of reality:

"Mrs. Starmont, I must now tell you, given the importance of Jordan's role in an FBI operation, our stay will be a brief one."

Maggie was in a huff:

"How brief? This is not what I expected. I hope you understand this a family matter, one between mother and son. We have a lot to catch up on."

"Those are all valid points, but we wouldn't be able to come this far without a limited contact arrangement. But, let me emphasize, once this whole matter is cleared up we will accommodate a better time for you and Jordan to mingle with no restrictions."

Margaret still quibbled and was not about to be placated. Broadbent gambled that she would be just a little more rational, but he underestimated the steepness of the emotional rollercoaster she was on. It was obvious that the number one person in Maggie's thoughts was her son. She was told they would meet Jordan at the FBI office on Golden Gate Avenue. Knowing Maggie was not in a good mood, there was an eerie silence in the cruiser after Maggie heard the ground rules for the meeting. Minds were in motion, but words were at a standstill. The principals were either unhappy or unsure of what would evolve to talk much. Broadbent prayed the rendezvous location, a locale that was not warm and fuzzy, would not undo any cordiality and cooperation he needed from Jordan. When the drive across town ended at the steps of the FBI office, Broadbent had a sinking feeling that he was so close but yet too far to solve a crime and win a woman's affections.

Once inside the building, they were greeted by agent Ross Cargill. Cargill was more traditionally dressed, business suit, white shirt, and blue tie. Maggie's displeasure only increased internally being in an environment that did not seem apropos. She was hoping for one of San Francisco's renown restaurants or a respectable hotel. Even some hovel in Haight-Ashbury would have been acceptable. But she gathered herself as an office door opened. The first person she saw was her son, standing behind a desk with a look that caught her off guard. She ignored the outstretched hand of Chief Investigator Theodore Johnson who tried to initially greet her. Rather, she immediately went to and clutched her son, who was not dressed in the expected hippie garb, headband, beads, and a paisley shirt and pants. Instead Jordan had his old Princeton preppy look, with a button down dress shirt, a grey and white striped tie, and blue gabardine slacks.

Her heart was pounding with joy:

"Oh, Jordan, Jordan. This is a happy day to see you, alive and well."

Jordan responded like a loving son and kissed his mother on the cheek and held her for a moment. Then gently pushing back from the embrace, he calmly and clearly said:

"Mom, it's been a long time--too long. I promise to be closer to you, in both time and space. Please sit down."

Following close behind, Broadbent and Cargill found chairs against the wall. To give everyone some needed space, Johnson reserved the largest meeting room in his office for the gathering. He was the last to take a seat behind a long mahogany table, sitting directly across from Maggie, with Jordan seated at her side. She was in a bit of pique about the environment:

"This does not meet my expectations. This is rather cold and sterile. Will Jordan and I have a chance to visit alone?"

Before he responded, Johnson directed a purposeful glance towards Jordan:

"Mrs. Starmont, I apologize for the austere setting. This is just a starting point. I just wanted you to know that your son, Jordan, is an admirable and loyal young man. I don't know if you realize it or not, but I worked on a matter of national security with your husband, Martin at the end of World War II. Jordan has exemplified all of your husband's best qualities."

Maggie was thankful for that bit of history. However, she was resolute and wanted a private moment:

"That is all well and good. I know my husband was a true patriot. But when do we leave this starting point?"

"Right now. You can have my office. But I must tell you that Captain Broadbent will also want to meet with Jordan privately after you can get up to speed personally with him. As you know he is investigating a crime and has some questions for Jordan."

Maggie quickly acquiesced and took Johnson up on his offer. She excused herself, took Jordan by the hand, and was directed to Johnson's office by Cargill.

Once there, Jordan could see that his mother was flushed with anger. Seated in chairs in front of Johnson's broad and cluttered desk, they discussed how she came to San Diego in the first place. Jordan apologized for the unfounded fear it gave her, but he never did go into why a corpse linked to his name was on a San Diego beach.

Jordan tried to soothe his mother:

"Mom, this is not the way I wanted to see you again. It's all too formal and controlled."

"Jordan, I got that impression the moment we drove up to this office. You look more gaunt than the last time I saw you. Are they taking good care of you?"

"Yes, don't worry; I am provided three square meals a day. I must say the FBI work has been intriguing and something I am committed to doing."

"Maybe we should talk about commitment. You were doing so well at Princeton, an honors student in English. That you abruptly left is a mystery. Anything your father or I failed to provide you? Was there something more important than your formal education to complete?"

Jordan had a ready answer:

"As you can see, the world we live in is in tumult. The biggest convulsion is the Vietnam War, with black people rightfully demanding their full rights in society also very important. But it seems all of society is being questioned and even experimented with in the form of alternative lifestyles and new values that are a threat to the establishment. I had to go west, to come here to San Francisco and the Haight-Ashbury colony in search of a new age to see what the buzz was all about"

"Jordan, it's apparent that young people of today have a different approach to things. What was so wrong or bad with what your father and I provided for you?"

Jordan could see his mother was a bit tormented and almost rejected:

"Mom, you and Dad did nothing wrong and everything right. But the eyes of my young friends see things differently. It's more about being less materialistic, more accommodating to others, and generally more open to perpetuating peace and love."

"From afar, I have seen that philosophy expressed on television and in the newspapers. How about this free love and use of hallucinogenic drugs to make you feel better? To me, those aren't values; they are uncontrolled appetites that do more harm than good."

Jordan could see the conversation was not an ingratiating one. He tried to overcome her concerns by explaining that he did not take drugs, respected the opposite sex by not taking advantage of them, and was becoming a better person with a more relaxed outlook on life. However, when approached by the FBI, he took a leave of absence from his world of idealism and became aware of the practical realities that all was not harmless. There was evil in the world that needed to be addressed. The wisdom and experience of his father kicked him into a new mindset. That seemed to resonate with his mother. But, he was reticent to tell her what he was doing in the service of the FBI:

"All I can tell you is that I am part of an effort to apprehend some Nazis in our country that mean to do great destruction to our nation. This will come to an end soon. When that happens I hope to go home with you for a time and be a better son."

"I guess I understand a little more this strange situation you find yourself. I trust you are not at risk to assist the FBI?"

"No, it's like I am more in the background and not on the front line of law enforcement."

They talked for another ten minutes about family matters. That's when Maggie brought up a potential bombshell:

"Your father mentioned in his letter your half-sister, Sela Danby. What can you tell me about her? Have or will you see her?"

Jordan was as protective as a threatened ewe guarding her lamb:

"I don't want to sound cold and insensitive, but Sela and I are working in confidence. There will be a time, and I hope soon, when we can all come together."

Jordan was glad there was a knock on the door to avoid further talk about Sela. This prompted them to get up, kiss each other on the cheek, and both go to the door. Waiting in the opening was a dour looking Damon Broadbent. His presence convinced Maggie that this was the only moment she would see her son for now. Broadbent gave her a wry smile and said he would not take too long asking Jordan some questions. She gave him the look of a woman scorned when she passed him and returned to the meeting room. Closing the door softly behind him, Broadbent wanted to be engaging and non-threatening. But he knew he had to be comforting and contrite at the outset:

"Jordan, on behalf of the entire San Diego Police Department, I want you to know that we deeply apologized to your mother for what we put her through at the morgue recently. This whole scenario has been a weird experience for both of us. Your name was linked to a dead body. As wrongful as that was, it still is for my purposes considered a homicide within the confines of my department."

Knowing the reason for all the sub rosa, Jordan tried to repress a disingenuous smile:

"My Mom just told me the reason she knew it wasn't me was that the corpse was uncircumcised."

"I guess we can say that your parents' religious beliefs were rewarded by sparing your mother from future pain and suffering."

"Interesting. I never looked upon it that way. So, do I call you Captain or Mr. Broadbent?"

Broadbent saw an opportunity to make their t'ete-'a-t'ete more relaxing:

"Just call me by my first name, Damon, similar to how I greeted you."

Jordan than reacted with a bigger, more sincere, grin and a nod. Broadbent briefly explained that it was long overdue for him to bring him and his mother together, but he emphasized that the FBI had momentarily tied his hands to do this. Jordan concurred that he also had his behavior controlled and monitored, but it was something he agreed to do. Broadbent found this the right time to drill down a little:

"So, can you tell me your specific role with the department? They have been very secretive about their activities, which frankly has hindered my investigation."

What Broadbent immediately realized is that Jordan was well-scripted and schooled to be judicious and vague to all questions posed to him:

"Damon, I don't know how many questions you want to ask me. But, up front, don't be disappointed if you don't get the information from me that you are seeking. Maybe Chief Johnson could be more helpful."

"Jordan, he has been as open as a stone wall to our inquiries. Let's start with what I know about this case and see if you can fill me on the facts. A body linked to your name was found on one of our beaches, a shock to the community that we are keeping a lid on. Through eye witnesses, we discovered that two AWOL Marines were drawn to the corpse in the cabana on Windansea Beach. With corroboration from the US Marine Corps, we know their names: Yancey Bixby and Monty Crawford. Are they familiar to you? More importantly, who are they linked to?"

"Never heard of them."

"We can make a specific case that they were at the beach, and possibly linked to a bigger suspect we are trying to get a bead on—a Nazi in our midst who is up to no good. What can you tell me?"

"The FBI tell you that?"

"Yes, they confirmed that. But it would be helpful if we had a name."

"Let me just say the FBI is aware of him and is keeping close tabs."

"What can you tell me about his background? Is he a Nazi?"

"You'd be surprised who he really is. I don't know where he lives or what he does."

"Does he fit the description of someone who works with avocados? Where does he live in our area?"

"Since I have been living out here I have learned to like avocados, especially with chips and salsa."

Broadbent had to counter the sarcasm and the regression of the dialogue:

"That may be humorous to you, but this is all dead seriousness for us. I hope you appreciate that our efforts to stop a serious crime are just as genuine as the FBI's. We want to help, not hinder what has and may happen."

"Okay. I am sorry for sounding like a wise ass. But I took an oath to be loyal to my superiors. The little the FBI gave to you is not much more than I can shed light on. I hope you understand that I have been spoon fed myself as to what's going on here."

"Yes, I do understand and sympathize with you. I must say you are a faithful servant."

"Not exactly a servant that comes free --I am being paid."

"Good. That is money well-spent. So, let's move on. Who is Sela Danby? Where does she live?"

"Why is she important?"

"Come on, Damon, your mother has made her a central figure to be de-mystified. What part is she playing in this Nazi connection?"

Jordan was intransigent:

"Captain, now you are talking about a very private and personal matter. All I can tell you is that she is above suspicion and should not be considered a criminal--nor abetting one."

"Hmm. That still doesn't tell me if she is close to one. Why do I feel she is a key person who can help lead us to the kingpin Nazi living and working with avocados?"

"You are a smart cop. This has not been easy on me. I am glad this is all going to end sooner rather than later."

Jordan slipped a bit by revealing time was of the essence. But knowing that Jordan was too guarded and uncooperative, Broadbent brought the proceedings to a frustrating close. He learned little. At least what he did know was not discredited. He was gracious in defeat, knowing he needed all the good will he could gather for any unforeseen cooperation he may get from Jordan:

"Young man, I commend your spirit. My generation has been challenged by yours, but I trust you to have my back any time. Here's my card if you need my back."

Taking the card, Jordan gave a cryptic answer that may unlock a few things if followed up on:

"Damon, not only your back, but my father's as well."

San Diego and Fallbrook, September 1969

Back in San Diego the following late afternoon, Damon Broadbent got to his office after dropping off Margaret Starmont at the La Valencia. It took the ultimate in persuasion for him to convince her to not stay any longer in San Francisco. The clincher to return was a tip he got in private from FBI agent Ross Cargill after his interrogation of Jordan Starmont. Cargill told him Margaret's son would likely be in San Diego soon, which would allow the two of them to have a more meaningful and unrestricted time to be together. Broadbent pressed Cargill for more details about when and why Jordan would be venturing south. There, however, the conversation ended. It was apparent the FBI was adamant about not divulging any significant information to aid Broadbent's investigation. He still was stuck with skimpy clues: two AWOL Marines and an avocado grower.

Broadbent held a debriefing in his superior's office, Chief Howard Moore, when things quieted down in the office near 6:00 P.M. Moore wasn't particularly upset that his homicide head came back to home base without any real breakthroughs. He wanted Broadbent to relax a bit:

"Damon, loosen your tie and light one if you have one."

Broadbent took the cue and lit up a Kool. Then Moore turned to a small cabinet behind his desk, took out two glasses, a jigger, a bottle of George Dickel Tennessee Whisky, and put these items squarely on the center of his cleared desk. Moore started their session a bit off task. Holding the bottle up and bringing it closer to Broadbent, he queried:

"What's different about this labeling?"

Taking a drag from his cigarette in one hand, Broadbent took the bottle, rolling it in the other hand, and then zeroed in on the peculiarity:

"This brand spells whisky without an 'e' in it. What's the significance, Chief?"

"You are so perceptive. It seems, primarily in America and Ireland, whiskey is generally spelled with an 'e' in it. A few brands, however, George Dickel in particular, in our country dropped the letter. It's consistent with their Scottish founder, who traditionally spells his product the way you see on his label. The moral of this story: in every case, it's always about consistency."

"So, what can we say about our mysterious case that makes things consistent?"

Before the chief answered, he requested the bottle back to refill both glasses for each of them to partake. He took a sip and waxed objectively:

"When you called me yesterday right after your questioning of the Starmont lad, it is consistent with our investigation that two AWOL Marines are linked to an avocado grower in North County, and a third person. Linking the three is no longer a question—it's an answer. Sela Danby, is in the middle of this. There was no denying that. So who are these three revolving around that ties them together?"

"That's the sixty-four-thousand-dollar question I've been trying to ascertain."

"Damon, we got our man—Friedrich Vogel, alias David Percival. With you out, Detective Sandoval contacted me this morning and uncovered the name by interviewing several business people in the Fallbrook and Bonsall areas. They all point to him. It seems he's the only guy up there with a distinct English accent that grows avocados—on the Sunshine Ranch."

"Detective Sandoval does good work. Let me think. The German sounding name, Friedrich Vogel. That's consistent with being a Nazi--and in disguise, which most of them are wherever they escaped to."

Moore was beaming seeing how things were coming together with what pieces of information they had:

"And there is more to make this a consistent, corroborative identification. Several days ago, I contacted an old military buddy who works in Pentagon intelligence. I asked him what they could bring up, now that their files are becoming streamlined by computer, about both Martin Starmont and Friedrich Vogel."

"Yeah. Mrs. Starmont did say her husband was a former Navy officer."

"You ready for his?'

Moore proceeded to relate the story of Vogel escaping with a nuclear canister from a surrendering German submarine at the end of World War II. Martin chased him across country to Los Angeles, before he disappeared. It stood to reason, based on witnesses, that this mysterious stranger spoke with an English accent from the time he entered the country at the Portsmouth, New Hampshire Naval base to when he arrived on the west coast. And then another critical, consistent link from Moore:

"Damon, in the files a cooperating FBI officer in the hunt at the time in 1945 was none other than our San Francisco friend, Theodore Johnson, working at that time in L.A.."

Broadbent saw the connections and could not help himself from interrupting this revealing tale:

"Chief, this is all, as you would say, consistent, with unfinished business. Johnson now has a chance to finally, almost twenty-five years later, to collar this Nazi living among us and he enlisted the familial help of Martin's son, who confirmed his loyalty to his father at the end of my interrogation."

Moore made an emotionally charged confirmation of Broadbent's analysis:

"And dammit, about keeping us in the dark to not interfere with what looks like a personal vendetta. This is all so sad for law enforcement."

But Broadbent surmised the severity of the situation:

"Holy smokes, Chief! We are dealing with a potentially catastrophic situation with a madman threatening our community with a nuclear device."

"Exactly, Damon. And we may be looking at a doomsday clock with little time left on it."

Approaching noon the next day, it was a dangerous time for detective Rick Sandoval to be snooping around a volatile location. He got directions to the property of David Percival from a Fallbrook banker. On a bright sunny morning, he drove his cruiser through groves of avocado trees on De Luz Road, looking for a sign that said "Sunrise Ranch." When he got there, he made the turn onto a narrow asphalt road. After a quarter mile, he came to the property, which had its name spelled out in an arched frame over the driveway. Things were quiet, almost spooky. The only thing that moved was the dust stirred up by Sandoval's cruiser. He came to a stop in front of a large two-story rancho styled house. Perhaps it was an omen, but he heard a cock crow when he came to the front door. There was no doorbell or other device to signal a visitor was present. The screen door was unlocked, and he slowly opened it, with an eerie squeak to this movement. Sandoval drew back his suit jacket so he could put a hand on his holstered service revolver—just in case. He knocked even harder a second time. No answer. He turned the big brass doorknob with no results to gain entry. Then he left the front porch and circled the house, trying to peer in windows. It was fruitless because the shades and drapes were tightly drawn. However, when he walked to the rear of the property, he thought he saw someone stirring in a large open shed about twenty yards away. A bronzed looking man with a wide-brimmed straw hat, clad in denim shirt and pants came into view.

Sandoval cautiously approached him:

"¿Habla inglés?"

The response was soft and shy:

"A little."

"Okay. Let's speak a little Spanish and English."

"Sí."

"Who lives here?"

"Señor Percival."

"Do you work for him? For how long?"

"Yes. Quince anos." (Yes, fifteen years)

Seeing that the man was adept at English, he continued to speak it:

"The house is locked up tight. Where has he gone?"

"I don't know -- he will return."

"When?"

"I don't know."

"Have you seen anyone else in the house lately with Señor Percival?"

"Sí, dos hombres jovenes." (Two young men)

"And where are they?"

"With Señor Percival."

"When did they leave? Where are they going?"

"Early this month. To San Diego. They drove their three cars."

"Hmm, what color and make of the cars?"

"A Ford pick-up, color blue, a black car, and a red car – muy rápido (very fast).

Sandoval thought he struck gold after what the laborer told him. He went immediately to his car and got on the radio to page Broadbent:

"Captain, I think we have much to chew on with what I just found on an avocado farm, owned by David Percival, over."

"Rick, glad you stayed camped up there. You are getting results. Anybody home? Over."

"His house is sealed tight; window coverings block looking inside. But one of his farmhands, a migratory worker who has been with him for fifteen years, confirmed Percival had two young men stay with him recently."

Broadbent stayed on the consistency wavelength:

"With Fallbrook so close to the eastern end of Camp Pendleton, it's consistent that the two in question have to be Bixby and Crawford. What else of note did the worker tell you? Over."

"My witness told me they left early this month, driving three vehicles off the property: a blue Ford pick-up, a red sporty car, maybe a Mustang or a Pontiac GTO, and perhaps a large black sedan. Could be in the Cadillac or Lincoln class."

"Yeah, the black car could be a Lincoln, according to one Windansea witness who was there when he saw two men picked up by this vehicle. I'll get this on the APB wire immediately. What's your next step up there? Over."

"I think there may be a way in the house. There is a slanted trapdoor on the back side of the house off the rear patio that looks like it may lead into a cellar. Over?"

"Okay. But be careful. Get back to me after you leave the premises. Over and out."

Sandoval approached the trapdoor, but there was a lock on the hasp. He asked the farm hand for a hammer. He came back with something better--a maul with a weighted metal head. Sandoval struck the lock with a powerful blow, which did not break the lock but undid the hasp. Just as he opened the angled door, a force of hot air and dust blew him violently backward ten feet. When he hit the ground, the concussion made him lose consciousness for a few seconds. With debris flying in the air and raining down upon him, he felt a tug behind his suitcoat and sensed he was being dragged away from the blast. Pedro had come to his rescue and pulled him into the shed to get out of harm's way. With both of them keeping their heads down, they saw the house was leveled and in flames. Fortunately, most of the heavy materials from the house's construction blew almost straight upward and came back to earth in a mangled heap. Still dazed, Sandoval tried to get his bearings and instructed Pedro to follow him to his car, which he hoped was not buried.

Once he got there, he was in luck. He parked far enough away that only some tile shards blown off the roof of the house landed on the car. Sandoval, weakened from the explosion and likely injured internally, crawled into the cruiser and hit the radio:

"Officer down. Explosion and fire around me. Looks like it might spread into the dry hillsides and cause a major brush fire. Use radio beam frequency Quincey, Niner, four one, one to find me. Hurry. Out."

39
CHAPTER

San Diego, The Seal's Lair, San Francisco, September 1969

Rick Sandoval's call for help was picked up by the San Diego Police Department's communication hub. Miles away from the distressed officer, the SDPD radioed the San Diego Sheriff, which mobilized units from their nearby locations of Fallbrook, Poway, San Marcos, and Valley Center substations. In addition, the City of Oceanside had a cruiser about fourteen miles west of Sandoval's call beacon and sped east on Highway 76 and then went due north to Fallbrook. The first on scene were sheriff deputies from San Marcos and Valley Center. The billowing smoke in the air helped guide them as they approached the scene. The first two arriving officers came to the Sunrise ranch driveway and had their Glock service revolvers drawn as they left their car. The two other deputies from the second unit came with added firepower in the form of their Remington 12-gauge shotguns. One officer immediately hurried to Sandoval's car, with the other three taking protective positions scanning the area for other lurking adversaries. Sandoval was weak but conscious when his car door opened:

"Man, I am glad to see you. I think I am hurt inside but don't know where. I'll make it."

The rescuing deputy was reassuring:

"Don't worry, the Fallbrook hospital is nearby and has been alerted that you are on your way. Any bad guys around?"

"No, the place was deserted, save for this field hand named Pedro. He saved my ass after the house exploded."

"That's good, but we will hold him for questioning."

"All right, let me call my boss in San Diego while I still can."

Back on the car radio, Sandoval got through to Damon Broadbent's office. He wasn't there to take the call, but his assistant took the message"

"Captain, Sandoval here and assisted by County Sheriff. On way to Fallbrook Hospital. Injured but not seriously. One more thing, Percival's house explosion has ignited a brush fire. This whole area will be engulfed by flames, especially with the east winds picking up. Send Forestry Fire units ASAP."

Back in his office later that afternoon, Broadbent came up to speed as to what happened to detective Sandoval. He called the Fallbrook hospital and was apprised that the force of the explosion inflicted a ruptured spleen on his colleague. He felt better when told Sandoval's condition was stable and would require a few days for treatment and observation before any release. But the whole incident made him aware that he was dealing with a perpetrator capable of inflicting surprising and devastating blows to anyone on his trail.

With nothing further to do of any merit in Haight-Ashbury, detective Dan Herlihy also was on the flight back from San Francisco after the Jordan Starmont questioning. Broadbent called him into his office with a sense of urgency:

"Dan, after what happened to Rick on the David Percival property in Fallbrook, we know we are dealing with a deranged mind. I told you that this guy is the presumed Nazi scientist who escaped into this country with a nuclear device. He detonated one explosion, but it will pale in comparison for what he may happen with a second one. Have any of our units stopped any suspicious vehicles listed on the APB wire? This is a manhunt we cannot afford to lose."

"Captain, I just checked with the active desk. In just three hours we've stopped approximately thirty-five vehicles that match the description of the three suspicious cars. None of the drivers looked like an AWOL Marine or an older English accent individual."

"Any help from the sheriff's office or any of the other law enforcement agencies in the county?"

"A few stops, but no results."

"Keep up the vigilance--into the night. These guys just might slip up."

After Herlihy left his office, Broadbent had a woman on his mind. He dialed Margaret Starmont's room at the La Valencia, hoping she would be in just before the dinner hour.

He was in luck when he heard her subdued voice:

"Maggie, I hope you got some rest. This is a bittersweet time for you, I know. You are not with Jordan, but at least you know he is safe and working in the service of his country--a fact your husband would deem very patriotic."

Something had changed within her by being more formal with him:

"Captain, I can't say I am happy. I feel used. I am taken on a trip to see my son but can't spend enough time with him to satisfy the long absence we've had with one another. It seems we are in a tangled web."

"Yes, I know. Sometimes I feel like a heel. But I hope you appreciate the severity of the fix we are in. We are chasing a Nazi capable of horrendous things. In fact, he apparently planted a bomb in his house that nearly killed one of my investigators."

Margaret had some sympathy:

"I hope he is okay. I guess it's easier to repair our feelings than it is our bodies."

"He's going to be fine. But, again, Jordan will be back before you know it. Believe me, I will do everything in my power to have you two free to go about your personal business."

"I can understand the importance of your work. You know that I am not a heartless woman. In fact, I must tell you, when this whole dizzying world comes back into balance then I can also get to know you better."

Broadbent felt the air had been cleared when she became personal:

"Maggie, that would be my ideal. However, the present situation might be grave."

"Grave? How grave?"

He laid it on the line:

"Enough that I may not have a city to protect if this Nazi unleashes a catastrophic devise in his possession."

David Percival's plan to destroy his residence and create a regional emergency with a major brush fire was working. Being September, the driest and the hottest part of the year, there was plenty of fuel to burn in the form of water-parched grasses, chaparral, scattered eucalyptus trees, scrub oaks, and avocado trees. Just before supper, Casey Douglas returned to Seal's Lair and had the news Percival was looking for:

"Just saw a report that there is a major fire burning in the Fallbrook area. It has spread to almost 500 acres in a few hours."

When Percival heard this, he knew what it was--his timed explosion of his house was the source of the blaze. Without admitting his arson, he probed for more specifics:

"Casey, is it out of control? Is it causing a stir with law enforcement and fire fighters?"

"Right now, it was reported out of control. For sure it's requiring a major commitment of equipment and manpower. There is urgency here because there are rural residences at risk, as well as the community of Fallbrook. It's not an ordinary wildfire out in the back country."

"Anything else on this fire?"

"Yeah, it was reported by a San Diego police detective, who said it started with an explosion when he was investigating in the area."

That was a red flag for Percival. The law was getting too close by searching on his property. It only reinforced his decision to vacate his permanent residences and put up stakes in the Seal's Lair. But his suspicions were further aroused. The only two members of his cohort who knew where he lived were Yancey Bixby and Monty Crawford. Percival's paranoia was always at the surface. He couldn't really be sure, at a time when he had to, of unquestioned loyalty. To placate his doubts, he started by visiting the two Marines passing time in the living room by playing gin rummy. Douglas conveniently left the Lair to go to the commissary for the night's dinner. It gave Percival the privacy he wanted. He knew he had to be delicate as to not appear accusatory:

"Troopers, in two days we will need to perform at a high level of execution. Are you prepared and ready to meet our mission?"

Crawford replied first:

"I guess so. But it's a little different to perhaps fight on your home ground instead of a war zone."

"If it comes to a fight, Monty, don't be deceived. The country we live in is a war zone, as long as it does not support the efforts of our fighters overseas and fails to arrest and stifle dissidents who do us no good."

Percival shifted his focus:

"How about you, Trooper Bixby? What's your level of readiness?'

"That beach episode was spooky. Some unseen folks were trying to intercept us. I'm not sure we can be successful at the airport."

'Have you shared these perceptions with others?"

"No, not in our immediate group."

"So, maybe outside our group?"

"Oh, I guess I am a constant worry wart. I may have mentioned something in a letter back home to Louisiana that folks should not worry about me. My Mom cautioned that I should be wary of outsiders."

"Was I one of them?"

"No, not you. I just said you treated Monty and I kindly and had an avocado ranch. Didn't mention your name."

Bingo. Percival realized the leak, as inadvertent as it might have been. Although he recalled that Bixby did not take his oath to the group until a week after he met him, there was no good reason to impugn his fealty. Besides, he proved what he could do in a tight spot at Windansea. Rather than make a big deal of this and question Bixby further, he got off the subject by stating they would do well because they have the element of surprise. However, when the rest of the cohort was present after dinner, Percival was more demanding:

"Troopers, it's close to zero hour, when we will have the ability to make our demands with a weapon that will strike fear in the hearts of all those in authority, both civilian and military. You all know your assignments at the airport. After you pick up my son, we will take up a position in the cover of dark at the Coronado Hotel. Trooper Douglas will debrief you on specifics. Lastly, for those of you still at duty stations, I trust you will have taken leave, effective tomorrow. This will be the end of your service to the American military. From that point forward you will be dedicated to the Nazi cause. One of our demands will be that we are free to advocate our ideas as a sanctioned political party in any public forum, without the fear of arrest or legal interference. We will insist on honorable discharges for you all from the military, without any threat to court martial you. Failure to comply with our wishes will have serious consequences.

"So, now, to show our dedication to our cause, let's salute the Fuhrer."

Percival then stepped front and center before the group and exhorted: "Heil, Hitler!"

The refrain was repeated by the cohort with feeling. Although one member of his band may have provided more than he should have about his identity, Percival was confident he would pull off the greatest threat to national security in America's history. To him, the Third Reich was alive and well, and ironically, undetected and ready to strike one of its biggest and most important military bases. He then excused himself to go into Douglas's bedroom to find his bag. In the bag was his warlike costume, ready to be worn again. In two days he would look like a classic Nazi: black shirt, with a black pistol belt draped over his shoulder to his belt, his red, white, and black Swastika armband, black riding pants, black jackboots, and a black Wehrmacht field cap, with the Nazi breast eagle placed above the brim. To make him more menacing, he would have his holstered German luger on his hip. He would appear like a haunting likeness a soldier American forces thought they eradicated over twenty-four years ago.

⊰•◉•⊱

Jordan Starmont felt chagrin an hour after his mother left the San Francisco FBI office. To him, it could have gone better. On the other hand, after being questioned by Damon Broadbent, he felt it could have been worse. Sitting around Chief Theodore Johnson's desk, with Ross Cargill also in attendance, he indicated in his debriefing that he was quite comfortable about not specifically answering any of the San Diego detective's pointed questions. The Chief was more than pleased:

"Jordan, given the strain of seeing your mother after what she went through and quickly followed by the detective's interrogation, you are up to the task."

Jordan was feeling fatigue from all the duress:

"Is it okay if Ross takes me back to my place? I am a bit strung out—didn't sleep well last night."

"Sure, that's understandable. But just a few more things to confirm and go over."

"Shoot. I am fading. What you got?"

"Sela Danby and Ian Bright are scheduled to land in San Diego the night of Friday, September 13 at 11:00 P.M. To be sure you are in a position to identify her, and also picking out Bright, assuming he is he close proximity to her, you, agent Cargill, and four other agents from this office will fly to San Diego to arrive in the early afternoon. Our force will be met and will be reinforced by San Diego agent Joe Pizzo and four other staff members."

Jordan than became cynical:

"Is that enough bodies? Percival it seems slipped through your net in La Jolla."

"Not an issue. These are all top-flight personnel. Given we will be covering a tighter security area, we should avoid the curveball thrown at us on the much wider beach area. As long as our targets are on foot, we will have things under control."

"That's some good muscle, but where do the San Diego cops, especially Captain Broadbent, play a role? You have to agree the unusual activity has occurred in his backyard."

Johnson didn't like to hear support for the local police:

"Jordan, because we have one individual of interest from England, and the prime suspect who was the object of a national manhunt, this is a federal, not a local law enforcement problem. Captain Broadbent's people will be called on if needed."

"You sure you are not underestimating Percival? He's got to have some other bad guys there like he had at the beach."

"I have full confidence we will net our quarry. If need be, we will break out the long guns, available in camouflaged cases in the airport, to give us enough firepower. We will control the roadway leading to the terminal, as well to prevent any outside interference or assistance. Besides, this time it's going to work--I'm coming along to direct the capture of Percival and any other accomplice he brings along."

Jordan felt Johnson a bit arrogant and still worried that Sela Danby may be harmed in any potential abduction. He made his reservations:

"That's all well and good. But I hope you will have the safety of my sister at the top of your priorities. Bright and whoever comes to meet him are nasty people."

"Jordan, we've been well trained on how to safely intercept a bad guy who is accompanying an innocent individual like Sela."

Hearing that, Jordan excused himself and signaled Cargill to take him back to his humble hangout on Columbus Avenue. When they got into Cargill's car, Jordan could see the lack of law enforcement cooperation:

"You know, Ross, I still think the San Diego cops could be an important backup force at the airport. It's like Chief Johnson is making this personal, with the FBI front center, and unassisted."

"Jordan, you know the history here, with your father a big part of it. The Chief has lamented to me more than a few times how he regretted letting that Nazi slip through his fingers. From time-to-time, he's even taken his own vacation time to do his personal investigation to pick up the trail. But it was as cold as an iceberg. Did he tell you that when we found you, it was like a new lease on his crime fighting life?"

"No. Never did say. But he talks like a man with an exclusive inner drive. What is it?"

"It comes from an old but appropriate Italian word: 'vendetta'."

40
CHAPTER

In Route to San Diego, September 1969

Josh Hannigan had been bracing himself for a return to his homeland, one where he was a wanted man. Perth, Australia has been a safe haven for him for nearly ten months. But that was now his past, with an uncertain present in front of him the moment he stepped on American soil in Los Angeles in two days. A vulnerable English woman, Sela Danby, had captured his heart, a new experience for a man who was cautious to enter into any close relationship. However, Hannigan was not living in a simple world. The woman he was falling in love with came with unforeseen complications. It wasn't enough she was involved with someone else, Ian Bright, but this triangle was in a tangled mess that was more than high crimes and misdemeanors. The flight to America would have its risks, but once there it could be eclipsed by an apocalyptic outcome.

Hannigan squeezed what personal clothing and possessions he could into two pieces of luggage. When he arose on this morning the mirror told him his visage had changed, as it was now covered by three weeks of facial hair that was rounding into a decent beard. The passport and driver's license identification photos of the identity he assumed, Rex Murtaugh, were of a clean-shaven individual. He felt confident he could finesse his way through American customs without incident. But the hard part, which has been vexing him, was the strategic plan he needed to begin his life again in America as a free man removed from the law. If exposed upon his return, he likely faced five to ten years in prison. Given the freedom he was enjoying, incarceration was a bad option. At least the weather in Southern California was similar to Perth--warm, dry, and sometimes hot, and if things went wrong even hotter.

Across the hall from Hannigan's flat in Perth, Sela's choice to leave Australia in the company of her boyfriend was also full of uncertainty. Being held on a tight leash by Ian Bright, Sela had little wiggle room to escape the literal hold he held on her. Trusting Hannigan to help her break this bondage, by traveling to America, she was both anxious and relieved that a better future would await her as she packed her bag.

Bright had his reservations as well about the trip. Ideally, he wanted to go back to England to continue his musical preoccupation with his band. If it were not for his cooperation to assist his step-father, David Percival, he would rather be traveling to Europe than to North America. However, of these three disparate passengers, Bright's journey was significant by not what personal items he packed in a suitcase. The oddity was an eighteen-inch by eighteen-inch carton he would tote as a carryon item on the airplane. It was more than a Pandora's Box, for it had the potential to ignite an explosion of mass destruction. The world had only seen such a blast twice before in 1945 Japan. It was headed for a third cataclysm in 1969 southern California.

It was an early wake-up call for the three westward passengers. To keep things above suspicion, Hannigan left his flat at 4:00 AM by cab. He did not want to get too close to Sela at this point—even if by chance, the happenstance that got them together in the first place. She and Bright departed about forty-five minutes later. The Perth Airport terminal building was opened in 1962, in time for the 1962 Perth Commonwealth Games. On the exterior east side of the terminal was a large courtyard with gardens, grassed areas, and a pond for Black Swans, the state emblem of Western Australia. There was an outside viewing area upstairs to observe departing aircraft on the nearby tarmac and arriving passengers below. Hannigan checked in and needed to get a bit of air to calm himself, so he went to the viewing area. Dressed in a new light leather black jacket, he needed to zip it to shield him from the cool morning breezes generated both by nature and the engines of nearby aircraft. At daybreak, Hannigan had enough light to spot two floors beneath him Bright and Sela vacating a cab at the curbside. Simply dressed in a mid-length light blue jacket and wearing a scarf, she still sparkled in the dawn's limited glow. Bright looked like a Sharpie, dressed in monkey boots, denims, and a tight black leather jacket. His hair was slicked back with a pointed crown, the look of a skinhead more than a Sharpie. The driver took out two large suitcases from the trunk. When Bright got out to pay the driver, he set his carton next to the bags. An unsolicited airport baggage handler placed all three items on a cart. When Bright saw this, he stopped the movement to the terminal and abruptly took the carton off the cart. Hannigan understood the defensive posture Bright was taking. He did not want this item out of sight and touch.

This was going to be a long time in the air. Because Perth was on the other side of the International Dateline, they would take off and land on the same day, following the sun from their 7:00 A.M. take-off to their final arrival at night in San Diego at 11:00 P.M. The fifteen hour difference between Western Australia and western North America created the ultimate jet lag. Hannigan went down to the main terminal after Sela and Bright had entered it after he first saw them. Hannigan kept his distance from the two, but, as they had agreed, he and Sela would try to at least exchange glances and some furtive contact. When Sela and Bright checked their bags, and obtained their boarding passes, Hannigan followed them as they made their way to their gate. Terminal one was not that large, mostly for Qantas, Queensland and Northern Territory Aerial Service, flights and an occasional arrival for BOAC, British Overseas Airways Corporation. It seemed all the passengers in the boarding area were bound for Sydney on Flight 235.

There was a stir when the call was made to board the plane that would take them to Sydney, about five hours in the air. Hannigan let Bright and Sela board first. When Hannigan got into the cabin, he walked down the aisle and saw Bright in first class. Trying not to make eye contact with him, he surreptitiously directed his vision at the carton Bright had placed at his feet, where there was enough room to stow the item under the seat in front of him. That looked like the modus operandi Bright would use to keep his vital package close at hand on every leg of the journey. Proceeding up the aisle, he saw Sela some fifteen rows further back in coach. As Hannigan made his way to his seat, he smiled at Sela and simply patted her on the shoulder in passing.

The Qantas stewardesses, dressed in powder blue two-piece suits with a rounded hat with a curled brim around it, were hospitable and tried to seat the passengers as expeditiously as possible. After the safety instructions for the Boeing 707 aircraft were given, Hannigan simply took a deep breath in his aisle seat, not looking to make conversation to a young couple seated inside of him. His mind was moving as fast as the plane's speed thrusting down the runway to lift off the ground and into the air.

Hannigan prepared a note for Sela, which he put in her hand as she made her way back to the aft restroom about two hours into the flight:

> *Sela:*
>
> *Things going according to plan. You are in my sight and will be until we get to the United States. What is Bright's disposition? Has he talked much about the transfer of his package to his father? What's his next move after that?*
>
> *Please reply below and have the stewardess bring it to me in seat 30D. Have no fear!*
>
> *Rex*

Sela gently tapped him gently on his shoulder as she passed him to return to her seat. About twenty minutes later, the Qantas stewardess gave Hannigan Sela's response.

> *Rex:*
>
> *I am holding up, knowing that you are close. Ian has been grouchy for the last three days. Today no different. Think he wants to rid himself of the box as soon as he can. He's still vague as to what happens after he delivers it to his father. Get some rest.*
>
> *Sela*

Later in the flight, Hannigan managed to doze off for perhaps thirty minutes. He awoke as the plane was descending into Sydney. All along he has been plotting what he would do when this long journey would end. Coming to a halt and ready to deplane, Hannigan had to be more vigilant to keep within view of Sela, as she and Bright briskly walked through the larger and busier Sydney airport. The airport was undergoing an expansion, so there were construction workers to contend with and some narrow temporary passages to navigate through the concourse to the connecting gate to Los Angeles, Qantas Flight 150. The layover was only an hour, so, as bad as Hannigan needed to go to the restroom, he held firm until he saw Sela and Bright take separate seats in the gate area. He got relief just in time once he made it to the men's room.

Because Hannigan wasn't up for breakfast on the flight to Sydney, he now was caved in--he had not really eaten much since last night. The coffee on the plane from Perth exacerbated his hunger. Seeing an airport concession stand, he went for the quick fix of Bowen Mangos, a variety from the town of the same name in Northern Queensland. The British Army would bring the fruit from India and they gave them as gifts to the locals. He supplemented it with half a dozen Anzac biscuits, which also had a history. This iconic staple had high nutritional value and stayed fresh for a long time when they were given to Australian soldiers in the Gallipoli campaign in World War I. It gave him some refreshing vigor as he surveyed the seating area to catch a glimpse of Sela, looking at her lovely face in a small hand mirror. She looked back at Murtaugh and gave him a smile. He was relieved that she did not seem tense.

The call to board the second leg of the trip was made onto another Boeing 707. This would be a long flight--ten hours in the air. Fortunately, it would be broken in two for a refueling stop in Honolulu, Hawaii. The seating arrangement was similar. Bright was seated in first class, Sela was seated this time twelve rows behind in coach, and Hannigan's seat was six rows behind Sela. The plane was loaded with it seemed like a mix of Aussies and Americans, the latter with an anticipatory air about them of returning home. The same could not be said for Hannigan. This was the second time Hannigan had experienced the Pacific Ocean. However, this time, in the air, he was above it. The first time he was on it, on a tramp steamer that eventually brought him to Perth. In these moments of high altitude solitude, he had a chance to become introspective. The biggest question he had to ask himself was if he was a changed man from the time he was at sea to where he was now in the clouds. He thought so, if only by forsaking the villainy of the crimes he inflicted in San Francisco at the end of 1968. Finding Sela was an epiphany for him. Now he believed that his heart had softened, he could care deeply for another, and he was ready to atone for his past sins.

Given the length of the flight, the passengers were served two meals, with intermittent snacks and beverages. Hannigan thought about buying a cocktail before one of the meals, but he wanted to be as sober as a judge with the quick thinking and moves he was pondering to make upon arrival in the USA. He paged a stewardess and forwarded a note with some injected humor to Sela:

> *Sela:*
>
> *I saw you get up and stretch during the refueling stop and wander over to Bright. How's he holding up, given he doesn't want to be where he is? It's going to be a time warp when we land in LA. Just want to assure you that I am staying sharp to keep you under my wing when things are up in the air. Bad pun, huh?*
>
> *Need and want you.*
>
> *Rex*

Sela responded:

> *Rex*
>
> *You are a dear-- and a wordsmith, too. Ian may have had a few too many drinks on this flight. Not sure if he is drunk. Said he wants to sleep off what has got him in its grip. I've got a dull headache, but am trying to stay alert for what awaits*

us. Stay close to me when we arrive in LA and then on our way to San Diego.

Need you--more than you know.

Sela

The note gave Hannigan hope that Sela was bonding to him. More importantly, at this critical moment, he now believed that Bright's condition would play into his hands when the time came. Perhaps the alcohol would debilitate Bright's physical well-being. To protect himself, Hannigan had thought of buying a pistol before he left Perth to take on the trip. But that had unforeseen difficulties. It would be hard enough to resemble Rex Murtaugh from his passport photo. If caught with a weapon, he was done for. He was best prepared to use guile and deception with an idea that just crystalized in his scheming mind. Its first implementation stage began with a final note to Sela when the stewardess announced they would be landing in twenty minutes at Los Angeles International Airport, LAX:

Sela:

When we land, don't leave your seat until I reach you. I'll follow behind you as we vacate the plane. Meet Bright and go to customs. Again, I will walk right behind you both as we go to customs to gain entry into the US. Then we must proceed to baggage claim to re-check bags for the flight to San Diego. Remember. I'll be close. Ask Bright to take your bags off the carousel. What happens next will be a better way for you to finally meet Jordan. Show me a nod if you understand.

I'm here for you. Life is about to be better!

Rex

Hannigan wasn't sure he sold the idea, given that it might disrupt Sela's plan to meet an unseen half-brother. But it did not take long after she read the message to turn her lovely face up the aisle towards him with a nod of affirmation. It helped that the approach to LA was a bit bumpy. Perhaps it might tax Bright's hungover condition. On the plane's final approach, unknown to the other, Hannigan and Sela had accelerated heartrates as the aircraft was descending over thousands of ground lights beneath them. It was approaching 8:00 P.M. but LA defied nature's growing darkness after dusk with a radiant glow. Just before the wheels touched down, Hannigan could see through the window a distinctive airport building that looked like a flying saucer that had landed on four arched legs. It was an especially designed theme building for the airport. Hannigan just hoped his legs would be as steady and sturdy as the unique piece of space age architecture.

With the plane now stopped at the jetway, the departing passengers were instructed to follow the signs in the terminal to United States Customs. Because the three of them had a connecting domestic flight, the three were given priority near the head of the line. They were required to reclaim their bags, even though they were checked to San Diego. Hannigan was right behind Sela and was within earshot as a bleary-eyed Bright greeted her:

"Sela, I'm glad we are almost there. I'll need a day or two to recover."

That was music to Hannigan's ears. The bloke was not doing well. Were any of them prepared to satisfactorily answer a customs agent's pointed questions upon showing one's passport?

"What is your purpose of your trip?"

"How long do you intend to stay?"

"Where will you be staying?"

"What is your occupation?"

And then a loaded question that Hannigan was close by to see how Bright would answer:

"Do you have anything to declare?"

Bright must have been well-schooled for his passing answer:

"I have no alcohol, tobacco, or foodstuffs."

Whew, Hannigan thought. Bright finessed getting the carton through. Sela passed as well. When it came to his turn, Hannigan tried to look calm and collected.

He stated he was returning home after an extended stay in Australia, he was going back to his home in San Diego, was an export-importer, and had nothing to declare. The customs agent took a look at Murtaugh's passport photo, giving a puzzling look at Hannigan in his fuzzy-faced condition, and gave his decision:

"Looks like you need a shave. Welcome home, Mr. Murtaugh."

Hannigan had an internal sigh of relief that almost buckled his knees. After passing this critical test, he quickly caught up to Sela and Bright who were apace to get to baggage claim. Once the two of them got there, bags were available for pickup on the metallic conveyor belt. Hannigan had no intention to get his bags, but he stepped right behind Sela as she looked for hers. In a minute she spotted some bags, with the Red, White, and Blue sticker colors of the Union Jack British flag on the sides, and gave her command:

"Ian, please get our bags."

Then Bright made a fatal error. He dutifully put the carton on the ground next to Sela and walked about ten steps to the belt. With his back to Sela, Hannigan's strategic opportunity availed itself. He picked up the carton in one hand and clutched Sela's in the other.

He told her:

"Sela, we are on our way to free yourself from this creep. Just hold me tight and don't look back."

He whisked her away through a door that said ground transportation. Still, looking for Sela's suitcase, Bright was unaware that his female companion and his critical parcel were gone. Hannigan saw a cab parked at the curb. With the prized possession in tow, he opened the back door and gave her a little nudge to get her in. Sela was aghast and was confused:

"Rex, I am supposed to meet Jordan in San Diego, not get off here."

Hannigan said nothing and simply squeezed her hand as the driver called back:

"Where to, folks?"

Hannigan was comfortable in his skin that he had Sela to himself and was perhaps foiling a dastardly plot.

"Sela, rest easy. Don't worry. Jordan will be in our sights. We are just taking an indirect route. Driver, how much is the fare to take a longer ride than usual?"

"That depends. I have a reasonable rate. Where to?"

Looking at Sela with a look of reassurance to her, Hannigan said:

"San Diego."

41
CHAPTER

San Diego, September 13, 1969

The cab carrying Josh Hannigan and Sela Danby from the Los Angeles airport left the terminal for Sepulveda Boulevard, which led to a faster arterial—southbound on the 405 Freeway for San Diego. Hannigan negotiated a $75 fare with the driver to get them there. But Sela was not in a bargaining mood:

"Rex, what's this all about? I have to meet Jordan, which I can't do now."

Hannigan tried to rationalize his unexpected move:

"Sela, I could not take the chance that you would fall victim to David Percival when we got to San Diego by plane. Ian and the detonator is what he wants. You would only be in the way. Who knows what they would do to you?"

"But that is not what Jordan and I agreed to. You must know it is important for us to finally meet."

Hannigan drew closer to Sela to speak in a low voice in confidence:

"That's what we are going to do--at a less dangerous time and place. A safer plan is for us to go to the San Diego Police Department and explain who we are and to be assured that the detonator will not be used for mass destruction. Sela, don't you realize we may have saved thousands of people by what we just did?"

Sela reflected for an instant on the profound statement she just heard:

"Well, yes, I suppose the greater good is always best. But would not the federal people Jordan is working with be informed of our next steps?"

Hannigan did not want anything to do with a law enforcement component that likely had him on their "Wanted List". He would take his chances with the local police who could do what they wanted with the detonator, but only if they agreed to his terms of surrender of it. He needed time to talk in confidence with Sela as to his next steps:

"Driver, is there an open restaurant we can stop at some point?"

"Yeah, there is place called Tiny Naylor's about twenty minutes away when we come to Orange County. Open all night."

"That's fine. I'll even buy you breakfast if you step on it."

That prompted the driver to rev up to 70 MPH. He had company, for more than a few drivers were passing him on a roadway with a racetrack reputation to get people around the vast Los Angeles basin sooner rather than later.

When they arrived at the restaurant, the driver went to the counter and Hannigan and Sela found a booth. It was after midnight, but the place was busy on a late Friday night. Hannigan ordered coffee, but right now he needed something stiffer for what he was about to dramatically reveal:

"Sela, remember back in Perth we talked about secrets. You were very open to me, but I was not as candid. But first let me just say that what I will tell you in no way will jeopardize your safety. You are too precious to me and I want you in my life."

Sela could see the seriousness in his face:

"Rex, in the last few minutes, believe it or not, I have taken stock. I am ready for anything on this whirlwind ride I have been on ever since I got involved with Ian Bright."

Hannigan caught an opportune respite to gather himself when the waitress interrupted and wanted to take their order. Sela just wanted dried toast; Hannigan ordered eggs and toast, instructing the waitress that he also would cover the cab driver's order. As keyed up as both were, they each wanted coffee. After ordering, Hannigan cozied up to Sela's body, put his arms around her, and made an impactful nonverbal impression by giving her a deep kiss, something he had wanted to do for days. Sela was responsive to the emotional gesture. Because Hannigan had thought this through more than a little, he had enough composure to lay it on the line in a low voice:

"Trust me now and allow me to explain. Rex is not my name. My true identity is Josh Hannigan, and I am wanted by the FBI for some wrongdoing in 1968 I did in San Francisco."

Sela leaned back in the booth in stunned amazement. But Hannigan continued as calmly as he could:

"I stole the identity of Rex Murtaugh on a steamer that came to Perth. I got off the ship and started the life you came into when we met there."

Sela was perceptive:

"So this is why you are avoiding the FBI?"

"That's part of it. But I hope you will understand that I am on my way for redemption and to make amends with past wrongdoing. I think the best way is to try and cut a deal with the police. Whether the San Diego cops know it or not, their city is at great risk if Percival ever gets this detonator."

Sela thought he was vulnerable:

"Cut a deal? Are you in a position of strength to do this?"

"I have a hill to climb. The way I look at it, I likely can be convicted of kidnapping, drug dealing, and possibly extortion."

Sela gasped when she heard this, thinking she left one bad seed, Ian Bright, for another, Josh Hannigan. But he continued, knowing he had to dissipate the doubt she likely had from him now with a shocking revelation:

"Sela, I did something wrong, now I can atone by offering this bartering chip, the detonator, in exchange for either reducing or eliminating some of the charges against me. When you compare what I did to what destruction David Percival could inflict, it's night and day. I would hope the law would see it's as a remorseful individual who has now converted into a true patriot, rather than an outlaw who needs to be punished to the fullest."

"Rex, I mean, Josh. What should I call you?"

He instructed her immediately:

"Remember I told you when we come to the States that we might change our names. Well, to reinforce honesty, I'm back to Josh."

"Okay, Josh. But are you persuasive enough to sell your worth?"

"After we get out of here and get back on the road, I'll instruct the driver to bring us to an audience that will be sympathetic, if not downright thankful that we are coming to them with our incredible story."

"Will they have some influence? Would they give you a break--legally?"

"It's a gamble, but with their city threatened as never before, I have to think it's the best place to start--the San Diego Police Department."

"But, Josh, again, what about Jordan Starmont?"

"He's waiting for you at the San Diego airport. But when you don't show he's no longer needed by the FBI. Without you next to him, they likely can't intercept Bright. They would likely have to question all the departing passengers to bag him. They might get him in the process. I'm sure the local police will bring Jordan to you if we request it."

"Will this work?"

"It has to. It's likely a bittersweet homecoming for me, but a new beginning for you."

Ian Bright waited longer than he wanted for Sela Danby's suitcase at the baggage claim conveyor at the Los Angeles Airport. He still felt hungover from his airplane drinking to feel levelheaded. It did not register with him that leaving his crucial carton unattended, even for a moment, would be a serious mistake. He had to think Sela would be a loyal temporary guardian of it. With all the luggage in tow, he turned to where he was and saw no one there. Serious consternation came over him. Where was Sela? Where was his package? What would his step-father, David Percival, say or do to him? What should he do now? He left the bags and made his search around three other conveyors, which had few suitcases circling on them and no passengers nearby to claim them. Now with a fearful sweat enveloping him, he dashed outside the door that led to ground transportation. Several people were next to a cab stand. He asked each of them:

"Have you seen a lovely lass in the last few minutes carrying a box?"

No one could help him. He queried a half-dozen parked cab drivers, but they were expecting fares, not Bright's frantic questions. He found a curbside skycap and brought him back to the suitcases and accompanying them to the respective PSA gate for the connecting San Diego flight in another hour. Maybe Sela went ahead to this point without him. Still not there. Did she take ill and perhaps go to a restroom? Bright checked with the PSA attendant and asked if she had checked in. An answer he did not want to hear:

"Not yet."

He was an emotional mess, to say nothing of the physical malady pounding in his hungover head. Trying to think clearly, he decided to take a seat and wait. There was no need to check-in if she hadn't done so. Time raced by. The first call for boarding PSA McDonnell Douglas DC-9 aircraft was made thirty minutes before departure. Bright was close to where passengers gave their boarding passes for admittance to the plane. A few young girls were among them, but no one as pretty and winsome as Sela. Her absence was getting serious. But he stood firm. He was not going on the plane without her, and more importantly, without the carton.

The final call was made, with Bright frozen in fear. Standing close to the check-in station, the attendant asked him:

"We are about to close the door for entry onto the aircraft. Are you on this flight?"

Then, amidst all the internal turbulence he was feeling, Bright decided upon his radical next steps. He thought: was I a naïve dupe for a man who really has never been in my life and now comes into it asking me to partake in a plot that was unthinkable if executed? Percival's persuasive powers with money clouded Bright's judgment. And, at this trenchant moment, was it all compounded by Sela's likely abandoning him? And, if she took off with the carton, would she betray or implicate him? His mind was made up for a new aviation direction to get him back to his comfort zone of music and zany non-conformist confidantes. He asked the PSA staffer about the first day of the rest of his life:

"Could you kindly direct me to the airline in the terminal that books flights to London."

⊹⊱◉⊰⊹

The day of reckoning was upon the forces of good and evil. The anticipated arrival of a calamitous device was awaited by David Percival and his band of Nazis. The interception of it by FBI forces was lying in wait for it in the terminal of San Diego's Lindbergh Field, conveniently located near the downtown area and across the bay to the Coronado peninsula, which was the home of the Seal's Lair. Both groups had positioned their personnel to act either for or against this transfer.

For Percival, he would wait in hiding in the Seal's Lair on the Coronado Naval base, as his compliant pawns headed to the airport. Not sure if the description of Percival's three vehicles, the Lincoln sedan, the GTO sports car, and the Ford pick-up, were known by the law, he decided to send his people in Trooper Casey Douglas's cream-colored Chevrolet Camaro and Trooper Bobby Montag's beat up light green Ford Fairlane sedan. Douglas transported Troopers Yancey Bixby and Monty Crawford. Montag's group, which included Grady Dunhill, would be back-up support to Douglas. If need be, Montag had enough room in his car to pick-up Bixby and Crawford. They synchronized their watches to ensure their timing. Trooper Mack Smith and Curtis Wyatt, the youngest of the group, stayed behind in the Lair with Percival.

All the outbound troopers were armed with pistols, concealed under their Navy work jackets. For added firepower, Douglas had the two M-16 automatic rifles fully loaded in his trunk. To give the force a look of uniformity, each man wore a Navy-blue baseball cap so they could be identified at a distance by one another. Under cover of darkness, about 9:00 P.M., Douglas drove to the Lindbergh Field terminal off of Harbor Drive to let Bixby and Crawford get out at the curb. From there, Douglas drove to Harbor Island, a man-made peninsula created in 1961 from harbor dredgings, where he could park anonymously in a restaurant parking lot. To avoid detection, he would not approach the airport terminal until 11:30 P.M., when Bixby and Crawford should have Ian bright in their clutches and the all-important detonator. If they were not at the curb, Douglas would circle to eventually pick them up. If that failed, or if Douglas was somehow impeded, Montag would come from the east off the Pacific Coast Highway and drive west onto Harbor Drive to the terminal. The plan was redundant in the event of contingencies, but this was all predicated on the expectation that Bright's PSA flight would have an 11:00 P.M. arrival. When Bixby checked at the PSA counter, the flight from LAX was on time. Then he and Crawford were instructed to go and wait for Bright's appearance at baggage claim. To not draw attention, they went to a snack bar that was still open. They would only proceed to the PSA baggage conveyor once the Los Angeles flight came in.

┼══ ◎ ══┼

But there was another force ready in waiting for the same important passenger. FBI Chief Theodore Johnson had a team of agents strategically scattered throughout the terminal. Included in his group was Jordan Starmont, who would be vital to identify an arriving Sela Danby, who hopefully was in the company of Ian Bright. The day before the FBI working with the airport port authority had shotguns hidden at designated terminal counters. To blend in with the average person in the terminal, Johnson's crew were dressed casually, wearing jeans, khakis, or polyester pants, with long sleeve tops, sweaters, or light jackets. Two lead agents, Ross Cargill and Joe Pizzo, wore San Diego Padres baseball caps. At their side would be Jordan Starmont, dressed in a plain grey sweatshirt and olive-green slacks. Only Johnson, at a command post at the PSA desk, was wearing a suit, topped by a black fedora.

Lindbergh Field was not particularly large, with a rectangular main building for check-in and baggage claim. From it several concourse arms lead to the connecting passenger gates. Cargill, Pizzo, Jordan, and four other agents were positioned outside the arriving gate for PSA Flight 2777 from Los Angeles. Various others were assigned in the concourse and the main terminal, but they did not think it necessary to cover the baggage claim area, which meant Bixby and Crawford may not be spotted. The FBI did not want to locate there because they hoped to tail their target to wherever he ventured through the terminal or egress to be picked-up— probably by David Percival. Externally, two unmarked cars and a boxy truck, which was essentially an armored car, were parked at curbside. At 9:30 P.M., agents questioned individuals entering the terminal as a passenger, well-wisher, or someone outside at the curb to make a pick-up. Not knowing that Bixby and Crawford were safely inside, Johnson thought he had all bases covered.

It was 11:00 P.M. on the button when the high-pitched jet sounds of PSA Flight 2777 approached to dock at the Lindbergh Field jetway. To confirm if Bright and Sela were on their way, the FBI contacted customs up in Los Angeles. They corroborated that the two cleared their station almost two hours ago. Cargill and Pizzo had their men in position to look for their quarry the moment passengers entered the terminal. But the key operative was Jordan Starmont, standing next to Cargill, with the only set of eyes who could identify Sela Danby. Cargill had him primed ten minutes before the plane landed:

"Jordan, now we want nothing to happen to your half-sister, Sela. Let's stay back a bit and have the departing passengers stroll by us. Once you identify Sela, poke me and quietly point her out to me. But no sudden moves. When I lift my cap off it's the signal to our team to get behind them about ten paces. We'll follow where they take us."

"So you don't intercept Bright at this point?"

"Right, he's the little fish hoping to lead us to the 'Kingfish', perhaps Percival waiting to pick them up. Other agents in the terminal will be alerted that we are on the hunt and will provide reinforcement on our flanks and up ahead. We make our move when they are approached by who is there to greet them."

"And Sela?"

"When we intercept our target, you will tail off and Agent Pizzo and I will remove her from Bright's proximity and get her out of harm's way. Stay back and stay put. We don't want a hair from your young head ruffled as we make the collar. It's good the airport is basically empty at this time--the PSA flight will be the last one in with the airport's flight arrival limitations."

At 11:10 P.M. the first of eighty-six passengers made their way off the plane. Most were carefree recreation travelers, coming to San Diego to enjoy its many recreational amenities for the weekend and beyond. The first twenty or so looked pedestrian and no one caught Jordan's eye, scanning for a brown-haired young beauty. No woman could match that description as half the plane was emptied. Cargill was getting antsy. He nudged Jordan and whispered:

"She hasn't come yet, right?"

He nodded and was also becoming a little unnerved. Finally, the last arrivals, two boisterous couples who started their holiday on the plane with potent potables, passed by. Cargill knew something was wrong. He immediately bypassed the boarding station counter and ran down the jetway to the plane's entrance door, where three stewardess and the pilot and co-pilot were ready to leave. He confirmed his intrusion by flashing his badge:

"FBI. Is the plane empty? Anyone else back there?"

The flight crew said they did a final inspection and verified the plane was empty, save for some baggage being unloaded below. Cargill ran back to Pizzo. He told him to alert all agents to be on the lookout for anyone suspicious and stop them for questioning. Chief Johnson could see his people scurrying around with serious looks on their faces, as if a wild animal was on the loose.

Meanwhile, at baggage claim Bixby and Crawford saw no one that matched Bright's description. Fearing another trap, Percival ordered them to leave their station once it became apparent Bright may not show. Always the doubting type, Percival was pressing his luck putting so much faith in a young man he really did not know well. If things went similar to the Windansea episode, he had several contingency plans, only known to him. Not seeing Bright, the Marines asked the baggage handler if all bags were on the conveyor. Once he confirmed that they left through the automatic doors to the outside walk and began walking briskly east looking for Douglas's car. They were in luck, Douglas flashed his lights when he saw them, and they hopped in and drove off, past unsuspecting FBI vehicles at the curb. Several minutes later, the FBI sealed off all ingress and egress to the terminal and stopping approaching vehicles.

Bixby and Crawford were dumbfounded again. Bixby said:

"Casey, this is a bunch of dangerous shit. We risk our necks for a second time and no results. Let's get our asses back to the Lair."

Following Douglas in support, Montag drove to the terminal when he saw ahead of him only two individuals, not three, get into Douglas's car. While following Douglas, in his rear-view mirror, he saw barricades across the road way and flashing lights. He knew the plan had not been executed. By the skin of their teeth the neo-Nazis missed the dragnet. Evading detection was no consolation. They all knew Percival would likely be incensed when they returned empty-handed, not so much with a person, but a package that he wanted dearly in his possession inside the Seal's Lair.

Disappointed rage was also affecting Chief Johnson, with a reddened face, as Cargill, Pizzo, and an amused Jordan Starmont came to the command post. He inveighed:

"What the hell happened? Jordan, are you sure you did not see this Sela Danby girl?"

"Chief, no one I saw came close to a young, attractive girl--and we had a good look at everyone."

"Okay. Cargill, have your people halt everyone leaving or trying to enter the airport for questioning. Blockade the roadway and stop any car or taxi stopping to pick up passengers. If passengers claim they need to get to their cars in long term parking, follow them to their cars and search their vehicles."

The net Johnson had to catch a Nazi was failing again before his very eyes, as agents tried to obey his fast, furious, and almost unrealistic orders. After ninety frenetic minutes, there wasn't a trace of Ian Bright to apprehend or confiscate, although one of the agents pulled the last unclaimed suitcase of Sela Danby off the carousel. When Johnson got the news, he lamented by pounding on the PSA check-in counter:

"Damn, damned, and more damned!"

Jordan thought this was becoming an inept comedy, the second time around. He had to be careful to not reveal his cynicism. Standing close to a perplexed Johnson, he asked an innocent, profound question:

"Chief, are you going to need me any longer?"

Johnson took a deep anguished breath and barked:

"Kid, get out of here, but be sure you check in daily with Pizzo's office as to your whereabouts. Now go home to your mother!"

42
CHAPTER

San Diego, September 14, 1969

It was early morning, and Damon Broadbent was having a fitful sleep in his modest two-bedroom apartment in the North Park section of San Diego. It didn't help that he smelled a hint of smoke wafting through his open window on a warm evening. The burning residue of the Fallbrook fire was a reminder that David Percival was always in the air. Being close to his downtown office, it was convenient for him not to travel far from work, which was keeping him chained to either his desk or mobile duties around the area and depriving him of sleep. As he pondered in bed, his thoughts drifted to any number of matters, which affected both the head and the heart. The mental concerns centered on what he considered one of the worst performances of his professional career as a homicide detective. He had only gathered a few significant facts about a Nazi in his city with malevolent intentions. With little to go on, especially after Jordan Starmont was a disappointing source of information, it was unnerving to know that the unthinkable could happen imminently. After one of his competent detectives, Rick Sandoval, was nearly killed in Fallbrook several days ago on Percival's property, it was apparent there was something of great magnitude to hide from public view.

When it came to matters of the heart, he was spinning his wheels trying to curry favor with Margaret Starmont, a woman who came to mind often during the course of a day. She had her priorities straight. Her son, Jordan, was at the top of the list. Although sending some flirtatious overtures his way, Broadbent had work to do. Unless he could assure Maggie that Jordan was no longer connected to the FBI, he had little hope to really endear himself to her. With Jordan joined at the hip to the FBI, this likely meant Percival had to be arrested and prevented from performing a horrendous act. Right now, that prospect looked desperate.

Not an overly religious man, Broadbent was to the point of asking for divine intervention. His look to the heavens was about to be answered. It was almost 3:30 A.M. when his telephone rang. Insomniac for the last hour, he was clear-headed to hear the best news he's had since he took Maggie to the morgue almost two weeks ago:

"Captain Broadbent. This is officer Frank Oliver calling from the night desk at headquarters. Sorry to awake you at this hour, but I think I have something urgent you should know."

"Yes, officer Oliver, I was instructed to be called with anything of importance. What's brewing?"

"Well, a man and a young woman, walked into the station out of the blue and have been revealing some information that pertains to your investigation about that Nazi, David Percival. In fact, the young man said he has something in his possession that could save our city."

He sat upright in bed and pressed the phone close to his ear:

"You got names?"

"Sure the guy is Josh Hannigan and the young lass is Sela Danby."

Broadbent almost screamed on the telephone when he heard the last name and barked orders:

"Sela Danby! I've been trying to locate her for days. Tell them not to move. Make them comfortable and don't intimidate them at all. Put them in my office. Get the coffee on. Find something for them to eat. Send a squad to that all-night deli on India Street if need be. I'll be there in less than thirty minutes. Got any idea where they came from?"

"Yeah, I must admit I've never had people come from this location before--Perth, Australia."

He dropped the telephone and sprang into action. Dressed in skivvies, it didn't take Broadbent long to find his trousers, get a light sweater on, and jump into a pair of penny loafers without socks. He felt he hit the jackpot, if only getting close to Sela Danby, high on Maggie Starmont's need to know list. Despite light early morning traffic, when he got to his unmarked police cruiser, he put his siren on to not be impeded. Getting to his office in minutes, he quickly parked his car and made a jog down the tiled hall to his office. The door was open, allowing him to see two huddled figures sitting side-by-side on his worn, leather sofa. They were strangers in the night, but were about to reveal even stranger things that would make Broadbent start to connect the dots. He greeted them by warmly taking their hands:

"My name is Captain Damon Broadbent, in charge of investigating the activities of David Percival, a Nazi threatening our community. I really appreciate the fact you came to our office. Our work to protect the public depends on the assistance we get from the public at large. Thank you for being here."

Hearing this, Hannigan and Sela, both tired and a bit nervous, made a collective sigh of comfort, invigorated by some coffee and sandwiches officer Oliver provided for them. Sipping his cup of morning joe, Broadbent tried to temper his excitement by politely starting his interrogation:

"So, can you kindly introduce yourselves and convey your story, with no fear of intimidation from my office?"

Considering that Sela seemed overwhelmed by what happened ever since they stepped off the plane at LAX, Hannigan held her hand by making some brief remarks, careful not to share any confidential information at this point:

"My name is Josh Hannigan, an American citizen who had been living in Perth, Australia for the last nine months. I am currently traveling with Sela Danby, who I recently met in Perth. We are here to help your investigation."

Broadbent nodded his head and then beckoned Sela to speak. She spoke softly and briefly volunteered:

"I am Sela Danby, and as Josh said we are traveling together. As you might guess by my accent, England is my home, born in Tunbridge Wells."

When Broadbent heard the young woman identify herself, it confirmed his exhilaration that he was ready to take dramatic steps to nab Percival, with a side benefit of fulfilling Maggie Starmont's request to find Sela. He brought the two of them up to speed by reviewing what his investigation has discovered, from a corpse falsely thought to be Jordan Starmont, identifying several accomplices of Percival's Nazi band, and uncovering his hideout in Fallbrook, careful not to reveal at this juncture that he likely had a nuclear device in his possession. He then became pointed with his questions:

"So, for both of you, why did you come to us, and what can you tell us about David Percival and anyone connected with him?"

Hannigan, more composed and to enhance his value to the case, answered first:

"By chance, Sela and I met in Perth. We struck up a friendship and she told me that she came to Australia with Percival's son, Ian Bright, and told me that she is the half-brother of Jordan Starmont, who we hope is safe and well after, as you said, he was falsely presumed to be dead."

Broadbent confirmed that Jordan was fine and encouraged Hannigan to go on:

"Bright, Sela, and I all flew to the states on the same flights. But, as Sela will tell you, she was in a dangerous situation. I took some emergency steps to come to your department to get Sela away from Bright and find protection for her."

Broadbent directed his attention to Sela:

"Ms. Danby, tell us more about this, especially any recent contacts you may have had with Jordan."

"First of all, I trust Josh and, with his help, I am now glad that I am away from Ian Bright. With regard to Jordan, we have exchanged letters, telegrams and talked on the telephone. I made a connection with him when I discovered we are the children of Jordan's father, Martin, who I called earlier this year before he died."

Broadbent was amazed how the unusual state of events linked Jordan and Sela together. He queried:

"So, when you finally made contact with your father, Martin Starmont, what did he encourage you to do?"

"He apologized that he could not see me, and requested that I also not contact his wife, but he did want me to connect with Jordan. When he answered one of my letters, I learned Jordan was working with your Federal Bureau, and somehow they knew I was in a relationship with Ian, who as it turns out is David Percival's son."

At this point she began to cry and tearfully and meekly admitted:

"It's not pleasant to know that we are both illegitimate offspring."

Broadbent placated her with a paternal touch by gently holding her hand:

"Ms. Danby, that is no shame. You are first and foremost a human being. It sounds like this has been a trying experience for you. Take a moment before you say more."

Composing herself with a handkerchief, she continued:

"Jordan explained that Ian was up to no good and was to obtain a device to explode something terrible for his father. He wanted me to accompany him here, to San Diego, with this thing. Jordan hoped if that happened, then they would capture Percival."

Broadbent finally saw the consistency that Chief Moore emphasized that linked Sela with Jordan and Percival. However, he was very curious about Bright:

"So, the three of you flew from Australia to the United States. You broke away on your own, but where is Bright and, just as important, where is the device he had in his possession?"

Then Hannigan interrupted to clarify things:

"Captain, let me take it from here. Sela has been under much duress these last few days. Let me just say we have no idea where he is. We eluded him at the baggage claim at LAX and took a cab down here. It's anybody's guess if he took the connecting flight to San Diego."

Then Hannigan, gathered himself internally, and asked a profound question:

"What would you offer me in return for a deadly box I can give you, the one I know the law is looking for with much urgency?"

Broadbent seemed open to things:

"It all depends what you are looking for as a fair exchange."

"A means to obtain freedom to atone for some past crimes I committed in Haight-Ashbury in late 1968."

With Broadbent leaning closer to him, he looked him straight in the eye and then reviewed his trail of tears, which included drug dealing, kidnapping, and extortion, all making him wanted by the FBI. He explained that he ran off to Australia to avoid prosecution. Assuming a stolen alias, he slipped into the Perth workforce undetected. His chance encounter to meet Sela brought him to this moment in time. Then he waxed almost patriotic:

"You know, it's funny. Back in my college days, I protested against my country, thinking it was not worth fighting for in Vietnam. Now, I want to come to its defense to save it from a disaster."

Broadbent knew he was in no position to give Hannigan legal protection from his crimes. But, being in the criminal business, he offered a solution:

"Young man, I know some of the best criminal lawyers in southern California. I can get you connected to one to make the best deal you can with the feds. Not sure what that would be. Perhaps a plea bargain, any restitution you might make to your victims, and cooperation to help find the Corsican heroin dealers you described. Minimally, my guess is that you might have to serve some time, but with good behavior it might be months, not years."

On the surface, it sounded attractive to Hannigan, but he was not ready to do business:

"You going to hold me? Certainly not Sela! Can you commit to writing any quid pro quo we might agree to?"

"First, can you confirm that you have a device that David Percival is expecting? Second, yes, I will get your terms and conditions written up as soon as possible. Officer Oliver is both a good cop and typist. Third, I really have nothing to hold either one of you. There's no crime you have committed in my city. Now, where's the detonator? And how soon can I get it?"

"I appreciate your help. We are both very fatigued from this whole ordeal. Can you get us a room so we can rest and refresh? With a letter of understanding, we can set up a time to make the exchange."

"Okay. I'll do that. To give you a well-deserved rest, we can put you up at the U.S. Grant Hotel in a room we have on call for our witness protection program. You'll find it very appealing and comfortable. The stay and all meals are on me. Need a lift to the hotel?"

"Thank you for being so hospitable. No, call a cab. Please don't follow us out the door. Give me your telephone number and I'll call you to go over details where and when we will meet."

Broadbent knew he had the power of newfound supernatural law enforcement in his hands and did not hesitate to give his answer:

"Deal! Here's my card."

In about twenty minutes, Broadbent had a cab outside for Hannigan and Sela. The two of them left the police station, with Hannigan telling Sela to warn him if they were being watched. It was all clear. Just before they got into the cab, Hannigan, who had cleverly hidden the detonator inside a public waste bin on the sidewalk outside the station, had his gamble pay off. He knew there would be no early morning trash collection. Lifting off the metallic lid, he retrieved it and clutched it close to his chest with the confidence that he might have a way clear to eventual freedom. When they got into the cab, he held Sela tightly:

"My dear, dear, dear one. Thank you for staying by me through that tough spot. Again, it's against all odds, but maybe there will be a life for us together in the not too distant future."

She seemed less tense, smiled, and caressed his face with her hand:

"Josh, you just might be the bravest, smartest, and most trustworthy person I have ever known. I will be there for you, whatever happens to you."

Compared to what travails they experienced the last few days, this was a blissful ride to the hotel for the two of them.

Meanwhile, no sooner had Hannigan and Sela left his office, the station desk telephone rang. Officer Oliver took the message:

"San Diego Police, this is FBI agent Ross Cargill. This is big stuff. I have someone who wants to meet with Captain Broadbent. How soon can you page him to come to your headquarters?"

"Wait. He happens to be here now. I'll put him on the line."

Oliver stopped into Broadbent's office and said he would transfer an important call to this telephone. It would truly be a night to remember for Broadbent in all of his twenty plus years on the San Diego Police Department:

"Captain Broadbent here:"

"Damon, Ross Cargill. Recall we met several days ago up in our San Francisco FBI office. I'm not far from your location."

Broadbent couldn't avoid laying out the sarcasm:

"Yeah, yeah, Ross, you handsome devil. You are unforgettable. What's so vital at this early hour? And what are you doing in San Diego?"

"You'll find out shortly. Well, I must confess, I have been secretly rooting for you to get some cooperation from our office. We want to come by and give you some answers you are looking for."

"Ross, you coming with Chief Johnson?"

"It's better than that--I'm bringing you Jordan Starmont."

43
CHAPTER

The Seal's Lair,
September 14, 1969

David Percival's para-military band of neo-Nazis were coming back to base empty handed--again. Like the fruitless result at Windansea Beach earlier in the month, a man they were supposed to have met never appeared a second time hours ago at Lindbergh Field. There was some soul-searching among some of them on the drive back to the Seal's Lair. It seemed like Jordan Starmont and Ian Bright were elusive phantoms. With all the emphasis Percival put on meeting Starmont the first time and Bright the second, it made for both an uncomfortable and disbelieving feeling for troopers Douglas, Bixby, and Crawford in one car, and Montag and Dunhill in the other. They knew Percival would be livid with them, but it also sparked a bit of doubt if it was worth it to stick their necks out for a man advocating an extreme ideology. As Douglas's Chevrolet Camaro and Montag's Ford Fairlane sped away from the airport heading for the on-ramp to the I-5 freeway, the vehicles were side-by-side. Montag motioned to Bixby to roll his window down and he yelled out in the night air:

"Tell Douglas there is a Denny's on I-5 down in the South Bay. Go there. We need to talk."

Douglas got the message from Bixby and told him to respond:

"Tell Montag I'll go there, but this better be good. No bullshit!"

Bixby yelled Douglas's words back at Montag and then pointed up the road so they could move on. It was now after midnight and the start of new day. But, for this band of renegades, would it be business as usual to do Percival's bidding? After parking their cars, the five of them found an empty table at the back of the restaurant. It was empty, save for a few customers at the counter. They all were in a testy mood. Douglas tried to bring them to order:

"Let's all keep our voices down, as pissed as most of us are. Percival gave me some extra cash if we needed it, so whatever you order is on me."

That seemed to placate their ire a bit. Everyone wanted coffee, four of them ordered breakfast, and Bixby preferred a bowl of soup. They all groused over the futility of the evening. It seemed a mutiny was in the air when Montag bemoaned:

"Guys, we risked our asses for a guy's kid, who likely didn't make the flight. Is this worth it anymore? I feel like walking away while I still can."

Dunhill seemed supportive:

"Bobby has a point. In the beginning, I could see the value of supporting this Nazi cause, given all the crap I see that blacks are demanding, the bad results we are getting from Vietnam, and I did come to believe what Percival said that the Jews in this country have too much influence, given their small but big mouth numbers. Now, I'm not so sure."

Crawford wanted in with a different view:

"Yancey and I might be in too deep. We'll have our asses burned by the Corps if they find us. I believe in David, but I guess he really needs to level with us as to what this will lead to. Will any of us have a future--anywhere?"

Douglas then beckoned Bixby into the conversation:

"I'm with Monty on thinking my options are limited. Percival won't be happy when we get back to the Lair, but I don't think he can operate solo. Let's ask him what he wants us to do next, especially with whatever explosive gizmo he has."

They continued to argue over the pros and cons of their positions in a civil way and then quieted down for a few minutes when their orders came to them. Douglas then tried to provide a capstone for their current situation:

"Men, the Seal's Lair is a mini armed camp. No one can push us around without getting hurt, but I don't think we want a confrontation that could lead to bloodshed. Frankly, we were lucky that not a shot was fired at the beach and just now at the airport. The future? I'm not so sure if we can avoid casualties."

The men voiced their agreement as Douglas continued:

"For sure, Percival has to reveal his cards. Just how far he is prepared to go with this explosive package he has? I guess each man will have to decide if they still are onboard after we get specifics from him. But, remember, we swore to band together."

While consuming their food, the men voiced their worries that they likely would find it hard to get away from their regular military duties without consequences. This wasn't a concern for Bixby and Crawford, who went beyond the point of no return when they went AWOL from the Marine Corps. Having no fallback position, for better or worse, they were wedded to Percival for their ability to hide from the Marine MP's. As they all vacated Denny's restaurant and headed to their cars, they were a mutinous bunch on the return to the Seal's Lair.

Earlier around midnight, Percival was uneasy with a silence that permeated the Seal's Lair. His troopers should have been back by now, making for jubilation upon greeting his son, Ian Bright, and the possession of the detonator, the lynchpin for his malevolent plan. Percival's other accomplices, Curtis Wyatt and Mack Smith, were asleep on the floor, oblivious to the storm that was to come. With men living in close quarters, the place had the funky aroma of an overcrowded locker room. Another telling smell was apparent when he opened a window and could get a whiff of the smoke from the Fallbrook fire he started by destroying his avocado estate. He thought that would divert attention from what he was all about, but he was unaware that his scheme to inflict terror was coming apart. He was dressed for the part, in his classic Nazi black uniform. Little did he know he was all dressed up for a celebration that would not happen.

It was approaching 3:00 A.M. when Percival's dejected band pulled up to the Seal's Lair. Hearing footsteps on the stairwell, Percival was there to open the door and greet them. Contrary to what the men expected, Percival was not filled with animus towards them. Rather, he calmly asked them to sit down in the cluttered living room. With Ian Bright not among their numbers, Percival knew there was a problem:

"Men, I asked you to accomplish an important assignment. With my son, Ian, not among you, it is apparent either you failed, or someone else failed us. Can someone tell me what happened at the airport?"

With expressionless, almost lifeless faces, there was little energy to report the empty results. Douglas, always the one to speak generally for the group, took the cue when no else looked like they wanted to say a word at this tense moment:

"David, sorry to inform you, but I believe you are puzzled why Ian did not show at the airport. Either he had a change of heart by not making the flight to San Diego, or perhaps someone else has him in tow. We waited a sufficient time for his arrival, but it never happened. Besides, we believe the law was also waiting for him."

Percival interrupted in an upset, inquisitive tone:

"This is drivel. How do you know that?"

"We were lucky to avoid a blockade into and out of the terminal just as we picked up Bixby and Crawford. We saw plenty of flashing red lights as we drove by the terminal. There's no way in hell at that time of day that the law could assemble the big-time stakeout they had in place. We were lucky we had no confrontation with them."

"Okay. No Ian. Any sign of a cardboard carton at baggage claim?"

That's were Bixby confirmed:

"He didn't show. We stayed until all the bags, save for one or two suitcases, were picked-up. In reality, I sensed something was wrong, so Monty and I got out when we could—by the skin of our teeth."

Percival had to acknowledge a wise move:

"Well, I'm glad your gut seemed to be right. But, how come it took you guys this long to get back here?"

Montag then came to fore to lay it on the line:

"Sir, we'll get to that, but isn't it time for straight talk. We risked our butts again--for nothing. Either this is all a great hoax or someone is on to you, which means they are on to all of us."

"Trooper Montag, it's what you last asked. But, with regard to you fellows, except for Bixby and Crawford, I think they really may not know all of your identities or where you operate from. It's likely a federal operation, backed by the FBI, bent on getting me. You see none of you really know who I am and why they want me."

This revelation seemed to placate the men a little. Percival saw the apt moment to give his history, from his education in England, his work as a Nazi nuclear scientist, to his escape from a surrendering German U-Boat, and his masquerading as an avocado farmer to avoid detection. When he mentioned he had the smuggled uranium cylinder in the trunk of his car, there was a gasp or two among the men. He confessed that Ian was to bring a detonator so he could have the ability to create a nuclear explosion. This prompted Douglas to ask the vital question:

"To what end or overall purpose, David. You could kill us all if things go bad!"

"Trooper Douglas, I appreciate your alarm. But my purpose is the power of suggestion, by laying at the feet of the United States nuclear blackmail. Instead of demanding money in return for not conveying damaging information, we will not explode our device in return for several things you blokes need to know at this critical point. How could one be sure it wouldn't go off? Just by showing it should put the fear of God on their minds."

Perhaps, in a small way, this diminished some of the men's self-doubts, but there were reservations, first expressed by Montag again:

"That may be all well and good, but aren't you gambling that they will call your bluff?"

"Trooper, Montag, that's perceptive. Again, would anyone in authority want to take a chance on an atomic bomb being detonated in a highly populated area, especially here in San Diego on a major military installation, close to a densely populated civilian region? Given a choice, a wise government would take the course of least resistance--letting us, as they say in the popular expression, 'do our thing'."

Then Percival took a moment to compose himself to give a mini oration on the Nazi gospel, designed to justify what his movement was all about:

"First, you, as current members of the armed forces, must be granted clear separation from the military, without fear of prosecution. Second, we must be guaranteed that we have the right to hold public meetings and assemblies, wherever they may occur, without the fear of disruption or arrest, to spread our message to expose the shortcomings of the American government in military affairs, the quieting of dissidents, primarily leftist, quasi-communists in this country, and to call out Jews and their undue influence in Hollywood, the media, and as elected officials. Lastly, we must not be hindered to increase our numbers, to the point we can become a viable political option for the American people to consider."

Douglas then felt compelled to express their reservations:

"David, you asked about the delay to get here. We have to tell you that we had a meeting at a restaurant after we came up empty at the airport. Without mentioning names, some of us are having second thoughts about our further involvement with your movement. Just too must risk, especially with the close calls of being apprehended or getting into a shootout. For myself, I believe in your philosophy, but have at your disposal, I want out."

This cast a silent pall of shock on the group. Percival seemed stunned as much as anyone. Douglas's decision caused the others, one by one, to announce their intentions:

Montag wanted out. Dunhill, a close friend of Montag, said he was through. The youngest members, Smith and Wyatt, peeped up to avoid suspicion that it might be best to go back to duty while they still could. But Percival still had loyal partners, Bixby and Crawford. Bixby spoke first:

"Monty and I have been talking this over. You guys are still in good standing on active duty. We burned our bridges when we went AWOL. I love my country, but I don't like what is happening to it. I'm with David."

Crawford seconded the motion:

"Yeah, you guys are all pretty solid and trustworthy. For sure, I would go to war with you. But Yancey and I see a way out if Mr. Percival can make his case and clear our names with the military and can return as civilians to do as we please. We believe in Mr. Percival and will stand by him."

Douglas then posed a momentous question at this minute of crisis for all of them:

"So what happens next? We can't stay on banded together and remain at the Lair? We need a clean break tonight."

Percival, who had given prior thought to a possible insurrection by his members, brought closure to the discussion:

"Some of you have to look deep into your souls as to what you are loyal and devoted to. I guess taking an oath means little to you. That's too bad. Nevertheless, rest assured I will not divulge, for those wanting to leave me, your identity, but only if you do not relate anything that has happened these last few months with our association. The three of us will vacate this place as soon as we can. Be sure to return your weapons and load into the truck. We'll drive our vehicles off base."

Douglas cautioned:

"You sure you won't be stopped? The cops are still looking for your vehicles."

"Casey, that's always a possibility. But we will be armed and dangerous, ready to defend ourselves. You know this town better than most. I want to stay off the freeway as much as I can. Suggest some side streets to travel to my next base of operations."

"I can do that if you tell me your destination."

"To a place where I think the bastard who has interrupted our plans, Jordan Starmont, may be lingering--the La Valencia Hotel."

44
CHAPTER

San Diego, September 14, 1969

FBI chief Theodore Johnson was beside himself. After his plan failed to bag David Percival a second time, he needed to gather his downtrodden force of a dozen special agents inside the Lindbergh Field terminal. But before he did that, he released Jordan Starmont from his commitment to help the FBI. For Starmont, the break was sudden. He had no definitive place to go in San Diego. He knew his mother was staying in La Jolla at a posh hotel; maybe he could try to reach her there. But he still felt dedicated to what his father could not accomplish--arrest David Percival. While he gave Captain Damon Broadbent the cold shoulder the only time they met, he liked his sincerity and dedication to bring criminals to justice. Perhaps a second encounter would be more fruitful in the quest to nab Percival. As the agents were huddling to hear what Johnson had to say, he came over to agent Ross Cargill for assistance:

"Ross, could you step away for a minute from the group. I need your help."

They stepped off to the side of a group of agents that were assembling in front of the command post at the PSA counter. Cargill seemed cooperative:

"I heard the chief tell you to basically kiss off. Yeah, I can help you after we break up. You are probably free and clear from us."

"Who knows? I am hoping you could give me a lift to San Diego Police headquarters. Frankly, maybe there is a better way to stop Percival, given these last two fiascos."

"Hmm. I don't know. The local cops don't have much to go on—by our design."

"I think I can change that a little. Besides, I have a gut feeling Sela Danby is much closer to us now than she was in Australia. To me, she is the common denominator in this whole affair. It's important to find her. I think Broadbent's people need the opportunity to close this thing down with what I know about Sela's involvement."

"That's a change of heart. You wouldn't give us the ultimate in cooperation, but you would give it to the local cops. Why?"

"As I told you, it is a family matter. My mother is closer to them than she is to you. And my mother is connected to my father, whose memory we have to honor."

After hearing this, Cargill had to grant Jordan's request:

"You know, I have not known you long, but for a young man your age you have shown me intelligence, courage, and devotion. In this troubled world, don't change that, kid. It will take you far. I'll give you a ride to detective Broadbent's office. Let's hear what the chief has to say."

Jordan felt a sense of relief. His association with the FBI was a reluctant one. But a chance to start anew in a different direction, on his own volition, made him confident he could do more to stop Percival's devastating plan. But first he had to bide his time while Johnson spoke to his people:

"Are we all here?"

There was a confirmation from Cargill that he counted all the heads who assisted the operation. Johnson continued:

"Right up front, you all did your job to cast a net to collar a Nazi and his henchmen bent on destruction. I'll take the hit here--this was my ill-conceived plan. I just confirmed with PSA Airlines and the LAX terminal that Ian Bright and Sela Danby never boarded the flight to San Diego, but they did land in LA. Her whereabouts are unknown. However, she must have wanted to come to San Diego, because her bag was headed this way and went unclaimed at the Lindbergh baggage claim carousel. We have it in our possession. But nothing that is linked to Bright, either luggage or the important parcel he was carrying, has been found. Did anyone see anything or anyone unusual in the terminal?"

One of Pizzo's agents raised his hand and volunteered this information:

"Chief, I did walk over to cover baggage claim and things seemed normal. Passengers looking for and picking up their bags. There were, however, two younger men, rather lean and lanky, that stayed until just about all the bags were claimed. They never went to the carousel. Rather, they were looking around the general area, maybe waiting for someone. They walked briskly to the terminal exit. On a hunch, I followed them and was not in position to stop them. Once outside, I saw them make a dash for an awaiting car that picked them up and sped off. Maybe there was a reason for all this unusual activity. Then the general alert went off to seal the terminal and I took up my position at the door to seal the building."

"Interesting. There's a chance, based on their behavior, that those two may have been waiting for Bright as well. Too bad you were just a bit late to hold them."

Then Johnson had further directives:

"Agent Pizzo, thank you for all your cooperation down here. After I am through, I want you to drive immediately to LAX with the five agents in your San Diego office. That's because I do have good news. We have mobilized our LA agents to get to the LAX terminal and to see if Danby and Bright might still be walking around up there. Customs confirmed they cleared their station when they came in from Australia. We have a loose description from Customs as to what they look like. To help better define their appearances, we have arranged to hold the Qantas crew who flew them to LAX to be questioned to perhaps give us more clarity. Please support our people at LAX and cover as many departing flight gates as you can--on the lookout for Bright and Danby!"

Cargill injected a question:

"Chief, do we have any idea if they were tipped off to not come to San Diego?"

"Good thought, Ross. Not really sure of that. It's possible some unforeseen event or person prevented their arrival. Bright and Danby technically had their bags checked through to San Diego. But Customs prefers, but does not require, that all bags be taken by arriving passengers from their foreign flight to the airline of the connecting domestic flight. As I said, Danby's belongings made it here, but Bright's luggage is still unaccounted for. There's a chance the two might have separated, for whatever reason."

Johnson then wrapped things up by encouraging his personnel to not give up hope to bring Percival and anyone else assisting him to justice. That was Cargill's cue to go to a counter telephone to call Broadbent's office. Starmont stayed back a little and liked the fact Cargill was becoming a friend. After Cargill arranged with Pizzo to have one of his local agents provide transportation, he and Jordan were directed to an FBI staff car at the curb right outside the terminal. As he stepped outside, Jordan was basking in the warm night air, a welcomed contrast from the cooler climate in San Francisco. He started a conversation with Cargill in the back seat as they headed to the Broadbent's office, only a short drive from the airport in downtown San Diego:

"Ross, again I appreciate this, I am a bit bummed, too. I wanted to have Percival, Bright, and that deadly package all bound up out of harm's way. Again, I looked at all the arriving passengers and no one at least matched Sela's description. Sela did describe what Bright looked like, tall and gawky, but I didn't see a match there either."

"Jordan, you did your best for what assignment we gave you. Let's hope for better hunting. I caught the chief's ear before we left. He said you're not obligated to assist us going forward, but, if by some crazy chance you stumble upon Sela Danby or Bright, contact agent Pizzo's office. Here's his card."

"Ross, rest assured I will comply. But you have to appreciate, right now, Sela has to be in a delicate, fearful state. She was very hesitant to come to San Diego with Bright in the first place."

In less than ten minutes, they arrived at Broadbent's Market Street headquarters. Jordan got out of the car, thanked the driver, and shook Cargill's hand. He then resolutely walked to the entrance of the police station, ready to be as truthful and cooperative as he could. The first person he saw inside was officer Oliver, behind his desk with a beaming smile who greeted him:

"At this early hour the only person you could be is Jordan Starmont. Right?"

"Yeah, you'd be right. When can I see Captain Broadbent?"

"Come on. Let's go down the hall to his office. He's expecting you."

Seated behind his desk with a lit cigarette in his ashtray and a steaming coffee mug in front of him, Damon Broadbent was writing his report on what just happened on this eventful evening. He was about to be a crime detective superstar. Hours ago, he had crumbs for clues to get Percival in custody. Suddenly he had Sela Danby, a strategic stranger with a prized possession, and now the return of a prodigal son to a woman he felt deeply for. They were all key ingredients in the most bizarre case of his career. The moment he saw Jordan walk in, he sprung up and shook his hand, thanked him for coming to see him, and ordered Oliver to bring coffee and whatever sandwiches were still consumable for Jordan. Broadbent was jubilant when he opened the dialog:

"Jordan, I trust you came because you wanted to. So rather than me start a grand inquisition, like the only time we met, why don't you tell what I should know at your own pace."

"Captain, thank you for sheltering and caring for my mother. She told me what you have done. As her son, I am indebted to you."

Broadbent just shook his head positively with a smile and awaited what was to be said next:

"Sela and I are the same children of our father, Martin, who, as I will explain, tried to apprehend David Percival after he got off a surrendering Nazi U-boat in 1945. It's a long, winding, almost unimaginable story."

Jordan then narrated the family ties he had with Sela, based on his father's letter, the unsuccessful chase his father made to capture Percival, how he looked for an alternative lifestyle in Haight-Ashbury, how the FBI found him and made him a part of their investigation, what really happened at Windansea Beach, how he was hamstrung to not say much to Broadbent, and what just went wrong at the San Diego airport. Broadbent was suddenly aware of the disparate pieces that were fitting into place, as his boss Howard Moore would say, a "consistent pattern." To better comprehend the wealth of new information conveyed to him, Broadbent qualified what he heard with soft, non-threatening questions. After Jordan had a chance to relax with some coffee and something to eat, Broadbent made for a dramatic revelation:

"Jordan, that's all unbelievable stuff. You have answered the call to elevate your father's memory to a patriotic level. Your country is proud of you. And, young man, I think it's time you get rewarded for your noble efforts."

Jordan was amused:

"What? You going to pay me like the FBI?"

"No, it's better than that because it is priceless and can't be bought. There is a lady who awaits you. I will bring her to you as soon as I can."

"Oh, my mom? I need to make amends for what happened in San Francisco. I can't wait."

"Well, we'll accommodate that, but this other lady, who you will see as soon as possible, has been waiting anxiously to see you for the first time--Sela Danby."

45
CHAPTER

The Seal's Lair and La Jolla, September 14

About an hour after a tense meeting had ended at the Seal's Lair, the bulk of David Percival's band of neo-Nazis had vacated the place. Bobby Montag, Mack Smith, Grady Dunhill, and Curtis Wyatt peeled away from any further involvement with Percival. Montag's roomy Ford Fairlane accommodated the transportation for the four of them. He took Smith and Dunhill to their quarters at the Coronado Naval Base. They were assigned to the *USS Ticonderoga*, a carrier that still was at sea, but due into port in ten days, returning from another Vietnam air support cruise in the South China Sea. Smith and Dunhill avoided sea duty and stayed in Coronado for special training. They hoped they could seamlessly slip back to their routine duties, assuming their superiors had no idea they were potential traitors. As active duty Marines, Montag and Wyatt drove off the Coronado Peninsula to get back to the other side of the bay at their duty station, the US Marine Corps Recruit Depot (MCRD). This base was adjacent to the Lindbergh Field runway. Hours earlier the Marines had broken their pledge to be "always faithful" (Semper Fi) to the Corps at the civilian airport. Deep down they had to recommit themselves to an oath they broke following Percival's directives.

Remaining at the Seal's Lair, the other Marines, Yancey Bixby and Monty Crawford, were packing their belongings and the weaponry: the long guns, the pistols, and the recoilless rifle, into the Ford pickup. However, Percival's arsenal was still in abeyance. The super weapon, the uranium canister, never left the trunk of the Lincoln sedan. Without the detonator he hoped to have obtained, the nuclear device was an idle threat. Percival knew that, but it still was a trump card in his stacked hand to inflict massive damage.

With Bixby and Crawford waiting outside, Percival had a final moment alone with Casey Douglas, who also renounced his affiliation with the Nazi group:

"Casey, I must say, out of all the guys who left the ranks, I never expected that you would be among them."

"I'll be honest, I didn't think it would come to me breaking away. But your nuclear device gives me the creeps. I don't know exactly how it works, but from what discussions we've had about in the Navy that stuff is volatile and dangerous."

"Your perceptions aren't wrong. But, as a scientist who has worked on developing an atom bomb, uranium safely encased, as what I have in my possession, is docile and harmless."

"So, without a trigger, or a detonator, it will not explode."

"That is an accurate assessment. But let's get back to you. I think the commitments we had from most of the troopers was not to the intense fervor I would like. When the going got tough, or off course, they bailed. You still committed to the Nazi ideology?"

Douglas, who was standing in the kitchen, gravitated through the opening to the living area where Percival was sitting on a sofa. He went to a lampstand drawer and pulled out a symbolic sinister sash and let it hang down from his fingers as he answered Percival:

"What appeals to me is the racial part. I saw the differences between blacks and whites while living in Georgia. It's not that I think blacks are inferior--they are just different, especially when it comes to their culture and how they view the world. To me, there is value to keep our distances from one another--to not mix or blend."

Percival was obliging, seeing he had a disciple:

"From my German roots, we emphasized being one people, set apart from all others who would threaten our stock. One of those threats was the Jews, who bred within their own numbers. Some did cross over the line to breed with Germans, but that was a condemned practice."

"You really don't like those people, do you?"

"If they would tone down their arrogance, 'God's chosen people', and be less assertive. Too many, I found, wanted to be in charge and play boss. They deplored a subordinate role. That's why they avoided the military if they could. Jews like giving orders, not taking them."

"Yeah, I see some of that here in the States. I haven't come across too many of them in the Navy. Maybe they think they are too good to serve."

"You know what is ironic, in Germany today it is outlawed to give the Nazi salute, a hangover I believe from their defeat in World War II."

"Hmm, seems inconsistent that you could do that in America and not really be breaking any law. Free expression does count for something in this country."

"No, it won't really be free until our movement grows and has more converts to see the power of a truly unifying force that will rid this place of its enemies and silence its critics. Again, that's where the loud-mouth Jews, communists, ultra-liberals have to be restrained."

Douglas turned the subject to Percival's disappointment:

"I'm at a loss why Ian Bright did not show at the airport. How does that affect your next steps?"

"I have to concede something terribly went wrong. Before he left Australia he said he was committed to delivering what I wanted. I am not hopeful I will see him or the detonator. I have to devise an alternate scheme, or, as you say in America, plan 'B'."

Percival then got up from his seat, prepared to leave the Seal's Lair for what would likely be the last time. He addressed Douglas with final advice:

"It's plain to see that we are on the same wavelength. Stick to those core beliefs. It's important that you spread our thinking. I encourage you to get in touch with Matthias Koehl, who leads the party in this country."

Douglas read something significant in the recommendation:

"So, how active will you be as an advocate for Nazism?"

"Casey, with all that has happened in the last month, my days might be numbered. It's not coincidental that things have gone wrong at Windansea and just tonight at the airport. My adversaries are closing in. I have to make a final stand to survive. Unfortunately, I just lost much of my force, but I'll persevere."

"I admire your bravery and dedication. I wish you well."

The two then vowed to keep their identities private. Percival told Douglas he might contact him again, but had to move on to his next objective: the La Valencia Hotel in La Jolla. Douglas did have a map of the City of San Diego. To avoid being spotted by the police, he brought Percival to a table and plotted a route to avoid main thoroughfares after they got across the Coronado Bay Bridge. Once off I-5 in San Diego, they would drive through the Ocean and Mission Beach districts. From there, they could wend their way, as time consuming as it would be, by taking side streets, eventually getting them into La Jolla. The sun would be up in a few hours, so Percival and the Marines readied their departure from the Seal's Lair.

Before Percival left, he took off his Nazi uniform and told Douglas to keep it, perhaps for a future convert. He gave Douglas a hug and went down the two flights of steps to the awaiting Bixby and Crawford. They would only drive two of three of Percival's vehicles, the Lincoln Continental, loaded with the uranium in the trunk, and the Ford pick-up, which had the weaponry and their personal belongings. Douglas was instructed to dispose of the Pontiac GTO at a later time, keeping it parked outside the Seal's Lair. With Bixby behind the wheel in the Lincoln, Percival was next to him up front giving driving instructions from the map. Crawford followed behind in the Ford pick-up, but was told to follow at a safe distance, just in case one of them was stopped. If that happened, Percival commanded:

"Shoot to kill!"

With deserted early Saturday morning streets, this deadly caravan made its way to La Jolla without incident, although the Lincoln found itself driving behind a police cruiser while in the Pacific Beach area. Bixby ended this encounter by turning off to a less traveled side road. They waited ten minutes and then proceeded northward to La Jolla without incident. It was nearly sunrise, 6:45 A.M., when they came to the front of the La Valencia Hotel on Prospect Street. Percival directed Bixby to a parking lot off Prospect on Ivanhoe Avenue, where he had parked last month during the

Windansea misadventure. Once cleared by the attendant, they found two side-by-side parking stalls. Percival instructed Bixby and Crawford to stay put. He walked from the garage to the front desk of the hotel, which was unattended at this early hour. He rang the desk chime and a reservationist appeared in a few moments. Percival had a case of déjà vu:

"Haven't I seen you before? My name is Wilfred Tanner, and I stayed here last month."

The hotel staffer reflected for a moment, then recalled:

"Yes, I do remember you. I do appreciate your generosity".

This was an acknowledgment of the bribe Percival paid to see if Jordan Starmont was a hotel guest. Percival then made the same devious inquiry, ensuring an answer by placing a $20 bill on the counter:

"Again, I ask you. Is Mr. Jordan Starmont a guest?"

The staffer answered immediately:

"He's not here, but we do have a Mrs. Margaret Starmont. She's been with us for an extended stay."

It wasn't the right Starmont he was looking for, but this one had possibilities for Percival:

"Good. Book me into a two-bedroom suite."

46
CHAPTER

LAX, September 14

FBI agent Joe Pizzo did not dally after Chief Theodore Johnson gave him orders to rush to Los Angeles International Airport (LAX). Johnson alerted agents at this investigative site that Pizzo was on his way to apprehend Ian Bright, who was thought to be wandering around the terminal, looking for a way out. In three FBI vehicles, with dashboard emergency lights brightly circling, they quickly made the short jaunt from the airport terminal to I-5. At speeds approaching 85 MPH with traffic light in the wee hours of the morning, they reached the airport in ninety minutes. Exiting the freeway and coming to Sepulveda Boulevard, at nearly forty-three miles long, connecting Long Beach to the San Fernando Valley, they came to the main terminal. However, Pizzo and his colleagues would have an arduous search to find Bright. The LAX layout dwarfed the more diminutive San Diego airport. Once inside, uniformed police were used this time to restrict passenger movement. One of the interdicting officers directed Pizzo to the TWA counter, the command post for the FBI already in place. Agent Luke Volz debriefed Pizzo:

"You guys have wings? It seems you flew up here."

Pizzo wasn't in the mood for levity:

"Yeah, can't you see the wings on my back? Agent Volz are you aware how serious the capture of Ian Bright is?"

"Calm down, Joe. I know you guys down south are pissed that he never made it to San Diego. And, of course, anytime you are dealing with extremists bent on terrible destruction we are all in."

"Okay. What's the situation?"

"To review, we confirmed from Qantas that Bright and his female company, this Sela Danby, arrived from Sydney earlier. What is it now? 3:00 A.M. That would make it last night. Conferring with PSA they indicated neither boarded the flight to Lindbergh, but somehow Danby's bag was checked through. We theorize a sky cap saw the baggage connection tag and put it on the connecting flight. Right now, no sign of Bright, his luggage, or the all-important box we were told he was carrying."

"Did you talk to the Qantas crew about descriptions for both of them?"

"They were very cooperative. Based on what descriptions we had for both, one stewardess was certain she served Bright in first class. Said he was on the gaunt side and is likely over six feet tall. He was wearing a tight fitting black leather jacket. With a black spiked pompadour head of hair. Looked odd. Likely was loaded. Drinking hard all the way to LAX. The stew said for an Englishmen he did not have the dashing looks of a Cary Grant."

"That's enough to make him stand out in a crowd. How about the girl?"

"One of the crew working coach thinks she was wearing something in blue. A jacket or sweater. Whatever she had on, she was described as 'drop dead gorgeous.' Seemed serious. Maybe on edge. Nothing else to go on."

"That's Qantas. What did PSA give us?"

"Nothing. No one matching those descriptions came to the gate for the San Diego flight. No one came to the counter to rebook if they missed that flight."

The two operatives then checked in with the Los Angeles police. No one of interest had left or entered the terminal since the time they were put on alert. Pizzo requested to extend the ingress and egress search until further notice. With over twenty foreign and domestic airlines serving the airport docking at multiple passenger concourses, it was going to be a difficult operation to cover adequately. On a hunch, Pizzo suggested to assign agents to concentrate on carriers that fly overseas, which included TWA, Pan Am, Qantas, Air France, and BOAC. Somewhere a rat was lurking, and with all these possibilities the FBI was not in a good position to trap him.

Earlier, when Ian Bright knew Sela and the detonator were gone, he was in a tough position. There was no way he was going to San Diego empty handed, lest he face the wrath of David Percival. With his suitcase in hand he went to a sky cap station and instructed that they hold it for him until he reclaimed it. He was told his best bet to go to London was via TWA, Pan Am, or SAS. While still not clear-headed from too much alcohol and in a state of extreme angst, he tried TWA first. He discovered a flight to New York would connect to London Heathrow Airport, but it wasn't leaving until 8:00 A.M. It was after midnight and he would have a long wait. He decided to book it; then changed his mind. It was too early in the process and his cash for payment, Travelers Cheques, were in his suitcase. He thought he would have time to get them. Bright was a misnomer for the innate intelligence he did not have. But he was wise enough to assume his moves might be monitored. Something this unusual was at play. Not sure what happened with the sudden disappearance of Sela and the detonator, Bright found his survival instincts kick in. Was someone following or interfering with him, knowing he was carrying contraband?

To stay out of sight as much as possible and kill time before the London flight, he found a vending machine and selected a ham and cheese sandwich and some potato chips. He washed it down with a Coca-Cola, served by an adjacent machine. The terminal was not especially crowded, so he had to find cover. But where? He let nature's call provide a potential safe haven. Finding the nearest men's room, he found the widest stall in the lavatory. There was enough room, as uncomfortable and unseemly as it was, to lie down on the floor, with his feet resting next to the commode and his head propped against the corner of the stall panels at the door. The odor was bearable, especially if he flushed the commode to freshen the air in his cramped quarters. Bright hoped that no one would need the larger stall for relief. He ate his sandwich and then dozed off.

After spending three hours checking with the reservationists at the major airlines, Pizzo found nothing for a Bright departure. He surmised he had to be ignorant of American geography, so where else could he escape to, besides a European destination? He placed his bets by assigning an agent to the TWA and Pan Am counters, which had morning flights for

London, to monitor any passenger activity. However, given the early hour no airline employee was at the counters, to say nothing of empty waiting areas at the gates. At least people clutter was not a problem. For now, it was a waiting game to see if Bright would rear his head.

An uncomfortable and fretful Bright looked at his watch in his humble hangout. It was 6:10 A.M. Fortunately, no one bothered him, but it was time to get out of a tight spot and seek freedom by finding a flight back to England. Leaving the men's room, he made a path to the red cap station where he checked his bag. He was glad Percival told him to carry American dollars on his trip, but it wasn't a large amount--$100. That was enough to tip red caps and buy some concessions, but not enough to buy a plane ticket home. He had to get to his bag, where he placed his Travelers Cheques. They amounted to $1500, the sum of money Percival gave him and the conversion of his lingering English Pounds and Australian Dollars. No one was on duty to help passengers with their luggage. This increased his angst, imagining there was no way out for him. With a look of paranoia, he looked around to see if anyone was watching him as he sat upon a nearby bench. After fifteen nervous minutes, a sky cap came to his post. Bright clutched his claim check in a sweaty palm. He called for his bag:

"Here's my ticket. Can you find it as soon as possible, I have a flight out shortly."

The red cap, a black man with a friendly face, was inquisitive:

"Where you from, boy? You talk a little different."

"I hope it is not a big deal—I am from England. Please don't dally. Give me my bag."

The sky cap gave a wry smile and dutifully went to a storage room. Returning in five minutes, Bright took his bag and gave a $5 tip. Immediately lifting his bag to a nearby metal table, Bright opened it in a flash, sifting through his belongings hurriedly. Bright decided he had to travel light, so he wasn't going to lug it with him. He would miss the Sharpie clothing he bought in Melbourne, but he was more than satisfied with the clothes on his back. The Cheques were in a side suitcase pocket, which gave him consolation. Having what he needed, he was off to the TWA counter for the London flight. Bright was astute enough to rip off the luggage I.D. tag, but in his haste he failed to remove the baggage tag. Drifting away, the sky cap called out seeing what Bright left behind:

"Young man. Your bag!"

Bright yelled back:

"Give it to charity. I'm out of here."

A few minutes later, a surveilling FBI agent came up to the sky cap:

"Have you seen a skinny looking guy with spike-like hair in a black jacket come by lately?"

"Yes, sir, I think he left minutes ago and didn't take his bag. It's at that nearby table."

The agent quickly got there and saw an opened suitcase. Inspecting it he found a Qantas baggage tag on the handle. This aroused the agent's suspicions, prompting him to use his mini walkie-talkie to contact Pizzo at the TWA counter. After he heard the details, Pizzo guessed it had to be Bright as the owner of the luggage. He alerted via radio his other floating agents to head to the TWA or Pan Am locations, giving this command:

"Be on the lookout for our quarry! Apprehend anyone who meets the profile you were given earlier!"

With no one asking questions or hindering his movement, Bright was starting to feel good about not being stopped as he made his way to the TWA departure gate. His sense of security would be short-lived. Passengers were beginning to check in for the London flight. Based on the description the FBI had for him, he clearly stood out. Two agents seized him from behind and handcuffed him. One of them barked out:

"You have the right to remain silent. Anything you say can and will be used against you in a court of law. You have the right to an attorney. If you cannot afford an attorney, one will be provided for you. Do you understand the rights I have just read to you? With these rights in mind, do you wish to speak to me?"

Bright had deaf ears to the legal advice and continued to struggle to free himself. When he realized that he was overwhelmed by the strangling strength that restrained him, he yelled out with an English flourish:

"Get your bloody hands off me. What is this batshittery?"

After Bright was frisked, they found his passport. Pizzo then came up to him and demanded:

"Ian Bright, why did you enter the United States? Where can we find what you were bringing to David Percival?"

"This is not right, you bastards. Let me go. I don't know what you are saying."

Pizzo made a final warning:

"Look, punk, if you want to see England again you better come clean."

San Diego, September 14, 1969

Damon Broadbent seemed like a travel agent, booking people into elite hotels. But when two of them were individuals who had brought him to the promised land of cracking a conundrum of a case, it had its rewards. He made a second reservation at the U.S. Grant Hotel, for a third major piece of a criminal jigsaw puzzle--Jordan Starmont. Margaret Starmont's son was fatigued from a night with unbelievable outcomes. Broadbent told him the stay at the hotel would have a double payoff: some welcomed rest and an eventual introduction to his half-sister, Sela Danby. Broadbent saw Jordan off as he left his office in the early morning:

"It's only a short hop to the hotel. Officer Oliver will take you there in my car."

Jordan had his expectations at high alert:

"When do I see Sela? It's long overdue."

"In due time, Jordan. Soon, I hope. Tell your Mom hello when you get settled and have her call me."

"Can I see my mother?"

"That's not a problem. But please stay overnight at the hotel until further notice. That will facilitate you seeing Ms. Danby."

"That won't be a problem."

Knowing that Sela and Jordan were staying at the same place, there was the possibility they could bump into one another before Broadbent wanted them to meet. If so, so be it. Broadbent was enjoying orchestrating this drama and walked with a light, jovial step back to his office. The sun wasn't up, but he thought he would awake his boss, Chief Harold Moore, with a welcomed telephone call that would not annoy him when breaking his sleep. Broadbent was on the edge of ecstasy when Moore answered his phone:

"Chief, Broadbent. You won't be grouchy from a ring this early when I tell you news we have all been waiting for."

"Damon, I am sure it is not the second coming of Christ, but it better be close. Tell me."

"I would ask you if you were sitting down, but I trust you are somewhat awake sitting in bed when I tell you pieces in the Windansea puzzle came into my office this early morning."

Moore gave a wild, bold reaction:

"Percival walked in and surrendered with his cronies!"

"Not quit that good, but links to him voluntarily came to me separately. First, Sela Danby, accompanied by a new character, a fugitive named Josh Hannigan, who claims he has the prime object of our investigation--a nuclear detonator intended for delivery to David Percival."

"Holy smokes! I am glad I went to confession several days ago to atone for all the cussing I have done about this case, both out loud and to myself. Go on."

"I have the two of them safely stashed away at the U.S. Grant. An hour or so later, the second fortuitous find came to my office. He's Jordan Starmont, you know the kid who wouldn't talk to me up in San Francisco?"

"You have been repenting for your sins, too. Did you also go to confession to receive these blessings?"

"No, but I might turn Catholic if this good fortune continues. At any rate, he wants to talk and assist us. I also put him in the Grant for safe keeping."

"Yeah, I am glad we have that posh hideaway in our meager budget to shield key witnesses. Stay at the office. Give me several hours to get dressed and eat something. I'll be there with bells on my toes."

"Chief, I can't tell how good I feel about this case now."

"Damon, that goes without saying for me as well. Have officer Oliver make a fresh pot of coffee."

As the two dedicated law enforcement officials ended their call, their frustration level had diminished exponentially. Broadbent did keep a set of clothes in his office closet, in addition to his formal police dress uniform. It included a white shirt, a red and blue striped tie, a pair of black gabardine slacks, two pairs of black socks, and two Jockey briefs. Also there was a personals kit, with shaving supplies, toothbrush and paste, and some aftershave balm. After a flurry of almost non-stop activity, he needed a refresher. The regular line police officers had a locker room and shower in the lower level of the building. Broadbent found solace with a shower and shave in this off-duty oasis for crime stoppers. He exchanged his casual garb for the formal dress pants, white shirt and tie. Looking into the mirror, making a Windsor knot for his tie, he gave himself an egotistic smile—he thought he deserved it.

It was approaching 8:00 A.M. with the aroma of Oliver's new brewing pot of coffee in the air as Chief Moore walked into police headquarters. This would be a different entrance into the building. He generally was dour, critical of whoever made the coffee, and always headed straight to his office. The atmosphere changed after Broadbent's good news. In passing by Oliver's desk, Moore had a sweeter face, he complimented Oliver on the coffee aroma, insisting he bring him a cup pronto, and this time headed to where the action was--Broadbent's office. The two men shook hands when they met and sat down with an air of relaxation for a change. Moore spoke first at the same time Oliver brought him his coffee:

"Damon, if what had not occurred this morning, all hell would have broken loose in the papers, alerting the public to possible panic. We've kept the mayor as calm as we could and we have been feeding the press drivel. If this Hannigan guy has the detonator, then we are on firm ground to have no fear for the greater population."

"Well let's just say that the hyper fear level is essentially gone. In a way, all it boils down to finding a Nazi with evil intentions, who just had his explosive balls cut off without a detonating device."

"I did get wind of what happened late last night at Lindbergh when I checked the news wire from my car radio. The papers got a reporter there when they got a tip from a passenger that the 'cops were restricting movement' in and out of the terminal. I don't know what the *Evening*

Tribune will report in their afternoon edition, but I think we can do damage control if they have inaccurate information or inflate the story."

"I have no way of knowing if the FBI has been interviewed, but their policy is to hear, see, and speak no evil to the press. Despite the damage, I'm glad the papers have committed most of their print to that Fallbrook fire."

Moore was shaking his head in agreement:

"Percival did us a favor to create the distraction by starting it as you reported with the blowup of his house. By the way, is Rick Sandoval on his way to resume his duties?"

"I spoke with him yesterday at his home. He got mucho TLC from his wonderful family. He could be back on Monday."

"Good, good. Let's get to the chase. First, we need to get that detonator ASAP. Are there strings attached to that happening?"

"Sure is. Josh Hannigan is a bright young man. Seems he fled to Australia after a drug deal went wrong, compounded by kidnapping and extortion, up in hippyland in San Francisco in December of '68. Fell into the middle of this Percival escapade by chance by encountering Sela Danby. Wants a criminal attorney to help with a plea in exchange for the detonator."

"That should be no big deal. We know more than a few lawyers who make our lives miserable trying to free guilty creeps we arrest. Might I suggest Channing Williams."

"He's top drawer. Won't come cheap."

"True. But once we let the cat out of the bag, giving the okay that he helped an individual avoid a nuclear calamity by helping his client, he'll get big time national exposure for his practice. For sure, the details are not public until we safely have the device and, if we are lucky, have Percival in jail."

"That's a plan. Let me whet Williams's appetite this morning."

Then Moore unexpectedly divulged his own bit of sensationalism:

"Buried under the pile of problems on my desk was a report from the morgue I finally read two days ago. It seems our Bay area FBI honcho, Theodore Johnson, has some deep connection to the corpse found at Windansea."

"That's news. The dead body is another unaccounted detail in this case."

"The report said that after two weeks, with the body still on ice and unclaimed, that Johnson made a request for the remains. He justified his request by claiming, among other things, that he knew the individual and was on scene after he hung himself last month."

"Wow! We are on a hot streak to answer the profound questions that piece things together. Did the deceased have a name? Any other details?"

"His name is Nick Petrie, who Johnson claimed was an orphan and left his foster care home in New Jersey over five years ago at age eighteen, and gravitated west to Haight-Ashbury. It was there that Petrie and Johnson struck up a relationship."

"Don't want to be presumptuous. But is this what I think this might be--two males with an intimate relationship?"

"That was my inclination as well. I called San Francisco P. D.s' Blake Sheridan and he said there has been whispers about Johnson's sexual inclinations. He never married."

"This is mind-boggling. How something, on the surface, seemed so complicated has become so simple."

"As usual, your good philosophical deductions are on point. But what's the improbable clincher for the morgue to release the remains in their chilled black box to Johnson?"

"Is it, as you say, 'consistent' to hold this case together?"

"Damon, it's the ultimate in consistency. Margaret Starmont said the body was not her son for the same reason Johnson said the body had a unique physical identifier--the guy is uncircumcised."

48
CHAPTER

La Jolla, September 14, 1969

Margaret Starmont was developing an aversion to telephones. Lately, their ring signaled unpleasant developments at the other end. The next call may have changed all that. It was approaching 11:00 A.M. Maggie had just returned to her suite from a light breakfast on the La Valencia Hotel patio on a clear, warm morning. Septembers in La Jolla are not generally blanketed by low clouds and overcast. It is the most sun-filled time of the year. Unsure what her day would bring her, another source of sunshine came into her life with an unexpected telephone caller:

"Mom, Jordan. Guess what?"

"From the lilt in your voice it sounds like something significant."

"Sure is. I'm here in a nice hotel in downtown San Diego--the U.S. Grant."

"Yes, I am familiar with it. Your father and I have dined at the Grant Grill in the past."

"I have so much to tell you: why I am in town, how I hope to help catch that damn Nazi, and to finally meet someone we both have an interest in--Sela Danby."

Margaret made a gasp when she heard Sela's name:

"My heavens! Is she going to be a reality we can finally meet and embrace?"

"Yes, ma'am. The plan is to meet her, location unknown, very shortly. This incredible turn of events has been made possible by a man I declined to help when I first met him—Captain Damon Broadbent."

Margaret had her emotions overrule her better judgment:

"Damon, I mean Captain Broadbent!"

Her son detected an affection for Broadbent.

"That makes two of us that are impressed with him. I had a good meeting with him early this morning in his office. He set me up at the hotel."

"Jordan, I must confess that I am impressed with his ability as a detective and the high character he exhibits. Now, when do I see you?"

"I'm not in the lockstep that I was with the FBI in San Francisco. I want to check with the Captain to see what's my best course of action."

"All right I understand, dear. I'll stay patient. When the time is right, I'll take a cab and get to the hotel. Then we can work out what we decide to do next. I've been thinking. I am open for you to stay in California, go back home to New York, or wherever you want your life to go."

"That's up for discussion. I am unsure of my future plans. By the way, the Captain wanted me to be sure I contacted you, and he says hello."

"That is good to know. He's always so attentive to my needs."

They closed their conversation by recalling how they have been on a roller coaster of emotions and recalling some memories of a young man's father and a widow's husband. When she put down the telephone, Margaret was trying to not be impulsive. But rather than let things unfold in a timely way, she decided to force the issue and call Broadbent's office. She was in luck to reach him, for Broadbent was staying in-house awaiting calls from several criminal lawyers, including Channing Williams. She was more emotional than rational:

"Damon, I mean Captain. Forgive me, I am so happy."

"Maggie, remember, between you and me, we are on a first-named basis when no one is around. Let me guess? You just heard from Jordan?"

"Oh, the joy! I just spoke with him and he said he's in San Diego, staying at a very nice hotel—the U.S. Grant."

"I won't be modest on this accomplishment. Your son is at the center of much of this Nazi problem we have. I had to be sure he would be out of harm's way. He'll be safe and sound there."

"Thank you so much for that action. Now, how soon can you arrange for a meeting with my son?"

"It likely won't be today. Jordan, Sela Danby, and a third party are all tied at the hip to help our investigation. They have to be debriefed further before I can have you meet again with Jordan."

"All right. I'll be good and await your approval when to see Jordan. Have a nice day!"

After ending her call, Margaret went to her wardrobe in the closet, enhanced by several new outfits she bought at some pricey La Jolla women's wear shops on Girard Street, to select some celebration apparel. She was just about ready to step into the shower when the telephone rang:

"Mrs. Starmont, my name is Wilfred Tanner, a former business associate of your husband when he managed Smith Barney's British accounts. I hope I am not intruding on your day."

Margaret was puzzled:

"Why no--not now. How did you know where to find me?"

David Percival did his homework prior to the call. He discovered Margaret's New York address from his La Valencia desk crony. That led him to Margaret's New York residence and her home telephone number. When he reached Lois Carson, Margaret's housekeeper, he was on the prowl for details, many of which pertained to Martin Starmont's professional work. Carson was tragically verbose, telling Percival he was a successful Smith Barney executive. And the ultimate faux pas was telling him that Margaret was off to see her son, Jordan, in San Diego. Hearing this, Percival was constructing a clearer picture of the plot trying to ensnare him. He had plenty to get Margaret's attention:

"Pardon me, Mrs. Starmont if I was too imposing, but I was told by your housekeeper at your New York City home that you have come to California for a stay at the La Valencia."

Margaret was disappointed her whereabouts were made public. However, in her anxiety to come west, she overlooked that caution and assumed that Lois Carson would keep her business private. She was guarded:

"Mr. Tanner, I must say this is a surprise. But I don't recall Martin ever mentioning your name with his business dealings. He kept his work private for the most part, but there were those he mentioned that he shared if we might have some social involvement."

"When you frame it that way, it's understandable that your husband kept me from view. If you might fit me into your schedule, I would like to meet you to discuss an important matter that I think you should know."

"Important? With Martin gone? Is there something that has lingered into the present?"

"Oh, yes, Mrs. Starmont--and it is alive and well."

Margaret was now intrigued but almost threatened:

"Some person? How is this important at this point in time?"

"Rather than belabor this conversation, and I thank you for hearing me out, could we meet--say for lunch at a time best for you?"

"Before we go further, Mr. Tanner, who is this live person?"

"Sela Danby. All I can say she might be trouble for your future, and likely your son, Jordan."

Upon hearing this, Margaret could feel the onset spiral of an emotional freefall, something she felt was in her past, now that Jordan was close at hand. But she quickly got a grip, acceding to a stranger's invitation:

"Okay. Maybe in a day or two. I'll call for a convenient time."

"That will work. Please call the hotel; they know how to reach me. In conclusion, I am only trying to bring some tranquility to honor the memory of your husband, whom I regarded as a true friend in life. Have a pleasant day."

When Margaret put the telephone down, she had to review what unexpected drama just unfolded. A stranger from left field entered her field of play. What did Wilfred Tanner portend for her? Why couldn't her life be so simple and predictable? She thought of calling Broadbent back again to get his advice on the matter. No, the man is just so busy. But she got careless with a false sense of security. She thought if and when she would meet Tanner, it would be her private affair--just between the two of them.

On the other hand, the mysterious man had a more premeditated, predictable approach to the situation. Percival had a devilish smile as he turned toward Yancey Bixby and Monty Crawford, who had just devoured their room service breakfasts in the hotel suite. He wanted to redirect his evil intentions:

"Troopers, with the conversation I just had, we just might unravel this Jordan Stamont no-show at Windansea Beach, and perhaps also determine why Ian Bright did not show at the airport."

Bixby wanted clarity:

"David, did you just talk to this Starmont character?"

"No, but this individual is close to him."

"How close?"

"Right now, I can't tell you. But here is what we need to prepare for next. There is just too much danger for the three of us being apprehended. It's to the point that we have to leave this country to free ourselves of the forces we want to destroy."

Both Crawford and Bixby had troubled looks when they heard this. This time Bixby queried:

"I sure hope it's not by airplane. We haven't had much luck with airports."

"No, that won't work. I came to this country by boat; I'm leaving it by boat."

49
CHAPTER

San Diego, September 14/15

Precipitated by a whirlwind late evening and early morning, Sela Danby awoke from a deep sleep of nearly five hours inside her U.S. Grant Hotel room. Josh Hannigan still found it hard to sleep with a redirection for his life that might have major consequences. He managed to shower, order some food, and appreciated seeing the young woman in his troubled life slumbering in peaceful beauty. Arising from bed, clad scantily in her bra and panties, Sela was bound for the bathroom. This titillated Hannigan, who was only wearing a hotel provided bathrobe. He became aroused and reached out for Sela before she could make it to a long-awaited shower. Embracing her warmly, Sela did not resist his touch and could see he was ready for intimate contact when Hannigan's robe opened. Giving him a deep kiss, she was open to a sexual encounter:

"Josh, let me freshen up a bit and I'll be ready to get stuffed."

Hannigan knew what that British expression meant:

"From the likes of it, you aren't talking about food. I'll be waiting for you in bed."

Having endured a frenetic last forty-eight hours, sex would be a welcomed tonic for the two of them. After taking her shower, Sela increased her allure by coming to Hannigan with a splash of perfume across her neck and shoulders. Hannigan clutched her with a tender touch and entered inside her without forceful thrusts. Interspersed between their sighs of joy, they exchanged words of love:

"Josh, I like your touch. Hold me."

"Sela, squeeze and hold on tight. This is a great ride."

They came to climax, almost simultaneously. Allowing some moments for the paroxysms of pleasure to subside, Sela fell back on her pillow and stared at the ceiling in a reflective mood:

"Josh, I admire what you told the detective. It seemed you are risking it all to come clean."

"Sela, as long as you don't back away from the commitment you made to me earlier, I am armed with the courage to face whatever my fate will be."

"Even jail?"

"Not looking forward to that, but I'm counting on Captain Broadbent to find me a lawyer who can make any incarceration minimal, if at all."

"I hope that will be so. But what do we have to fear with Ian and his stepfather, David Percival, rearing their ugly heads back into our lives again?"

"After what we heard from the San Diego cops and what the FBI is doing, it's obvious Percival is a hunted man. He doesn't dare raise his head recklessly; it will be knocked off. And Ian Bright? The guy is a wuss, right?"

Sela made a mocking smile as to how Hannigan described Bright. She did not offer a different impression:

"Yes, Ian is at times no brighter than a button. But he's not exactly what we call gormless and you Americans call clueless. Deep down he can be course and unpredictable."

"I just wonder what happened to the bloke when he saw you and the detonator left him at LAX? My hunch he was not in a strong position to meet his step dad empty-handed."

The two of them went to the courtesy bar and fetched a refreshment. They seemed more relaxed as they resumed the conversation. Hannigan was curious:

"As you recall, how much did he know about your background? Again, I take it he was unaware that Jordan Starmont was alerting you to the danger in your life?"

"Along with you, Jordan was my secret. However, he did know I was a fatherless child, just like him."

"By chance, did you mention, by name, who your father was?"

"I may have dropped his name when Ian and I first met in London and we queried about our backgrounds. Where are you going with this?"

"We have to assume Bright told Percival as much about you that his devious mind would want to know. That's why it is good that you are now safe. Percival would not be your friend--you know too much about him."

Sela felt a shudder of fear when she heard this. She changed the subject:

"Josh, back in Perth, you said it might be best if we changed our names when we got to America. Is that part of your plan?"

"I'll get a better sense of that after I talk to a criminal lawyer. I want to clear my name before I assume another one."

They broke off the serious talk and got dressed. Told to remain in the hotel by Broadbent to stay secure, they hoped they could venture out. San Diego looked warm and inviting, with a climate similar to Perth. They preferred to be outside rather than inside. They also complained about staying in the same clothes more than their noses could tolerate. A potential release from their confinement came when the telephone rang late that afternoon:

"Josh Hannigan, Captain Broadbent again."

"Captain, glad you called. How are we coming on the letter of understanding? When can we move about?"

"Please try not to be fidgety. The stakes are too high for premature steps into the outside world. Sela has to stay put in your room. Are you in a position to come to the lobby in thirty minutes so we can pick you up and bring you to police headquarters?"

"That will work. But what you want won't be with me."

"I understand. Let's move forward to the terms and conditions we want you to review before the exchange. By the way, some legal help will be at our location for you to consider."

"Great. Who's coming for me?"

"It will be me and another detective. I want to keep you in my sights as much as possible."

They ended the call with Hannigan telling Broadbent they needed some fresh clothes. Broadbent said he had a surprise for him about that. Hannigan explained to a disappointed Sela she had to be duty bound to the room. He told her to open the door to no one and hang up on any caller.

To give him a "good boy" look, Hannigan was clean shaven and borrowed a touch of Sela's perfume to repel the odor of his almost three-day old attire. Despite his limited time in the hotel, Hannigan grew to appreciate its history and old-world elegance as he sat in the lobby waiting for Broadbent. Built by Ulysses S. Grant, Jr., the son of the 18th President of the United States, it opened in 1910. Its décor was accented with hanging crystal chandeliers, marble columns, lush, potted ferns throughout, some almost tall enough to reach the fifteen foot lobby ceiling, and a courtyard that looked out across to Horton Plaza and a beautiful fountain. The scenic view across the bay brought the Coronado peninsula into focus. When Broadbent came by and took Hannigan to his police cruiser, he gratuitously offered his historical perspectives of the place. Perhaps to allay the fears of Hannigan and Sela, Broadbent said the hotel is so secure it meets Secret Service standards to house presidents. One of the most famous, Franklin D. Roosevelt, delivered his first "fireside chat" outside Washington, D.C. from the hotel's 11th floor radio station. But, for Hannigan, that was enough about the past. He asked Broadbent about the present meeting at his location:

"So, can you tell me about the legal assistance you mentioned?"

"I hustled like crazy to get one of the best criminal lawyers in town to join us--Channing Williams. He'll be there with an assistant. Also, our Chief of Police, Howard Moore, feels your cooperation is so vital that he wanted to be in on the meeting."

"I like your energy, Captain Broadbent, to make things happen. But I need the desired effect."

"Mr. Hannigan, I want that to happen as well, in the worst way."

Hannigan was beginning to appreciate Broadbent's earnestness. In a matter of a few minutes they were at police headquarters. Broadbent brought Hannigan to a conference room that looked out onto the bay in the background. But, in the foreground, the individuals sitting around a long, rectangular table made Hannigan seem out of place. He was dressed for a casual evening; they were dressed as if attending a Fortune 500 board meeting. Chief Moore had a dark brown suit, white shirt, and a black tie. Williams had a most distinguished look, a younger version of Melvin Belli, the renowned San Francisco personal injury "King of Torts," with gray hair at the temples, and donned in a three-piece black suit, white shirt, and a power red tie. His assistant, an attractive redhead introduced as Deirdre Powell, wore a dark grey suit with a deep blue ruffled blouse. Having the time to go to his place, Broadbent slipped into a gray suit, white shirt, and blue tie. After exchanging the introductory formalities, Moore began the discussion:

"Good afternoon everyone. Ms. Powell, are you ready to record these proceedings?"

Giving a nod with her court reporting machine at the ready, Moore continued:

"Mr. Hannigan, first let me say our entire community owes you and your companion, Sela Danby, a debt of gratitude. Based on the details conveyed to those here today by Captain Broadbent, you have risked much. It is our firm hope we can satisfy your pre-conditions to surrender the nuclear detonator in a timely fashion. Do you want to say anything right now?"

"Yes, thank you, Chief Moore. I indicated earlier this morning to Captain Broadbent that I committed past crimes. What are the consequences of self-admisssion?"

This impactful legal question was immediately seized upon by Williams:

"Mr. Hannigan, were you admitting to the crimes or were you confessing to them?"

"I guess I am not sure. I just brought them into the conversation."

"Captain Broadbent, were you aware that Mr. Hannigan committed any crimes before you first met him? If so, did you charge him?"

Broadbent wisely paused a moment to jog his memory, especially since nothing was committed to writing while he spoke to Hannigan:

"Mr. Williams, based on what I recall, I made no charges. I just let Mr. Hannigan make his statement."

Williams stared at the ceiling, arose from his chair, and walked around the table in pensive thought. As if he was addressing a jury, he directed a pointed question to Broadbent:

"You let him talk without informing him of the consequences of what he might be saying? In other words, did you cite his Miranda Rights?"

"I generally state them to an accused if I press charges. Not knowing Mr. Hannigan is a past criminal, it didn't occur to me to inform him of his rights."

"Fine. At least that's out of the way. Gentlemen and lady, I don't want to be legally presumptive based on the reality I have not had the opportunity to interview Mr. Hannigan to establish a client/lawyer relationship. However, with just cursory knowledge of the situation, I like his prospects. There are more than a few moot points that affect his status. To wit, no one in this room is a witness to or knew of his alleged criminal activity last year."

Chief Moore jumped in for clarification:

"So, we can't say we are obstructing justice or withholding evidence by not alerting any law enforcement arm, specifically the FBI, by not charging Hannigan with anything. For sure, he has broken no crime in my jurisdiction and no one has come forward to claim he is a criminal."

"Chief Moore, that's a good way to frame it. Now, Mr. Hannigan, with the serious threat to domestic security in this vicinity, we have to confirm that you are willing to surrender the detonating device to the San Diego Police Department in exchange for a legal defense, if necessary. Is that still on the table, sir?"

Hannigan was squirming inside but trying to maintain a calm demeanor. He stroked his chin and replied:

"My intentions are honorable. The trade still is legal help in exchange for the detonator. However, in this limited discussion as to what my rights are and the criminal liability I might face, is it wise to not go to the Feds and admit wrongdoing? In other words, keep my mouth shut until I might be accused of a felony?"

Williams was amused at what he heard:

"Mr. Hannigan, why did you say anything to Captain Broadbent in the first place? You were in hiding in Australia. Your trail was cold to link you to wrongdoing. Considering what you wanted to surrender, you were making a heroic act, not something a criminal mind would entertain."

"Mr. Williams, I am not a religious person. But, in my Jesuit education in high school a passage from the *Gospel of John* applies to me in my current state. It goes like this: *Ye shall seek the truth and the truth shall set you free.* It's time for my soul to rest easy."

Williams was impressed but was practical, too:

"That is truly exemplary, but, in the world we live in, legal statutes overrule religious dogma. To get on point, you should know that I will confirm, in writing, to come to your legal assistance if and when it is required. Anyplace, anywhere."

"I understand you are a high-priced lawyer. I am in no position to cover your fees."

Williams gave a philosophical response, with a warning:

"Mr. Hannigan, don't worry. I am a man of principle as well. It would be a patriotic act on my part to help you, given that you have potentially saved our country from a calamity. It's also a way of honoring my brother's memory, who was lost at Iwo Jima. If this comes to a head, and there is value for everyone present to keep this episode quiet, lest it create an unwarranted panic, I'll be prepared to be proactive on your behalf. Legal fees? Don't worry, I'll profit both extrinsically and intrinsically."

That was convincing for Hannigan:

"Okay. Let's not delay. Draw up what you promised to do. With that in hand, I'll surrender the detonator to Captain Broadbent."

There was a general sigh of relief around the table that an equitable arrangement had occurred. Chief Moore ordered coffee brought in to those who wanted it, although he sensed a stronger potion he had in his liquor cabinet would not be out of place. Broadbent was assured by Williams that a letter of understanding would be drawn up, perhaps ready for delivery in two days, on Monday morning. Hannigan looked forward to it. Then he brought Broadbent aside and asked what the surprise was. It seemed the luggage for Hannigan and Sela was brought to Broadbent's office when he sent officers to the airport terminal to obtain their unclaimed belongings. Hannigan felt refreshed, knowing Sela would also welcome her clothes. Then, after thirty minutes of idle chatter, Williams got up with Deidre Powell to make their exit. He turned to the group and made a revelation:

"Mr. Hannigan, please heed my counsel--lie low and go by your real name. Not knowing your true nature, I had an ace in the hole if you reneged on your promise. You see, we researched and discovered there is a person who would be very upset with you. He's back from sea duty, living in the Claremont area of town. Your alias--one Rex Murtaugh."

50
CHAPTER

The Seal's Lair/La Jolla, September 15/16, 1969

David Percival picked up the telephone in his La Valencia suite for some needed support. He still needed help from the Seal's Lair as his caller answered:

"Hello"

"Casey, David Percival."

"I take it you made it to La Jolla okay."

"Yeah. Had one close call, but your secretive route got us to the La Valencia undetected."

"That's good to know. I am curious as to your next steps."

Percival tried not to sound too demanding, considering he had lost most of his accomplices:

"I know that I have barely left your presence, but, as I left it, I mentioned I might need your help. To be sure, it won't be too risky for you."

"Okay. If I can help, what is it that you need?"

"Since you are probably off duty on Sunday, I need you to drive out this afternoon to the La Valencia and pick-up Monty Crawford. From there, I need you to transport him to the Lair for a couple of days. Is that doable?"

As a Navy man, Douglas could not resist to deride a Marine:

"You know, David, the guy is a slob. They train those jarheads well, but they have poor table manners and general etiquette."

He then quickly added with a laugh:

"No. Not to worry. I can have him for a stay, providing he's out of my place by Friday. Have my living quarters inspection coming up this weekend."

"That will work. He should vacate in a couple of days. When needed, I'll call so you can take him to H and M Landing, which is just off Harbor Boulevard before you reach Shelter Island. You familiar with it?"

"Never been to H and M Landing, but I am familiar with Shelter Island. I can get him there."

"Great. Appreciate your help. Can you get Crawford about 4:00 P.M.? He'll be waiting outside the hotel at the valet stand."

"Done deal. But what are you really up to?"

"Casey, sorry to be evasive, but you'll know it when you see it. Stay by the telephone until you leave to get Crawford."

"Fair enough. Keep me posted."

Percival was relieved to still have Douglas at the ready. The Navy Seal still was unknown to those wanting to corral Nazis in their midst. Percival was gambling that Margaret Starmont would agree to meet him in the next few days to orchestrate his next calculating move. Crawford and Yancey Bixby were sprawled out on the sofas in the suite watching the early NFL football games on television. Percival broke up their amusement:

"Troopers, please shut the TV off and listen up."

The Marines sat up in an attentive manner:

"Just got off the phone with Casey Douglas, who still is loyal enough to our cause to give us a hand. Monty, pack your personal belongings, to include the .45's and long-barreled Colt pistols. Use the canvas bag in the truck to pack the rifles and recoilless. Include the ammo that goes with these weapons. Bixby and I will still retain the Glocks and the Berettas."

Crawford was a little puzzled to be on the move again:

"Sounds like I am a one-man battle group. This won't be another wild goose chase?"

"At ease, Monty. Keep your powder dry. Have your strong body and these items in position at the valet stand, to await a 4:00 P.M. pick-up by Douglas."

"Where am I bound?"

"Back to the Seal's Lair to await further instructions. By the way, I'm providing $1,000 to be used as I direct you to spend it. You've got enough pocket change to get by?"

"I'm fine. Probably have $60, but I'd have more if Bixby would pay me back the $100 he owes me from the craps we rolled at the Lair."

Bixby had a rejoinder for his fellow Marine's misguided humor:

"I owe you money? You never could add in your head."

Percival then got his cohorts on task:

"All right, all right! Now order us some food from room service. Tell them I need some fresh coffee."

Percival needed the caffeine to keep him sharp and alert. His sleep had been disrupted since he left the Lair. What would happen in the next few days would determine if he would stay a free man. The formula for freedom was in his head; all he needed was to meet Margaret Starmont to make it work.

+⊶ ◉ ⊷+

Jordan Starmont was the same cloistered guest of the San Diego Police Department at the U. S. Grant Hotel. However, he did not waste much of a beautiful sunny San Diego day, so he thought he would surprise his mother with an unannounced visit. He took a cab ride to La Jolla and enjoyed the scenic ride on I-5 first past Mission Bay on the left and then the ride up the ridge off Ardath Road. At the summit, he could see, below and straight ahead, the beauty of the palm trees in the foreground and the azure blue of the Pacific Ocean in the foreground. When the ride brought him to the coastal level of Torrey Pines Boulevard, he thought to himself that his mother chose a great neighborhood, filled with sumptuous cliffside residences and high-end homes throughout, to rest and relax. What he did not know is that his euphoric feeling would be fleeting, with danger lying in waiting at the La Valencia.

It was nearly noon when Jordan got to the lobby of the hotel. He used the house telephone to give his mother a sudden rush of joy:

"Mom. You ready for me--right here, alive and well in La Jolla?"

Margaret Starmont's heart raced with excitement:

"Oh, Jordan, I am so thrilled to hear you again. You are in La Jolla? Where?"

"Just beneath you--in the lobby of the hotel. Are you coming down or am I coming up to see you?"

"As a matter of fact, I was half dressed, ready to have lunch on the patio. It's another gorgeous day for it. Give me fifteen minutes and I'll come down."

Jordan had a flair for making his mother feel good:

"Mom, don't overdo the make-up--you are lovely just the way you are."

"Jordan, you are so kind. I think, someday, you'll be a good catch--you know how to make a woman wanted."

After ending the call, Jordan needed something to calm his excitement a bit. He strolled into the bar and took a seat in a rounded-back chair and asked the bartender what drink would go well this time of day. He suggested a mimosa, a drink Jordan never heard of. However, since the described ingredients had a two-fold benefit, the healthy orange juice and the elixir of champagne, he ordered one. The first sips had the desired effect. It seemed it relieved much of the intense moments he had lived through for weeks. It only took fifteen minutes for his mother to find him. Dressed in a two-piece white suit and beige blouse, Margaret had the look of lovely leisure. She came upon Jordan unseen and poked him gently on his shoulder:

"My, my, you found a good place to unwind. Give me a hug, will you!"

Jordan immediately vacated his seat and put his arms around his mother and kissed her on the cheek. They looked at each other, head to toe, in a look of amazement that now the rest of their lives could be more tranquil. Margaret decided to match Jordan's mimosa and suggested they have lunch in the Med restaurant, hoping they could get a table on the balcony. Despite a nearly filled dining room, they were in luck. Margaret had gotten to know the maître d' during her stay to gain some favor from him. With the sun beaming down upon them, a soft wind blowing in their faces, and the blue Pacific beneath them, it was a classic setting for conviviality.

At about the time Margaret and her son were ordering their meals, David Percival came into the hotel after a brisk walk that included the heights above La Jolla Cove, the open Pacific vista at the lifeguard station, with a gaggle of sea lions barking at its base, and the narrow green parkway that straddles the ocean. With Margaret Starmont on his mind, he pondered during his walk what he would say when they met. He was in luck when he went to the front desk, for his complicit desk man was on duty. Percival was pointed, as he surreptitiously slipped a $20 bill to the clerk:

"Any idea what Mrs. Starmont is up to lately?"

The clerk was a willing font of information:

"Just one telephone call this morning, a room service breakfast, and a visitor who came in forty-five minutes ago."

Percival was intrigued by a possible impediment to get to her:

"A visitor? Any idea who that would be?"

"Her son, Jordan Starmont, who asked to be connected to her room from the house phone."

The name struck Percival like a thunderbolt. Finally, the real Jordan Starmont was at hand and ready to be confronted. He asked the obvious:

"Is her son still on the premises?"

"As a matter of fact, he is. He's having lunch in the Med restaurant."

"How would I find him?"

"If you look around, you'll find the young man dining with his attractive mother. She's stunning for her age. I saw her come to the lobby in a lovely white suit."

He gave a diabolical smile to the clerk and slipped him another $20 bill under a folio on the counter. Walking to the restaurant, he told the maître d' he was looking for a friend. Trying not to be too obvious, he casually looked over the dining clientele, with indirect glances. When he looked out into the doors that led to the balcony tables, he spotted his quarry. There they were: an attractive woman with a young man in rapt conversation, oblivious to the glare of a demon spying upon them. Finally, clarity was now in focus for what had been vexing him. Jordan Starmont was a ruse, much younger than he ever imagined. This called for an adjustment to Percival's plan. With animated awareness, he quickly exited the restaurant and used the house phone to call his suite. Bixby answered:

"Yancey, I am glad you picked up. You know where the Berettas are?"

"Sure, in the drawer you stored them in."

"Good. Bring them under cover down to the lobby ASAP. Tell Crawford to leave now to get the Lincoln and park it out front of the hotel, immediately!"

"Hey, this sounds big."

"It is. We are going on a hunting expedition to bag the pain in the ass who has made us look like fools."

51
CHAPTER

San Diego, September 16, 1969

Damon Broadbent had had the weekend of his life as a law enforcement officer. It was a unique experience to have a dramatic turn of events to have the most vital case of his career bring such positive results in such a fortuitous fashion. He was beating his head against a stone wall, but when Josh Hannigan, Sela Danby, and Jordan Starmont appeared, from out of nowhere, it was an unbelievable twist of fate. To keep the forward momentum, he spent his Sunday following up on details and coordinating critical players involved to capture a nuclear madman.

The paramount goal was to have Josh Hannigan turn over the uranium detonator to get it in a safe place. In preparation for this transaction, Broadbent would send detective Dan Herlihy to the Physics Department at the University of California, San Diego, first thing on Monday morning. Someone there had to know how to handle the device without consequences. Then, as promised, attorney Channing Williams was to have a letter of understanding to defend Josh Hannigan, if needed, to cement the canister transfer deal. It was nearly 10:00 A.M. on Monday when Broadbent was paged on the intercom by officer Oliver:

"Captain Broadbent, you have a Deidre Powell here to see you."

Broadbent felt reassured that Williams was committed to help the cause:

"Great. Please send her in. Ask her if she wants a cup of coffee."

"Will do, although she just went to the ladies room. Captain, she's a real looker. Lately you have been doing business with some real beauties. Some guys get all the breaks."

"All right, Oliver. Let's not use your imagination. This is all business."

In several minutes, Powell walked through Broadbent's open door with Oliver's coffee in one hand and a portfolio in the other. She was dressed in a grey midi skirt, the same colored blouse, and an avocado velvet Westcott jacket. She had the look of a well-paid paralegal, which didn't question Broadbent's belief that Williams paid his people well. He got up from his desk, seated her in front of it, and returned to his seat with an ingratiating attitude:

"Ms. Powell, I am so happy you are here in a timely manner. Please tell Channing that I really appreciate the extra effort he made to make the whole City of San Diego a safer place."

"Captain, Mr. Williams is committed to helping your investigation and to, as you say, make our city breathe easier. We worked all day yesterday to prepare what I have for your consideration."

She opened her portfolio and handed Broadbent a two-page document. Broadbent thanked her and asked for a moment to read what was prepared. The essence of it summarized the Saturday discussion they had with Hannigan. The salient points included: A.) Hannigan was to fully cooperate and assist with Broadbent's investigation; B.) Along with his companion, Sela Danby, they were not to leave the San Diego area until cleared by the police; C.) That he was not to volunteer any admission of guilt to any past crimes; D.) If confronted by any Federal or any local law enforcement official with criminal charges, he was to immediately invoke his Miranda rights and to enlist the Williams law firm for legal counsel before making any statements; E.) If he needs a legal defense, for any alleged criminal activity, that he had retained and would be defended by the Williams firm, pro bono; F.) It impressed upon Hannigan and Ms. Danby to talk to no one about this entire episode until so directed by the Williams firm; G.) By agreeing to these terms and conditions with his signature, he would turn over the detonating device in his possession to Captain Damon Broadbent.

Broadbent beamed with approval:

"Ms. Powell, this is clear, direct, and persuasive for Mr. Hannigan to consider and approve. I hope to take this proposal to Hannigan, your client, this afternoon, if possible. I take it Channing would have no objections to not be present when I put it front of Mr. Hannigan?"

"We expected you to request this. There are no objections if Mr. Hannigan follows through. But, if he refuses to cooperate, we must be contacted immediately. In no uncertain terms must you press the matter to your liking."

Then, Broadbent could not resist asking about the Rex Murtaugh revelation:

"Ms. Powell, who contacted Murtaugh? What does he know about Hannigan and his whereabouts?"

"I called him, carefully following the script given to me by Mr. Williams. Since we represent several shipping firms in Southern California, always looking for experienced deck hands, I asked him he if he was interested in an employment opportunity."

"What was his response to you?"

"Naturally, he was surprised we found him, but he opened up a bit and said he wanted some time off from the sea. I discovered he generally hires on with trans-Pacific freighters, which take him to the Far East, New Zealand, and, what do you know--Australia."

"He give any bad vibes about Australia?"

"Didn't press him there when I heard Australia. We assumed he's the man Hannigan lifted his I.D. from."

"Did he ask you for your name and contact information?"

"I simply said, if he ever needed a job to contact me at the separate business number I retain for special activities."

"Hmm, that's funny. I never knew your firm is a diverse organization."

Powell knew Broadbent had to have his cynicism straightened out:

"Let's be real here, Captain. Our firm has a vetting process for potential clients. Hannigan conveyed a sensational story. We had to separate fact from fiction.'

"Sounds to me your firm likes to take on clients that can beat the odds and win their cases if they go to trial."

"You could say that, but Hannigan is a good client to bring into court. Based on what we know about him, he seems to be truthful, a quality many people who come to us don't have."

"Yes, it's a rare quality. And, as far as I can tell, he's honest and I believe reliable enough to deliver the goods."

As they concluded their meeting, Broadbent was satisfied that Hannigan's cover was not blown and that lawyers used devices that sometimes stretched the limits of ethics. He thanked Powell for her help and saw her to an awaiting car outside the police station. When she was seated inside, he brought his head around to make a parting comment:

"Tell Channing I'll contact him when I have the object in hand. And, let's hope we won't see each other in court."

To not dally, Broadbent immediately went back to his office and called Hannigan at the U.S. Grant Hotel. They agreed to meet in Hannigan's room at 1:00 P.M. Then he telephoned Margaret Starmont, simply to say hello and find out if Jordan visited with her. No answer. He left a message. Might as well call Jordan at the U.S. Grant. Again, no answer. He left a message. His disappointment was reversed when a familiar face walked into his office shortly thereafter. Rick Sandoval, with his usual big smile, sauntered into his office and was raring to go but started out a bit sardonic:

"Captain, I think that fire I started out at Percival's place is finally under control. What a blaze, and I didn't even use matches."

Broadbent smiled at the wry humor. He just was happy his trusted colleague was not more seriously hurt:

"Sure good to see your smiling face again, Rick. Guess we sent you into a hornet's nest, or should I say a TNT debacle. What you discovered has likely made Percival and his cronies more cautious in their movements."

"I just found out from Oliver that you guys may have cracked the Windansea case without me. I find that hard to believe."

"We'll see. More work ahead of us before we are out of the woods. Percival still has the uranium at his disposal; just can't set it off right now--we hope. The break we got with Hannigan's heroics was a big benefit. What else you got?"

"I found out a little more as to what happened Friday night at Lindbergh from the FBI's Joe Pizzo. Guess their trap to nab Percival getting the critical delivery from his son went awry."

"I'm just relieved the papers didn't say anything about that fiasco."

"It seems Percival's kid, this Ian Bright, was nabbed at LAX trying to get back to London. He's being held as an accessory at the U.S. Marshal's office in L.A."

"That's good. One less desperado to worry about. They get anything out of him?"

"No, he's a scared puppy. Claims he was just a pawn doing his father's bidding."

Broadbent had no sympathy for a group who had little for him:

"I'll let the FBI figure out what they want to do with the bum. They never really apprise us of their activities. If they only knew we scooped them for the prize they were looking for."

"I take it that's not for Pizzo and his lads to know?"

"Exactly. Say, can you drive up to La Jolla and see if Margaret Starmont needs anything? She's another kind spirit that I hope is resting easy after her son came in to help us."

"Will do. What's Herlihy into?"

"He's up at UCSD to enlist the aid of some faculty person who knows how to safely handle a nuclear detonating device, which I hope to get shortly from Hannigan."

Not knowing what a Nazi thug was up to, Sandoval was unaware and naive:

"Good luck with that. I'll give you my report from La Jolla. It seems nothing exciting really goes on there."

52
CHAPTER

La Jolla, September 15/16, 1969

David Percival did not want to pass up a golden opportunity to bring Margaret Starmont into his devil's den. As an added bonus, he got an unexpected prize in the form of her son, Jordan, oblivious to the latent danger he faced. Grabbing these two would be his ticket to ride to live another evil day. Mobilizing Yancey Bixby and Monty Crawford into position, he had Bixby at his side in the lobby, armed and dangerous, and Crawford idling the Lincoln, in front of the hotel. Percival told Bixby that as soon as Margaret and Jordan left the restaurant and come into the lobby, he would try to lure them outside. Once there, they would force them into the waiting Lincoln. He instructed Bixby to be sure no one blocked the exit to make a smooth transition out of the lobby.

A beautiful midday brunch between mother and son belied the imminent peril about to befall them. For the most part, the conversation over their meal was about the future—for both of them. However, Margaret had to reminisce about her good times at the La Valencia:

"You know, your father and I always enjoyed our stays here in La Jolla in general and this hotel in particular. Its charm and beauty always eased the pressures and hectic pace of things in New York, although we thrived on its pulsating pace."

"I do recall father talking about your satisfaction with the place. I can see why you have fond memories. Didn't you think of retiring here?"

"I think that was one of your father's options after he left Smith-Barney, but he still had a good ten years before retirement. Things could have changed."

"Well, I am glad I changed my order to your--eggs benedict, with the beautiful fruit and pastries to delight us both. Those Mimosas were good. You having another?"

"No, son, I think it wise to limit drinks with a kick to them. Speaking of changes, what do want to do after this bizarre experience is over?"

"Just get back to normal. Perhaps go back to Princeton."

Margaret was hoping her son would rekindle his education:

"Jordan, I hope you do that. You know your father set aside enough funds for you to complete your education. You are fortunate. This war in Vietnam has interrupted the lives of many boys your age."

"You know, it's funny. Some of my friends were selected by the government to go into the military. My flat feet gave me an out for the draft, but the government still got me—for a little while anyway."

"This Vietnam thing still weighs heavily over the heads of your generation. It all seems so senseless. At least your period of involuntary service to the government was short and, in the end, safe."

"You must know that Sela Danby's work for our country came at an emotional price. It's important that I meet her for the first time. I want to console her, apologize for putting her through the wringer."

"She's kind of delicate, you think?"

"Yes, I believe it is her kind nature. You'll see it when we meet, which I hope is soon."

"When might that be? Has Captain Broadbent cleared it for you two to finally get together? You know, I would love to meet the girl as well."

"Soon, I hope, in the next day or two. It's all dependent on coordinating with a Josh Hannigan, who rescued Sela from this Ian Bright I told you about earlier."

"Yes, I hope that happens quickly. It's been nice out here, but I have to get back to New York, knowing that you are safe."

As Margaret signed off on their meal, she suggested they go her room and continue the discussion about both of their next steps. But that pleasant plan was about to be rudely interrupted. In the lobby off the restaurant, Percival had his Beretta positioned in the right pocket of a sweatshirt.

Bixby had his at the ready in the pocket of his jacket. Margaret and Jordan were in rapt conversation as they came into the lobby area. It helped that no one was at the front desk or congregating in the hotel entrance hall. At that moment Percival stopped in front of her and got her attention:

"Mrs. Starmont? I don't mean to be gauche, but I am Wilfred Tanner."

Margaret was taken aback, but answered:

"Yes, I recognize your voice from our recent conversation. I thought I was to contact you when I had the time to meet?"

"Again, I am sorry if this is rude, but the hotel staff told me where I could find you. There is an important person outside the hotel who wants to meet you and the young man at your side—who I presume is Jordan Starmont?"

Looking somewhat bewildered by this stunning encounter, Margaret was compliant:

"You are correct. Jordan, this is Mr. Tanner, an old business associate of your father."

Jordan did not know what to make of this blatant stranger, but was hospitable and cautious:

"Mr. Tanner, this is all so sudden, but it is a pleasure to meet you. But who is it that we absolutely have to see at this awkward time?"

"She's important to you both--Sela Danby. You might tell that I am from England. She told me she was coming to San Diego. You see, I am her uncle, trying to help her at a tough time."

Percival said the magic words, Sela Danby, and gained instant credibility from them both. Margaret was now motivated to accede to Percival's request:

"Oh, what a delightful coincidence. By all means, let's go out to see her."

The four of them headed out the hotel entrance into the bright sunshine of the afternoon. Percival directed them to the Lincoln at the curb and gave this instruction:

"She's in the back seat of the Lincoln that brought her here. Percival suddenly took Margaret's arm, opened the rear door and shoved her into the back seat. Concurrently, Bixby strong-armed Jordan, opened the front door, and shoved him next to Crawford at the wheel, who immediately locked the car doors and drove off up Prospect Street. Margaret was in a huff:

"What's the meaning of this?"

Jordan was more blatant:

"Stop this car and let us go!"

He wanted to struggle but Bixby had the ultimate in persuasion when he clutched Jordan's head and brought him forcibly into his lap with his pointed Beretta at his temple:

"Kid, you feel this barrel. Settle down or it's the last thing you are going to ever feel."

Then Percival, who was holding Margaret's right arm firmly, tried to allay the panic of his passengers:

"Please do not be alarmed. We are going for a little ride to calm down a bit and then go back to the hotel—to my room to better get to know one another. Crawford put on the radio for some musical merriment."

That turned out to be a bad suggestion. The first lyrics from the radio were Jim Morrison's mournful tones from *The End:*

This is the end, my only friend, the end.

The end for whom?

53
CHAPTER

San Diego, September 16, 1969

Perhaps the most eventful moment of Josh Hannigan's young and perilous life was about to unfold. Contacted by telephone by Captain Damon Broadbent earlier in the day, a meeting was arranged at 4:00 P.M. in the room Hannigan was sharing with Sela Danby at the U.S. Grant Hotel. To reinforce his intent to surrender the detonator he had in his possession, he went to the closet door and brought the box that held its contents. Hannigan made a dangerous assumption that the detonator was in there, since he never opened the box when he pilfered it from Ian Bright. Putting the box on a coffee table, he held his breath when he broke the seal of the package and opened up the top cardboard lids. As they opened he could see a round object wrapped in bubble wrap. Then he turned to Sela, who came to his side, sensing this was a big deal:

"Dear, I just hope this is what I think it is."

"Sela, it could be a huge problem if this falls into the wrong hands. Let's be sure."

He excitedly unwrapped what turned out to be a metallic sphere, gold plated, and with a series of wires connected to small rods that surrounded the outside surface. It looked like an ugly face with pox marks on it. The object felt like a brick, but it seemed like he was holding the weight of the world. After carefully unraveling this sinister device, he saw a six-inch lever at the bottom of the sphere. To Hannigan's unscientific mind, this seemed like the connecting piece that would be attached to the uranium canister. Lifting it completely out of the container it gave him a cold sweat to feel it in his trembling palms. It was if he was present when Robert Oppenheimer, the "Father of the atomic bomb", first saw the catastrophic effects of the initial nuclear explosion, he quoted Hindu scripture running through his mind:

Now I am become Death, the destroyer of worlds.

He sat down, put the detonator in his lap, and wiped his brow in disbelief:

"This puts me in total shock, Sela. To think we have in our possession an instrument that could inflict such unthinkable results hits home. It will be good to get rid of it, to give us a sense of relief."

"Josh, it is all those terrible things, but look at the bright side. It represents a chance for a new lease on life for you when you give it up."

"Let's hope so."

After rewrapping and re-packing the detonator, Hannigan needed a cold shower to dissipate the tension descending upon his body. Sela was limp, realizing they have a lethal means of harming many in their possession. She rested for a bit and then got dressed. They decided to go down to the Grant Grill to have something to eat. It was a venerable gastronomical spot with wooden panels and floors. Sela commented on the place when she was seated by the restaurant host:

"This reminds me of home, back in England. There is a restaurant in my home town, Tunbridge Wells, that comes to mind."

Looking over the top of his menu, Hannigan took the opportunity to broach an important topic:

"We've talked a little about our life after we disengage from this bit of fix we are in. I take it England is still close to your heart?"

"You would find it a delightful place. It's about 50 kilos southeast from London, close to the Kent/East Sussex border. It's an easy train ride to London, which is so alive these days, especially with all the gaiety of Soho's Carnaby Street and the music: the Beatles, the Stones, Dave Clark Five, Herman's Hermits, and so many more musical blokes."

Hannigan could see that Sela was on a euphoric ascent. He kept it that way:

"You mean I might have a chance to get Twiggy's autograph there?"

"You have the good looks that she would not pass you by. Just don't cozy up to her."

All this mirth made them laugh heartily, something that they hadn't done for a while. He bent over to kiss her softly on the cheek and said:

"Perhaps that might be our next destination. You think we could make a go of it?"

"I've been gone for several years, but I still have a few friends and one aunt who lives in Tunbridge Wells. They would open their arms to us, and I think won't ask too many questions."

"And, if I go abroad again, I can leave my past behind me."

Then Hannigan moved on to Jordan Starmont, who Sela really wanted to meet:

"Are you disappointed you have not met your half-brother, Jordan, yet?"

"Given what the two of us have gone through, sight unseen, it would be a fitting tribute to a tortuous, long-distance relationship. I guess once you give the police what they want and you get what you need from the attorney, I'll get the okay to meet him."

"For sure, this has also been on my mind. Four o'clock can't come soon enough to clear the decks of all obstacles and start to go on with our lives."

Having laid out some alternatives for their future, they finished their meal with anticipation that the worst would soon be over. They went back to their room to await Broadbent's arrival. Meanwhile, Broadbent was stirring in his office. It concerned him that Jordan and Margaret Starmont still had not returned his calls, and it was approaching 2:00 P.M. He got on the radio dispatch to Rick Sandoval for some clarity:

"Rick, you got a fix on Margaret Starmont, over?"

"Captain, I was just ready to contact you. I'm at the summit leaving La Jolla about to enter I-5. Sorry, but Mrs. Starmont is either unavailable or has left the confines of the hotel, over."

"I take it you did the routine stuff, checking with staff up there, over?"

"Sure, but the desk clerk did clarify something. He said the last time he saw them was yesterday when they went to lunch. Checking with the maître d', he saw them leave the restaurant together about 1:30 P.M."

"How about messages, over?"

"Nothing given to the hotel, either incoming or out-going. They have been unseen for, what is it, over twenty-four hours, over."

"I don't like the sound or looks of that. It's too long to be gone without a trace. Come back to the office. When you get here we have an important visit to make with Hannigan and his girlfriend at the Grant, over and out."

Broadbent knew that only half of the danger was allayed. The detonator would soon be his, but David Percival and his cronies were still at large, with an unaccounted nuclear explosive. Detective Dan Herlihy soon returned to the station from the UC-San Diego campus after consulting with a physics professor. He reported that that the detonator was not volatile, but, and it was a big exception, an encapsulated container of uranium still had the capability of doing horrendous damage. It was latent, but its potency was never going to diminish. All it needed was a spark to blow things to the high heavens. That didn't make Broadbent breathe any easier.

About 3:00 P.M, Chief Howard Moore came to his office. He was to accompany Broadbent to the hotel to make the exchange with Hannigan. He was a bit fidgety, knowing something could still go wrong:

"Damon, how we doing? No surprises, right?"

"Chief, relax. When this is over we'll come back to your office, open your private reserve, and sample a relaxing fluid without an 'e' in its name."

"That will be just fine. In fact, I am so confident that I have a fresh bottle, just in case we have company to celebrate."

"Oh, you sent out invitations when we have the prize in our hands?"

"Yes, the mayor, Channing Williams, and his lovely assistant. It's a party, but the rest of the world won't know about it. I don't know if we have been living a lie or keeping the best kept secret since the Manhattan Project, the development of the A-Bomb."

Picking up a portfolio, Broadbent exited his office by placing a comforting arm around Moore's shoulders. Sandoval was at the ready with a police cruiser as they came outside. Moore commented about the atmospherics:

"I'm glad I can't smell smoke anymore from the Fallbrook blaze. It was a constant reminder, as they say, where there is smoke there is fire. One fire down; one to go."

Hearing this, Broadbent smiled as he opened the rear car door for his chief. Sandoval dutifully chauffeured them to the Grant Hotel. Once at the front desk, Broadbent called up to Hannigan's room, telling him to wait for three knocks on the door. He also instructed the clerk to have room service provide ice water, coffee, tea, bread and butter, and some scones. Having gone through the emotional mill, Broadbent felt he had his emotions under control as the elevator took them to Hannigan's eighth-floor room. After the three raps on the door, Hannigan opened it and enthusiastically invited his guests in. He had a formal look, buying a tie and a white shirt yesterday at a hotel shop, to make it appear this was all business. Broadbent wanted to take the edge off the proceedings up front:

"Josh, Ms. Danby, thank you for agreeing to meet with us again. In a moment, room service will provide some refreshment. With a pleasant English lass in the room, isn't it time for 'high tea'?"

Sela nodded in agreement. They went to the suite area, which had two loveseats flanking the coffee table. Upon it was the topic of conversation--the detonator carton. Sela intervened at this point to increase the group comfort:

"Let's wait for room service. Back in England, important matters are not discussed until everyone has a cup in hand--tea, coffee, or something stronger."

The three men all laughed in agreement. While awaiting to be served, the badinage covered the beautiful weather, the great ambience of the hotel, and the guests thanking Broadbent for the great accommodations. In ten minutes, they helped themselves at the serving table for the provided refreshments. The men all reached for coffee, with no additives to give it an efficacy of making one attentive. Sela, as expected, went for the tea, two lumps of sugar, cream, and a scone, since she ate little at lunch. Broadbent opened the formalities:

"I believe everything is in order. Based on our department's review, the letter we have received from the Williams law firm covers the talking points we agreed to the other day. There are two copies: one for you; one for the firm. Here is your copy, Mr. Hannigan. Please take a moment to study its contents."

After opening the portfolio, Broadbent reached in and handed Hannigan his copy, printed on premium bond paper. Standing up and reaching across the table to accept it, he sat right back down next to Sela. He gave her a smile and lightly squeezed her hand as he began to read it. At that point, it was if the air had left the room. Hannigan perused it carefully, reading it twice. Then he made a comment coming from right field, aiming to satisfy Sela's desires:

"When will we be introduced to Jordan Starmont?"

Broadbent looked nervously at Moore, justifying the chief's angst that things could go wrong, and replied:

"As indicated in the agreement, upon the department's consent, facilitated by your signature, you are free to go and seek out whomever you wish to see."

"Do you know where Jordan might be?"

Broadbent had to stretch the truth:

"Like you, he is staying at the hotel. You can seek him out with the help of the hotel, staff."

Hannigan nodded, looked into Sela's eyes, and made a request:

"This looks fine. Could you kindly hand me a pen?"

Broadbent had to subdue a big sigh of relief and pulled out a fountain pen, which the Williams firm provided, and gave it to Broadbent. Both he and Moore rested easier as they heard the sound of the pen affixing its image on the letter. With that, Hannigan handed the carton to Broadbent, who took the liberties to inspect the carton. He looked for the details Herlihy received from the UC-San Diego physics department. Broadbent then gleefully reached across to shake Hannigan's hand with a lilt in his voice:

"Mr. Hannigan. It was a great pleasure to do business with you to uphold the motto of our department: 'To protect and serve'." Chief Moore, I defer to you."

Moore also shook Hannigan's hand and finished with the proceedings:

"You have the copy of what you signed, Mr. Hannigan. Captain Broadbent will also give you a letter from my office, which summarizes, from our perspective, what just transpired and allows you to go about your business. Again, thank you. Oh, by the way, you can keep the pen--it's a souvenir of your patriotic act."

The group then shared what was left of the food and drink in a relaxed mood. Sela was beaming, happy for her beau's opportunity to now walk to the beat of his own drum. Broadbent and Moore got up to leave about fifteen minutes later. As he got to the door, Broadbent turned and needed to satisfy his curiosity:--

"You can stay at the hotel for two more days, then you'll be on your own dime. Where might you be bound?"

Hannigan thought about it, whispered in Sela's ear for approval of what he was about to say, and then replied:

"Not really sure. The agreement made no limitations on where I can go. You'll know where we are--if and when we need you."

54
CHAPTER

La Jolla, September 15, 1969

A captured pair, Margaret and Jordan Starmont were filled with fear. David Percival had them in his clutches inside his black sedan. He instructed his driver, Monty Crawford, to take them to the rear of the La Valencia Hotel to off-load the Starmonts, where they would be closely guarded as they were escorted to his suite. Percival gave his intimidating orders:

"Nothing will happen to you if you stay quiet. We are going to my hotel accommodation. We'll rest for a bit and get to know one another better. Am I clear?"

Margaret was in no mood for compromise:

"Who the hell are you? Why are you holding us?"

"This is not as bad as it looks--if you cooperate. If not, I am your worst nightmare."

The conversation ceased as Crawford slowly navigated to the back side of the hotel on Coast Boulevard. Margaret's heart was pulsating as she tried to calm herself by hoping for the best. Jordan settled down but was thinking of ways to free himself. For now, he would stay silent and cooperate. When Crawford parked at the side of the hotel, Percival instructed their exit:

"Remember, pistols will be pointed at your backs until we reach my room. We are going to quietly leave the car, take the service walk to the fire exit of the hotel, and all without saying a word. Got it?"

At this point, the captives were too anxious to utter a word. Percival got out first, prodding Margaret to walk in front of him on the walkway. Then Yancey Bixby left the front of the sedan with Jordan walking in front of him. The four of them made it to the door of the fire stairwell and walked up the metal steps to the second-floor landing. Bixby opened the door to the hallway and observed:

"The coast is clear. Everyone stay here until I open the room."

Percival then pulled a second pistol, his German Lugar, out of concealment and pointed it at the Starmonts:

"You see this? I mean business. When we are called to move, we will go quietly into the hall and into my room. One peep and it's curtains."

The Starmonts remained frozen for what seemed like an eternity. Then Bixby opened the stairwell door and beckoned them to enter the hall. It was just a short walk into Percival's suite. Once inside, Percival told the Starmonts to take a seat and remain quiet. He offered them refreshments from the service bar. Trying to ingratiate himself, Percival had a calm demeanor, but he asked a loaded question:

"Again, my intent is not to harm you both. But I am curious. First, what brings you both to La Jolla, Margaret and Jordan?"

Margaret was flippant with the first response:

"It's a beautiful place. Can't you tell with the warm sunshine?"

Percival fluffed it off and was after bigger game by directing his words to Jordan:

"And, young man, why are you in this vicinity?"

Jordan simply rolled his head a little. He answered with some venom:

"It sure wasn't to meet a madman like you."

"Hmm? Madman, huh. Weren't you to have met me at a La Jolla Beach several weeks ago? Somehow you were a no show. Or were you the corpse that suddenly came back to life?"

"I don't recall arranging anything with you. You have the right person?"

"Maybe not, because the Jordan Starmont who planned to meet me is an older man, not a naïve lad like you. But somehow your name is at the center of all this. Who's been using you? Or are you the Messiah the Jews have been waiting for?"

Margaret, hiding the fact her husband had a Jewish father, came to her son's defense:

"Jordan is joining me here. He's been living out here and came in to see me. He's not involved with anything."

Percival didn't want to push too hard:

"Everyone doing okay? You'll find things will improve if you open up—just a little. Let's move on. Do the names Sela Danby and Ian Bright ring a bell?"

Hearing those names hit Jordan with increased emotion. It convinced him that the man they were talking to was the center of the FBI manhunt: David Percival. He still had to be coy and not reveal his cards:

"They sound like they might be English. Judging by your accent, are they acquaintances of yours, back in England?"

"Young man, you are wise beyond your years with these evasive answers. So, let me be blunt for the two of you: you only gain freedom by giving me the truth. Give it some time. If you don't give better answers, perhaps we make things more uncomfortable for the two of you. Understand?"

The Starmont's both winced but stayed tight-lipped. Percival told Bixby to guard their unwilling guests while he took Crawford into one of the bedrooms. Closing the door behind him, Percival had a change of plan:

"Monty, there's not much time. Your bags and weapons packed and ready to go?"

"Yeah, I did it when you told me to."

"Good. We all have to leave when Douglas gets here. It will be later than planned. I'll pack my stuff. Go out and relieve Bixby and tell him to come in here."

Percival trusted his survival to impromptu but calculated moves. The La Valencia was not an ideal place to keep the Starmonts without unforeseen problems. Time to go back to a place of comfort. He got on the telephone and called Casey Douglas:

"Casey, glad you stayed close to the phone. Change of plan. Come to the hotel at 8:30 instead tonight. We need the cover of darkness"

"Will comply. What's prompted the time change?"

"I've got company that I need to keep out of sight. They are hot commodities."

"Who can be that be?"

"Margaret Starmont, the mother, and her son, Jordan--you know the phantom we did not meet at Windansea?"

"Let me see here? A mother of Jordan Starmont? How old is she?"

"Not that old. In fact, she's rather attractive. Her kid is college age. It confirms the ruse the law people tried to pull on us."

"Where are they now?"

"In my room, being guarded by Crawford and Bixby. They are tight-lipped and won't tell us about Ian and this Sela Danby."

"How long you intend to keep them?"

"They are my hostages until I see a way to get out of the country—in a few days."

"Out of the country, David? How?"

"That's where the H and M Landing I told you about comes in."

"Don't the boats that go from there only offer day trips, or limited overnight bookings?"

Percival had a grander voyage in mind:

"Casey, between you and me, they can take me to Ensenada. From there I think I can find passage to a safe haven--somewhere in the Pacific."

Douglas was curious what Percival may take with him:

"You going to take along that explosive package you have at your disposal?"

"Of course, Casey. It's the best self-defense I have. It doesn't look like I will use it here in San Diego. I still have hopes, someday, I'll obtain the desired effects to gain acceptance for our Nazi movement."

"But getting back to the Starmonts. What might prompt them to play ball with you?"

"I think we need a change of scenery."

"Where could that be?"

"The one place that keeps them out of sight and out of mind and has been good for me--the Seal's Lair"

55
CHAPTER

San Diego, September 16/17, 1969

Approaching 8:00 P.M., Damon Broadbent was feeling the effects of too many George Dickel Whiskys after a victory celebration at Howard Moore's office. He reflected back on what concluded. Joining Broadbent and Moore to celebrate the acquisition of the detonator from Josh Hannigan, were the San Diego Mayor, Channing Williams and Deirdre Powell. The mayor was relieved that they kept a potential nuclear attack from the public by keeping the press in the dark. It also helped that the FBI gave no specifics on the failed capture of Ian Bright and what he carried at Lindbergh Field last Friday night. At one point, Williams inquired about the object:

"So what are you going to do with the grand prize?"

Moore responded with a sense of elation:

"It's been a while since I have felt this good, especially knowing that detonation monster will be stored in our evidence locker until further notice. We are also getting scientific advice from the UC-San Diego Physics department as to how to handle it."

"Sounds like you have that well in hand. If all else fails, I am sure the Atomic Energy Commission can help you dispose of it. But how about Hannigan and his, as I understand it, his English beauty?"

Broadbent got his cue:

"He plays his cards well. They have a destination unknown. I doubt he's going back to Australia."

"If he was smart, which he is, maybe he leaves the country. Given the relationship he is in, I'd guess to the Mother Country--England."

Powell, always with an eye and ear to important details, offered what she was into:

"I have a contact who works for PSA in town. She will be scanning the airline bookings in and out of the city. If they show up, we'll get some idea where they are headed."

Broadbent questioned why the importance of accounting for them? Powell replied:

"To say this has been a bizarre episode is an understatement. Our reputation is not on the line by defending a potential felon. If Hannigan stays in country, he could be an embarrassment, not to our firm, but to the City of San Diego."

Williams was quick to support Powell:

"No matter, we'll be at the ready to give him legal help--if he needs it."

Then the seriousness abated when the mayor thanked Moore and Broadbent for their outstanding efforts to avoid disaster, as fortunate as this all turned out to be. But he asked the obvious question about unfinished business:

"We got the fuse to prevent disaster, but what about the Nazi--this David Percival?"

Broadbent responded with some sense of objectivity:

"We think Percival and his cronies are on the run. He destroyed his house in Fallbrook; likely has nowhere to hide."

The mayor wanted more specifics:

"Any idea if Percival and his bad boys are still lingering around?"

"My hunch he's still in the general area, hoping that Ian Bright will show up with what we have. Our units are still looking for the vehicles he has in his possession. Maybe we will get some help, finally, from the FBI to see if Bright could help lead us to him."

As the festivities came to an end, Powell sidled over to Broadbent and got personal in a silent, sultry voice:

"What does a handsome man like you do when he's off duty?"

Broadbent wouldn't take the bait:

"Ms. Powell, I'm always on duty."

The following morning, Broadbent, nursing a hangover, returned to what seemed like his continual high anxiety: where was Margaret Starmont? This was compounded by the loss of contact with her son. He mobilized detectives Dan Herlihy and Rick Sandoval. Herlihy was to scour anything he could find from staff at the last place Jordan Starmont was located, the U.S. Grant Hotel. Sandoval was instructed to work with the police field force, the California Highway Patrol (CHP), and enlisting help with the MP's through an "old friend", Captain Julian Desmond at Camp Pendleton. All eyes were ratcheted up to be on the lookout for Percival's automobiles.

Broadbent directed his efforts to Margaret. After consuming some dried toast, black coffee, and two aspirins, he headed out to the La Valencia about 10:00 A.M. The weather was changing. Not as hot and clear, especially over La Jolla, with onshore overcast skies. He hoped the hazy atmospherics were not harbingers of potential problems. With Hannigan out of his world, Broadbent was losing objectivity by having an affair of the heart. The woman he was enamored with could be in difficulty.

Parking his cruiser in the usual La Valencia slot reserved for valet services, Broadbent stayed outside the hotel and started his investigation by going to several adjacent shops on Prospect Street. They included a gift shop, a woman's boutique, and a jewelry store. The proprietor at the boutique indicated a woman matching Margaret's description did buy several garments three days ago. However, Broadbent was coming up empty for recent sightings until he spoke to a hotel valet. The young man revealed he saw a person matching Jordan's description come by cab to the hotel around noon on Sunday. That gave Broadbent hope that Jordan came to visit his mother, possibly to assist her in some way.

He then went inside to the hotel, questioning as many staff members he could find. The best information he got was from the maître d' at the Med restaurant, who recalled seating Margaret and Jordan for Sunday brunch. He told Broadbent that Margaret was a regular diner at the hotel. The maître d' had taken an interest in her these past few weeks and tried to keep her in his line of sight. When Margaret and Jordan left the restaurant, he went to the restaurant entrance and saw them go into the lobby. From afar he saw them stop to talk to two men at the hotel entrance. When pressed for specifics about these individuals, all he could say was that one was an older man. The other was a lean, younger person.

Broadbent was not ready to jump to any false conclusions. He went to Magaret's room and found the maid that was assigned to her, who happened to have the door open when he got there. She indicated that Margaret did not sleep in her suite the last two nights. Broadbent, with gloves on, meticulously scanned the three-room suite. There were no instructions left behind on her nightstand, where the maid said she generally requested a variety of amenities. Knowing this, the sum of all fears was upon Broadbent. He surmised that Jordan was with his mother, they encountered some shady individuals, and had to be presumed missing. However, of significance, on the desk was a scribbled note that said: *Wilfred Tanner?* That prompted Broadbent to rush back down to the front desk to press for information about Tanner. Discovering that he was a hotel guest, he asked the clerk, the confidante who assisted Percival, for more information about him. He was tight-lipped, but did say Tanner had an English accent. Broadbent enlisted the help of the La Valencia manager when he showed him his credentials to go to Tanner's room. There was no answer when they knocked at the door. Gaining entry when the manager unlocked the door, Broadbent was a whirling dervish looking around. The place was well-lived in, probably more than one person staying there. Food and drink on room service serving carts were still not completely consumed.

Broadbent then got on the telephone and called Moore's office. He told him that things were afoul and there was a strong chance that both Starmonts were missing. Moore indicated he would send a crime lab unit to the La Valencia to dust for finger prints in the Starmont and Tanner rooms. Broadbent said he would have the two rooms sealed, marked as a crime scene, to keep all contents secured. Moore was supportive but cautioned his detective:

"Damon, I think we know we are dealing with a crafty, dangerous critter. It's desperation time for Percival, which will make him lethal. Like the song says: *Fools rush in where wise men never go.*"

"Chief, don't worry--I'm looking before I am leaping. But we are on the verge of finishing this case by bagging this Nazi and hopefully his explosive."

"Good hunting. I will stand by to give you all the resources you need."

Continuing to search in Tanner's room he found nothing of substance. Then a glint of light on a sofa caught Broadbent's eye. It was a diminutive clear glass perfume applicator. It was a fragrant container of Chanel No. 5. Margaret Starmont wore it. That was a terrifying reality for him. She had to be in the company of David Percival. How could this terrible set of circumstances be possible? Broadbent was full of self-flagellation, questioning why he did not better protect Margaret. A fortuitous series of events brought him in contact with the Starmonts. Would he be so lucky to see them again? That would only be possible if he finally confronted a nemesis--David Percival.

56
CHAPTER

The Seal's Lair,
September 15, 1969

As nightfall was approaching, David Percival's hostages were getting testy. Margaret and Jordan Starmont complained about the cramped quarters. Percival reiterated that things would improve if they answered his pointed questions. Margaret was coming down with a bad headache and requested some aspirin. Percival had some in his personals case and told Jordan to find another seat so his mother could lie down on the sofa. He then updated them as to what would happen next:

"In a short while we will leave this location. The fresh air will do you good. As bad as this looks, I and my associates are not vicious men. Our goal is not to harm you--just stay quiet and only speak when spoken to. Okay?"

Percival was about to gamble again by driving his Lincoln sedan. He had too much baggage and it was the only vehicle that could transport five people like it did yesterday. Discussing this risk with Bixby in the hallway outside their room, the Marine came up with a better means of driving to Coronado without being detected. Bixby recommended:

"This is a swanky place. I've seen some big buggies pull up to the hotel. You think we could borrow one?"

Percival resonated to the alternative means of transportation:

"You mean we somehow commandeer a good-sized car that the valet parks in the nearby parking garage?"

"These guys have an easel on the sidewalk with hooks on it to store the keys and locator numbers of the cars they park. I can snatch the keys of some comfortable wheels after I size it up after the valet parks it."

"Great idea, Yancey. The valet parking in the same spot we have the Lincoln. You can then transfer our stuff from one trunk to another. Do it now!"

Bixby immediately went down to the hotel entrance, stationing himself behind a palm tree about fifteen feet from the valet stand. He was close enough to see the keys on the parking board. Then a good substitute automobile came to the valet stand. It was a light green four-door Cadillac De Ville pulled up to the hotel. A well-dressed couple exited from it and the gentleman gave his keys and what looked like some cash to the valet. The valet parked the car, returned to the board, and Bixby saw where he placed the keys and locator tag. He waited until the valet had to park the next car. With the board unattended, it was easy pickings for Bixby to pilfer the keys and head to the garage around the corner on Ivanhoe Avenue. In no time Bixby found the Cadillac and then drove it to where the Lincoln was parked. Bixby immediately transferred the contents from one trunk to another, to include the satchel with the uranium canister. He found a spot to park adjacent to the side of the hotel on a hilly street facing the ocean off Prospect, making an abrupt departure from the car and returning to find his accomplices. Once inside the La Valencia, Percival was stunned at the speed of Bixby's theft when he knocked on the door. Percival greeted Bixby and immediately went into the hall to chat secretly before they both returned to the suite:

"Yancey, you are a magician. Douglas should be here in less than an hour. We'll transport the lady and her son to the Cadillac. Then we will all go to the Lair."

Percival had telephoned a reluctant Douglas earlier about housing him, Bixby, Crawford and the Starmonts at the Lair. Douglas acquiesced but stipulated they had to be out by Thursday morning. Percival calculated that three full days seemed sufficient to make a getaway from San Diego for points unknown on the Pacific. After about sixty minutes, Bixby went down to the front curb to await Douglas. When the Navy Seal pulled up in his Chevrolet Camaro, they went to the Ivanhoe parking garage to shift the contents of Crawford's Ford pick-up, which included the rifles and recoilless. Once that transfer was complete, Bixby instructed Douglas to park behind the Cadillac around the corner of the La Valencia. Bixby told Douglas to wait in the Camaro and returned to the suite to assist Percival in bringing the Starmonts down the back fire escape stairwell. Jordan was still very annoyed when he and his mother were ordered from the hotel at gun point:

"You guys will pay for this."

Percival had his own stiff rejoinder:

"Kid, quiet! All the money in the world won't save you and your mother if you call out when we get outside. Button it up. Got it!"

Once off the fire escape, there were no utterances as the five of them hurried across the front deck of the swimming pool, which led to a walkway and a wooden security door that opened to the street. As they got into the parked Cadillac, there was levity echoing from above them at the outdoor café and poolside bistro. The hotel guests were oblivious to the pernicious behavior not far from their enjoyment. With the Cadillac loaded, Douglas took the lead and the two cars drove back to Prospect, which eventually brought them to Torrey Pines Boulevard, the gateway to I-5, and then up Ardath Road.

The ride inside the Cadillac was subdued. Margaret was still tormented by a pounding head and Jordan was getting fatigued as a hostage. Douglas stayed at the speed limit on the interstate as to not invite speeding problems. In fifteen minutes the lights of the Coronado Bay Bridge came into view. This did cause Jordan to speak once the vehicle began traversing the bridge:

"From my brief exposure to San Diego, are we headed to the big Navy base on Coronado?"

Percival was sarcastic to the nth degree:

"I told you that we don't want to harm you. Now you will have the whole US Navy to give you safe keeping. If you start answering my questions, we might even put you on a carrier."

Margaret inwardly waxed nostalgic as they drove past the Hotel del Coronado down the Silver Strand to the Naval Amphibious Base. The hotel was another former place of joy both she and Martin once frequented.

Presently, she was on the brink of collapse with fear and anguish. Once at the gate to the base, Douglas stepped out and had a brief discussion with the SP. It was obvious he had some leverage as a Seal, for he came back with a visitor parking pass and instructed Crawford to put it on the dash. The two cars then made the short drive to Douglas' location on Tulagi Road. Percival instructed everyone in their car to be quiet and wait until Douglas gave the all clear to exit and go to his quarters. The pistols still were in the backs of the Starmonts as Percival and Bixby ushered them up the stairs into the awaiting open door Douglas had prepared for them.

Always a martinet for cleanliness, Percival noticed things were uncluttered and had a pleasant aroma. Douglas even took the time to light some incense, which gave the place a mystic feel to it. Jordan took his mother to the couch and requested some water. Always ready to give aid and comfort, Douglas told Margaret she could have privacy in the bathroom to shower if she wanted to. He offered her a warm white Navy issued robe to rest in. He found sweatpants and a sweatshirt for Jordan. Finding some solace with fresh clothing, Jordan spoke with a less maligned inflection:

"What is this place?"

Percival had a ready answer:

"The Nirvana for all those who seek a safe haven--the Seal's Lair."

57
CHAPTER

San Diego, 17/18, 1969

Damon Broadbent thought he was through with sleep-deprived nights. The hour was late and he still was scanning the field reports that came across the wire. No unusual activity was reported, to include no spotting of any of the Percival vehicles on the roadways by the San Diego Police or the CHP. The crime lab was instructed to expeditiously process the fingerprints they picked up at the Starmont and Percival hotel rooms. At best, he would see their report tomorrow. The lab was also instructed to coordinate with the Marines up at Camp Pendleton for fingerprint confirmation for the AWOL Yancey Bixby and Monty Crawford. Broadbent surmised that Percival had them at the ready.

Almost at the door to leave for home, he got a telephone call. It was from a police officer in the La Jolla area. Calling from outside the La Valencia the officer reported:

"Captain Broadbent, this is officer Nolan Francis reporting from La Jolla. With regard to this lookout for this Percival guy, he might be changing the horse he's riding."

"You mean he might be using different vehicles?"

"I was called to the valet stand at the La Valencia earlier this evening and they confirmed it. A light green Cadillac De Ville was stolen from a hotel guest and he was flabbergasted when they could not find his car."

"Any suspects, by chance?"

"No, but the valet seems to think it could be the driver who abandoned one big car for this newer one."

"Such as?"

"This Cadillac for a four-door Lincoln Continental. The parking garage indicated no one has claimed it or paid its daily fee. We are also checking out a Ford pick-up truck that has not been claimed or paid its parking fees."

"That's good work, Officer Francis. Radio the dispatcher to put out an A.P.B. for the Cadillac. Complete a full report when you get back to your Northern Division H.Q."

Broadbent was spent, emotionally and physically. In a matter of days, he had traversed a road with mountain highs and valley lows. He managed to tie a few more business matters together and then left his office. As hyped as he had been, the fatigue in his body put him soundly to sleep at 1:00 A.M. It took his usual 7:00 A.M. clock radio to awake him in the morning. From what he heard on the newscast, it appeared the blackout on the Percival caper was lifting. He heard the news reporter convey:

The San Diego police have been called to the La Valencia Hotel in La Jolla. The hotel management became suspicious when one of its guests, a Margaret Starmont from New York City, has disappeared without notice. She was last seen with her son, Jordan, in the company of another guest, Wilfred Tanner, and one other man early Sunday afternoon. Tanner has also unexpectedly left the hotel. Both the Starmont and Tanner rooms have been sealed as possible crime scenes by police. Police are trying to connect whether the four in question may have left in a stolen Cadillac De Ville, the vehicle of another hotel guest.

Broadbent turned the radio off in anger knowing that his investigative operation had lost its secret cloak with media coverage. He took a quick shower, found his cleanest dirty shirt, and draped it in a wrinkled grey suit that was in bad need of dry cleaning. Finishing knotting his tie in his police cruiser, he got on the radio to his office. Officer Oliver heard him call out:

"Officer Oliver, alert detectives Sandoval and Herlihy to come to the station as soon as possible, over."

"Any special instructions for them, over?"

"Yes, tell them to arm their vehicles with shotguns. Alert all neighborhood units to be extra vigilant for a light green Cadillac De Ville. I'll be in the office in minutes. Over and out!"

Broadbent was surprised that Chief Howard Moore was in his office, a place he generally did not reach until 8:30 A.M. The two huddled together there and lamented that things were going public about the Percival case. It was really unavoidable the moment they cordoned off two La Valencia rooms. Broadbent sized up the situation:

"As I reported, I suspect Percival and his Marine accomplices have kidnapped Margaret and Jordan Starmont. Just minutes ago, I picked up a report from our La Jolla unit that they found an abandoned Lincoln Continental in a parking garage near the La Valencia. I'll make a big assumption and say they traded that car for a Cadillac that they stole from that same garage."

"Captain Broadbent, I am glad you are still making great connections. I believe that is likely true. They are on the run—but where?"

"Frankly, I am at a loss. They kidnapped the Starmonts on Sunday; today is Wednesday. They have a three-day head start on us."

'We know Percival is involved with military types--the two AWOL Marines. We have alerted Pendleton to help us. How about the biggest military show in town?"

"The Navy?"

"This Nazi is so slick that he may have abandoned his civilian base in Fallbrook for a military one to give him a shield from regular law enforcement."

Broadbent brought his open palm to his head as if a brilliant idea just hit him:

"It's the last place we would look. I'll alert the command on Coronado to start searching for a green Cadillac DeVille. We are going to go hunting for it as well. It's a stab in the dark—but we are desperate."

"And I will alert our newly formed SWAT team and the bomb squad to react at a moment's notice."

It was about 9:00 A.M. in Broadbent's hectic office. He ordered detective Dan Herlihy out to the La Valencia to keep the lid on and not make the commotion any bigger than need be. He asked Detective Rick Sandoval if there was anything new on what the FBI may have learned from Ian Bright, held for questioning in Los Angeles. Bright revealed that his stepfather was surrounded by military types--Marines and Navy individuals. The kid was sorry and felt he had been a pawn in this whole matter. Hearing the Navy mentioned reinforced Broadbent's belief it was the black-hole in his investigation. He told Sandoval to stay in the station for possible assistance.

Fifteen minutes later, a telephone call came to the station. Officer Oliver told Broadbent that FBI agent Ross Cargill was on the line:

"News travels fast. Congratulations on intercepting the detonator--you scooped us."

"You know, Ross, it really did not have to shake out like that. We are going to have to stop being in competition. What do you have?"

"I guess the explanation why we were in competition. Theodore Johnson made the hunt for Percival a vendetta, given that he has a history of chasing him back to 1945 when he eluded his pursuers, one of them, by the way, was Jordan Starmont's father, Martin, a naval intelligence officer at the time."

"Yes, I know this. I just hope Percival does not know this."

"What's up, Damon? Is Percival in Jordan's life?"

"Unfortunately, as preposterous as this all seems, this Nazi menace may have kidnapped Jordan and his mother."

"Wow! This is the weirdest crime investigation I have ever been a part of. Do you need our help?"

"Will Johnson let you assist us?"

"That's why I am calling. He's not a player anymore. You see it's been rumored that Johnson was a homosexual, there are more than a few of them, for better or worse, walking our streets here in San Francisco. Just a few days before this whole Percival affair started, he was down in the dumps about something."

"Boyfriend problems?"

"Big time. It was the corpse you found on the beach in La Jolla—Nick Petrie."

"The same guy Johnson claimed from our morgue?"

"Roger. You see it all becomes clear in a letter we found in Johnson's Van Ness Street walk-up. He lamented the break-up the two had, which drove Petrie off the edge to hang himself. Johnson did wonders to keep Petrie's body as glued together as possible with his morgue friends. It was a marvel we drove him down to La Jolla in one piece."

"Oh, oh. This doesn't sound like a happy ending."

"In the letter, Johnson looked for a way to venerate Petrie by using his remains to lure Percival into a trap. An act of redemption that went wrong. After the second attempt to capture Percival failed, Johnson went into a shell."

"And?"

"It's over, Damon. We just found him with his Smith and Wesson in his hand and a bullet through his forehead."

58
CHAPTER

The Seal's Lair,
September 16, 1969

Life in the confined quarters of the Seal's Lair was at best tolerable and at worst unbearable, especially for kidnapped Margaret and Jordan Starmont. A world of captivity, compared to the comforts they had in their Manhattan home, was unknown to them. However, the benevolence of Ensign Casey Douglas proved to be a saving grace. He was mindful of them by providing food, at least one hot meal a day. He offered to wash and dry their clothes and gave them clean clothes in the form of sweatshirts and sweatpants for Jordan, and a wool sweater and a pair of loose fitting navy dungarees for Margaret, which were wide enough to clear a woman's hips. When bedtime came, he wanted no part of standing watch over them. The Starmonts tried to sleep, fitfully so, in the living room: Margaret on the sofa; Jordan in a sleeping bag on the floor. Guard duty was left to rotated shifts of David Percival, Yancey Bixby and Monty Crawford. Douglas thought the less belligerent he appeared, the better. His kind approach would keep the panic level down for the captives.

On Monday morning, September 16, Percival was ready to make a major move to facilitate his escape from the Seal's Lair. After a boring, uncomfortable day of watching over the hostages, Percival needed to get some fresh air. Originally, he wanted Douglas to take Crawford to H and M Landing on Shelter Island, the site of several fishing and cruise boat operations. But since that plan was scrapped, he decided it would be better if he made his own accommodations. Percival decided to take Bixby, rather than Crawford, since Bixby talked about his seagoing excursions from his Louisiana home in St. Tamany Parish on the north shore of Lake Pontchartrain. Bixby had a familiarity with seagoing craft that Crawford didn't. Percival asked Douglas if he could get off duty mid-afternoon so he could go to Shelter Island. Leaving Crawford alone to watch the Starmonts might be risky. As reluctant as Douglas was to hover over the hostages, his mere presence made for better security. Douglas also needed to be in his quarters when the SPs called to allow Percival and Bixby to gain reentry onto the base.

By not being detected with their stolen Cadillac DeVille, Percival had Bixby drive him to Shelter Island with impunity. It was like the two of them were getting inured to being residents on the amphibious base. The drive to the main gate was a simple one down Tulagi road to Lavella Road. The main gate was only a simple left turn away to get them to the Silver Strand then back to the mainland via the Coronado Bay Bridge. Bixby was curious as to Percival's seagoing plan:

"If I knew where you were intending to go, I could recommend what type of vessel to get you there."

"Yancey, that's why you are with me--to help select one. As a minimum, we have to get to Ensenada. From there, maybe we can find something bigger and better to go further south."

"Where might that be?"

"I have been thinking about South America, where we have some Nazi sympathizers."

Bixby took a moment to digest what he heard before he responded:

"Hmm? I don't know much about those countries. If we leave the States, I guess we are never coming back?"

"Yancey, you, me, and Crawford have burned our bridges. It's either start a new life or face the long arm of the law in this country. Besides, the one we are living in is going to hell anyway. Wrong people running it or have undue influence."

"Yep, I see what you mean. Looks like we have no balls to destroy North Vietnam and win the war. I saw that firsthand over there."

Driving on Harbor Boulevard it gave Bixby bad vibrations passing Lindbergh Field. That feeling quickly passed because just beyond it was Shelter Island, which was not an island but was linked to the mainland by a narrow parcel of land. Once a sandbank, only visible at low tide, the landmass was increased from dredging material from San Diego Bay. Private housing was prohibited but it was the locus of hotels, restaurants, public parks, and marinas, one of which was H and M Landing. Percival was looking for an excursion boat possibility. His eye was drawn to Kari's Kruises, if only because the name Kari reminded him of his late Uncle Karl in Germany.

They pulled up to single one-room white framed office. When Percival got out of the Cadillac, he could see across the bay to the mighty naval base on North Island. He once diabolically thought of destroying it with the nuclear device he had in his possession. But, that was then, this was now. He went inside the office with Bixby and saw a crusty redhead in her 40's with a cigarette hanging from her lip sitting behind her desk with what looked like a mug of coffee. She bluntly sized up her guests:

"You land lubbers need a ride on the waves? This is the place to be. I am Kari Hebert, sole proprietor and operator."

Bixby was the first to react to the invitation:

"Afternoon, Ma'am. You sound like you might be from down south."

"Better than that, son, Louisiana, a sportsman's paradise."

That excited Bixby, a native Louisianan:

"What part? I grew up on the north shore of Lake Pontchartrain. Got out to the Gulf often to relax and do some deep-sea fishing."

"If fishing is what you are after, this is the place. After my daddy came back from the war, he raised me on a shrimp boat not far from Venice, Louisiana, in Plaquemines Parish. You know the place they call 'the end of the world' because it's the final spot you can get to by car along the Mississippi."

Bixby asked what brought her to San Diego. She replied:

"My daddy was a Navy man stationed in San Diego during the big war. Decided to come out here to start this business. And he gave it to me when he retired. Lives not far from the Naval Hospital in Balboa Park."

Percival liked the genuineness of the owner, someone he could make a deal with that would not be broken. He then interjected into the folksy conversation:

"Ms. Hebert, I need a means to get to Ensenada, and possibly farther south. It's a one-way excursion. Is that your boat tied to the pier behind your office?"

"Sure is. A beauty--the Kari Anne. Fairly new, too. It's a 52-foot Santa Barbara glass hull cruiser that sleeps six"

Percival needed some guidance from Bixby and whispered to him:

"Will her boat get us to where we want to go?"

Upon which Bixby whispered back:

"It will be fine to stay within sight of the shoreline."

The boat owner needed a passenger total:

"How many in your party?"

"Just us two and one more person. Tell me, how far could you take us, say beyond Ensenada?"

"Been down to the end of Baja at Cabo San Lucas. Heck, one time I took a group to Manzanillo. Have a reliable crew of two that can help me get you there."

That location spiked Percival's interest:

"That's a big-time port for trans-Pacific freighters, right?"

"Got that straight. Big time facility that serves Mexico City. When do you want to leave?"

A distant place and a major port was what Percival had in mind:

"Today is Monday. How about Wednesday--late afternoon? Is Manzanillo doable?"

"Yes, that would work. Take us about three days to get there. One group tomorrow and I am free for the next six days after that. I can get back-up from other excursion folks if I need more time to cover my other reservations next week."

Percival cemented an agreement with the owner for $500—cash. As he wished, it looked like he was about to leave America the same way he arrived—by water. But landlocked issues were still paramount. After leaving Shelter Island, he told Bixby to drive back to the Lair. Having no trouble getting back on base, it was nearly supper time when they walked up the steps to Douglas's quarters. The smell of oregano was in the air.

Douglas, a better-than-average cook, was preparing a spaghetti and meat sauce meal. Anticipating a good meal took the edge off things for the captive Starmonts. The group of six ate in shifts at the small kitchen table, which barely had enough room for three to eat comfortably. After dinner, Percival was in an interrogating mood, enough to cause indigestion for his captives:

"You two have had some time today to think about cooperating and answering my questions. Again, Jordan, who are you working for? You were supposed to be dead at Windansea. Remember? What was that all about?"

"Maybe someone has the same name as me."

Percival didn't appreciate the insult. He got right into Jordan's face:

"Look, kid, my self-control prevents me from bending your nose to your ear. We've been treating you and your mother with kid gloves. Do you want that to change?"

Sitting next to her son on the sofa, Margaret began to quiver. Jordan had to compromise to make her more tranquil:

"Okay. I'll tell you a few things. But only if you tell us when and where you plan to release us?"

"Soon, kid, soon. Maybe in a couple of days. You won't be released from here. Is that enough for you to talk?"

Jordan took a moment to compose a reply that might placate Percival but not reveal all his cards:

"I agreed to help the FBI, but it was not my scheme for that Windansea fiasco. They planted my name so I would be beholden to them."

"Then who was the older fraud I talked to that pretended to be you?"

"I don't know for sure, but it was good enough to lure you to the beach."

"Yes, I must say I was duped by a clever guy on the telephone. Let's go on. Are you connected to Sela Danby and perhaps Ian Bright as well?"

Jordan had to still measure himself and not be completely candid:

"Sela Danby is my half-sister. I found out she was visiting Perth, Australia. She indicated she was traveling with Ian Bright. The FBI convinced her to come to the States with him. As far as I know, they never got here."

"Trying to nail me, I suppose. Mrs. Starmont what do you know about all this? Why did you come to San Diego?"

Margaret had calmed herself sufficiently to sound convincing:

"I'm like you. I thought my son was dead when the San Diego Police called me. Don't you see? The FBI has used both of us. It was not our intent to harm you."

Percival resonated with this and backed off his questioning. After several painful minutes of silence, Jordan pressed for their release:

"We've given you what you want to know. Can you assure us we will be freed and not be harmed?"

"That will happen if and only if you stay compliant and act as a protective shield during our departure. But if things go wrong, this will have a violent and very unhappy ending--for all of us!"

59
CHAPTER

San Diego, September 18, 1969

Just two days ago, Damon Broadbent thought he had things under control. Completing the transaction with Josh Hannigan, a nuclear detonator was out of the hands of a deviant David Percival. It seemed Jordan Starmont was about to permanently reunite with his mother, Margaret, a woman Broadbent was very fond of. Despite the fact Percival was still at large, it was a story that appeared to have a happy ending. However, with the Starmonts unbelievably in Percival's malicious hands, Broadbent was still on a continual merry-go-around. When would this ride end? Given the gravity of things, he used to think he had hours, perhaps minutes, to resolve things. But time was more precious--down to seconds when a rash act by Percival could be inflicted on the Starmonts.

Around 10:00 A.M. the lab report from the fingerprint dusting came in. Trying to ascertain if David Percival, a German Nazi masquerading as an avocado farmer, was present at the LaValencia, the San Diego lab used the fingerprint system of a German: Henry Roscher. Roscher was credited with the first positive criminal identification in 1892, when he successfully extracted a set of prints off a door that identified a woman as the perpetrator of a double homicide. Although the report could not specifically identify Percival's prints in his suite, the clincher was that the other two sets, cooperating with great speed with the Marines at Camp Pendleton, matched those of Yancey Bixby and Monty Crawford. A set of Crawford's prints were also found on a glass in Margaret Starmont's suite.

The lab detected two other sets of distinct prints in the Starmont suite. While there was no match either from the FBI or military fingerprint records, it was presumed they were the identifiers for Margaret and her son, Jordan. For Broadbent, it removed all doubts that Percival had kidnapped the Starmonts.

An hour later, Deirdre Powell called Broadbent with an update on Josh Hannigan and Sela Danby. Hannigan called Channing Williams law office late yesterday afternoon and said that before he and Sela left San Diego they wanted to meet with Jordan Starmont. Powell asked a beleaguered Broadbent if he could arrange the meeting. He had to tell Powell in confidence of the serious reality of events. To her, this was incredible--Jordan and his mother are missing. However, to keep the shock within the confines of the San Diego Police Department, Broadbent did not tell Powell they were Percival's hostages. Broadbent counseled Powell to tell Hannigan and Danby to find a place to stay after vacating the U. S. Grant until such time Jordan could be brought to them. He pressed a bit on Hannigan's and Danby's plans:

"Did they give any indication where they are bound after leaving town?"

Powell was a skilled investigator herself, but had only a cloudy idea:

"I asked them directly, but they admitted to no specific destination. It sounded like it may be out of the country. But are you ready for my nugget of improbable realities?"

"Ms. Powell, at this point, nothing would shock me. Humor me."

"I told you that we like to get a good background profile on any client we represent. I discovered two significant facts about Hannigan's alleged criminal activity. First, he is not on any FBI Wanted List. Second, and more importantly, when I contacted San Francisco PD they have a record of several people being held against their will at a Haight-Ashbury residence in December 1968. However, it seems the apparent victims did not press any charges and no arrests were made, despite the appearance of criminal intent."

Percival was almost at the point of apoplexy:

"My God, when will normalcy return to crime! Did you tell Hannigan this?"

"Channing told me not to, and you shouldn't either. We are all joined at the hip with regard to confidentiality. Right?"

"My lips are sealed. If I told anyone about what's happened in this case, they would not believe me. Go on."

"By keeping Hannigan oblivious to what I discovered, it may compel him to follow the straight and narrow, thinking any false step may force him to confront his past sins. Besides, Channing and I do not want to pour cold water on a budding romance."

Broadbent relieved some tension with some levity:

"It's good to know you are both hopeless romantics! You can always go into advice to the lovelorn if your law practice goes south. Seriously, Deirdre, that is great stuff. Again, it's under my lock and key. I'll keep you posted as to what we find on the Starmonts."

After ending a conversation with another impossible chain of events, Broadbent was in need of military assistance. The lab told him that Captain Julian Desmond was instrumental in assisting with the fingerprint confirmation for the AWOL Marines, Bixby and Crawford. To thank him and ask for help, Broadbent called Desmond's Camp Pendleton office and discovered that he was unavailable until early afternoon. Given the urgency of the situation, that seemed like an eternity. The military had its hierarchies and protocols and could not easily be circumvented by the civilian sector. To Broadbent, it was just another reason for better coordination between law enforcement agencies, no matter who ran them. Nevertheless, he was going to take some independent action to drive over to the huge North Island Naval base after lunch.

But first Broadbent had to face the realities of a big news story breaking. Moore called him down to his office and was in need of a strategy:

"Damon, the *San Diego Union-Tribune* is sending a writer to my office in thirty minutes about what happened at the Las Valencia. I need you at the ready."

"Sure, Chief, I started the process. I guess I am best able to walk through the landmine questions they pose to us."

Before this press interview, Broadbent ordered Sandoval and Herlihy to contact the base officer at the North Island Naval base to get permission to surveil their parking areas for vehicles driven by both officers and enlisted men. The primary search would be outside the barracks of enlisted men, plus married and bachelor officer quarters. Once that occurred they would drive immediately to Coronado and begin the hunt for the autos owned and driven by Percival, to include the stolen green Cadillac De Ville. Broadbent would join them as soon as he could after the answering the questions from the press.

The press interview in Moore's office started with simple introductions between the Chief, Broadbent and the *San Diego Union-Tribune* reporter. Moore had coffee and some sandwiches for all to consume. The Chief said that since Broadbent is the lead investigator on the case, he will defer to him for answering questions. The reporter, Graham Underwood, was a veteran beat writer who covered the local scene. He got down to business with his first question:

"What prompted the police activity at the La Valencia?"

Broadbent was front and center:

"We were called when a stolen vehicle was reported."

"Fine. But how about the sealing of two hotel guest rooms. Why was that step taken?"

"After discovering from the hotel management that two guests, a Margaret Starmont and a Wilfred Tanner, it was highly unusual that they had not returned to their rooms. Because they were last seen together in the hotel lobby Sunday afternoon, we probed to see if they had colluded to abruptly end their hotel stay."

"On the surface that does not seem suspicious. What might that crime be?"

Broadbent had the perfect red herring to throw at the reporter:

"It looked like they left the hotel without paying their respective bills. The incurred charges for well over $950, which according to the California Penal Code makes it possible grand theft, punishable by up to three years in prison."

"Looks like that was reasonable to assume. But back to the car, the Cadillac De Ville, the reason you were brought in the first place. Is there a linkage here between the Starmonts and Tanner, who was reported accompanied by a younger person?"

"Mr. Underwood, Tanner's car was still at an adjacent parking garage, in arrears for daily parking fees. We have reason to believe he no longer wanted his car and 'traded it in' if you get my drift, for the Cadillac. The person with Tanner is considered a person of interest."

"So, where are you on the investigation?"

"If we find the Cadillac, we believe we'll find the principals involved here. You'll be the first to find out."

"Well, fair enough. I guess there is not much more to this?"

Broadbent wanted to wrap this up sooner rather than later:

"You're right. If you don't mind, I have a pressing matter to attend to. Any more questions?"

"Not really. But a surfing friend of mine told me there was some unusual activity with the police at Windansea Beach last month. What can you tell me about that?"

Broadbent made this short, sweet, and evasive:

"Simply a dead body, likely a suicide, the remains which have been claimed and accounted for."

After the reporter left, Moore complimented Broadbent for his adroit handling of the questions. To the Chief's satisfaction, the front-page story they were working on would still not be reported as headline news. It had enough specificity without explaining the reason for cordoning off the La Valencia rooms. Moore then asked about the central issue: how was the search for Percival and the Starmonts going. Broadbent brought him up top speed:

"The naval complex across the bay is out next hunting grounds. If we find our prey, we will likely need more than all available officers, to include the SWAT Team, and another special contingency unit."

"What's that?"

"Percival still has that canister of uranium. We'll need the bomb squad."

60
CHAPTER

The Seal's Lair,
September 17/18, 1969

Tuesday night, September 17, was gut check time for an unlikely amalgam of people assembled at an even more unlikely hideout for criminal activity. For David Percival, it was about making exit plans. This had to be the last night he would be living in a country where he had hoodwinked authorities as to his true identity for over twenty-four years. With his plan to threaten the American establishment with a nuclear weapon gone awry, he thought it best to regroup—off shore. But his getaway to an unknown destination has strings attached. Percival's freakish intuition, and a bit of luck, brought Margaret and Jordan Starmont into his life. As a vindictive act he kidnapped them, bringing them to the Seal's Lair. If the law got in the way, they would be the shield to get him to a boat that awaits him tomorrow afternoon. But, first, he still had unfinished business with the Starmonts.

After dinner, Percival asked Margaret to come outside with him on the landing, warning that his Luger would be pointing at her at all times. Once outside, Margaret appreciated the fresh air of a clear, breezy evening. She felt less threatened when Percival put the gun in his belt. It was almost relaxing, hearing the breakers of the nearby Pacific that bordered the

Navy Amphibious Base. Percival began the conversation with a different perspective:

"Mrs. Starmont, I find you a handsome woman. Even though I know you detest me, can we talk with candor, now that you are away from your son?"

Margaret was a little better composed after two days of captivity. She started a guarded discussion:

"Your flattery has limits. I guess I can be more open if you tell me what you are hiding. You don't use names when you talk to one another. Is it a secret organization you belong to?"

"Secret? Our cause is famous; it just has to go underground now before we get the recognition we deserve."

"Jordan told me the FBI was chasing Nazis. Are you one of them?"

Percival couldn't resist to be pompous:

"Yes, and proud of it. We have the best chance to save the world from detestable Communists, Socialists, Jews, and dangerous revolutionaries. Tell me, do you belong to one of those groups?"

"I belong to the human race, the best place to be if you have love in your heart."

"That philosophy is ideal, but it doesn't work. We are all made unequal, and we believe we have the supreme attributes to rule the world."

"Good luck with that one."

"We have not harmed you, we have not taken your money, and we have treated you with some compassion."

"Yes, I appreciate that. The individual who lives here seems to be a caring person."

With Margaret speaking in a relaxed manner, Percival pressed on:

"Does it trouble you that your husband had a child with another woman?"

Margaret was repulsed but firm in her answer:

"My husband was involved with another woman before I ever met him."

"Ms. Danby is English. Was it during the war when your husband was stationed in England?"

"All right. You seem to have the answers. It happened when he was in the Navy."

Percival tied together his suspicions of who Martin Starmont was. He reached into his shirt pocket and opened a yellowed newspaper article, which was scotched taped to prevent it from crumbling. It was a telltale memento Percival kept in his satchel. He read off a *Los Angeles Times* article from May, 1945, a piece he had retained for years. It reported that an escaped Nazi scientist, a Friedrich Vogel, had been pursued by a Naval intelligence officer, Martin Starmont and was still unaccounted for. After reading other bits of the article, Percival moved closer to Margaret and intoned:

"Isn't it amazing? Your husband could not find me and now we are face-to-face. Aren't you glad I have great restraint with you and your son? Now, tell me, where is Ian Bright?"

Margaret was taken aback by hearing this. Fudging a little, she relented, hoping it would eventually give her and Jordan safe passage:

"Jordan told me that the FBI set a trap here in San Diego for Sela and Ian upon arrival from Australia. Like Jordan told you, they never arrived here. We have no idea where they are."

Then, making a sudden move, Percival leaned forward and put his hand around Margaret's waist and gave her a kiss. She broke away with a sigh of disgust. Percival had exacted his pound of flesh:

"There, now I feel vindicated. I have won out over a man and his family who have been trying to destroy me."

Margaret had a biting reaction to this unwanted sexual gesture:

"Was that your English charm or your German brashness?"

"Neither, my dear. Just something to remember me by."

They went back into the house without further conversation. Percival then instructed Crawford to put the Starmonts into the bathroom, closing the door to keep them out of earshot. Percival gathered his cohorts together and in voice just above a whisper:

"Tomorrow we leave the Seal's Lair. We need to pack our belongings now and load into the Cadillac. Casey, thanks for getting the clothesline we need to control our guests. I also want to thank you for being flexible and giving us safe haven. Perhaps one day we'll reconvene, but I think that is doubtful after we leave tomorrow."

"David, I hope you make it without incident. You have to assume the police are looking for the Cadillac you took from the La Valencia. But, when you release the Starmonts, won't the cops come looking for me?"

"You are a smart man, Casey. You'll just have to talk your way out of it. You could tell them you were at the wrong place at the wrong time and we somehow found our way to your place—against your will and to your displeasure, of course."

"That's a stretch. But I'll be working on something creative to absolve me. Is it one last dash to Shelter Island without being detected."

"No worries, Casey. As long as we have the Starmonts in our possession we have big bargaining chips on our side. Besides, I still have the power of suggestion."

"What's that?"

"How would they know I can't still detonate the canister?"

The following morning, Wednesday, Douglas said goodbye to Percival. Bixby, and Crawford to report to his duty station on base. Before leaving, he glanced back at the Starmonts, sitting at the kitchen table having toast and coffee, and said:

"I'm sorry you had to be put through this. You'll be all right if you just comply with what you are ordered to do."

Giving a half-hearted wave as he left, it was if the Starmonts were losing the only trusted person they'd known for nearly seventy-two hours. Around 2:00 P.M. Percival then told them to change back into the clean clothes that Douglas washed for them when they arrived on Sunday. Percival did not want his captives in a rag tag condition. If anything, it was a benevolent gesture that might help with Douglas's alibi if the police came a calling. After Margaret and Jordan alternated using the bathroom to change clothes, they sat down on the sofa with the anxious expectation they would finally be free. Percival had changed into the all black he left with Douglas: jackboots, Nazi Storm Trooper jodhpur pants, belt, and a shirt with a swastika lapel pin on it. It was symbolic of the true dark essence of the man. He gave a preview of what was to come:

"We will be going to the mainland. I am afraid we have to tie you together and drop you off at a public restroom. Don't struggle and try to do anything rash. We'll be out of your life soon enough."

Directing his comments to Percival, Jordan was filled with bravado:

"Do you really think you can get away with this?

"Kid, we've come this far without being discovered. If anybody asks, just tell them you were in the company of individuals who will be heard from at another more convenient time to discuss mass destruction."

Jordan knew what that meant and stayed silent to not antagonize his captor. Percival didn't smoke, but he asked for a cigarette from Crawford. He went outside to light it on the porch. As he took his first puff, he looked up Tulagi Street. About seventy-five feet away, he saw a parked Oldsmobile Cutlass, with an aerial banded over the top of it, connected at the rear bumper. It gave him a start, for cars with antennas have radios. Sucking intensely on his cigarette, he locked in on the vehicle. A man in a grey suit and a black fedora got out of the car and went around to the passenger side of the car. Leaning up against it, he gazed up to the third floor landing of the Seal's Lair. Finally, Damon Broadbent was looking eye-to-eye at his elusive quarry--David Percival.

61
CHAPTER

Shelter Island,
September 18, 1969

After his interview with the newspaper reporter and debriefing Chief Howard Moore, Damon Broadbent managed to finally join fellow detectives Dan Herlihy and Rick Sandoval in Coronado. They were looking for the stolen Cadillac, operating on a gigantic hunch that it would be found on U.S. Navy property. The forty-four acre base on North Island had four gates to choose from. Having received permission to enter government property on official business, Herlihy entered the one furthest west on Ocean Street; Sandoval entered the one furthest east on First Street. With maps given to them by the SPs at the guard shack, they scanned any and every parking lot on the base, to include the ones at the golf course, athletic fields, swimming pool and the enlisted men's and officers's quarters.

Broadbent was almost an hour behind them, so he went to the Navy facility closest to where he exited the Coronado Bay Bridge—the Navy Amphibious Base on the Silver Strand. Including the main base, training beaches, a recreational marina, and a nesting sanctuary for terns, it covered about one-thousand acres. Broadbent had neither the time nor the personnel to cover all this ground. So he asked for some help from the SP at the gate:

"I think you have clearance for me to search your base for criminals at large. My name is Captain Damon Broadbent, San Diego Police Department."

The SP checked his manifest and approved entry:

"Yes, sir. You are on the clearance list. How can we help?"

"This is no small operation you have here. I am looking for a suspicious vehicle, a light green Cadillac De Ville. It's a car I think the average naval person does not drive. Seen one like that?"

Broadbent received a well-deserved break:

"As a matter of fact, I was on duty last Sunday night when a car you described was brought on base by Ensign Casey Douglas, who lives at 88 Tulagi Road. Here's a map with his circled location."

Broadbent saluted the guard and drove about a half mile on Tulagi. When he got there, cars were parked in a single row, perpendicular to the three-story building. There was also a larger lot on the side of the building, where he struck gold. Parked near the far corner of the building was the light green Cadillac De Ville, gleaming in the waning afternoon sun. Not knowing how many individuals he may be confronting if he went to Douglas's quarters on the third floor, he radioed Herlihy and Sandoval:

"Call off your search at North Island. I found our objective outside a bachelor officers quarters at the Navy Seal base, over."

Herlihy responded on the open microphone so Sandoval could tune in:

"Captain, where exactly is your position, over?"

"I am east of the main gate at the end of Tulagi Road, over."

Sandoval was out for revenge:

"I'd like nothing better than return the favor to a guy who almost blew me away, over."

"Rick, maintain focus. Here's the plan. I will stay outside the building until someone comes for the car. When that happens, I will tail it. Rick, you station your car inside the gate; Dan, you position yourself halfway up Tulagi for a possible blockade of the roadway, over."

Both officers complied with the order. Broadbent then got out of his car and looked at the third-floor landing, where he spotted David Percival. Broadbent got back into his cruiser and alerted Chief Moore for back-up.

The only way off Coronado by land was on the bridge. Special units would be positioned at the San Diego exit.

+⊱═ ◉ ═⊰+

Percival's recent frozen gaze at the car and the stare from the person leaning on it paralyzed him for a moment. But he made an about face back into the apartment. He barked orders with a heightened intensity:

"Put the Starmonts back in the bathroom."

When that occurred, he brought Monty Crawford and Yancey Bixby close to him with fire in his eyes:

"Look, Marines, this will test your battlefield abilities. I just saw what looks like a cop and his squad car positioned outside the building. We have to leave immediately."

Bixby was ready for action:

"We are locked and loaded. The car is packed and ready to make a run for it."

"Good. Monty, when we all go down the steps, we'll be right behind you with the Starmonts. Go to the car and move it to the grassy area so it can't be seen from the street level."

"I understand. We bound for the boat on Shelter Island?"

"That's the objective. Bring the Starmonts out and tie their wrists and loop their waists so they are linked to one another. I also want them gagged with strips from a bedroom sheet. Clear?"

Both men nodded in agreement. Upon hearing the order, the Starmonts were stiff with fear when the bathroom door opened. They sensed it was time for a big move. Bixby tried to be as gentle as he could as he tied them up. Crawford brought two inch bands of white cotton and wrapped them around their heads and across their mouths, tight but not suffocating as Percival instructed. Crawford told them to be quiet when they left the apartment. Ready to move out, Percival opened the door to the landing leading to the stairwell. It was covered so no one could see their movements from the street. Crawford went ahead to move the car into position. Percival had the rope leash tied to Jordan, who was linked to his mother. Bixby was tethered to the captives at the rear as they quietly moved down the steps.

At the ground floor, Crawford had the Cadillac in position. Percival instructed the Starmonts to get in the car after the tethered ropes were untied. Jordan was placed again in the front seat next to Bixby. Margaret was seated in the rear, beside Percival. As before, Crawford was at the wheel. The car drifted out from behind the building onto Tulagi Road. This caught the eye of Broadbent, now at the wheel of his car ready to react. He radioed ahead to Herlihy and Sandoval that there was movement.

In the Cadillac, Percival orchestrated what was next:

"Drive slowly as we leave the base. We will be followed. Be ready for a shootout if we are stopped. If not, speed through the front gate. Jordan keep your head down; same is true for you Mrs. Starmont. Otherwise we will have to push them down. If we are free and clear past the gate, make way for Shelter Island."

As the car moved up Tulagi Road. Broadbent got on the radio:

"The Cadillac is coming your way. No intercept at this time. Remember, the Starmonts are likely in the car. Follow my squad. Over and out."

Crawford drove at the posted speed and passed Herlihy's cruiser parked on Tulagi without incident. Percival saw it:

"Troopers, that's the second police car looking for us. They are following us."

Crawford was scanning his side and rear mirrors and confirmed that the car parked near the Seal's Lair was about three car lengths behind them. Nearing the gate, Sandoval's cruiser was set back and could not be sighted. Crawford calmly waved at the SP at the gate, turned onto the Silver Strand, and headed for the Coronado Bay Bridge. Crawford updated the surveillance upon them as he approached the entrance to the Bridge:

"From what I can see, there might be three cars tailing us. Do I try to shake them? What's my speed?"

Percival cautioned:

"Don't speed. Don't evade them. It's good we have the Starmonts for cover."

Hearing this Margaret clenched her fists and tried to get some air through her nose. Her heart was pounding, not knowing her fate. Jordan was in an uncomfortable physical and mental state. Being bound up was no picnic for the body, questioning why he ever got involved in this whole mess in the first place. He and his mother wouldn't be here if he had not succumbed to the wishes of the FBI.

Broadbent opened his radio to the general scanner, which connected him to the general patrolling police force and police headquarters:

"To all units. In contact with suspect vehicle. Using Code 2 (no lights or sirens). Suspect turning off Coronado Bay Bridge, northbound on I-5. Proceeding with caution. From what I can see, multiple people in the vehicle, perhaps the Starmonts, over"

Howard Moore was told to stand by when Broadbent went to Coronado. He got on the horn:

"Captain Broadbent, advise as to other assistance. Do we bring in the SWAT Team and Bomb Squad, over?"

"Chief, get them in position. Start their engines. Not sure of suspect's route. Will advise. Let's see where the suspect takes us, over."

"Will comply. Out."

Crawford was driving at the posted limit. It was only a short drive to the Hawthorne Street exit off I-5. He updated Percival.

"Still have the heat behind me. Where to?"

Percival was concerned but calm:

"Follow directions to the airport. That will take you to Shelter Island. Make no evasive move."

Broadbent alerted his force that the Cadillac had exited I-5 and was turning unto Harbor Drive. He updated Moore, who commanded the SWAT Team and Bomb Squad to head for Broadbent's latest position. Crawford was driving deliberately and waited patiently for the traffic signal to allow him to proceed to Shelter Island off Harbor Drive. Broadbent and his detectives were filed behind, about twenty-five yards off the Cadillac's rear bumper. Broadbent got back on the radio:

"To all units, suspect driving past the airport, heading for either Harbor or Shelter Island. Head in that direction for possible intercept. Out."

Broadbent's force was now joined by two trailing SWAT vans and a vehicle that looked like an oversized armored car--the Bomb Squad vehicle.

Broadbent was getting animated. As harmful as this could be to the Starmonts, he was prepared for a shootout. He had a shotgun leaning across the front seat and a holstered pistol. He needed more firepower, so he switched his .38 caliber pistol to a .45 caliber, which would have greater velocity and force when fired. Meanwhile, Percival gave another command to his Marine cohorts:

"When we get to Shelter Island, head for Kari's Kruises. Trooper Bixby, tell Trooper Crawford how to get there."

It was the first time he addressed them by name in the presence of the Starmonts. He continued:

"Stop the car at the boat pier. Offload everything in the trunk and put on board, but not my satchel. Place it outside the office door. Take two envelopes out of it, one for each of you. Get on the boat ASAP and tell that female captain to warm it up. We leave immediately! I'll handle the cops."

Broadbent was following his target as it turned onto Shelter Island. He alerted his following posse of police:

"Suspect is now on Shelter Island. Not sure why. All units should head that way. Out."

As the Cadillac approached H and M Landing, Percival directed a pointed threat to the Starmonts:

"When the car stops, stay inside. Allow the troopers to vacate and off load. Once they have done that, we will exit the car. No sudden moves after I cut the rope that ties us together. I'll get out first, then you follow. Remember, my pistol is still pointing at both of you."

Crawford brought the Cadillac to a halt within feet of the office door for Kari's Cruises. Both he and Bixby left the car and went immediately to the trunk, unloading three bags, a canvas case holding the rifles and the recoilless, and Percival's satchel. Bixby went into the office and found a startled Kari Hebert when she was at gunpoint:

"Drop everything, get in your boat, and warm it up. We have to get out of here--now!"

She obeyed and went through a side door directly to the pier where the Kari Anne was docked. Back outside, Crawford brought the bags to the pier and came back to the car with its three occupants:

"Sir, I'd use caution. There are at least three squad cars behind you."

"I know. Just get on board with Trooper Bixby--I'll get there. Did you take the envelopes out of the satchel?"

Crawford nodded his head and scurried back to the pier to board the boat. The envelopes contained $2500 in cash for the Marines. Up the road, Broadbent stopped his car, got out, and raised his hands for the trailing police vehicles to stop. He motioned to Sandoval and told him to get a package out of the back seat of Broadbent's cruiser. This puzzling development was made clear when Broadbent said:

"Rick, stay close and follow me about twenty paces behind me. I'll call you if I need what you are carrying."

Meanwhile, Percival vacated the car with a pointed Luger at the Starmonts as they struggled to get out of the car with bound hands. When that happened, Broadbent, with his .45 caliber pistol drawn in one hand and a shotgun in the other called out as he approached them:

"Percival, it's over. Hand over the Starmonts and drop your weapon."

Margaret was so frightened she wet herself. Jordan had shaky legs and sweaty palms. Percival had fire in his eyes and was resolute. He told the Starmonts not to move as he sidled to the satchel near the office door. The Cadillac partially hid Percival when he reached down to get the satchel. Bixby was at the stern with two Remington rifles. Crawford was coming to join him with the recoilless, loaded with a rocket. Bixby called out as the diesel inboard engines were firing up in the background:

"Sir, we are almost ready to sail. When you getting onboard? I think we could shoot our way out of here."

Percival wasn't ready to leave just yet.

"That's good, Yancey. I'll be there. I want to make a point."

Broadbent edged closer, within thirty feet of the quivering Starmonts and the defiant Percival. Broadbent stopped and demanded again:

"Let the Starmonts go and drop your weapon. You'll never get away."

Then pointing his Lugar at Broadbent with one hand he brought the satchel out with the other and dropped it at his feet. In one last act of bravado and intimidation to a country he wanted to change, Percival used the power of suggestion. While staring at Broadbent he reached down and lifted the pointed tip of the uranium canister and let it rest skyward in the bag:

"Come any closer to me and this whole part of the world goes up in atomic dust."

Broadbent wasn't buying it:

"You and I both know you can't detonate that thing--it's impotent without a fuse."

"You think, smart ass? I put one round from my pistol into a blasting cap I have next to this bomb and it's so long San Diego."

Broadbent gambled and looked for an opening to take Percival down. He called Sandoval over and told him to take the detonator out of the box and come to his side. He was dealing with the devil and hoped to outwit him. Pointing to what was in Sandoval's hands he called out:

"You see, David, I have what Ian Bright was supposed to give to you".

Percival took umbrage when he saw the detonator. In a moment of fatal weakness, he lowered his Luger, reached out, and stepped forward wailing:

"That's mine, you son of a…."

Before he could finish his sentence, Broadbent spent two rounds that hit Percival fatally. One into the abdomen that penetrated the liver; one just above his heart. Percival fell to the ground in agony. That was a sign for Jordan to elbow his mother and have them head for Broadbent and a number of police who moved up to the scene. Seeing this, Bixby was in a survival mode when he called to Kari Hebert at the wheel of the boat:

"Let's cast off, and gun it."

Making sure that the Starmonts were unbound and ungagged, Broadbent ran up to the dying Percival. He was face down when Broadbent turned him over. With the pall of death upon him, Percival's dying words were:

"Deutschland Uber Alles."(Germany over all).

Broadbent got up and looked out upon the bay as he saw the glistening purple and gold letters of the Kari Anne on its stern as it made for open water and the Pacific. Herlihy came up to him:

"Captain, should we call out the Coast Guard to interdict that vessel?"

Broadbent paused for a moment and then waxed philosophically:

"No, Dan, let two wayward Marines go to an uncertain future. In the end, they were betraying their country, but the way their country has been treating them in Vietnam, maybe they need a reprieve. We finally got who and what we wanted today, and the guy on the ground can't poison their minds anymore."

Broadbent then turned and went back to the Starmonts. He reached out for Margaret, who was still shaking when she admitted:

"This is the most terrifying experience of my life. I am just so glad Jordan and I survived it."

Broadbent consoled her and brought her and Jordan to an awaiting ambulance that would take them to the hospital for observation and treatment. After things cleared a bit at the landing, Chief Howard Moore came forward and sized up the situation:

"Damon, you finally connected all the key parts of the danger that threatened an entire city. Everything is packaged together at this spot: the madman, his detonator, and his weapon are all safely put away. You took a gamble and won. The Bomb Squad wasn't sure if the canister was going to explode. Great work, detective!"

"Thanks, Chief. I'm glad I spoke yesterday to the UCSD physics professor who told me that the canister was basically harmless, save for a little emitted radiation. But I think the biggest accomplishment we made today was killing some hate. Far from all of it, but a big step in the right direction."

"Damon, thanks to your fine work the world avoided a catastrophe."

Broadbent's response was not sanguine:

"For now."

After two days, the tumultuous events on Shelter Island settled down. Back in his office, Damon Broadbent was trying to get back into the routine by filling out a myriad of reports as to what transpired on Shelter Island. Officer Oliver came over the intercom:

"Captain, there is a nice lady and her polished son who want to see you."

Broadbent knew who his guests were. He gleefully opened his office door and brought them in. Out of the hospital for a day of treatment, both Margaret and Jordan looked a little tired but were in good spirits. They both thanked Broadbent for saving them from a harrowing experience. Sitting around his desk, enjoying one of Officer Oliver's famous cups of coffee, Jordan touched on something profound:

"As a witness to what happened, it calls to mind the most serious of the seven deadly sins: pride. In a philosophy class at Princeton, I learned the Greeks called it hubris, which is futility and corrupt selfishness, putting one's desires, wants, and urges without caring for others."

Broadbent admired Jordan's wisdom:

"Jordan, stating it that eloquently, Percival's contempt for his fellow man came to the fore. When he dropped his weapon and reached for the detonator, it was if the world had to be beholden to him. I'm glad I took a chance and appealed to his deranged vanity."

"What if he decided to forget about the detonator and get on that boat with his cronies?"

"We were in a compromising position. At that point all of us were vulnerable, especially with that recoilless looking down our throats."

Jordan looked down at his watch and it was approaching 10:00 A.M. He blurted out:

"Whoops! Got to get over to the U.S. Grant Hotel for a date with Sela Danby and Josh Hannigan. They extended their stay. It will be a chance for all of us to finally meet. Mom, don't stay too long. They are expecting you, too."

With Jordan gone, a good vibration was apparent with Broadbent and Margaret finally alone again. Broadbent, however, brought up an important outstanding matter:

"Are you still sure you don't want to press charges against Ensign Casey Douglas?"

"Yes. Jordan and I agree that the man had a sense of decency and civility. Men can think evil thoughts, but if they show you kindness it reveals their truer self. I think he knows Percival's view of the world is a losing cause."

Then Broadbent was speaking from the heart:

"Maggie, what about us?"

That triggered her to come to his desk, have him stand up, and put her arms around him, putting her lips firmly onto his. Softly breaking away she cooed:

"Damon, I have to go back to New York to tend to some matters, one of which is to get a new housekeeper. I want you to come out and stay a bit. From there, we'll decide who, what, and where we want to be."

Broadbent realized he could be headed to the romantic relationship he wanted:

"That's the best proposition anyone has ever made to me. I hope you feel good about yourself after what you and your son survived."

"It hasn't all sunk in yet, but I am thankful you rescued us from what was a diabolical person and a place I will never forget--David Percival in the Seal's Lair."

ABOUT THE AUTHOR

J.A. Gasperetti was born and raised in Milwaukee, Wisconsin. He earned a bachelor's and master's degrees from the University of Wisconsin, with course work at both the Madison and Milwaukee campuses. A Vietnam veteran, he served there with the 4th Infantry Division in 1966-67. He is retired and lives with his wife, Anne, in Iowa City, Iowa. The Seal's Lair is his second historical fiction novel after his well-received first book, Landon's Odyssey, about a returning Vietnam veteran's epic journey through time and space during the turbulent 60's. The Seal's Lair brings back the villain of Landon's Odyssey for a chance for redemption.